LITTLEVILLE

JIM BOB SALLY

ISBN: 1-4196-9478-2
ISBN-13: 9781419694783

Visit www.booksurge.com to order additional copies.

ACKNOWLEDGMENTS

I was born and raised in a small town. One of the things I learned early in life was people loved to gossip. I didn't really have to do any research in writing this book. What I did need were all the stories I'd been told over many years of living. I would like to thank a good buddy and his Mother for their editing skills. I will never be confused with an English scholar. I'll just say thanks to Chad and Momma for taking the time to edit my work. Thanks to the people at Book Surge for putting it in the proper form to print.

LITTLEVILLE

CHAPTER ONE

Jimmy Martin was facing life-threatening surgery. It was real serious and he was a nervous wreck. Jimmy was quite a character around Littleville. He was a lifelong resident with quite a tale to tell. The fact is that Jerry Springer could not manufacture Jimmy or his family in a million years. The entire Martin family was in an uproar over problems covering Jimmy's surgery, cheating wives, drug charges and fading health. The drama built over two decades was all coming to a head. The families' nerves were on edge and things were getting out of control. Jimmy knew his luck was about to run out two weeks before. He had packed his clothes and gone to the hospital for major heart surgery. His girlfriend Shirley had wailed as the hospital staff ran tests the entire day. He thought it strange when the nurse told him to get dressed.

"Peggy Sue will be in to talk to you, Jimmy."

"What time is my surgery tomorrow?

"Peggy Sue will tell you everything, Jimmy," Sharon said.

Sharon turned and almost ran out of the room. The man knew something was very wrong when she turned around and shook her head. Peggy Sue came in two minutes later and gave him a warm embrace. Jimmy didn't hesitate to return the favor.

"Damn, you are looking fine girl. What time is my surgery tomorrow?"

"Jimmy, I don't know exactly how to say this, my friend. You can carry your pretty ass on home now. Doctor Wind won't be here tomorrow. He has gone on vacation to Hawaii with that bitch, Nancy Thomas."

Poor Jimmy looked like he had seen a ghost. "You have to be bullshitting me."

"Hell, I wish I were. Jimmy, the stupid fool took off without even looking to see if he had surgery scheduled. It is not the first time the crazy bastard has done this crap. That man is not playing with a full deck of cards if you know what I mean. His little head is constantly over running his big head."

"Jesus Christ, what the hell am I supposed to do about this mess? It's not like I can just forget about my heart."

"Are you sure you want this man to cut your chest open? Jimmy, you better wake up and smell the roses, sweetheart. This is serious business and you could come up on the short end of the stick."

"That man ran off with Nancy and left me to die. I thought you took some kind of oath when you became a doctor. Christ, I'm about to have a fit."

"I could be fired for telling you this baby." She looked around to make sure no one was listening and continued. "Littleville General is the lowest rated hospital in the state. We are losing a lot of people in these operating rooms. The state board of medical examiners is camped out here. This place and half the doctors are on the verge of getting shut down."

"Hell, Peggy Sue, my crap insurance has the Doctor and this hospital on their approved list. I can't go to Cartridge General or Southern Medical. They may as well be in China. I am going to have to have it done in Littleville with this crazy man."

"I hope to hell you don't buy the farm. A lot of women are going to be very let down," she whispered.

"Yeah, I know exactly what you mean. I'd be very let down myself. By the way, I was supposed to have a private room when I got here. The first thing I saw on the door was a sign saying caution. When I walked in there was a man half dead looking at me. Two minutes later the man died right before my eyes. Shirley had a fit and I almost fell dead myself."

Peggy Sue held poor Jimmy's hand and looked him dead in the eye and spoke. "I know, Jimmy, that was Charley Hastings and he bought the farm. He came in three days ago for knee surgery and the worst case unfolded. His wife and family are fit to be tied. Charley had never been sick a day in his life." She reached out and touched Jimmy's cheek. "Well, the good news is you are going home right now. The bad news is you went through all these tests today for nothing."

Jimmy stared at her and put his hand over hers. "Christ, I have to do all this blood work again when I come back? I look like I'm a heroin addict."

"Every last one, Jimmy, I'm telling you, this place is bad news. All the terrible stories you've heard about this hospital are true. You have one life to live and you don't want it to end here."

He grabbed his jacket and threw it over his shoulder. "Well, I guess I have no choice but to carry my ass back home. Give me a call and we'll have a drink."

"What's the best time to call?"

"You can call anytime after five in the afternoon. Shirley is worse than a blood hound tracking me. I'm about ready to have the woman hit the road. I'll look forward to hearing from you."

"You think you're up to a little trip back in history big boy?"

"You bet your pretty little ass I'm up to it."

She put her finger in her mouth and smiled. "I'll leave the garage door open for you. Let's say tomorrow night at seven if that works for you. Carol brought back some good weed from West Palm."

"Baby, I'll be there and bring a quart of Crown Royal."

"I'll be ready, Tiger. Make sure the beauty patrol doesn't catch you before you get to my house. Tell your girlfriend you will be out of town for the night. We have a lot of catching up to do, baby."

"Damn I feel better already, Peggy Sue."

The Martin family loves nothing better than to share stories among themselves. They were a colorful bunch to say the least. They all loved to talk about each other. Lord have mercy did they loved to talk about each other. Someone once said their entire vocabulary was made up of four-letter words. I myself, found that not to be true. But, in Cases where they did I've tried to clean up the language. Anyway, within hours everyone in the county knew about poor Jimmy's ordeal. Faith Hudson was playing a round of golf with her husband, Don, and another couple at their country club in West Palm Beach. Faith had left Littleville after graduating from high school and gone to work in Miami as a flight attendant for American Airlines. She had meet Don two years later at a party thrown by mutual friends. It was love at first sight and they married six months later. Don was a hugely successful trial attorney and they lived an opulent lifestyle in their south Florida mansion overlooking the ocean. Don loved his private jet and they traveled constantly around the country playing golf with friends and business associates. Don and Faith were both stunningly good looking and make quite an impression everywhere they went. They walked in their home after having drinks at the club. Faith checked her phone messages and walked in the living room. Don was reading a story in the newspaper and looked up to see his wife clearly agitated.

"What's wrong, Faith?"

"Renee left me a long message about our brother." She repeated the story of Jimmy at the hospital in graphic detail.

"Faith, things like this don't happen in the real world. Jimmy must be crazy to have that doctor operate on him in that hospital. I would never walk in that place in a million years. Something is just different about your family and Littleville. I can't put it in words. The people are really nice, but it's like a third world country."

"He has crap for insurance, Don. He has no choice. I cannot believe any doctor or hospital could be this irresponsible. My poor brother is so sweet and it is a crime what those people are doing to him. I am going to shower and get dressed. I'm ready for dinner and drinks. My nerves are shot to hell after hearing about Jimmy."

Faith walked out of the room and Don shook his head. "Jesus, I can't even believe it."

The older and younger generation of Martin's all had grown kids. They, in turn, had been through several marriages and produced lots of children. The girls were all lookers and loved sex which should have been great for the husbands. Unfortunately, the girls seemed to have missed the never cheat and never lie vows they took somewhere along the way. Faith was the only sister who chose not to have children. The rest of her sisters had turned them out on a regular basis. They had collectively turned out some real characters.

In Littleville the local police stayed under federal investigation for taking bribes and beating prisoners. The Mayor hated the Sheriff and the feeling was mutual. The Sheriff said that he didn't have a clue his deputies were beating prisoners to death. He wondered aloud to the press if the Littleville police might be the ones to blame. The Littleville police swore they never laid a hand on their prisoners. The Sheriff suggested the prisoners must have been beaten by the Littleville cops on the way to the county jail. Since the jails were three blocks apart most people were having a little trouble buying the story. Drugs were everywhere and the Martin kids and grandkids loved to participate.

The Mayor was a redneck who stayed one step in front of the law. Mayor Huey Cox thought he was the king of Littleville and his you-know-what didn't stink. The man was as ugly as home made sin and thought he looked like the late Rock Hudson on a good day. Tattoos covered a smooth running eighty percent of his body. Huey was famous for his front page quotes in the newspapers around the state. When his grandson was busted for possession of marijuana the mayor didn't get upset. When the press asked for a comment he gladly responded.

"Everyone smokes marijuana," he said. "Some people have the misfortune of getting caught. Every young person deserves another chance. You people need to start reading the bible and going to church."

Now, that certainly makes sense to most folks who smoke marijuana. It left those who didn't smoke the stuff scratching their heads. The problem was that it was the young man's fifth drug bust in two years. When the scandal broke that seventy percent of the city employees were convicted felons and six were the mayor's relatives he addressed it head on in a news conference.

"You people in the press need to climb down from your pedestal. These people are doing a good job and need to be left alone. Not a single one of these people has robbed another store since they went to work for me. You need to find some Christian forgiveness in your hearts."

The press conference was going strong and Huey as usual didn't disappoint. Jane Morgan, a reporter with The Littleville Democrat had the first question. "Mr. Mayor, over sixty items up for votes on zoning have been pulled off the agenda illegally. The council members and city attorney say you personally directed this to be done."

"Hell, that's nothing but a big lie, Jane. You're listening to C. Jacob and my enemies and repeating their trash."

"Your opponents say you packed the boards with your friends and cronies and they do exactly as they are told. Four different developers are suing the city alleging they were turned down for refusing to pay kickbacks," Bob Pratt with The Town Talk said.

"Hell, that's nothing but a big lie. That old fat ass C. Jacob is spreading that garbage. I appoint these good folks to the boards. They don't take orders from me. You need to quit putting that garbage on the front page of your paper."

"Mr. Mayor, are you aware the national press is painting you as a red neck buffoon? You have insisted AT&T must come see you personally and not deal with the state legislature."

"Listen Bob, I am Huey Cox. The C.E.O. can bring his butt to Littleville if he wants to service my town. For your information nothing gets done in this town without my blessing."

"The News of The World is reporting in today's edition you will be indicted," Mona Craft said.

"Listen, I'm late for church. I have to help christen a baby. My enemies have been saying I will be indicted forever. Do you see a pair of handcuffs on me?"

Huey had a bad adversary in Councilman C. Jacob Cattleman. Old C. Jacob had his heart set on taking Huey on and sweeping him out of office. He loved to say the mayor thought he had an enemy behind every tree. The problem for C. Jacob was he was arrogant and ugly as home made sin himself. Obese just wasn't a strong enough word to describe him. The man had the social skills of a drunken sailor. If you ever met someone and just wanted to kick their ass that would be C. Jacob. The man was a lawyer by trade and loud by nature. A newcomer to town had commented he couldn't understand how Huey ever got elected. Two days later he met C. Jacob in a local bar and understood completely how Huey had managed to win.

The sun had gone down and the night was as black as the ace of spades. Folks in Littleville ate early and most were settled in to watch the ten o'clock news before calling it a night. Channel Four news had been tipped off about an imminent drug bust and the crew stood ready outside the house on Whitfield Avenue. The cameras were rolling as the drug bust played out on live television. Anne was a breathtaking beauty and was quite a sight as she made her television debut live across the state. The policemen walked next to her on each side as she shot the cameraman the bird with both hands raised. She looked around and saw another camera ten feet from her face. Anne was in no mood for all this attention and let her feelings be known.

"Screw you!" she screamed.

Her Aunt had just put down her glass of Jack Daniels. "Oh Lord," Florence shouted. "R.E. come in here now."

"Stick that camera up your butt, you sorry piece of crap and get a life."

Her husband came around the corner and stood next to her. Rufus was quite a character in his own right. He was never at a loss of words when it came to discussing anything. Everyone had called him R.E. for years.

"What is it, Florence?"

"Anne has embarrassed the hell out of the family. She got busted and shot the bird to the whole state. She was cussing like a drunken sailor spitting out four letter words at every turn! My poor baby sister is going to be down at the jail trying to put up her bail sure as hell. The woman don't have any money."

"Those damn kids are going to put Renee in her grave. I'm surprised Carol and Sammy Joe didn't get busted with her."

"Carol is in Las Vegas gambling and Sammy Joe is out of town on a construction job."

"Renee has raised three of the worst kids in the whole damn county. I'm going to bed and get some rest."

The phone lines came alive as the news of Anne spread across the countryside. The seven Martin sisters and poor Jimmy were busy comparing notes. Florence called her daughter to make sure she was not involved in the drug bust before calling her sisters. Another sister, Vicki Minter, was doing the same thing. There was nothing like a little drama to get the Martin's stirred up and on the move.

Emily Franks was the straight arrow of all the sisters and her husband Jake was even straighter. She had called Renee, who was in trauma over her daughter's arrest and barely able to talk. She hung up and tried to reach Faith in Florida but no one was home. She left a detailed message and moved on to her other sisters.

The baby sister was Kate Manley. Kate was a bulldog with sharp teeth. She was sitting with her husband Chuck watching the wrestling match when the phone rang. She checked the caller I.D. and picked up the phone.

"What's on your mind, Vicki? Talk fast; I'm watching my favorite wrestler on pay for view."

"Kate, Anne got busted live on statewide television thirty minutes ago. She was carrying on something awful," Vicki said.

"Busted for what?"

"She was smoking dope at Cindy Jackson's house with eight other fools."

"Have you spoken to Renee?" Kate asked.

"She and Paul left for the jail five minutes ago to try and post bond."

"I have to go now and watch the match. Let the little devil stay in jail."

She looked at her husband and rolled her eyes. "Who got busted this time?" Chuck asked.

"Anne put on a show for the cameras tonight. See why I keep to myself, Chuck? They are all a bunch of crazy sons of bitches. I don't mess with nobody and I damn sure don't want those crazy bastards messing with me. I keep my ass at home and they all know not to come around here."

The Martins were no ordinary family. Their parents had eight kids spread out over thirty years. Florence, Vicki and Joan were now in their late seventies and still ready to go in a minute.

Florence had completed her calls and looked at her husband, asleep in bed. She wanted to talk and shook the poor man. "Damn, we have to go to the square dance tomorrow night R.E. Everyone will be talking about Anne and her drug bust."

"Damn you woman what the hell do you think you're doing waking me up to talk this trash. Florence, if you're not snoring your talking." The old boy had about had enough and jumped out of bed mad as a wet hen. "I told you those kids stay in trouble. Renee has a heart of gold and her kids are wearing her ass out. Thank God Beverly didn't get into the drugs and booze. Her husband does enough for five people. Woman I hope to hell you have satisfied yourself."

"Bobby Jack is never going to settle down," Florence said.

R.E. hauled ass into the living room and turned on the television. "Good God, are you ever going to give me a minute's rest?" he screamed.

Florence walked in the kitchen and looked over her shoulder to see where R.E. was. She reached under the counter where she kept her flour and pulled out a pint of Jack Daniels. She looked again to see R.E. with his back turned and turned up the bottle. She had been a closet drunk for years and fooled no one including her husband. R.E. watched as she hid her whiskey and shook his head. "I've been married to a drunk for fifty years," he said.

Down in the sunshine state Don and Faith's jet landed and they got in the limousine for the ride home. It was past midnight and she knew something was terribly wrong when her cell phone rang and saw Emily was calling.

"Faith, Anne has been busted live on television for using marijuana."

"Oh, my God! How is Renee taking the news?"

"She is a basket case, Faith. Jimmy goes in for surgery tomorrow and Jake and I are driving over from Lilleyville."

"I'm in the car on my way home now. Don will make sure Anne get's out of jail immediately. I'll call our sister as soon as I get home."

Don was staring at her when she hung up. "What was Anne busted for, Faith?"

"Smoking marijuana."

"Why the hell are those brain dead cops busting people for smoking a joint?"

"Will you call Ben Rollins baby and get her stupid ass out of jail? Renee doesn't have any money to post bail or hire a lawyer. Her Boyfriend won't come up with a dime."

"I'm not calling Ben in the middle of the night. I'll take care of her in the morning."

The next morning he picked up the phone and called Ben on his cell phone. Ben was the most powerful man in the state and a famous attorney. He and Don had become close friends over the years and had a great deal of respect for each other. Ben came on the line and said hello.

"Ben, my wife tells me Anne Childress got popped for possession of marijuana. Get her out and make sure this crap goes away."

"I understand the whole state got to watch the bust, Don. I missed it myself but I will take care of everything. The Mayor is up for reelection and he has the cops out busting people. When are you and Faith coming this way?"

"In three weeks, Ben. Send me a bill for your services."

"Let's play a round at my club when you are here and have dinner. There will not be a bill coming for my services. The Clausen case was a gold mine and I owe you big time."

"I'll look forward to playing a round, Ben. Make sure Tom leaves his guns at home."

"He is still trying to run the geese and groundhogs off. I have to go and take this call from Senator Ford."

The men hung up and Don looked at Faith and shook his head. "Why don't the cops spend their time catching real criminals?"

"They do catch them baby and you get them out," Faith said.

Jimmy was back and under the knife as the scene unfolded at the Littleville hospital. Jimmy had a lot of family members including his three daughters. He had several former wives and a live in girlfriend. The girlfriend had a former husband who also lived with them. Jimmy didn't think much of the situation as he had one of his former wife's living with them from time to time. Rumor had it in Littleville that the girlfriend's former husband was really Jimmy's son. But hell, you could hear all sorts of tales in Littleville. Anyway, the ex-wives and girlfriend were jawboning pretty well in front of the daughters. Doctor Wind came out to give them the news on Jimmy's surgery.

"Ladies, the surgery went very well and I am quite pleased. Jimmy is going to make it to see another day. The man is going to need a nurse to monitor him and provide medical care for two weeks when he leaves the hospital. I want him up walking and he damn sure is not going to be in the mood to go for a stroll."

"I used to work at a nursing home. I'll take care of him, Doctor Wind. I don't want anybody over at our house kissing his ass. I got to watch him twenty-four seven," Shirley said.

"Doctor Wind, I am Susan Warden. I am his daughter and I have full authority to make any decision concerning my father. This bitch is a damn live in and you do not listen to a word she says. I want a registered nurse with him around the clock. My husband and I will pay for my father's care."

"Susan, I will get you a list of nurses to choose from."

Shirley started to speak but thought better of it and zipped her mouth. A nurse approached Doctor Wind with a frown on her face and whispered in his ear. The Doctor stared at the nurse and his face turned bright red. His voice was suddenly cold and hard as he spoke to the women.

"Nurse James just informed me there is a man who came in with you. That man is in Jimmy's bed passed out. One of you has to get the man out of his bed right now. Jimmy will be in intensive care for several hours. We will not tolerate anyone passed out in a patient's bed."

"We will get the drugged out bastard out of Jimmy's bed immediately," Shirley said.

"Make sure you do young lady. I want that man out of this hospital immediately."

He turned and walked away shaking his head in disbelief. He walked with his clipboard and a nurse to complete his rounds. Dr. Wind had only been in Littleville for three years but had already heard stories of the Martin clan.

"I'll get the stoned fool up right now. You would think the years in prison would have gotten Billy away from staying messed up," Shirley said.

Jimmy's first wife looked up and snapped at his second wife. "Go on and get him out of Jimmy's bed," Wanda said. "You're sleeping with Billy, Doris. Get your fat ass in there with Shirley and get him up."

"Bitch, Jimmy is paying your rent. You get your uppity old butt out of my face. Who the hell do you think you are talking to me this way? If we weren't in a hospital I'd kick your ass," Doris shouted.

The ex-wives never saw eye to eye and things had gotten worse over the years. It never was a good idea to take turns living with Jimmy and Shirley. The Martin's had started to arrive in mass as the two women headed for Jimmy's room.

Being at the right place at the right time has always been overrated. On the other hand being at the wrong place at the wrong time can never be underrated. R.E. and Florence had started in the hospital when Florence realized she left her purse in the car. They went back and got her purse and headed back from the parking lot.

Doris walked in the room with Shirley and stared at Billy who was in bad shape. His eyes looked like they were in backwards. "Billy, you have to get out of Jimmy's bed and sober up fast. The Doctor is going to be calling the cops, sure as hell. The man is pissed off as hell at you for pulling a stunt like this," Shirley said.

"Come on, Billy, and move your lazy ass! Shirley is right: you're going to be in jail before the night is over. You know better than to come up here all drugged out."

"I got some bad stuff and my head is about to fly off. Why do I have to get out of the bed?"

"You are embarrassing the entire family, you jerk. Doctor Wind wants you out of the hospital right now. Billy, if you had a brain you would take it out and play with it," Doris said.

"Man, I'm telling you, I'm really messed up. I can't see a foot in front of me and my head is spinning. I should have known better than to buy this crap from that bitch, Carol."

"You look like you are about to OD," Shirley said.

The women helped him out of bed and on his feet. Poor Billy looked like he crawled out of a cave as he started for the door. Doctor Wind was talking to two nurses when he looked up and saw Billy staggering out of Jimmy's room. He turned his attention back to the nurses as Billy started to make his way down the hospital corridor.

"I fell like I'm getting ready to go any second. Airplanes are flying around right over my head and the band is playing. There must be ten thousand people standing over there watching me."

"There are not ten thousand people watching you're drugged out ass. Hang in there Billy. We will get you to the car and drive you home. When will you ever learn to quit using dope?" Doris asked.

Billy was barely moving and his eyes almost popped out of his head as he looked down at the floor. "Watch out for the snakes. There all over the floor," he screamed.

"Shut up before you get arrested," Shirley said.

Everyone in the hospital started looking at the floor. One poor woman backed into a metal serving cart and let out a scream thinking she had been bit. Shirley and Doris had an arm on each side of Billy and were almost to the elevator when it happened. R.E. and Florence were coming off one of the four elevators. No sooner had the elevator door opened when Billy let out a blood curdling scream. "Snakes are on the floor, R.E. he wailed. Someone dumped rattlesnakes all over the floor. I've been bit by two of them."

R.E. and Florence started screaming themselves. Suddenly Billy collapsed and fell head first into Florence. She looked up to see

Billy with his arms over his shoulders and a wild look in his eyes. His whole body fell forward and Florence hit the floor with Billy on top of her screaming at the top of her lungs.

"Where are the snakes, Shirley?" Rufus shouted.

"There ain't any snakes, Rufus, the bastard is wiped out."

A nurse came running from the nurse's station fifteen feet away. Shirley, Doris and R.E. were frantically trying to remove Billy from Florence. Florence tipped the scales at two hundred thirty two pounds while R.E. hit the scales at one hundred fifteen soaking wet. Florence was screaming bloody murder tying to get out from under a passed-out Billy. The elevator doors kept trying to shut, hitting Billy's legs and reopening. Billy's body was pressed against her and the girdle was killing her.

"Get him off of me R.E., she shouted. Damn you Shirley get this piece of trash off of me."

"We're trying to get him off of you, Florence. The damn boy is passed out," R.E. shouted.

"Shirley, we have to get Billy off of Florence and out of here. The boy is dead weight," Doris said.

"O.D.!" The nurse screamed at the top of her voice. "O.D.!"

"Billy, what have you done?" Shirley shouted.

The nurses all ran out of the station and over to Billy. R.E. and the women had finally pulled Billy off of Florence and she was fit to be tied. Her wig had almost come off and was turned sharply to one side of her head. She was trying to kick poor Billy with both feet.

"Quit trying to kick the boy, Florence. Can't you see he is about dead already," R.E. yelled.

"I want to make sure the bastard dies. This no good freak is worthless."

Billy's head was cut badly as Doctor Fox and Doctor Wind rushed to help him. All the sisters and their husbands stood mesmerized as Florence dusted herself off. Billy was wheeled into the emergency room on a stretcher as the two Doctors followed.

"Are you alright Florence?" Vicki asked.

"Hell no, I'm not alright. I think my back is messed up. I'm going to sue this damn hospital. What hole did that rat crawl out from under? Jimmy is a fool to let that boy hang around."

Emily's husband, Jake, was an ordained minister and he looked at Florence and started to speak. "The Lord works in mysterious ways, Florence. There is a reason for everything," he said softly.

"Jake, I don't want to hear another word out of your long lanky mouth. There is nothing mysterious about a no good drug addict."

"He must have gotten some bad stuff. The boy freaked me out when he started yelling snakes were on the floor," R.E. said.

"That boy is one messed up puppy," Vicki's husband, Howard, said. "You have got to cross the fence and get on the side of the Lord. I used to stay messed up until I found the Lord. I was a worthless sinner who ran around on my wife. I tried to drink every drop of whiskey in the county."

"Bless you, Howard, the good Lord has shown you the way to eternal salvation," Jake said.

"Thank you, Brother Jake."

Faith was getting constant reports from family members at the hospital. She was having a fit when Don came in the room. "Don, the sleazy bastard Shirley was married to goes in my brother's room and got in his bed. When the Doctor forced the family to get him out he fell on top of Florence in the elevator and overdosed. They have him in the emergency room."

Don shook his head and looked at his wife for a good twenty seconds before speaking. "I love you baby and I'll do anything to help you. I have to tell you sweetheart, your family is so screwed up its unbelievable. Can you even believe the man showed up at the hospital drugged out and got in a man's bed? Faith, I'm telling you these things do not happen in the real world."

Back at the hospital the family was busy getting there two cents worth in about the situation. One of the nieces was under indictment for writing a false prescription for drugs. Carol was the oldest of Renee's children and a piece of work. The family viewed her with utter contempt. Carol had watched the scene with her husband Morris. Morris was a laid back easy going fellow who stayed stoned twenty-four hours a day.

"Morris, that piece of crap is totally wasted. Billy is one step away from the grave yard."

"I wonder where Billy bought that stuff from. I hope to hell I never stumble across any of that stuff."

Carol was in no mood for any crap from anyone. Six to twelve years in the state pen has a way of getting you a little uptight. She looked over and saw Renee staring at her with contempt in her eyes.

"What are you staring at? I didn't give him that crap. Don't be staring at me like I gave him the drugs."

"You stay messed up, Carol. You stole my pain pills Thursday when you were at my house."

"That's a damn lie, Momma. You are hooked on those pain killers. You are a bigger druggy than me. You can't even keep up with how many pills you are popping every day."

"You lying low life bitch!" Renee screamed.

"It takes one to know one, Momma."

The entire clan was now watching the two of them glaring at each other. Carol looked at the family and screamed at the top of her voice. Patient's, doctors and nurses two floors down could hear the exchange.

"None of you give a damn about me. I have to have five thousand dollars, Momma, for the lawyer. None of you cheap asses will up a dime!"

"Shut your filthy mouth!"

She grabbed her coat and looked at Renee. "I'm calling Don in Florida right now. He will give me the damn money."

"Don't you dare call Don and bother my sister. I caught you in a bald faced lie for the hundredth time last week. You don't have cancer and there are no treatments going on anywhere. I called the damn clinic and they never heard of you. You are the biggest liar in the state!"

"It takes one to know one!"

"If you say that one more time I'm going to shut your nasty mouth for good!" Renee screamed.

The Martin's started to spread out across the room. They all felt it prudent to put a little distance between themselves and Carol. They knew all too well a cat fight could break out any second.

"Your ass has been in and out of rehab and jail and you are going to prison. You better stop telling everyone Don is going to fly you out of the damn country. Your Aunt Emily called Don yesterday and told him you said he paid five thousand dollars and got you off. Yesterday, you come squalling in my house telling me Davis won't give you the money. That old married bastard has been sleeping with you for ten years. I'm broke and living on disability. Don't ask me for any more money."

"Screw you! Screw all of you!" Carol screamed at the top of her voice.

Everyone was staring at her now. The hospital staff was starting to become very uneasy and Jake said a quick prayer asking for a quiet ending.

"No good pricks!" Carol yelled. "Get your stoned ass up Morris and take me home."

"Okay, I'll take you home Carolyn."

Lou Horton was in charge of the hospital's nurses and she had just begun her shift. The head nurse came off the elevator and witnessed the scene. She turned and addressed her staff standing next to her.

"Oh, my Lord, the Martins are here. The last time they had a family member here they emptied the hospital. Get the administrator on the phone and tell him to get down here right now. Call security and have them come up before they get in a brawl."

"Yes ma'am," Charlotte said.

Morris was a good worker and was crazy about Carol. The man just was not sure if Littleville was in the United States; if you know what I mean. Carol walked out with Morris following meekly behind.

"I'll see all of you later. Carol wants to go home now," Morris said.

Kate was taking the scene in and not enjoying it one bit. "I'd kick her ass if she was my daughter," Kate told Renee. This damn family belongs on Jerry Springer, but no one would believe it. Come on Chuck, we are going home before I kick someone's ass."

"Calm down Kate before you cause a scene. You are showing your red neck ass."

"Watch your mouth, Chuck. I'll shut it for you if you're not careful. I'll do and say anything I damn well please! I hate even being around these fools. Jimmy is the only one I care a damn thing about."

"Honey please don't go upside anyone's head. I don't want to go to the jail and bail you out."

"Chuck, I don't want to hear another word out of your mouth. Don't you let me catch you turning into a wimp-ass."

Kate was a bulldog who kept to herself and stayed away from the rest of the Martin's. She did not suffer a fool and long ago realized the family was big trouble. While the family members loved nothing more than to stick it to each other; none of them had the nerve to mess with Kate. The woman would kick any one of their butts, including the brother in laws. Faith once asked Kate if she had a security system in her home. Her reply pretty much summed up Kate Manley. "What the hell do I need with a security system? I got a 357 Magnum and a 16 gauge shotgun. If a son-of-a-bitch comes through my door it will be the last door he walks through."

The preacher stood trying to ignore the women with his wife. Jake had married Emily thirty years ago and they had three normal kids with families of their own. Jake tried to keep his distance from the rest of the Martins. He was a very religious man and never got along with the cursing and fighting. The Martin's father enjoyed the name, Wild Buck. Old Buck must have slept with half the women in Littleville before he died. Liquor sales plunged upon his death. Old Buck hated Jake with a passion and every thing he stood tor. Wild Buck had pulled a gun on Jake before he died. That had proven to be the last straw. He loved his wife dearly, but the Martin family was a different matter. His wife shook her head and spoke her mind. She always spoke her mind.

"That's disgusting, Jake. Carol is totally out of control. Poor Renee has done everything for those kids. Look at what it has gotten her. My sister's health has gone to hell and her children are responsible."

"Try to stay calm, Emily. Get Renee and we will drive down to the Outback and have some supper."

Emily walked over to Renee and held her hand. Renee was fit to be tied after the latest exchange with Carol.

"Come on, Renee; let's go have some supper at the Outback."

"I'd like to choke that damn Carol."

"She used to be such a good kid. She was just a little angel and pretty as a picture. I don't know where you went wrong, Renee."

Renee glared at Emily but said nothing. She cursed her life as they left the hospital. She couldn't wait to get outside and have a cigarette. Her kids were on the verge of driving her completely insane.

CHAPTER TWO

Emily and Renee walked outside as Jake went to get the car. Jake never used valet parking. Jake tried hard to never do anything that cost him money. The word cheap didn't come close to describing Reverend Jake Franks. The man had plenty of money but he bought all his clothes from the Goodwill store. Jake loved to brag about putting three hundred thousand miles on every car he owned before getting a new one. Jake was once seen going through a garbage can looking for coupons. When the police were called and arrived on the scene Jake calmly explained a promotion was going on. He had managed to collect enough coupons off the boxes to win a nice prize. The police gave him a pass but the word spread like wildfire through the community.

The girls waited for Jake outside on the sidewalk. Renee had a cigarette going and was puffing away. "My back is killing me,

Emily. I need a pain killer in the worst way. That damn Carol stole my pain pills and I can't get anymore until the first. I'm about to die I'm hurting so bad. I didn't get a wink of sleep last night the pain was so bad. I sat in front of the television watching old reruns all night. I think I know every line in I Love Lucy."

"How did she steal your pain pills?"

"I went to the bathroom and both Carol and my pills were gone when I came out. The little bitch has been stoned for a week. I've called the little thief ten times a day and she will not answer her cell phone. When she get's stoned the bitch just disappears. You can't let her out of your sight for one second. I'm surprised she showed up at the hospital."

"Lock your pills up where she can't get to them."

"I hid them in my panties at the bottom of my dresser. The damn girl can smell a pill five miles away. She is like one of Howard's coon dogs when it comes to sniffing out drugs."

"If one of my kids did something like that I'd take a baseball bat and put it upside their head. On second thought I think I'd just put a foot up there butt. That girl is out of control."

Emily looked like a bouncer in a rough nightclub and she had a personality to match. The family loved to say it was Emily's way or the highway. The woman was so aggressive it was downright scary. If Emily didn't approve of something she let you know in no uncertain terms. She was a Mary Kay saleswoman and she guarded her territory with an iron hand. Her voice was louder than a bullfrog. She once had a physical confrontation when she discovered another sales person on her turf. You can trust me when I tell you the woman never came back.

Jake, on the other hand was quiet as an ice cube. The man said nothing unless someone addressed him directly. The man was six four and weighted a solid one hundred forty pounds. It was pretty safe to say Jake was the world's quietest preacher. Jake and Emily both had one thing in common. It was not that they were good in bed. They both drove so slowly it was downright frightening. Jake pulled up and the women got in. The three of them left the hospital and headed for the local Outback. Now the Outback could only be reached by driving down the interstate. Jake was about to pass the exit to the freeway and Renee spoke up.

"This is your exit, Jake."

"Thank you, Renee," Jake said.

Jake came up the ramp and onto the highway at thirty five. The problem was Jake kept right on driving thirty five. The cars and trucks started blowing their horns and shooting Jake the bird.

"How rude," Emily shouted. The cars are right on our bumper. I hope a policeman comes along and writes them a ticket. It seems like they get worse every time we drive."

"Emily, the speed limit is seventy and Jake is doing thirty-five."

"He has to find the exit, Renee."

"The exit is six miles down the highway, Emily. Jake, the speed limit is seventy," Renee said.

Jake just smiled and kept right on driving at thirty-five. A man in his green pickup truck pulled up beside them and rolled down his window. He was waiving his fist at Jake and screaming at the top of his voice.

"Drive you stupid asshole. You are on an interstate highway. Pull off the road before you get someone killed," he shouted.

Jake had both hands on the wheel and never took his eyes off the road. Traffic was now backed up a mile behind Jake in the right lane. Renee said a silent prayer for their survival as Jake continued to ease along with horns blowing and birds flying. Cars began to pull over as the Littleville chief of police, Mike Thomas, turned on his flashing lights. When he finally reached Jake he turned on his siren and Jake pulled over. Renee hung her head and waited as the policeman approached the car.

The cop got out and walked up to Jake's car. "I need to see your driver's license, sir."

Jack started for his billfold and was trying to have a conversation with the Chief. "Was I speeding officer."

"Don't get cute with me. You were driving thirty-five on a seventy mile an hour freeway. You have traffic backed up to exit ten. People like you are causing wrecks all the time."

"I'm sorry officer."

He looked in the car and saw the two women. "Are you smoking anything?"

"No officer, I don't smoke. I never smoked a day in my life."

Thomas looked at Jake's license. "Are you taking any pills?"

"No sir."

"Is something wrong with your car? Why are you driving so slowly?"

"I'm from Lilleyville and I get very nervous on the freeway. I'm really sorry if I've caused an inconvenience to anyone."

"Mr. Franks, I'm going to give you a pass this time. You cannot drive like a turtle. An interstate highway is not a school zone. Are you getting the message?"

"Yes, officer, I will pay more attention to the speed limit."

Thomas handed Jake his license back and leaned in the window. "Go on now and don't let me catch you trying to be a turtle again. You are going to fool around and get run over."

Jake drove off and the Chief shook his head. It didn't take much to be the Chief of Police in Littleville.

The Chief thought it was a good idea to lower the speed limit on the interstate himself. Matter of fact, Thomas brought it up at the city council meeting one night six months ago. He had requested permission to address the council. His time had come to speak and he stepped forward. The chief walked to the front of the council chamber and eased up to the mike.

"Good evening, Chief Thomas. What do you wish to speak to us about tonight?" Mayor Cox asked.

"I would like the council to lower the speed limit to fifty miles an hour on the Interstate within our city limits. In my opinion it is creating a safety hazard for our citizens."

"Son, that's a federal highway. You can't just lower the speed limit through our town," the city attorney said.

"Hell, why can't we make them do what we say? It's our town and the cars and eighteen wheelers are going much to fast. Lilley Mae Jacobs is constantly complaining about almost getting run over. The woman is scared to death to get on the interstate."

"Son, the federal government paid for the highway to be built. They make the rules. Believe me, I don't like anybody trying to tell me how to run my town," Mayor Cox said.

"Why can't you go talk to those guys and tell them we want to lower the speed limit? Hell, I'd be willing to drive over to the highway department and talk with them myself."

"Son, just put it out of your mind. You have to go to the capitol to talk to those boys."

"That ain't but seventy five miles, Mr. Mayor."

"Son, the capitol is in Washington."

"When did they move the capitol?"

"Son, I'm talking about the nation's capitol. It's in the District of Columbia." Anyway, a prominent attorney suggested after the show that night at the council meeting that someone needed to check and see if the Chief was brain dead. Sadly, no one ever followed up on the suggestion and Chief Thomas kept his job.

The first generation of Martin's was still at the hospital. It turned out they were just getting warmed up. Florence was still trying to settle down from the elevator incident. The old gal had excused herself and gone in the restroom to freshen up. She adjusted her wig and looked around the room. Florence pulled out her bottle of Jack Daniels and took a good shot. This visit to the hospital to see Jimmy was not going well at all. She came back out and saw R.E. speaking to Howard and Vicki.

"They are all treating Shirley like bad medicine. Jimmy would string his girls up if he knew they were acting like this."

"You're right R.E. and I've had enough of the young ones calling me mother. Hell, I'm in the prime of my life. Faith is the worst one in the bunch."

"They are just being respectful. They have always looked at you as a mother figure," Vicki said.

"I don't hear them calling you Mother, you old bat. You are two years younger than me and Joan is three years older. They don't call Joan and you, Mother."

"You old drunk! Get a life. I'm not in the mood to put up with your crap tonight."

Florence looked at her sister and was ready to fight. She pointed her finger in Vicki's face and got on a roll. "Where do you come off telling Jimmy the devil has gotten a hold of him and that's why he's sick? You ought to be ashamed of yourself scaring the boy like that. Ever since you and Howard got religion you've been a pain in the ass. Daddy would whip your ass if he was still alive."

"Florence, I never said such a thing. What the hell is wrong with you coming in here and jumping all over me?"

"Yes, you did Vicki. You are nothing but a lying hussy. Faith told Renee that Jimmy told her you said it. It upset the boy to no end. Emily doesn't ever lie and she said it too. Ever since you and Howard joined that crazy church you have been saying bad things about everybody."

"You old fool I never said any such thing. You have been nipping on the whiskey and you are showing your ass. You need to start going to church and straighten yourself up. Your fat ass is the laughing stock of Littleville. You are an embarrassment to the entire family carrying on with that Jack Daniels."

"This fat ass will bust your skinny ass across this damn floor. The nerve of you to talk about my drinking."

"You ain't never seen the day you can whip my butt. Take your damn false teeth out. I'm going to splatter them all over this damn hospital!" Vicki shouted.

The family rushed between them before tragedy could strike. The hospital staff stood and watched in horror as the men pulled them apart.

"Florence, you need to settle down. The boy is in there fighting for his life and he don't need your big mouth running all over the damn hospital," R.E. said.

"The Lord will lead us away from temptation," Howard said. "You have to cross the fence R.E. You can't stay on the wrong side of the fence, my friend."

"Howard, why don't you take that line and stick it up your ass," R.E. shouted. You old bull shit artist; you chased more strange tail than the Mayor. You're ass has been beaten and shot at a dozen times by irate husbands. You're worse than a reformed smoker carrying on about that crap."

Howard was Vicki's husband of fifty plus years and a reformed sinner. Old Howard had finally found the Lord after years of drinking and looking under women's skirts. He was yet another brother-in-law and he loved to talk. His favorite subject was his coons and buck dancing trophies. Most folks suspected old Howard had consumed one to many drinks along the way. Still another group was convinced the shock of being shot at so many times had taken a toll. He seemed to be in his own little world when it came to commenting on anything.

R.E. had not gotten any sex from his wife in twenty years. Florence was cold as a freezer working overtime. The woman was a hundred pounds over weight and had the sex appeal of a Rhino in June. Unlike Howard, he was still on the make when it came to women. R.E. loved to read and tried his best to keep up with events around the country. He was a blue dog democrat and damn proud of it.

Florence and Vicki were now nose to nose again and heading for a showdown. It just was not a good night to be a Martin. R.E. was doing his dead level best to keep them apart to no avail.

"You old bitch! You are lazy as hell and have never worked a day in your worthless life. Florence you are a closet drunk and you smell like a whiskey factory. You are not fooling a damn soul; you old wine head!" Vicki shouted.

"I don't tell people the devil has gotten control of them because they don't live right. R.E and I. raised damn good kids. Our kids are not messed up like yours."

"You bitch I never liked you since we were kids. You get fatter by the day, you old pig. You're ugly as death warmed over and everybody in the family knows your crap stinks."

"My husband didn't try to screw every married woman in town. You must not be so damn hot yourself!" Florence shouted.

Joan stood watching with her guitar in her hand. She played in a country band with her boyfriend. Joan was quite a sight at seventy-eight playing her ass off on Saturday nights. She was the oldest sister and never participated in the family feuds. Her life was her music and listening to the police scanner. One of her sons, Herb, was a Littleville cop and stood ready to jump in the middle of Florence and Vicki. Herb had seen this show many times over the years. By the grace of God the local minister showed up and the women calmed down. The Reverend told everyone to hold hands and he would lead them in a prayer. Florence and Vicki moved away from each other and bowed their heads.

"Let us all join hands together and say a prayer for Jimmy's speedy recovery. Lord, be with poor Jimmy in this time of need.

Give him the strength to pull through and carry on his life," Brother Garrison said.

"Amen, praise the Lord," Howard said.

Over at the Outback Jake and Emily were seated with Renee. The waitress came over to take their drink order.

"Can I get you something to drink?" Ramona asked.

"Sweet tea," Jake and Emily said.

"Double scotch on the rocks. Johnny Walker," Renee said.

Ramona had the misfortune of waiting on Jake and Emily before. She cringed at the thought of Emily's big mouth and no tip from Jake. Jake was the worst tipper in the state and Emily was so aggressive it was downright scary. Needless to say she was not a happy waitress as she walked over to the bar and ordered the drinks.

"Why are you so up tight?" the bartender asked.

"I've got a loudmouth woman and a cheap tipper."

"Man, that ain't good."

She came back with their drinks and asked if they were ready to order. Renee's nerves were completely shot and she wanted to relax and have her drink before ordering. Emily and Jake on the other hand were ready to get started with the food. Jake liked to get in and out of a restaurant as fast as possible. One of the family members once commented that Jake thought he had a clock on him. If he didn't get in and out in thirty minutes something terrible was going to happen.

"I want the filet well done. I'll have a baked potato and the house salad. I got two coupons with a discount for my meal. Do you want them now?" Jake asked.

"Sure, give them to me and I'll take it off your bill."

Jake pointed at Renee and spoke. "I'll be paying for me and my wife. Give Renee her own check."

Emily could not eat meat and she was looking for chicken. Nobody was completely sure if Emily was half deft or she just liked to talk loud. Her voice carried across half the restaurant when she spoke. "Can you cut the chicken in half?"

"No, we cannot cut the chicken in half."

Emily had a set of lungs that put a bull frog to shame on a good day. She shouted at the top of her lungs and the patrons all jumped. "I can't eat a whole chicken!" she screamed.

"Whoa!" The drunk shouted from the bar. "Some bad ass is going to kick butt," Frank said to his buddy.

"That's a woman screaming over there," Junior said.

"We are going to see a cat fight at the Outback," Frank said.

Everyone seated within twenty feet of Emily jumped up from their tables. Children started crying as the parents scrambled to get out of the way. One little boy was terrified and was clinging to his Mothers' leg.

Ramona recoiled and glared at Emily. "You uncouth red neck bitch," she said to herself.

The people seated at the three adjoining tables literally got up and left their tables. One of the men walked to the front and confronted the manager. "Seat me and my family somewhere else. The woman sitting next to us is completely crazy. I don't care if you have to seat us in the smoking section. You get me as far away from that woman as you can."

"Yes, sir, we will move you immediately. I'm so sorry about the disturbance," the manager said.

Renee wanted a steak but knew she had to save the day. She had seen this movie before and knew it was going to get worse very quickly. The three families were now up and watching them from a distance. The little boy was crying and pointing at Emily.

"That bad woman is going to get me and eat me up. She's loud and mean."

"The woman is not going to get you. She is in need of a little chicken," his father said.

"I'll split the chicken with you, Emily. Calm down before you empty the damn restaurant. You are embarrassing me and Jake."

"I am not embarrassing anyone. I own my own business and I know how to handle people." She stood up and glared at Jake. "Am I upsetting you, Jake?"

"Emily, please lower your voice if it wouldn't be too much trouble. Please sit back down people are staring at you. You are about to empty the restaurant."

"Well, it sure doesn't bother you when we're having sex, Jake. You are always saying, 'Moan, Emily. Tell me how good it is, baby. Scream when you have an orgasm, Emily."

"Emily, you are embarrassing me to death. Everyone in the place can hear you."

"Well, the truth shall set you free, Jake. These people need to cut the chicken in half. The rest of the bird is not going to fly away. I have to go relieve myself."

"Oh my Lord in heaven! That woman is describing her sex life to the whole restaurant. The woman is completely crazy," the manager said.

"You need to get that foul mouth fool out of the restaurant. This is the third time she has done this since we opened. She needs to carry her ass to Kentucky Fried Chicken and go through the drive through window," Ramona said.

Ramona brought their food and Jake and Emily did their usual thing. They gobbled the food down like it was a contest to see who could finish first. Poor Renee tried her best to keep up to no avail. Jake sat staring at her clearly ready to leave. The two drunks at the bar were taking it all in.

"That big old girl is a hell cat," Junior said.

"That skinny ass she is with can't do her any good. The old gal is crying out for help," Frank said.

"Are you going to make a move on her, Frank?"

"Watch me put a smooth move on her ass, Junior."

Old Frank made a move alright and he won't soon forget it. He carried his two hundred seventy pound ass over to the table. Renee was looking dead at him when he put his hand on Emily's arm. Jake looked up and was overcome with fear.

"Baby, oh baby. How would you like to come home with a real man?" Frank asked.

Emily looked at Frank with his hand on her arm. "I'd like to tell you what I think but I'm a believer in the Lord. I'm just going to show you what I think."

"Show me what you got baby."

She stood up and looked Frank dead in the eye. She reached out and grabbed Frank by his shoulders. Well, the right boot went flying between the man's legs and down he went. He opened his mouth and tried to scream but nothing came out. The manager rushed over with the staff and carried old Frank outside withering in pain. It wasn't easy trying to pull almost three hundred pounds of dead weight across the floor. The patrons and staff watched in disbelief and shock. Emily calmly sat down and looked at Jake and Renee.

"Jake, why on earth did you sit your butt down and say nothing."

"The man was twice my size," Jake whispered.

"Jake, you have to stand up and defend your woman. If one word gets out every man will be hitting on me."

Renee's cell phone rang and she looked to see it was Carol. "What do you want, Carol?" she snapped.

"Tell Morris my car got hit in the parking lot at the shopping center. I have to put some loving on David and try and get the damn money. If Morris calls tell him I'm running errands for you and my cell phone went dead. I should be done with the old bastard by ten o'clock."

"Carol, let me finish my dinner. I'll cover for you if he calls."

"Thanks, Momma. I think I can score some pills from Charley C. and I'll bring you some."

"Alright Carol let me get some food in my body."

Emily was all ears and naturally she had to make a comment. "You need to confront that girl and get her off the drugs."

"Emily, I've had her in rehab three times in five years. What else can I do for her?"

"Whip her tight little ass."

"Emily, she is not a child anymore. Carol is thirty years old. Please lower your voice everyone in town can hear you."

"Everyone in town already knows she is a druggie," Emily said.

Ramona brought the separate checks and sat them on the table. Jake looked at his bill for five minutes. He pulled out his billfold and left a whopping five percent tip. Ramona came back to the table and picked up the money. She looked at Jake and wanted to spit. "Preacher, I want to thank you for the big tip. I'll try my best not to spend it all at one time."

She walked straight to the manager and confronted him. "Never again will I wait on those people. You can fire me if you want. That cheap sucker is no more a man of God than Charles Manson. That crazy bitch screams one more time and I will choke her to death."

"Hell, I don't blame you Ramona. I just wish there was a way to ban both of them from coming in. Two tables just got up and left the restaurant. The man with the little boy was madder than hell. He said his child will have nightmares about the woman. I'm sure she has to be completely crazy."

"I'll tell you what we should do boss. The next time they come in, I'll have my boyfriend cut the tires on their car. Let that pig bellow in the parking lot. She can run all the wildlife across the interstate."

"We can't do something like that, Ramona. I have to figure out how to keep those people out before they run everyone off. The paramedic told me the guy is finished for life. The woman just flat de balled him."

Emily, Jake and Renee finished and made their way to the parked car. Jake eased out of the parking lot and onto the road. Renee's phone rang and it was Anne.

"Momma, I need you to come down to the city jail. Sammy got cute and I popped him in the mouth at the Silverstone bar. The sorry wimp called the cops and they arrested me."

"Jesus, Anne, do you think I could have one day of piece in my life. I don't have any money to bail you out."

"Damn! I knew I should have called Don. You would let me rot in this hell hole. I have to be at work in the morning or I'll lose my job."

The line went dead before Renee could say anything. Emily was all ears and immediately put her two cents worth in. Jake drove them home without saying one word.

Anne turned to the jailer. "Winston, I need to make another call to Don in Florida."

"Sure. Don bought the whole department dinner when he was here. If he says the word you will be out of here in one minute."

Faith was having a glass of wine when the phone rang. She looked at the caller I.D. and saw Anne was calling. She picked up and spoke. "How is my favorite niece?"

"Aunt Faith, I'm in the Littleville jail. I need Don to make a call. Sam got in my face and I had to defend myself. He started pushing me and I popped him right between the eyes."

"Poor baby," Faith said. "Let me get Don for you."

Don was taking a shower and had just stepped out. He looked up and saw Faith holding her glass of wine and the cordless phone. "Baby, Anne needs you right now. She hit Sam and the police arrested her." She handed him the phone and left the room.

"Anne, how can I help you?"

"I need you to get me out of this place. Can I put Winston on the phone?"

"Put him on."

"Mr. Hudson, this is Winston Morgan."

"Winston, I need you to release Anne. What do you need from me?"

"I'll release her now if you will guarantee her court appearance."

"I'll be happy to guarantee her court appearance. I will call Ben Rollins tomorrow and have him represent her."

"Yes sir. I'll have her out the door in five minutes."

They hung up and Winston looked at Anne. "Come on Anne, I'll drive you home. Man, Faith's husband is cooler than an R C Cola and moon pie."

Anne looked at Winston and shook her head. "I think I'd put it a different way, Winston, but I get your point."

Don got dressed and went in the living room. "Call your sister and tell her Anne is on her way home."

"Thank you so much, sweetheart."

Faith watched Don go in his study and close the door. She called Renee and Emily answered. "Emily, please tell Renee that Anne is on her way home. Don took care of everything and I don't want Renee worrying."

"These kids are out of control, Faith. Don needs to quit helping them. They need to spend some time in jail. It might bring them to their senses."

"How can you say such a thing, Emily? The girls are crazy about Don and he adores both of them."

"Faith, all of Renee's kids is worthless drug addicts and they are all going to O.D. and leave this world. Both of you are making a big mistake bailing their sorry butts out of trouble."

"Give me the phone, Emily," Renee shouted. "Quit answering the phone at my house. You didn't raise perfect kids either."

She jerked the phone from Emily's hand and spoke to Faith. "Please tell Don how embarrassed I am. I wish the girls would quit calling and bothering him."

"Don't be silly, Renee. Don would do anything for Carol and Anne. Honey, I have to run and get ready for dinner."

"Thank you again, Faith. Give Don a hug for me and tell him we all love him. I will never be able to repay him."

They hung up and Renee saw the look in Emily's eyes. "Don't say a word, Emily. I can't stand one more second of stress. I'm going to bed before something else happens."

The Martin family had lived in Littleville forever. They were all well known by law enforcement officials. They spanned decades in age as the parents had two generations of children. Wild Buck Martin had long since moved on to a better world. Well, he probably didn't, but you're not supposed to talk bad about the dead. The man's legend had endured the passage of time. The Martin girls had all married and were blessed or cursed depending on the situation with the numerous kids. The children in turn had kids of their own when they grew up. Old Buck was not much to look at for sure. However, it didn't seem to slow him down when it came to the ladies around town. Buck was the town drunk and he was damn proud of it. Buck was white trash and everybody in Littleville knew it. He had eight kids by his wife and dozens more with other women. Rumor had it that one of the ladies killed his old ass over the skirt chasing and boozing. Wild Buck was a drinking and partying fool and loved moonshine whiskey. He was a practical joker of legendary proportions. The stories of his drunken mischief carried on to this very day. Jimmy took up where Buck left off, but for now women were the last thing on his mind. He was one scared dude and death was staring him squarely in the face. He lay in the intensive care unit hoping tomorrow would come.

Florence and R.E. had six grandkids, but their pride and joy was Bobby Cage. Bobby's best friend was James Holley whose dad was the Sheriff in Littleville County. The boys loved to pop pills, smoke dope and chase girls. They were both nice looking young fellows and played football at the local high school. Sadly, neither was blessed with much of a brain. It was getting late as the boys cruised around the shopping center parking lot.

"I have to take a leak," James said.

"I'll pull around back and stop behind the pharmacy," Bobby said.

"Hurry up, I'm about to piss in my pants."

"Hold your horse's man I'm moving as fast as I can."

Bobby whipped in and parked the car. The boys got out and started to relieve themselves. Bobby looked at the back door of the drug store and could not believe his lying eyes. He pointed to the wide open back door.

"Son of a bitch, can you believe it, James?"

"Hell no, come on Bobby. I can't believe we could get this lucky."

"It could be a trap," Bobby said.

"No way, the damn owner forgot to lock the back door. I would never have believed we could get this lucky in a hundred years."

In they went never hearing the silent alarm. They were loading up on the pills when James looked up and saw the building was surrounded by police. "Bobby, someone was here before us."

"Crap, we got to figure out something fast."

"We have to escape, Bobby. My father will kill me. I hope to God he is not out there in the parking lot."

"We have to dive through the glass window and make a run for it. Whatever you do don't stop running."

"What about the car?" James asked.

"We'll tell them we left it and went with some friends. We have to get out of here."

Bobby grabbed a display and put it in front of him. He took off and crashed through the plate glass storefront with James on his heels. A small miracle happened and they escaped into the night with the police in hot pursuit.

"Damn crazy bastards ran right through the window," the stunned policeman said to his partner.

"Let their bloody ass haul it on down the road," his partner said.

The boys ran two blocks and crossed over to a residential neighborhood. They tapped on the window in their buddy's bedroom. Davis looked out the window and saw Bobby bleeding and James with a wild look in his eyes. Long story short, Davis got dressed and took a towel outside.

"Davis, we need a ride home. Bobby had to jump through a window at the pharmacy and he is cut up pretty bad."

"Take this towel and press it to your head, Bobby. Did you break in the store?"

"The door was open and we walked in. It turned out to be a trap the cops had set," Bobby said.

"I'll take both of you home but we have to be quiet. If my father hears us he will kill me."

The next morning the Sheriff and his wife were having breakfast when James walked in. "James, someone broke into Millar Pharmacy last night and got away," Sheriff Holley said.

James never looked up as he ate his eggs and toast. "I can't believe it," James said.

"Jumped through the window and escaped with twelve officers surrounding the building. We know there were two white males in their late teens or early twenties. The Mayor wants to see me this morning. The press is having a field day with the story of the getaway. R.E. Cage's son called to let me know your friend Bobby was all cut up this morning."

"How did Bobby get cut up?"

"He said someone threw a beer bottle and hit him in the head. His car was parked behind the pharmacy. Strange it would happen the same night someone ran through the front window in the store. It is even stranger that his car was parked out back. The odds of him not being involved are a million to one."

James felt himself starting to shake. The phone rang and his father answered. He came back in and sat down.

"Who was that dear?" his mother asked.

"That was Chief Thomas. They caught the guy who broke in the pharmacy. It was Judge Baxter's son and he confessed to breaking in and stealing the drugs. He swears he was alone and went in and out the back door. I know damn well someone else came in the store after he left."

Sometimes you catch a break in life. Bobby and James damn sure caught a big one that night in Littleville.

Bobby's father was on the phone with Florence giving her the news. "Mother, I didn't want you and Dad to hear this from someone else. Bobby got hit with a beer bottle and he is cut up real bad."

"Oh my poor baby," Florence said. "Is he going to be okay?"

"He is going to be fine, Mother. We had to take him to the hospital early this morning to get stitches. He didn't tell us when he came in last night. He seemed to be very scared about the whole ordeal. I told him to quit hanging around that old shopping center. That is a rough crowd of kids that go over there every night. They sit around and drink beer and smoke dope until the wee hours of the morning."

"Lord, I am so thankful our children and grandchildren are normal. I almost came to blows with Vicki at the hospital last night. She and Howard have the worst kids. Renee is the same way. Ours are just perfect."

"I wouldn't go nearly that far, Mother. I'm running late and have to go to work now. Bobby will be fine," Morgan said.

They ended their call and Florence looked over at her husband staring at her. "Poor little Bobby got hit with a beer bottle by some thug last night. R.E., I just heard on the radio Judge Baxter's son got caught breaking in Millar's last night. He jumped through the window and they caught him. That boy is the biggest pill head in town."

R.E. had just gone for his walk and ran into a neighbor who was a cop. The policeman was telling him the story of the robbery at the pharmacy and the chain of events that had occurred.

"No Florence, the boy didn't jump through the window. The police think someone else came in later and jumped through the window. Apparently, it was nothing short of a miracle they escaped."

"I can't believe we live in a town where people throw beer bottles at innocent kids."

R.E. nodded his head and went out on the porch. He sat down in his rocking chair and looked as the cars went by. The old man leaned forward and shook his head. R.E. was not the brightest star in the sky, but he smelled a rat. Bobby was a little wild ass and R.E. knew it. "Beer bottles my ass," he said.

CHAPTER THREE

Bobby Jack Cullen was the luckiest man alive. He was married to R.E. and Florence's daughter, Beverly. The man was a skirt chasing, drinking and partying fool. Beverly knew he was up to no good but chose to tolerate his actions in order to spare her children the trauma of a divorce. Bobby Jack was a good provider and worked for the local cable company as a manager. For twenty years, Bobby had managed to avoid running afoul of the law. He and Jimmy were best friends and had been in many a tight spot together.

If he was drunk and speeding the cops stopped the car in front of him. He had escaped once by pulling his car over at a checkpoint and been lucky enough to have a wrecker come along. Bobby Jack flagged the man driving the wrecker and had him tow him right past the checkpoint. But, all good things must come to an end. This was the night it ended for the cock hound of Littleville County. Bobby had been partying fifty miles away in another county. It was time to call it a night and get his ass back home. He got in his car and put the petal to the metal.

The state trooper sat waiting at the top of the hill next to the interstate. Brian Watkins was a bad ass cop and he liked his work. For weeks, the sports car had been flying down the highway traveling well over one hundred miles per hour. Each time he found himself in pursuit of another car when the sports car sped by him going in the other direction. He was determined to catch the rascal and bring him to justice. The car was taking the Littleville exit to leave the freeway and he was sure of it. He glanced at his watch. It was almost midnight and he was ready to pounce. Bobby Jack came roaring down the highway on his way home. He was drunk as a wine taster on the job nonstop for two days. Bobby Jack was no fool and knew he better get home before Beverly killed him. He had no sooner fired up a joint when the red lights went off. The BMW was traveling at a hundred and twenty miles an hour and the cop took off after him in hot pursuit.

"Damn, the S.O.B. has me dead to right," Bobby Jack shouted. He threw the joint out and started to slow down. Bobby Jack pulled off the highway and the state trooper pulled in behind him. The trooper opened his door and walked up to Bobby's car. He had a look of total satisfaction when he looked at Bobby Jack.

"I've been waiting on your ass for a long time," Trooper Watkins said.

Bobby Jack was a friendly sort of guy and he thought he would try his luck. "I know officer. I got here as fast as I could."

"Get out of the car and give me your driver's license, smartass, before I whip your butt."

Bobby Jack got out of the car and nearly fell down. He handed his license to Watkins and leaned against his car.

"Boy, your eyes are blood shot red. You don't even need your headlights. I'm going to write you a ticket for doing a hundred and twenty and being totally intoxicated. I'd have you try to walk but you would kill your damn fool self. I am taking your butt to jail."

"Well, I guess I have it coming."

"It is a damn miracle you haven't killed yourself or some innocent person."

Watkins pulled out his handcuffs and started to slap them on Bobby Jack. "Turn around and put your hands behind your back." Bobby Jack started to turn around when all hell broke loose. The explosion was so loud both men jumped and turned to see a horrible wreck on the other side of the freeway.

"Jesus Christ, all those people are going to die."

"Don't you move," Watkins said.

He called for help and ran across the freeway to administer help. Bobby Jack watched as ambulances started to arrive and flashing lights went off everywhere. He looked down the freeway and saw the Littleville exit a half mile away. Being the dumb ass he was Bobby decided to drive away; completely forgetting the trooper had his license. He was one drunken dude as he pulled into the open garage at his house. He closed the garage door and went inside only to find Beverly staring him in the face.

"Where have you been?" Beverly shouted.

"I've been here all night if the cops come to the house."

"You drunken fool what have you done!"

"Honey, please just do as I asked for once in your life. I'll make it up to you. My ass is in big trouble."

"Get your butt in bed Bobby and don't say another word. Why I stay married to you I'll never know." Beverly was so angry she couldn't go back to sleep. Their kids were all spending the night with friends and for that she was grateful.

Trooper Watkins had his hands full working the scene of the crash site. He was joined by two more troopers and five squad cars from the Littleville police department. It took well over an hour to untangle the wreckage and free the victims. The care flight helicopters went back and forth and the tow trucks were brought in to clear the cars from the freeway. Traffic was backed up ten miles and after much work the cars were finally able to move again. Watkins was walking back across the freeway and saw the BMW sitting on the side of the road. He pulled the driver's license out of his pocket and approached the car. He looked around for Bobby Jack but no one was in the car. He started to walk back to his police car when it hit him right between the eyes.

"Son of a bitch!" he screamed. "The bastard drove off with my car."

"The man must be a maniac," Trooper Jordan said.

"I always knew the man was crazy. Even I didn't think he would steal a state police car," Officer Williams said.

"I'm going to hang Bobby Jack Cullen," Watkins shouted. Watkins looked at the address and handed it to Littleville officer John Henry Williams. "Show me where this bastard lives."

"Come ride with me. I'd bet my life he drove the damn car home and parked it. That boy is the biggest party hound in the state."

"The bastard will not be partying for a long time when I find his ass. This is the most embarrassing moment of my law enforcement career," Watkins said.

It was quite a scene at two in the morning. Half the Littleville police and two state police cars arrived at Bobby Jack and Beverly's house. Their lights were flashing and sirens blaring. All the neighbors were up and outside in their yards as Beverly answered the door.

"Beverly we need to see Bobby Jack," John Henry said.

"He is asleep, can I help you."

"Open your garage door, Mrs. Cullen," Watkins said.

Beverly opened the garage doors and there sat the state police car. The keys were still in the ignition and Watkins backed the car out of the garage. Beverly watched the police car being backed out and almost fainted.

Herb Heller had been in law enforcement his entire adult life. The Littleville cop looked at Beverly and sighed. "Beverly, get Bobby Jack out of bed. I have to take him in and book him."

Herb was Joan's son and this was not his finest moment in law enforcement. Beverly went in the bedroom and tried to get Bobby up from his drunken sleep. The man was snoring so loud the walls were starting to shake.

"Get your sorry ass up!" she screamed. "The cops are taking you to jail."

The word jail seemed to bring his drunk to sobriety fast. Bobby came up out of the bed fast. "Whose here?"

"Half the cops in the town and four state cops are here. My cousin is taking you in so they don't beat you to death. You stupid fool; how could anyone be dumb enough to steal a state police car?"

"I stole a state police car? Call Ben Rollins and your Daddy, I'm in big trouble."

"You jerk, if it were not for our children I would love to see you rot in hell. I'm leaving your worthless ass today."

Herb stood waiting as Bobby Jack came in the living room. He had a shit eating grin on his face. None of the policemen were smiling back.

"I'm sorry Herb. I have messed up big time. Please don't leave me alone for a second. I'm afraid the bastards will beat me to death."

"Bobby Jack, just keep your mouth shut. The trooper is ready to kick your ass. If you open your smart mouth he is going to jump your ass."

Bobby was cold sober now and fearing the worst as the cops led him to the squad car. Herb had put the handcuffs on him and off they went to the Littleville jail. By now everyone living within two blocks had their cell phones going. People in Littleville were early risers on a normal day. This kind of excitement didn't happen often and by four o'clock the whole town was wide awake and the stories were flying.

Beverly was so mad she could spit and she called her parents. R.E. answered and she got straight to the point. "Daddy, the cops have arrested Bobby Jack. He is on his way to jail and I am totally humiliated."

"What did he do, Beverly?"

"He was doing a hundred and twenty miles an hour, drunk out of his mind, and stole a state police car. Bobby left the scene of an accident and ran his big mouth to a cop."

R.E. and Florence were both wide awake now and taking it all in. "He stole a police car, Beverly?"

"He drove off with it at the spot he was stopped. I'm married to the dumbest sucker in North America, but I won't be for long. He wants you to bail him out and call Ben Rollins. Frankly, I don't care if you let him rot in jail. I'm going to bed and get some sleep. Don't try calling me because the phone will be off the hook. I am the damn laughing stock of the whole county. I should have left Bobby Jack years ago when he started running around and drinking."

R.E. put the phone down and looked at Florence. "Bobby Jack has stepped up and outdone Anne and Carol. The son–of-a-bitch has stolen a state police car. I have to get the crazy fool out of jail, Florence. I just invested sixty thousand dollars with him to buy the car wash on Lane Street."

"Oh, my God, say it ain't so Rufus. Mercy, it is going to be hell to pay. Where did he steal the car?"

"On the side of the interstate where he was stopped for speeding at over a hundred miles an hour. Beverly said he was drunk as a skunk. Get dressed, we have to go to the jail and bail him out before they kill him. We won't be going to the boat to gamble today."

"But our comps expire in two days."

"The hell with the comps from the casino, Florence; I have sixty thousand dollars about to go down the drain. I should never have invested a penny with Bobby Jack. I can just see myself running a car wash everyday."

"R.E. Cage, what are you doing investing my money in a car wash? Since when did you become a big investor?"

"Woman, don't you start in on me. You have never worked a day in your life."

"How dare you throw that in my face, Rufus Cage? Who the hell do you think raised our kids? You wouldn't know how to cook a meal if your life depended on it."

Renee was up having her coffee and listening to the police scanner for her morning entertainment. Jake and Emily were still asleep in the bedroom. She lit a cigarette and almost choked when she heard the news. Emily came out of the bedroom and saw the look on Renee's face.

"What have your kids done now?" Emily blurted out.

"My kids haven't done a damn thing, smart mouth. Bobby Jack got nailed doing 120 and drunk. He stole the police car and drove home."

"Oh, my goodness, land sakes alive! He stole the policeman's car? You better be joking, Renee. R.E. and Florence are going to have a cow. Why does our family stay in trouble with the law?"

"I'm not joking, Emily. The boy drove off in the police car."

Jake heard the women carrying on and got out of bed. He got dressed and walked in the living room. "Jake, Bobby Jack is in jail. He stole the police car and went home in it. He was drunk and speeding when the trooper stopped him," Emily said.

Jake was a man of few words until he reached the pulpit. He thought for a few seconds before he spoke. "Bobby Jack was drunk, speeding, and drove off in a police car. Your rotten father would be proud as punch."

"Watch your mouth, Jake," Emily snapped.

The press was having a field day with the story. It spread across the county and then the state. By ten o'clock it was national news. The Martin's didn't need to tell each other the story this time. They heard it on every radio and television station on the air. It sure as hell didn't stop them from talking to each other. Howard and Vicki were early birds and were one of the first to see the story on the local television station. They sat having breakfast listening to every word. Vicki was still mad as hell over the confrontation at the hospital the night before.

"The old bitch is always rubbing our kids in my face. That crazy son in law of hers should shut her big mouth for a long time. He stole the state police car and drove home drunk as a skunk, Howard."

"I'm going coon hunting with Jeff as soon as I finish breakfast. Bobby Jack better get Ben Rollins on the case fast. He has really outdone himself. Those damn cops are going to put a rubber hose on him sure as God made green apples."

The phone rang and Joan was on the line raising holy hell. Vicki listened as she sipped on her coffee. "That damn Bobby Jack has embarrassed Herb to death with his bad behavior. I hope that boy does time and straightens himself up. This is the second time in less than a month Herb has seen him show his ass. First he gets caught naked in the back seat of his car with the town whore in the church parking lot. Now he pulls this stunt and makes the national news."

"Bobby Jack got caught naked with a woman at church?"

"Yes, he has no shame. Herb said he was not even using a condom."

"Have you spoken to Florence?"

"Hell no, I don't want to talk to that big mouth bitch. I just got off the phone with Kate and she is ready to whip Bobby's ass.

Beverly is going to leave his sorry ass and it's long overdue. I have to call Renee when we hang up and give her the news."

"I feel so sorry for Renee."

"Carol and Anne are driving the woman crazy and flaunting their bad behavior in her face. It is just totally unacceptable behavior. They get their ass in a bind and pick up the damn phone and call Don. He and Faith think they are both little angels and can do no wrong. When he and Faith come to town they steal him away and we never even see him. Carol writes a false script and my Herb busted her. The next thing we know all the charges are dropped. Don got her butt off and she is free as a bird. They nailed her a second time three weeks ago."

"Don't say anything bad to Renee about Don. She thinks he hung the damn moon. Hell, who am I bull shitting; we all think he hung the moon. Howard thinks the man is the second coming of Jesus. Carol is going to keep the crap up and land in a spot where nobody can help her little ass."

Across town one of Jimmy's ex wives Wanda, had troubles of her own. Money was tight and her past due bill at the city was staring her in the face. Wanda had somehow managed to get a credit card and was starting to breathe a little easier. She picked up the phone and called city hall. A woman answered in the utility department. The city employees had the social skills of a thirsty elephant on the way to drink water.

"I got a pass due bill I need to pay. Do y'all take credit cards?"

"No, we most certainly do not," she snapped

"Bitch, you need to get laid. You must be one of the Mayor's relatives. I wouldn't hire you to scrub my floors."

"You probably don't have a floor to scrub. Why don't you kiss my ass?" Teresa said.

"I got a better idea. Why don't I just come down there and whip your rotten ass, you smart mouth bitch."

"I got your caller I.D., Wanda. I am going to press charges against you for threatening a city employee."

"Go right ahead you sleazy trailer park trash. I swear to God I'll beat your ass like a big drum."

"You will do it in the dark, bitch. I'm having your lights turned off the minute we hang up."

"I want need them bitch. Ten minutes from now I'll be wiping the floor with your ass," Wanda shouted.

I'm not pulling your leg. Things like this happened all the time in Littleville. Anyway both Wanda and Teresa were fit to be tied when the call ended. The city staff just stood with their mouths open and shook their heads. A daily cussing was something they had all grown accustomed to over the years. Anyway, Teresa wasn't taking any chances and called the police for protection.

Faith was asleep and had the phone turned off in her bedroom. Faith never worked and was a night owl who slept until nine or ten the next morning. Don was in Miami in the middle of a big murder trial. He sat with two of his paralegals having breakfast at the hotel. The trial was not set to resume until one o'clock. His legal secretary came in and joined them. She was laughing and told them the story she has just watched on CNN of the man driving over a hundred miles an hour, drunk and driving off in the state policeman's car.

"Where was the damn fool "at" when it happened?" Don asked.

"Some place called Littleville," Mary said.

"I never heard of Littleville," Rodger said.

"I know exactly where it is, Mary. Faith was born and raised in Littleville. Did you happen to catch the man's name?"

"How could I possibly forget? His name is Bobby Jack Cullen."

"Lord, I can't believe my wife's family. Let me have a few minutes to call Faith. She should be getting up right about now. I met the damn fool years ago. I think he is married to one of the older sister's daughter."

Don walked across the room and called Faith on his cell phone. Faith had a private number on one of her cell phones that only Don had. She heard it ring and rushed over and picked up.

"Good morning, baby. Have you heard the news from Littleville?"

"No baby. I'm making my coffee and the phones are turned off. I stayed up late watching a movie."

"Well, you will be hearing from everyone shortly. Beverly's husband got busted and made the national news. Faith, the man got stopped for speeding and drove off drunk in a state police car."

"Don, please tell me you are joking."

"Honey, Mary just saw it on CNN. You may not want to answer your phone today. How did you manage to turn out normal with all these crazy people around you? I love you. I have to get back to the courtroom. I'll see you tonight around seven. There is no way I am going to be involved in this mess. You do not give my private number to any of those people."

"Hell will freeze over before I give them your number. I love you baby and keep your record perfect."

Faith sat down in a daze. She could still see her late father passed out on the floor from an all night drunk. She poured herself a cup of coffee and sat down to read the newspaper. The phone rang and she saw it was Renee calling and picked up.

"I already heard the story about Bobby Jack. Renee, what is wrong with the Martin's?"

"R.E. and Florence went to the jail and they are desperate to reach Ben. We are sure he is avoiding us and the Judge is refusing bond. The pompous ass Governor is on every station that will stick a mike in his face raising hell. Will you call Don and have him call Ben? He will not help us unless Don calls him. The cops are in an uproar and want to kick Bobby's ass. Florence is drinking and R.E. has his hands full. Emily and I are on our way down to the jail."

"I am not calling my husband under any circumstance. That fool can stay in jail until his trial comes and they hang him. I could choke myself for letting Don bail Carol out. For your information it cost us a hell of a lot more than a lousy five thousand dollars to save her little ass. He gave Ben Rollins all the work on one of his big murder Cases and Ben made over four hundred thousand. He will not listen to me when it comes to Carol. Don says she is his little running buddy and she is just trapped in that hell hole. He comes home happy as a pig in shit when Anne and Carol hit the town with him. Don is not going to lift a finger to call anyone including the Governor. I don't want one more phone call to my husband from anyone in this family."

"Why don't you climb down off your high horse, Miss Prissy and calm down. For your information my daughters are crazy about Don. They are always protecting him from women hitting on him. The man is a damn magnet for women and you better be thankful my girls run their ass off. Give me his number and I will call him myself."

"I'm not giving you his number. I better never hear of you or your daughters ever calling him again or it will be hell to pay. For your information no one needs to protect my husband from women. Don only has eyes for me and he always has, Renee." "Goodbye!"

Emily stood listening to the conversation on Renee's end of the line. Renee was not a happy camper when she put the phone down.

"What was that about?" Emily asked.

"Faith hung up on me, Emily. I can't believe the nerve of my own sister telling me those awful things about my children. Come on Emily we have to go to the jail."

"Faith is right and you are wrong, Renee. Don needs to quit bailing your kids out of trouble. I don't approve of Don going to the nightclubs with them either. Married people have no business going out to clubs without their husbands and wives. In fact, they have no business going at all. All of you need to quit smoking and drinking. You set a terrible example for your kids. Do you ever ask yourself if you are the reason they are all messed up?"

"Why don't you pack your bags and take you and Jake's freeloading ass back to Lilleyville. You never offer me a penny when you come to my house. You both show up unannounced and disrupt my life. Both of you are messy as hell and it takes me a week to straighten out my home when you leave. You are both so cheap it is shameful."

"Well, of all the nerve. I've been giving you money for twenty years you ungrateful you know what. Families don't charge each other when they stay for the night."

"You and Jake have stayed over a hundred times at my house. Why don't you reach in your purse and do the right thing. You and Jake have half of every dollar you've ever made. Here I am a single woman living from month to month and you both take advantage of my kindness."

Jake stood with his mouth open looking at his wife. "Come on Jake we are going home. Renee thinks she is running a damn motel."

Jake didn't say a word as they headed for the car. She was mad as a pit bull sprayed with mace. Emily was so loud

Jake quietly eased the windows down as they headed for home.

"I'll never speak to Renee again as long as I'm alive."

"I guess she has a lot of pent up hostility towards us."

"I always use our car and gas to take her to the garage sales. I buy her something at the Goodwill Store every time we come. She is just like her worthless kids. The woman is ungrateful for everything I do for her. I wouldn't think of charging her to stay at our house."

"I sure hate to think of paying for a motel room."

"You don't have to worry about paying for a hotel room. I'm never coming back to see her again."

"Well, that's a relief. We need to save our money for a rainy day."

"Jake, it would take a flood to wipe out your money."

Speaking of the jail, the Martin clan had moved on it in full force. The sisters and their husbands along with the children and their husbands were there. The grandkids and their boyfriends had come along with the preacher. Bobby Jack was pacing the floor and apologizing to every cop in the station. The cops were in no mood to hear it. Well, I mean they did have their car stolen and the news was on national television.

Ben Rollins was a powerful man and controlled Littleville County. He was a brilliant attorney and had numerous high profile cases in his career. Ben was as far from a fool as one could get. He was not going to touch this case with a ten foot pole. He came in from court and his secretary, Brenda Mason, handed him his messages.

"R.E. Cage has left four messages for you," Brenda said.

"I don't want to speak to him or anyone in the Martin family."

"Bobby Jack made the national news."

"The man is going to do hard time for pulling this stunt. Get the Governor on the phone and let's start returning calls. By the way has my buddy Don Hudson called?"

"No sir."

"I didn't think so. Let's get started."

Jake and Emily were driving their old van home. Both of their cars were in the shop. She was still mad as a wet hen over Renee calling her and Jake out over being so cheap. It was dark and Emily needed to stop and relieve herself.

"Jake, I have to stop and relieve myself."

"There is no place to stop, Emily. We will be home in thirty minutes."

"Pull over right now and I'll go behind the trees."

"Emily, the tail light is out on the back left side. If the policeman sees it we are going to get a ticket."

"Pull over Jake I don't care if we get a ticket. I'm going to piss all over myself if you don't stop."

"Alright, hold your horses. I'm pulling over right now."

Jake pulled over and Emily got out and headed for the tree line. The ground was hilly and she had trouble getting her clothes off. Jake was getting nervous as he sat on the side of the road with his taillight out. Emily got tangled up as she squatted down and was relieving her bladder. Jake heard her scream and jumped out of the van and headed for the woods. Jake looked everywhere and kept calling her name. The noise from the cars and trucks going down the freeway were drowning out his voice. Emily had made her way back to the van and thought Jake had gone to relieve himself. He was panicked as he went back to the van alone. He opened the door and Emily sat naked in the front seat of the van.

"Emily, what are you doing?"

"I lost my balance and fell down. I got tangled up in my jump suit. All my clothes are covered in urine. Drive us home no one can see me."

"You can't sit here naked, Emily. We will both go to jail and be ruined if the cops pull us over."

"You're worrying about nothing, Jake. You are always trying to get me naked and now I am. Try to keep your eyes on the road and off my body."

"Emily, get in the back seat."

"I'm not moving one inch, Jake. Quit sitting here and drive the van back to Lilleyville."

Jake was a wreck thinking of the consequences of them being stopped by the police. His ministry would be ruined and he and Emily would be the talk of Lilleyville. They were less than five miles from their home now and he was starting to finally breathe again. But, as fate would have it things turned bad in a split second.

"Oh no!" he screamed. The trooper's flashing lights went on and he pulled over. "Get in the back and cover up Emily."

"There is nothing to cover up with."

"Oh my God I'm going to be run out of town on a rail."

Emily was scrambling to get over the seat and hide in the back of the van. Jake jumped out of the van and watched the officer get out of his car. The policeman was less than five feet from the back of the van when it happened. A car full of teens came roaring down the highway doing at least a hundred. The trooper jumped back in his car and took off after the speeding car. Jake climbed back in the van and took off himself. The poor man saw his whole life racing in front of him as he made his way home.

"Stay down, Emily. We are close to home."

"Hurry up Jake. I'm very uncomfortable back here. I need to get home and take a shower."

"Emily, I don't want to be stopped again. My heart can't take anything else happening tonight."

They finally made it in their driveway and the garage door would not open. Jake tried desperately to get it to open and finally gave up. He jumped out of the old van and almost fell head first on the ground.

"What else can happen?" he shouted. "Wait here Emily. I'll go in the house and bring you some clothes."

"Hurry up; I'm freezing to death Jake."

You are probably wondering why Jake was so panicked after making it home. People in Lilleyville and Littleville didn't call before they came over. Folks just drove right up and didn't even bother to knock on your door. They came right on in and made themselves right at home. Many a person had been caught in a compromising position because of such behavior. Jake was busy rounding up some clothes when he looked out the front window. His heart jumped as two cars pulled in his driveway and six members of his church got out. He ran out of the house and tried to head them off before they reached the van.

"Good evening, Brother Jake!" the Deacon said.

"We brought you and Emily a surprise," his wife said.

"You did?"

"All of your many years of service to our church are going to be rewarded Jake. We voted last week to buy you and Emily a new van. It is long over due," Deacon Brown said.

Jake looked up and the van was coming in the driveway. He felt the wave of nausea starting to sweep over him. His mind was racing to find a way out of the certain disaster soon to come.

"We'll just take the old one back to the dealer now for a trade in," Deacon Autry said. "If you will be kind enough to trade keys with me Jake we will be on our way. I know it is late and everyone needs to get home."

Jake looked at the van and his hands started to shake. He could barely whisper when he finally spoke. "I don't have the keys, Deacon."

"Now Jake there is no need to get emotional about this little gift," Deacon Butler said. "You certainly have earned it with your clean Christian lifestyle and the wholesome example you and Emily have set for all of us. We are all blessed to have you and Emily lead us to the promise land. You are a fine man, Jake. You are a man of God with the highest moral principals."

Jake could not speak as Deacon Butler's wife opened the back door of the old van and looked in. He felt his knees buckle and became light headed. Emily had gone in the house unbeknownst to Jake and showered. She came running out to find Jake passed out on the ground surrounded by church members.

"Call an ambulance Emily, Brother Jake is down. I fear for the worst," Deacon Miller said.

"Deacon Miller, he will be just fine. He forgot to take his medicine and when he get's excited he will pass out without it."

About that time Jake came to and saw Emily fully dressed. The men helped Jake to his feet. Everyone came in and had a glass of sweet tea.

"Jake, you scared us half to death. You need to be more careful and take your medication," Deacon Autry said.

"I will be more careful."

"Jake, your hands are still shaking. Are you sure we don't need to take you to the emergency room?" Deacon Brown asked.

"I'll be alright, Deacon Brown."

"I'm sure Jake will be just fine," Emily said.

"I hope you and Emily enjoy the new van. We went down to Mr. Pete's dealership and picked it out ourselves. He was very understanding of our needs and sold it to us at his cost," Mrs. Brown said.

"Well, it is getting late and we need to go and let you get some rest. We will see you in church Sunday morning," Deacon Miller said.

They headed out the door and Jake and Emily saw them to their cars. They came back in and Jake was still shaking. "Emily, I thought you were still in the back of the van naked."

"You took too long and I was freezing."

"I thought my life was over and we were facing public humiliation. All my life I wanted to preach the gospel. Tonight my dreams almost came crashing down."

"Well, it would have been embarrassing to get caught naked."

"I'm never going to get over this happening."

"Jake, just go to bed and forget it ever happened."

Jake stayed shook up for three weeks but Emily went right on about her business as though nothing ever happened. Of course, Emily had a big advantage. She was born and raised a Martin and nothing fazed her. Plus, it wasn't the first time the woman had been caught in an uncompromising position.

CHAPTER FOUR

The Martin's were in a class all by themselves when it came to the embellishment of a story. Call it bad ears or lack of a brain. Most folks thought it was lack of a brain. But, hell they elected Huey time after time. Who were they to be calling the kettle black? The Martin's were something else when it came to tall tales and they never let the truth get in the way of a good story. If you gave a Martin a story of a broken fingernail, it could turn into an amputation of the entire arm. Don was one of the country's top criminal defense attorneys. He represented people of questionable character, including those involved in murder and drug cases. Less than two years after starting his practice, he was besieged with high profile cases. The man was so good in a courtroom, prosecutors dreaded going up against him. He had never lost a case and it started with a visit Faith had with Vicki one night years ago. Vicki was much older and had experienced a bad hearing loss over time. Quite often she would misunderstand what someone said to her. Howard was even worse and he was practicing his buck dancing that night. Background noise exasperated the problem and Howard was playing his music.

Vicki thought Faith said Don had gotten away with murder six times. She also got the idea Don had beaten no fewer than sixteen separate drug indictments. Vicki was shocked that Faith would be married to the man. Faith was bragging about how Don got everyone off and was making a killing financially. Faith was excited that Don had agreed to come with her to Littleville to meet the family in a week. Vicki hung up and looked over at Howard as he danced. She was not a happy camper and she looked at her husband with a frown on her face.

"Howard, turn off the music I need to speak with you. Faith is bringing Don to town next week."

"I have been looking forward to meeting Don."

"Well, let me tell you something. You will not be looking forward to meeting him when you hear what I have to say. Faith told me Don has been involved in six murders. She said the man has beaten sixteen different drug arrests. He has managed to get all of his people off as well and is filthy rich. They are flying in on his private jet."

"Drugs and guns go hand and hand."

"I can't believe Faith would stoop so low to marry a man who is a murderer and drug dealer. The family stays in trouble, but we don't kill people. Our kids use the damn drugs, but they don't grow the crap. I bet he uses that jet to fly the drugs in from another country."

"I thought that girl had more sense than to marry a man like that. Did he kill all the men at one time?"

"Hell no, Don killed every one of them at different times. Faith said he won six different murder cases. He won three in Florida, two in Texas, and one in Mississippi. He must kill people all over the damn country. She said his best friend is a Judge in New York. You know damn well the Judge is getting him off every time. Ben has been doing the same thing for years around here."

Howard's memory was not as good as it used to be. He thought he remembered a man named Don Hudson shooting some gangster in New York last year. The man's real name was Don Huggins and the police found the body in the Hudson River.

He looked at his wife and told his story. "Now I remember, Vicki. Don murdered another Mafia guy in New York last year. They found the man's head chopped off and the rest of his body in some river. I never put one and one together until now. I watched the show on T.V. one night when you were gone. They call Don the headless monster up there in New York. I think he is the head of one of those bad families."

"Jesus Christ, that makes perfect sense. They are always going to New York for the shows. Now I know what the show is Howard. Don is in the mafia sure as hell. Lord, can you believe he chopped the man's head off? Why would that girl bring the man up here for God's sake?"

"Damn, there could be some tense moments for all of us when he gets here. Wayne killed those two girls and they sent his ass away for life. I don't know how that boy has gotten away with six murders. He must be using all that drug money to buy off all the Judges."

"You know damn well that's what the man is doing, Howard."

Vicki called Florence to relay the bad news that Faith's husband was a murderer and drug dealer. Florence answered the phone and Vicki dove right in with the story. Florence had put away a pint of Jack Daniels and was all ears. The Martin's loved to get the inside scoop and talk bad about each other. Florence was so messed up that she had the speaker phone on. R.E. sat next to her reading a story in the newspaper.

"Don is in the mafia, Florence, and he flies to New York to kill his enemies. He kills them all over the south on a regular basis. He is the biggest drug dealer in the whole country."

"Vicki, I think you are full of shit. That boy ain't running around the country blowing people up."

"Damn it, I heard it straight from the horse's mouth, Florence. Faith seemed to be enjoying telling me the stories. He has killed people all over the place. I bet you anything they double crossed him on drug deals. Howard said guns and drugs go hand and hand."

"I'm putting R.E. on the phone. You put Howard on the phone and let him tell the story. I think you must be taking the wrong drugs. You need to march your ass down to the Doctor and have him change your prescriptions. R.E., get you're ass up and talk to Howard."

R.E. put the paper down and took the phone from Florence. "Howard, what the hell are you and Vicki smoking over there?"

"I ain't smoking anything R.E.! The man is a killer. It is plain as day to me. I saw myself where he killed a man in New York City and got arrested. Faith told Vicki he has beaten six murder raps in three different states. He whipped the government on sixteen different drug cases. The boy has to be the biggest drug dealer in the country."

"Good God, Howard, he wants to go hunting when he is here with us. What the hell am I going to tell him?"

"There is no way I'm going in the woods with that man. Can you just imagine him carrying a loaded shotgun? I don't know about you R.E., but I'm getting very nervous about this business with Don."

"I've already committed for us to take him. We have to come up with a damn good reason why we can't go, Howard. God, why didn't someone tell me this before I opened my big mouth?"

"No! Hell no! We will tell him we would rather play golf. Tell him the damn birds are not here this year."

"Good God, why did Faith have to bring him here? Now that I think about it, Don told me he was bringing his shotgun. He told me he had his own shotgun and shells."

"You know damn well he carries his guns with him. The damn girl is proud as punch. She wants to show the boy off to the family. She told Vicki he is the love of her life."

"She better always feel that way. Once you get in one of those families, you have to stay forever. I've seen a dozen shows and they always say the same thing. There is no getting out once you have come in. I've read a lot about these people, Howard. If you treat them with respect, they generally don't harm you. If you cross them in any way, they will put your lights out for good."

"You can bet your ass I will be showing the man respect. R.E., this is one bad ass dude."

"Howard, we ain't seen nothing like him in Littleville. How many murders did you say he committed?"

"Faith told Vicki about six and I read about the fellow in New York. Lord only knows how many he killed that the cops don't know about."

They hung up and it didn't take long for the word to spread throughout the Martin family. Once it made its way through the family, it moved on to friends. From there it spread like a wildfire out of control with the wind blowing seventy miles an hour. A mass murderer and drug dealer was on his way to Littleville and it could be hell to pay. Family members started looking for excuses not to attend the dinner at Howard and Vicki's house. But, curiosity kills the cat and in the end they all had to come see for themselves.

Faith loved going out to dinner. She really enjoyed her fine wines. When she went home, she took her wine with her. Littleville was not known for carrying fine wines. She would order the house wine and go to the restroom and pour it out. Faith always carried a big purse that could hold her wine. The pilots always kept a case of her wine on the jet and never dared let it get too low. The family was stunned at the news and everyone was afraid to bring up the subject with Faith. Renee and her boyfriend had agreed to pick them up at the Littleville airport. They drove up and parked in the parking lot twenty minutes early. Both Anne and Carol had been to West Palm and spent a week with Don and Faith. They were both out of town and due back the next day.

"I just can't believe Faith has gotten herself in a mess like this, Paul. She is never going to be able to get out alive. Once you're in the family, you can never get out. I've watched shows about them for years on television. They will flat out kill you if you try and leave."

"I have a hard time believing the man is a killer. Your family is full of liars and I never read anything about Don killing anyone. Anne and Carol carry on about him like he is a rock star," Paul said.

"I know exactly what you mean. I told Faith not to take her eyes off either one of the girls for a minute. Christ, do you know how embarrassing that was for me? Where should we take them for dinner? They are staying in the new hotel on Freemont Street."

"I think Don would like Fish Hoppers. They have good seafood, but the servers are a little weird."

"I hope to God we don't get a goofy one this time." Renee stepped out of the car and lit another smoke. She looked up in the sky and saw the big jet. "Christ, the jet is getting ready to land."

"Renee, no killer flies around the country in a private jet. I still believe Vicki is full of crap and the rest of you are idiots for believing her. You should have called Faith and found out the truth. Vicki could turn a shoplifting into an armed robbery of the bank with ten people being murdered."

Jake and Emily were on the way over from Lilleyville. Jake had heard the story and gone straight to the internet. It took about thirty seconds for him to realize Don was a big time criminal attorney. The man was as far from a felon as he was. Jake had been waiting thirty years to watch the Martin's make a fool of themselves. He didn't say a word as they drove across the state. He was licking his chops at the prospect.

"Are you nervous about meeting Don?"

"I hope we make it back alive. This mafia business is deadly stuff. When you cross these men, they put the hammer on you."

"I don't even know what to say to him. I've never been this nervous in my entire life."

"Let the old ones take, the lead. They are much older and wiser than we are. Let us hope no one upsets the man."

"Thank you for coming, Jake. I felt I had to come and see Faith. She was always my favorite sister."

"I would not miss this for the world. I am at peace with my God and if this is the end, I am prepared to move on to a better life."

"Oh Lord, Jake! Surely, Don would never kill any of us."

"When you have wasted six people, you don't care about killing the seventh one, Emily. You know how much I love to read. The experts all say the hardest murder is the first one. From then on, it just becomes easier each time you kill. Once you have killed three or four, it becomes a necessity to continue killing in order to get the gratification you need. You and I better hope none of your family shows their ass. He might just put the hammer down on all of us."

"My God in heaven! What has Faith done?"

The big jet landed and Faith walked off holding Don's hand. Renee and Paul greeted them and everyone was introduced. They walked back to the car and off to the hotel they went. Renee kept looking in the mirror at Don as the men spoke. They pulled up to the hotel and got out.

"We will wait for you in the lobby," Renee said.

"Thank you so much for the ride. We will be down for dinner in fifteen minutes," Don said.

Paul looked at Renee as they sat waiting. She was a nervous wreck and was smoking nonstop. "I'm telling you Vicki is full of shit. No murderer acts like that Renee. That damn jet cost forty million dollars. I've seen the plane before in a business magazine."

"The girls are crazy about him. I can't reach either one of them. I have tried since Vicki and Florence told me the story. Don said we are going to dinner, Paul. Dinner is over. We are going to supper."

"People from the city refer to supper as dinner, Renee. Anne and Carol are both going to laugh in your face. You better be damn careful because you are on the verge of making a complete fool of yourself. If that man is a murderer, I am the damn Governor."

Don and Faith came down and the four of them drove to the restaurant. They were seated and ordered a round of drinks. Don had backed a friend starting a chain of hamburger restaurants in Florida. He noticed the manager was a real worker and sharp as hell. He wanted to get her name and the number of the restaurant. The four were making small talk when the waitress came back to the table. Don picked up a comment card off the table and asked the lady if he could borrow her pen.

"Sure honey," she said and handed Don a pen.

"Thank you very much. What is the name of your manager?"

"Sue Ellen Monroe."

"May I have the number of the restaurant?"

The woman dropped her shoulder to the side and stared at Don. She looked around as if to see if anyone was listening or watching her. "You want my number?"

"No. I want the number of the restaurant."

"I don't know the number of the restaurant, but you can have my number anytime you want." She started to walk off and turned to Don. "You're welcome," she said.

Don looked at Faith, Renee and Paul and shook his head. "Did I miss something?"

Renee and Paul looked at each other and the waitress as she walked away. "How can you work at a place and not know the number? That idiot has been here at least five years," Paul said.

"Jesus, I can't believe it. That ding bat broad is full of shit. We will get you the number before we leave, Don. How embarrassing," Renee said.

Anyway, Don had the comment card and a pen to write. So help me God, if Buck Beavers twin brother didn't walk up to the table.

"Did you use all the creamers I brought you last time?" he asked Renee.

"Yes, I did and thank you so much."

Buck placed two buckets full of the little creamers on the table in front of Renee and looked around. "Huh! Huh! Huh! Don't tell the manager or she will fire my ass."

Don picked up the card and pen and looked at the idiot. "Excuse me, could I have the number of the restaurant?"

Buck looked at the comment card and turned white as a sheet. "This restaurant?"

"Yes," Don said.

"445-7695. Are you going to call the manager?"

"Yes, I'm going to call her first thing tomorrow and have a chat with her."

"Oh hell, you're going to get me fired." Buck hauled ass across the floor like they were giving away hundred dollar bills and disappeared into the night.

"They need to fire his stupid ass," Paul said.

They finished dinner and Paul drove them back to the hotel. Once again Don thanked Paul and Renee for their time and trouble. They watched as Don opened the door for Faith and they went in the hotel. Paul drove off and headed for Renee's home.

"Renee, you are going to make a fool out of yourself if you say one word to Faith about Don. Those old fools need to be put in a mental institution. That man is a real gentleman."

"I'm afraid you are wrong, Paul. You just can't judge a book by the cover."

"Don't say I didn't warn you."

The next day, Renee and Emily picked up Faith to go shopping. Don went to play a round of golf with Jake. Vicki and Florence were busy preparing the meal for the evening. R.E. and Howard went for a ride and stopped at a garage sale.

When the three sisters got together, it was usually non stop chatter. Faith noticed both Renee and Emily seemed distracted and were saying nothing. "Why are the two of you being so quiet?"

"I think everyone is a little uptight about meeting Don tonight. We're just plain country folks," Emily said.

"Don is a little uptight about meeting the family. He is an only child and he has never been around a big family like ours."

"I hope everyone is on their best behavior. I don't want anything to upset Don," Renee said.

"I hope so too, Renee. Don has a terrible temper and when someone get's out of line it is really bad. My God, one night at our favorite restaurant, a man slapped his wife and knocked her to the floor. He was screaming at the poor woman and blood was coming from her mouth. It was an ugly scene and all the patrons were just mortified. Don proceeded to get up and put the man to sleep on the spot. He didn't even know the man. Don never said a word to the man before he wasted him. My husband helped the woman off the floor and handed her his handkerchief. Once he seated her, he sat back down like nothing out of the ordinary had even happened. He just looked at me and said the white trash wouldn't be slapping any more women. It was quite a scene when the ambulance came and they carried the man away. Everyone in the place stood up and applauded for two minutes. Don didn't even acknowledge the applause."

"Did he get arrested and have to go to court?" Emily asked.

"He never loses in court, Emily. I went to court and watched one of his murder trials. The man walked away free as a bird. He killed four people in a hotel room in Miami. Don claimed a drug deal went bad and he killed all of them in self defense. The jury bought it and came back in six minutes with their verdict. After the trial, all twelve jurors came out and hugged my husband. The women wanted his autograph and their pictures taken with him. You can't imagine how happy Don was when he won. Hell, I'm glad I went and showed my support. Two of those bitches were real lookers and crawling all over Don. It happens every single time he has a murder or drug trial. The women go crazy and he wins."

"Oh my God," Emily said.

"I can't believe it," Renee said.

"You both can believe it. I saw it with my own eyes and it wasn't a pretty sight. The restaurant owner came to our table and bought us a round of drinks. She insisted Don could not even pay for dinner. A woman walked over to our booth half dressed and told Don she would like to take him to bed. I told her in no uncertain terms to hit the road while she still could."

"Oh my God, Faith, I don't even know what to say," Emily said.

"Why do you think the women always let him off?" Renee asked.

"He flirts with every damn woman on the jury the entire time. It used to really bother me. But, after a while you realize it has nothing to do with you. He just has to win at all costs. He takes the bitches to bed every day in the courtroom. When a man's life is at stake, you do what you have to do. I know of at least fifty love letters women jurors have sent him."

"My God, did you find them, Faith?" Renee asked.

"No. He shows them to me. He is proud as a peacock and loves showing them to me."

"When did you realize what you had gotten yourself into, Faith?" Emily asked.

"It started as soon as we got back from our honeymoon. It wasn't three months before he had a murder trial. Don won and the District Attorney told the press if he didn't know better he would swear Don had been doing it all his life. I have to say I agree completely with the District Attorney. I would be completely freaked out if I was involved in a murder or drug trial. Don just thrives on going to the courtroom and kicking ass. The man is so good in a courtroom, it is just unbelievable. The prosecutors hate going to court against him. The only thing I don't like is that we can never be seen together in front of a camera or have our picture in the newspapers. We have to make all the women think Don is single and available."

"Why do you put up with him carrying on like that?" Renee asked.

"I have no choice, Renee. You cannot imagine in your wildest dreams how much money Don makes. It just blows me away how much the drug dealers pay him."

"I don't even know what to say, Faith," Renee said.

Emily's eyes were big as a saucer as she eased off and called Vicki. Renee could barely breathe as Faith went about her shopping. Vicki heard the anxiety in Emily's voice the moment she picked up the phone.

"Vicki, you and Howard better make sure everyone is on their best behavior tonight. Faith just told Renee and me about Don killing four people at one time. He has a violent temper and killed another man in a restaurant. He didn't even know the man, Vicki. Don just stood up and flat out killed him without saying one word. I'm worried sick about Jake out on that golf course with the man."

"My God, she told you he killed four people at one time?"

"She said she went to the trial and he walked free. One of his drug deals went bad and he blew them away in the local motel room. The strange thing was the jurors all came out and hugged him. The women wanted his autograph and a picture taken with him."

"They were probably all scared to death. I would never want the man mad at me. I better invite the Sheriff and the Chief to come tonight."

"Faith was carrying on about how much money his drug dealers bring him. She is going to fool around and get busted living with that man."

"Mark my words, Emily. That girl is in way over her head. Let me ring off Emily; Florence is foaming at the mouth over here."

Emily walked over to Renee, who was sitting down smoking a cigarette. "Renee, we are going to lose Faith. I can't believe she has gotten herself in a fix like this."

"My mind will not slow down thinking about the situation. I would just die if I found out my husband was a murderer. On top of that, it sounds like he is sleeping with half the women in Florida. The poor baby has to sit and watch him flirt with women right in front of her. Why is Faith so damn happy?"

"I'll just be honest with you, Renee. The man must have completely brain washed her. The nerve of the man, showing her fifty different women sending him loves letters."

Across town, R.E. and Howard pulled into Beth Ashley's yard sale and got out. Howard saw Vicki was calling and told R.E. to go on without him.

"I'll be looking for some tools, Howard. Come find me when you finish your call," R.E. said.

"Alright, let me answer the phone," Howard said. He picked up and Vicki's voice was breaking with fear.

"Howard, call the Sheriff and the Chief and invite them to supper. Faith must have lost her mind bringing that man to our house."

"What has happened now, Vicki?"

"The man killed four people at one time. He was in town doing one of his drug deals and it went bad. He killed a man he didn't even know in a restaurant right in front of everyone. Emily said he has a violent temper and the least little thing sets him off. I am worried sick about tonight. My damn head is spinning around like a top."

"Jesus Christ, put my pistol under my chair. I'll have R.E. bring his with him. He keeps one in his glove box. You call Scooter when we hang up and tell him to bring his gun. We have found ourselves in a hell of a bad situation here."

Vicki was so shook up that she got her story even more tangled up. "Damn, I would never have believed Faith would go off the deep end. I heard the sirens, but I didn't know what was going on. I can't believe the nerve of the man to kill four people and stay in town. Don has to be one bad son-of-a-bitch with no fear of the law."

"Let me go and get R.E. I hope to God we live to see tomorrow, Vicki."

Vicki looked up and Florence had the Jack Daniels bottle and a wild look in her eyes. "I never thought in my wildest dreams I would meet a mass murderer. This boy must get his kicks blowing people away. Hell, he just killed four men in the snap of an eye," Florence said.

R.E. was done shopping and put his merchandise on the table. He paid Beth her money and went looking for Howard. When he came back, a monster of a man was looking down at him. R.E. reached to pick up the things he bought.

The man laid his hand over R.E. and frowned. "I want that stuff little fellow. Why don't you go back home to your momma?"

"You're too late. I already bought and paid for it. My momma has been dead for ten years."

"I ought to take the tools and stick your skinny old ass under my foot. I ain't stepped on a bug in five days."

R.E. and the monster looked up to see Howard running over with a look of horror on his face. Howard had suffered from a hearing loss for years and when he got excited all bets were off. He was out of breath and shaking violently.

"R.E., Don just killed four men. The men didn't pay for the drugs and he wasted them in the motel. Faith has confessed to Emily that he has killed four men since he hit town."

"Jesus Christ, there must be a massive manhunt for him. I've been hearing sirens going nonstop for the last hour," R.E. said.

The monster started to back up and stared at Howard with a wary eye. He looked over and saw the look of shock on Beth's face.

"Vicki wants you to bring your gun and Scooter will bring his too. Shit, the man has been in town less than twenty four hours and murdered four people. Where in the hell are the damn cops."

"Is he bull-shitting?" the monster asked R.E.

"Hell no, Howard is giving you the straight skinny. The man flew in from Florida and he is having dinner at Howard's house tonight. The man is in the mafia and has killed a dozen people. Come on Howard, we need to get over there quick and get our guns placed. This son-of-a-bitch is worse than Wayne ever thought about being."

The monster backed away and didn't say another word. Howard and R.E. took off for the truck like a bat out of hell. Beth was taking it all in and called her husband in a panic. "Earnest, there is a mass murderer on the loose in our town. Howard Minter just told me he killed four people. Where are you?"

"I'm stopped on the interstate. The police have road blocks set up on both sides of the freeway. I knew some bad shit must be coming down."

"My Lord, what has the world come too."

"Get yourself in the house and lock the doors, Beth. I may be stranded on the highway for hours. Did Howard know who he killed?"

"He said the man's name was Don. He flew his plane in from Florida and killed four people over a drug deal. I don't know who he killed. I just know it was over drugs. Whatever you do don't get close to Howard's house. They got their guns and they are ready for him."

"Why is he after Howard?"

"I have no idea what Howard did to piss him off. I can tell you that Howard is scared half to death. R.E. was with him and is just as scared. Maybe the damn Martin's have done something to bring the killer to Littleville."

"You get my shotgun out of the closet and don't you move until I get there. That damn Howard probably slept with the man's wife. Stump Hacker tried to kill him seven years ago when he caught him with Elsie. Maybe we will get lucky and Don has already flown his plane out of town. My word here comes two police helicopters right over the top of me. I've never seen this many cops in my life."

"What am I supposed to do about all my merchandise in the yard?"

"Beth, if you don't get your butt in the house, you may not be alive to worry about your merchandise."

"Alright, I'm heading inside right now. Earnest, keep your ass in that car with the doors locked. I better not hear of you trying to be a hero."

"Woman, you must think I'm the dumbest bastard on earth. The chances of me trying to take down a mass murderer are zero."

Out at the golf course, Jake's cell phone rang. He excused himself and took the call from Vicki.

"Jake, are you alright? We are all worried sick about you."

Jake had been waiting for thirty years to get the Martin bunch and he was not going to miss the opportunity. The man had taken a lot of abuse over the years from Old Buck and the Martin clan. He had a big smile on his face when he spoke. "I think I will be alright. He got upset twice when he hit a bad shot. Once, he said he was going to beat the hell out of me if it happened again."

"Jake, you need to get Don back to the hotel and get over here. I don't want to scare you but Emily just found out about five more murders. Renee and Emily think Faith has gone off the deep end."

"Let me see if I can get Don to leave. We are almost finished with the round. I have to be really careful not to upset the man. Lord, he just missed a putt and threw his club in the tree. He is glaring at me like I caused him to miss. He is walking right towards me and this could be the end for me. Tell Emily my life insurance policy is in my desk drawer."

"Oh, my God! What is going to happen?"

"I don't know, but he has a mean look on his face. I should never have come over here. Tell Emily I want to be buried next to my Mother. I have to go before it is too late, Vicki."

"I'll tell her, Jake."

Vicki hung up and called her son. Jimmy Ray was famous for his smart mouth. Howard had always called him Scooter since he was a small child. Scooter had been drinking with two of his buddies at the Homer Watson bar all afternoon. Scooter looked at his cell phone and saw his mother was calling.

"Momma, I'll be over there on time tonight. Amanda is refusing to come with me."

"Scooter, your father wants you to bring your gun. I'm afraid we have a mass murderer coming for dinner and he has a violent temper. Son, please keep your mouth shut and don't say a word. I don't want to lose you tonight."

"Mother, are you drinking?"

"No, but I should be, Scooter. Your Aunt Faith has married a mafia man. We are all having a fit and scared to death. Jake is out on the golf course with him now. He doesn't think he is going to make it out alive."

"You have to be kidding me."

"I'm serious as terminal cancer. Get your tail over here and bring your gun. Don't you dare open your mouth when you get here. The man has just killed four men over a bad drug deal. You call Sarah and find out who got smacked. I think her drug source just got wiped out."

Scooter hung up and looked at his buddies. Wilmer and Jackie had been listening and had a look on their faces that was begging for an answer.

"My mother and father have completely lost their minds. I got to be going. They are telling me a mass murderer is coming to their house tonight. My father must be back on the whiskey. The dude put four men to sleep over a drug deal gone bad in a local motel. They want me to bring my gun and put it under my chair."

"I bet Bubba Fredrick got wasted with his men," Wilmer said.

"Good riddance to bad rubbish, Scooter. I never liked the sorry bastard. He finally got what was coming to him," Jackie said.

"Man, I can't believe this bad ass is coming to my parents' house. I don't want any part of this sucker."

"You better leave that mother alone," Jackie said.

"Scooter, I wouldn't even go over there if I was you," Wilmer said.

"I can't believe he is staying after killing four men. He must be one cold-blooded son-of-a-bitch. Man, it's like he is daring anyone to screw with him."

"That's what I'm talking about, man. If you or I killed four people, we would be hauling ass out of town. This bad ass is staying and coming for dinner. You better not go over there," Jackie said.

"What am I supposed to do, Jackie? I can't stand up my parents and let them be murdered."

"Man, y'all are all crazy as hell. Everyone needs to make a run for it and get the hell out of town while they can. The dude ain't going to hang around town forever," Wilmer said.

Jake dropped Don off at the hotel and headed over to Renee's house to get Emily. She ran out the door and hugged him. "I've been worried sick something terrible was going to happen, Jake."

"I'm happy to say everything worked out just fine."

"Jake, Emily and I think Faith has lost her mind. She flat out told us about Don killing a man in their favorite restaurant. He killed four men in Florida in a hotel room over a bad drug deal."

"I say both of you are full of bull," Paul said.

"Paul, you don't know what you're talking about. I told you Emily and I heard it directly from Faith."

"Both of you are as bad as the old ones. The man has not killed anyone."

"We need to get over to Vicki's house before Don arrives," Emily said.

"Emily, be very careful what you say to the man," Jake said.

They drove over together and went in the house. Everyone was nervous as a cat on a hot tin roof. At six o'clock sharp, the limo pulled up and Don and Faith walked in Howard and Vicki's house. Over forty family members were present and Don was introduced to all of them. There was tension in the house and Don sensed it immediately. He sat down with Howard and R.E. and started to visit.

"Are we going dove hunting?"

"The birds didn't come in this year," Howard said.

"I think we should wait until next year," R.E. said.

"Faith told me you love to hunt coons, Howard. I've never been coon hunting. I think I'd like to try it."

"Both of my coon dogs are sick. Their down and out today."

"Okay. You guys know about the hunting around here. I brought my shotgun and shells with me. I keep guns on my plane all the time. You never know when you will get the opportunity to use them. I love it when I get the chance to shoot my guns. How about letting me take you out for a round of golf?"

R.E. and Howard looked at each other, but said nothing. Both of them usually talked nonstop, but today they were at a loss of words.

Renee looked at Emily. "I can't believe a man that nice goes around killing people, Emily. I let both of my girls go spend a week with him."

"You can't judge a book by the cover, Renee. I'm keeping a close eye on Scooter with his big mouth. I told Jake not to get close to him. Thank God Moose didn't come with us this time."

Vicki and Florence were watching intently to Don's every move. Florence took a shot of her Jack Daniels she had in her paper cup. "He seems so nice, Florence," Vicki said.

"Maybe he has one of them split personalities. The Sheriff needs to get his ass on over here before all hell breaks loose. We're liable to wind up in a tight spot when he comes in. Don may figure out he has come to arrest him."

"The Chief can't come, but Rufus and Howard have their guns. Scooter has his under his seat and the boy has his hand under the seat."

"You better not be counting on those three to save us. Don will waste all their asses in a split second."

"I'm getting light headed, Florence. I think I'm going to pass out any second now."

"Would you just look at Don talking to Howard and Rufus? Vicki, he ain't the least bit worried about the cops showing up. Both of them are about to have heart attacks."

Across the room, Don sat talking to the men. "Y'all know Ben Rollins?"

"Everybody knows Ben. He is a legend in this neck of the woods, Don," R.E. said.

"Ben is picking me up in the morning and we are going to his country club. You guys are welcome to join us if you have an interest. The club professional is joining us for a round."

"Well, I guess it would be okay," Howard said.

"How do you know Ben," R.E. asked.

"We are both in the same line of work."

The front door flew open and Anne and Carol ran across the room and hugged Don. Everyone was staring and looking at each other. Jake had his camera and was filming the whole scene.

"How are my favorite girls?" Don asked.

"Are you ready to unwind and party?" Carol asked.

"Let's do it tomorrow night."

"I can't wait to see New York," Anne said.

The Sheriff came in with his wife and Vicki jumped up from the table. She sprinted across the room and gave him and his wife a hug. "Thank God you are here. Please be careful when you cross the floor to see the man."

"Did you just wax your floor, Vicki?" Sheriff Holley asked.

"You sure are one cool customer, Sheriff. Man, you must not be afraid of the Devil himself."

The Sheriff gave Vicki a strange look and walked straight over to Don. "I never would have believed Don Hudson would be in Littleville. I've heard every story about you."

"I'm here," Don said.

Everyone started to shake as the Sheriff reached and pulled his gun. Howard, R.E. and Scooter slid their hands under the seat and prepared for the worst.

"Oh no," Renee said.

"Get down behind the counter, Renee," Emily said.

"The Sheriff handed Don the gun. Don, this is a gift from the Sheriff's Association from around the country. You saved a good man from going to prison. He was a man who had no choice but to kill four men in self defense. That under cover policeman and every law enforcement person in America will always be grateful to you. The fact that you defended him and refused to take a dime will never be forgotten. If you ever need anything, you just say the word. There is not a police officer in this country that won't go to the mat for you."

"Thank you so much, Sheriff Holley. I'm glad I could help the man and his family."

"God, I loved going to the trial with Aunt Faith," Carol said. "You make Ben Rollins look like a rookie out of law school. You had me convinced that man killed those four men in self defense. You had those bitches in the palm of your hand."

The men and women looked at each other as Carol went on. "Don has never lost a case when he was defending a client."

"He is poetry in motion. You have to see him in action to believe it. Carol and I are crazy about you," Anne said.

Faith walked across the room and hugged the girls. "That's right, you all. My baby has never lost a single case. It is wonderful seeing you and your wife again, Sheriff."

"Faith, you got yourself a good man. I'm happy as hell for you and Don," Sheriff Holley said.

"We are all so very happy for you Faith," Mrs. Holley said.

Jake looked at Don and spoke. "Do you represent people involved in murder cases, Don?"

"I don't really like it, but it pays very well."

"You practice criminal law."

"Yes, I do Jake."

Paul looked at Renee and started laughing. He was pointing his finger at her and holding his stomach. Don looked around and everyone was laughing. R.E. looked at Howard and shook his head. Finally, Vicki came over and hugged Don.

"I don't know where my head was Don. I'd like to choke my fool self. We all thought you were a murderer and drug dealer."

"You crazy old fool," Carol shouted.

"Jesus, you people are sick," Anne said.

"Good God, Vicki have you lost your mind? Don is the top defense attorney in the country and the darling of policemen everywhere," the Sheriff said.

"How on earth did you come to believe Don was a murderer?" Faith demanded to know.

"Stupidity," Jake said." If they knew how to read and turn on the internet, there are sixty eight stories of Don's success."

Don stood and gave Vicki a hug. "Hey, that's okay. I'm not offended. I'm ready for your home cooking, Vicki."

"Lord, I'm never going to get over making a fool out of myself," Vicki said.

"I warned you, Renee. You were going to make a fool out of yourself. How dumb could you be? You crazy fools are going to be the laughing stock of the county when this story hits the streets."

"You go straight to hell, Paul."

Emily was not the least bit amused and was in her husband's face. "Jake, I ought to choke you."

"You got exactly what you deserved, Emily. Maybe this will teach you a good lesson. I've been trying to tell you for thirty years, your family is messed up. They are the dumbest people on earth."

"Don't you even speak to me," Emily shouted.

Scooter took a deep breath and started to get his gun from under the seat. The boy had no sooner touched the damn gun when it went off and shoot a hole in the sofa. Scooter yelled and everyone including the Sheriff hit the floor looking for cover. The women were screaming and the men were looking to see if they had been hit. Let me tell you, it was a hell of a scene.

"Who's shooting?" Howard yelled.

"It was me, Daddy. My damn gun went off."

"Damn, Scooter! You scared us all to death," Sheriff Holley shouted.

"Boy, don't you know to keep the safety on. My damn hands are shaking like a leaf," Rufus said.

It took some time, but everyone settled down. You can bet your life, Florence got her two cents worth in. R.E. wanted to crawl under the floor, he was so embarrassed. By the end of the night, Don had become a folk hero. The Martin's were their usual selves the rest of the evening. The women took turns cursing each other out privately and the men did the same. Emily was so mad at Jake, she could have spit. Scooter never got over the gun going off. Both he and his sister, Sarah, were sure their parents were both completely insane. Scooter was so shook up, he had to excuse himself and go home to change clothes. The Sheriff and his wife had seen enough and excused themselves as well. Carol and Anne were mad as hell and never forgave their mother. Don couldn't wait to get home and tell the story to his business partner. Renee went out side and smoked. She called Kate and gave her the whole story. It took Scooter a week to convince Jimmy the story was true.

CHAPTER FIVE

The next morning Ben picked up Don at the hotel and they drove out to the Twelve Trees Golf Club on the edge of town. It was an overcast and windy day, but no rain was in the forecast.

"The golf course looks beautiful from the air, Ben," Don said.

"You will love playing the course. It is the third highest rated course in the state. I have dinner twice a week in the clubhouse."

"Twelve Trees is an unusual name. How did someone come up with a name like that?"

"Two old families owned the land forever. The men were best friends for fifty years. One of them died and the other fellow bought the family out. Someone found out the fellow who bought the family out was carrying on with the widow. One of the grandson's didn't take the news very well. He proceeded to take a chain saw and cut down twelve trees along the road. Sam Meyers bought the land from the fellow and loved the story. He decided to name the club Twelve Trees."

"Hell, why not," Don said.

They pulled in the parking lot and the valet brought a cart and put their clubs on. They drove to the driving range and hit balls. Howard and R.E. drove up and parked their truck. They got out and a young man drove up in a golf cart just as a woman walked across the parking lot.

"Are you gentlemen playing today?" he asked.

Howard looked at the woman and shook his head. "Son, I had to give up playing when I found the Lord. I ain't going to stand here and lie to you about it. I still miss the hell out of casting around for strange fish."

"Damn you, Howard, the boy is asking if we are playing golf. He don't give a shit about your sex life."

Howard looked at the cart boy and spoke. "I'm sorry, young fellow, about the confusion. We are playing with Ben Rollins and Don Hudson."

"I'll be happy to put your clubs on the cart. Mr. Ben and Mr. Hudson are on the driving range."

"Thank you very much. Howard give me a dollar."

"Why do you want me to give you a dollar?"

"I need to give the young man two dollars."

"Is he with the church?"

"I don't know if the boy is with the church. Just give me the damn dollar."

Howard reached in his billfold and handed R.E. a dollar. R.E. gave the young man two dollars. They got in the cart and the young man pointed out the driving range. They climbed in and R.E. drove over to the range. They got out and walked over to Don.

"Good morning, it is a beautiful day," Don said.

"Praise the good Lord. R.E. and me just donated a dollar each to the collection."

"You must both be good Christian men, Howard. R.E., do you and Howard play very often?"

"I used to play a lot, Don. In the past year we probably only played twice. It was really nice for you and Ben to let us poor boys join you."

"Well, we are going to have an unforgettable experience today. I'm glad you both decided to join us."

"I am looking forward to a fun day," Howard said.

"Howard, what do you shoot?"

"I shoot mostly coons, Don. I used to shoot ducks and geese but I don't much anymore. I got a fine coon dog, if you're ever of the mind to go hunting. That dog can sniff a coon half a mile away."

"He means what kind of golf score you shoot, Howard," R.E. said.

"I can't rightly say I ever shot a golf score. What kind of animal is it?"

"Christ, Howard! You have started already," R.E. said.

"I haven't started anything."

They got in their carts and drove over to the first tee. Ben was laughing so hard he was about to wreck the cart. "This is going to be a golf outing we will not soon forget, Don," Ben said.

"I think he was serious."

"You can bet your last nickel he was serious. Howard lost his brain a long time ago."

Don stood on the first tee with Ben as the club pro joined them. Howard and R.E. stood watching at the back of the tee box.

"You have a beautiful club, Ben."

"Don, it is a pleasure having you here. I want you to meet Tom Morrow. Tom is our pro and does a hell of a job."

"Don, it is a real pleasure to meet you," Tom said.

The men shook hands and Don noticed a flight of geese flying over. "Do you have a problem with the geese? They have to shoot flare guns to keep them off our course in Florida."

"We are having hell with the geese and the groundhogs, Don. I have two flare guns in my bag. If the damn geese try to land on the greens, I'll fire on them. We have a hell of a mess with the groundhogs digging holes beside the greens."

"I've never seen a groundhog," Don said.

"They are big and ugly. They're low slung to the ground and sound like a herd of deer when they come running down the hill. We have been trying for three years to get rid of them."

Howard stood with R.E. looking over the golf course. "Howard, try not to make a fool out of yourself. We are out here with powerful men and I'm very nervous."

"Hell, I knew that boys father and he was one of the finest men I ever met. Don't you worry about a thing."

"What boy's father are you talking about?"

"I'm talking about the boy who brought our golf cart over to us when we got here."

R.E. had both hands on his hips staring at Howard as Ben walked over. "Do you boys care to make a wager on who wins the match?"

"We are bad golfers, Ben," R.E. said.

"Hell, we can play for a dollar a hole. That way, no one get's raped."

"Howard, I'll give you and R.E. a stroke a hole," Tom said.

"There ain't no way in hell you're giving me a stroke a hole."

"Alright, I'll give you two strokes a hole, Howard."

"Ben, tell this man R.E. and me are straight shooters. Ain't anybody but Vicki going to give me a stroke."

"Howard, if you don't stop making an ass out of yourself, these men is going to run our ass off," R.E. said.

"Howard, you missed your calling. You should have been a stand up comedian," Don said.

"Don, no one told me until it was too late. I started hearing about how funny I was when I hit sixty five. I'd gone and retired by then."

They teed it up and Don, Tom, and Ben drove their balls down the middle of the fairway. R.E. was so nervous he hit his ball straight up in the air.

"Hit a mulligan," Tom said

"What's a mulligan, R.E.," Howard asked.

"Another ball, Howard," R.E. said.

"I thought a mulligan was a fish. My Daddy said they taste real bad and weren't fit to eat. He said if you caught one to just throw the fish back in the lake. My Daddy said they weren't good for nothing."

R.E. shook his head and had a frown on his face. Anyway, R.E. hit it a little better and it was Howard's turn.

"You're up, Howard," Tom said.

"I was up since five o'clock, son."

"I mean it is your turn to hit," Tom said.

Howard got over the ball and took a swing. He hit is dead sideways where four men were standing on another green.

"Fore!" Don and Tom yelled.

"Fore? What are they talking about, R.E.?"

"Never mind, just hit another ball."

"Do I have to hit a mulligan like you did?"

"Hit the damn ball, Howard! You are embarrassing the hell out of me. You can't slow the course down."

"I was born at night, but, it wasn't last night. The damn ground can't move and I know it."

"I'm telling you, Howard could be a stand up comedian," Don said.

"Trust me Don, he is just being himself," Ben said.

Tom and Don were both excellent golfers and Ben was hanging in. R.E. and Howard were all over the course. They had played the front nine and Howard and R.E. had finally started to relax from thinking Don was a murderer. The cart girl came by on the next hole and Don bought Howard and R.E. another beer.

"Can you believe we are out here with Ben and Don?"

"R.E., you are always making fun of me. You must be trying to play a trick on me. Of course, I believe we are out here with Ben and Don. I'm looking right at them ten feet from me."

They teed off on number ten and Howard's ball landed about fifteen feet behind a tree. He walked over to his ball and pulled out an iron. He turned and looked at Don. "I'm going to give it a good whack."

"Howard, be careful if the ball hits a tree, it could come back and hit you."

"Thanks Don, I'll watch out for it."

Howard took a mighty swing and sure enough it hit the tree and came right back at his head. He was diving to get out of the way and landed smack in the middle of a pile of goose shit. Don and Ben had to turn away they were laughing so hard. Tom walked over and helped Howard up.

"I'm covered in goose shit, R.E."

"Golf is a rough game old friend."

They played the next two holes without incident and drove over to the thirteenth hole. Howard hit his drive way off line and it landed in a hazard. They drove the carts over to help Howard find his ball.

"There it is, in the ditch," R.E. said.

The ball was behind a big log and Howard reached down to move it. "Howard, you can't touch the ball. It is laying in a hazard," Tom said.

The man bolted straight up as if he saw a snake. "Don't you worry I know better than to touch hazard material. Man, they let y'all have a toxic waste dump on the golf course?"

Ben, Don and Tom were laughing so hard their stomachs hurt. Don tossed a ball on the ground for Howard. "Hit this one, Howard. It is safe."

"I'm just going on to the next hole, Don. This damn stuff is probably seeping under the ground all over the place. Ben, I have always been told you had a lot of clout, but this just takes the cake. A toxic waste site right smack in the middle of the damn country club."

When they got to the fifteenth green, both R.E. and Howard had put down four beers each and were feeling no pain. They all stood waiting to putt on the green. Howard and R.E. had their backs turned as the groundhog came barreling down the hill behind them raising nine kinds of hell.

"Tom has yelled fore a bunch of times when we're swinging. He don't ever yell when Don swings," Howard said.

"He is trying to warn the other players, Howard."

"Warn the other players about what, R.E?"

"Howard, he is trying to tell them your ball is about to hit them. Now that I think about it, have you ever been hit in the head with a golf ball?"

"That damn Ben has more clout than a bulldozer. Can you believe we were standing in a toxic waste site?"

R.E. was about to correct Howard about the toxic waste site when all hell broke loose.

"You sorry bastard," Tom screamed.

"Whoa, what happened?" R.E. said.

"Lord, I think another man may be after me," Howard said.

Tom grabbed his guns out of his bag and started firing away at the groundhog cursing at the top of his voice "I'll kill you son-of-a-bitch," Tom screamed.

R.E. and Howard turned to see Tom with a gun in each hand and firing at the groundhog. Ben and Don were moving fast to get out of the way. They didn't see the groundhog, but they damn sure saw the guns blazing in their direction. I can't say for sure what R.E. and Howard were thinking. They both took off running and never stopped until they got back to the clubhouse. Don, Ben, and Tom fell to the ground laughing for five minutes.

Golfers on the next three holes saw the two men running for their lives. The phones at the pro shop were going off as golfers on the course called to report the two men running.

"This is the Twelve Trees Golf Shop," Susan answered.

"I think two gay men got caught on the fifteenth hole in the woods," Johnny Irby told Susan. "They are running for their lives. You better call the police and get them out here fast. Larry and I both heard a lot of shots being fired. There has to be at least two guns going off."

"Where are they now?"

"There running up the sixteenth fairway. I almost hit one of them with my drive. One of them keeps falling down. The man may be hit."

"I'll call 9-1-1 right now."

"Can you believe this is happening right in front of our eyes?" Larry Norton, his playing partner asked.

"Those two wish they had stayed in the closet."

"I think you may be right, Johnny. The man just hit the ground again. Maybe we should drive up there and see if we can help."

"Larry, I'm not going to get shot trying to help two gay men escape. I'm not into that alternative lifestyle crap. I always heard they were not violent people and were more like women. I guess that is a bunch of crap."

"Those two men are running for their lives," Larry said.

"Keep running, R.E. They're hollering 'Fore back there!'"

"I'm running as fast as I can, Howard."

T.J Welch and Mitchell Blowback had hit their first shot and were driving down the seventeenth fairway on the cart path. Both of the men loved to drink and had each consumed a dozen beers. Mitchell looked out of the corner of his eye and saw them running. "Watch out, T.J.!" Mitchell yelled.

"What the hell are those two old men doing, Mitchell?" T.J. asked as he slammed on the brakes.

"There running for their lives, T.J."

Howard and R.E. had made a mad dash in front of the cart and almost been hit. The new addition was being built next to the fairway and the blasting was going on right across the hole at the top of the hill. The blast was very loud and R.E. and Howard thought it was coming at them. They dove on the ground. Mitchell and T.J. hit the ground as well. R.E. and Howard jumped up and started running again.

"Son-of-a-bitch! Someone is shooting at those two old men right here on the course," Mitchell said.

"I'm calling the pro shop right now. What kind of person would be shooting at two old men?" T.J. said.

"Can you see where the shots are coming from T.J.?"

"Hell, it looks like there coming from Old Man James house. He must have caught his wife with these two men. I hope I can still get it up when I'm their age. The old gal must be into threesomes. We ought to go up there and kick his old ass."

"That bastard has a gun you fool. What are we going to do; run up there with our nine irons?"

"I'm calling the pro shop right now."

"This is the Twelve Trees Golf Shop," Susan answered.

"Susan, this is T.J. and we have an incident going on. Two old men are being shot at right before mine and Mitchell's eyes. They are running for their lives and I don't know if their going to make it."

"I was just going to call the police. Mr. Irby just called and told me two gay men were being shot at. My God, snipers must be all over the course. Where are you and Mitchell?"

"We are on the next to last hole, halfway down the fairway. You better hurry, Susan. The bastard is shooting again and one of the old men just took a fall head first on the ground. These are two straight men that got caught by Harvey James."

Two members were signing in and listening to the conversation. "Is someone really shooting at people on the golf course," Ted asked.

"It must be horrible out there, Ted. Two gay men are being shot at on sixteen and two straight men are under fire on seventeen."

"Good Lord, there is no way we are going out there, Jack," Ted said.

"I have to go out there, Ted. My wife is playing with three of her friends. I have to get them out of harms way."

"Jack, I'm really sorry but I have to get out of here."

Susan had no sooner hung up when the third call came in. Janice Doggett stood on her back porch watching R.E. and Howard running past her home on the eighteenth fairway. She had known both the men for thirty five years and was not pleased that they were in her neighborhood.

"Golf shop, can I help you?" Susan asked.

"This is Janice Doggett. R.E. Cage and Howard Minter are running past my house. I think they have been caught by someone's husband. I heard lots of shots being fired and they're both running for their worthless lives."

"I'll call the police right now."

"You better get them out here fast. Those two have been cheating death for fifty years and their time may have run out. The shots are ringing out again as we speak."

"Oh my goodness! I hope we don't have a murder at Twelve Trees. Those men are not even members."

Susan was shaking as she called the police. Ted had his cell phone calling his wife. Jack took off down the first hole scared to death, looking to save his wife.

"Littleville Police Department how may I help you?" Sergeant Watt answered.

"This is Susan at Twelve Trees and we have six men being shot at on three different holes. Please get someone out here immediately."

"I will dispatch officers immediately, Susan. Sound the horn and try and get all the members attention. We need to get everyone off the golf course. It sounds like you have a sniper perched on a hill. Did you say they were firing from three different locations?"

"Yes, they are definitely shooting from three different places. Two of our members were under fire five minutes ago. There are six more men being shot at as well."

"Sound the horn and get those people off the course. We are on our way with help right now."

"Yes sir, I'll do it right now."

Watt hung up and hit the police radio. "Attention, all officers in the vicinity of Twelve Trees. We have multiple shootings on the golf course. Please respond immediately without delay."

"Car Seven. We are two miles away and will respond immediately. Do we know how many shooters we have? Over," Officer Cocker asked.

"My best guess is we are looking at the probability of three. At least eight men have been seen running for their lives."

Over the air came another call from policemen. "Watt, this is Warren with swat. We are on a training exercise four miles from the club. My men will respond in five minutes and I'm bringing in our sharpshooters in the helicopter."

"Roger. We have you, Warren," Watt said.

Joan's son, Herb, and his partner, Mary Ann Kidder, were hauling ass to the scene. Squad cars from across Littleville were on their way as well. "My bullet proof vest is in the trunk," Mary Ann said.

"Mine is in the trunk, too," Herb said.

"God, I hope we can subdue the shooters before they kill a bunch of people. The terrorists might have chosen our little town to strike. My uncle belongs to Twelve Trees. I hope to God he is not on the course."

The newspaper folks were listening to the police scanner and dispatched two reporters to the scene. Phil Kerry and Rudy Jenkins had been long time reporters at the Times. They had never encountered a situation like this before.

"We have a national story here, sure as hell," Phil said.

"I'm not going on that golf course and get my ass shot," Rudy said.

"God, I hope we don't get out there and find a lot of dead people."

"I can't believe we have a sniper shooting at people in the middle of the damn day."

Janice had turned around to see her husband listening after her phone call.

"I guess those two old rascals must have found some Viagra, Janice. I can't believe they got caught out in the middle of the golf course," Milton said.

"Howard's wife caught him with my cousin years ago. Vicki ran over him in a pay phone booth at the state park. She kept backing up and ramming the phone booth."

"Was Lucy with him in the phone booth?"

"She sure as hell was, Milton. Lucy was giving him a job on her knees. It saved her worthless ass from getting hurt badly. There was a ramp and the car hit the top of the phone booth. When it finally flipped over, she landed on top of Howard. Vicki got out, but they both ran for their lives."

The horn sounded and Tom looked at Ben and Don. It was an overcast day and people on the course thought a tornado warning was being issued.

"Why in the hell is Susan sounding the warning?" Tom said.

"There isn't any weather in the forecast," Ben said.

Tom called the pro shop and Susan answered. She saw his caller ID and sprung into her story. "Mr. Morrow, you need to get off the course. Someone is trying to kill eight men and I've had three separate calls from members. Shots are being fired on three separate fairways and the police are on their way. I took it upon myself to call for an ambulance."

"Nobody is shooting at eight men."

"I'm sorry to say you are very wrong. T.J. and Mitchell had to hit the ground to keep from being hit. They almost ran over the two men in the golf cart."

"Were they on seventeen, Susan?"

"They were on seventeen and Mr. Irby was on sixteen. Mrs. Janice called from her house on eighteen. Someone's husband is doing the shooting on seventeen, Mr. Morrow."

"Good Lord! I'm on my way to the clubhouse right now."

"What the hell is going on, Tom?" Ben asked.

"R.E. and Howard have created the perfect storm. Members are calling the shop telling Susan eight men are being shot at all over the back nine. She has the damn police and an ambulance on their way out here. T.J. and Mitchell must be drunk out of their minds. They think they're being shot at as well. I have to get up there fast and stop the story from spreading all over the damn state."

"You better get moving, Tom. A police helicopter just arrived and I hear the sirens in the distance," Don said.

Tom jumped in the cart and took off for the clubhouse. The word had spread and members were jumping in their cars and hauling ass off the property. Tom arrived at the clubhouse to find police everywhere and the press waiting with pen in hand. He approached the police and started to explain how everything went wrong. The press was all ears as he took them through the story.

Needless to say, R.E. and Howard had played their last round of golf. They had jumped in Howard's truck when they made it back to the parking lot and hauled ass for home. Three squad cars with sirens blaring passed them as they pulled out of Twelve Trees. The police helicopter came flying fifty feet over their truck. Less than a mile down the road, a half dozen more police cars were flying by them.

"There is a mass murderer on the golf course, Howard. We almost bought the damn farm. If that crazy Tom hadn't started shooting, we might not have been shot at by the damn fool. I wonder if anyone got killed."

"That's the scariest place I've ever been. We are blessed the Lord was with us. Praise the Lord."

"I hope the two men in the golf cart didn't get killed. They were moving fast trying to escape. They must have taken off in a different direction."

"I heard one of them scream at the top of his voice. He was shouting 'Watch out to his buddy."'

"We almost got shot when we came by those fellows. Man, they must have really pissed someone off big time."

"I'm sad to say I probably know why they were being shot at my friend. Rufus, when I was a sinner, I almost got killed a dozen times messing around with men's wives. They just don't take it well at all when they find out. Those boys probably got caught and the man came after them."

Fifteen minutes later Howard and R.E. walked in the house and looked up to see Vicki and Florence visiting. "What the hell happened to both of you?" Florence asked. "You look like you went swimming and saw a ghost."

"I ain't ever going to play golf again," R.E. said. "That damn pro at the club started shooting live rounds right where Howard and me were standing. I'll be damned if we didn't come up on two men being shot at themselves. There is a sniper at the club and the police are everywhere. We must have passed a dozen police cars hauling ass to the club. Howard saw a sharpshooter with his gun sticking out of the helicopter. I hope they nail the no good bastard."

"I swear to God, I thought we were dead men. I could see the flash coming out of the end of the gun. When I looked and saw those two men hit the ground, I thought my life on earth was over. The man kept shooting nonstop from the top of the hill. He must have a dozen assault rifles with him. He never ran out of ammo," Howard said.

"Is that bird shit all over you?" Vicki asked.

"Yes, I had to duck to keep from being hit and I landed in the bird shit."

"You ducked from the gun shots?"

"I ducked from the golf ball. Actually, I dove on the ground when the ball came back at me. Thank the good Lord that Don warned me before I swung. The gun shots came later when we were running."

"Where were Don and Ben?" Vicki asked.

"They were with us. I saw both of them running to get out of the way out the corner of my eye."

"We ran for our lives all the way to the clubhouse. I bet that damn Rollins put that son-of-a-bitch up to shooting at us," R.E said.

"Did Don run?" Florence asked.

"I don't think so, Florence. He was smart to stay where he was. All the shooting started two holes away. I damn sure wasn't interested in finding out where Don was heading," Howard said.

"Did you have any trouble getting away?" Vicki asked.

"My ass was stuck in the mud trying to wiggle free when I hit the top of the hill. They can take that damn Twelve Trees Country Club and stick it up their ass. Hell will freeze over before my little butt sees that place again. They got a damn toxic waste dump right on the golf course. I almost stepped right in the middle of the damn thing. The pro warned me just in the nick of time. I was going to touch it sure as hell."

"We almost got hit by a golf cart, Florence. I swear to God, I'm not lying to you. The two men were being shot at and we all hit the ground. That must be a rough place out there. Freddie Hickman over at the light department told me the city is always out there turning people's lights off."

"Where are your golf clubs?" Vicki asked.

"They're on the golf cart. We left the cart and ran for our lives. They can keep the damn golf clubs," R.E. said.

"Well, big spender you just carry your ass back out there and get the damn clubs. You can sell them and give me the money."

"Florence, I'm never going back out there. If you want your big ass shot at, you go get the damn clubs."

"Well, you damn sure ain't any macho man, Rufus. I'll go get the damn clubs but I'm selling them and the money is mine."

"You go right ahead, Big Mouth and get the clubs. Don't you come crying to me when those son-of-a-bitches start shooting at your big ass."

Don and Ben sat having a drink with Tom and one of Ben's partners in the Twelve Trees bar. The club was buzzing with stories of men being shot at by the snipers. T.J. and Mitchell were holding court with at least twenty members. All the members were stunned to hear Mitchell tell the story. T.J. damn sure backed him up in no uncertain terms. Of course the story got even better with the beer and whiskey flowing. They went from diving for cover to the bullets missing them by inches.

"That's the funniest thing I have ever seen in my life. I hope I can run like that in my seventies," Don said.

"Howard has years of practice," Ben said.

"Hell, I thought they heard me say I was going to shoot the groundhogs if we saw them. I was shocked when they took off running for the clubhouse. Susan is all shook up thinking people were being shot. It took me an hour to convince the cops and the press no one was being shot at anywhere. Mitchell and T.J. were swearing on their lives they saw live rounds being fired at R.E. and Howard. The crazy bastards are over there telling the bullshit story all over again."

"Those old rascals just have a guilt complex. Don, you will find out over the years the Martin bunch is a special breed of cat. Old Howard is the cat with nine lives. I know personally of seven men who tried to kill him. He just could not keep his dick in his pants and he loved screwing married women. R.E. still runs wild every chance he gets. Come on and I'll take you back to the hotel. Are you flying back tonight?"

"I think I'll go party with Anne and Carol. I promised them we would fly up to New York and let our hair down. Faith and I will fly back in the morning."

"You will have your hands full with those two girls. I don't know how much longer I can keep their butts out of jail."

Littleville was abuzz with stories of R.E. and Howard. Half had them getting caught with someone's wife. The other half had branded them both queers. Both the stories had live rounds being fired at both of them. The people living at Twelve Trees were all shook up about the shootings and spent a restless night with their doors firmly locked. The mass murderer named Don had somehow fled the county and escaped. Most people figured he had made it to the airport and flown away before the cops could find him. Numerous people said they saw the big jet take off into the sky. The story had gotten legs and people knew four men lay dead in a motel room. Every hotel owner in town swore it didn't happen in their motel. Most people assumed the man followed R.E. and Howard to Twelve Trees to finish his job. At least a dozen people saw a gunman in the air over the course. No one was able to find out who did the shooting at Twelve Trees but suspicion abounded as to who the man was. Mitchell and T.J. told their story to every member of the country club with absolute conviction. When one of the members questioned his honesty, Mitchell went right upside his head. Beth lost half her merchandise when she fled to the safety of her home. She told her story with equal conviction and got into a verbal shouting match at the church of all places. Her husband found himself defending her with friends and relatives. The local press was adamant in their coverage that no one was killed or even shot at for that matter. The newspaper was flooded with calls accusing them of being bald face liars. Of course, the locals knew better and figured Ben has used his power yet again to cover everything up. Howard, of course, confirmed along with R.E. that indeed all hell had broken loose that day at Twelve Trees. Florence and Vicki heard the stories of their husbands and watched with a careful eye. One thing was without question. Don never forgot his first visit to Littleville and neither did the family.

CHAPTER SIX

Jimmy was out of intensive care and Bobby Jack was still in jail. Sarah Watson was not at all happy with her husband. She had meet Jeff Carter at work several months ago and the two were getting real friendly. Sarah was Vicki and Howard's oldest daughter and a real firecracker. Jeff was married himself, but was not getting any sex at home. The two of them had finally decided to take the plunge. They drove over in separate cars and checked into the motel in Eastville. The town was about thirty miles down the interstate and almost at the state line. They both figured they could have a little fling and make it home by eleven. They both concocted what they thought were good stories. They had been romping in the bed for a couple of hours and smoking some good grass. Jeff looked at his watch and saw it was ten o'clock.

"I guess we better get dressed and head on home," Sarah said.

"Yeah, I can't wait to get together again. I feel young again for the first time in ten years."

"Baby, you are a world class lover. My husband is like a lawnmower cutting grass. You are a smooth lover and we have to do this again. You ain't much to look at, but you sure know how to please a woman."

"Sugar, you are the best I've ever known. Man, I feel like a million dollars! However, I sure wish you hadn't told me that I wasn't much to look at, Doll. My damn wife is always telling me the same thing."

"Honey, do yourself a favor and drop fifty pounds. You ain't trying out for the football team."

They got dressed and started to head out the door. Jeff's hand touched the doorknob when shots starting ringing out. It sounded like a war as bullets bounded off the building. They hit the floor and crawled under the bed as sirens started to blare.

"Jesus Christ, we are in the middle of a drug war," Jeff said.

"My husband is a cameraman for Channel Four. The station is going to dispatch him sure as I'm breathing. We have to figure out a way to get out of here. I can't believe my damn bad luck."

"Are you crazy? The shooting is still going on and the cops are here. They are going to be looking for eye witnesses."

"My damn car is in the parking lot, Jeff. Henry will see the damn thing when he arrives. The only thing I'm an eye witness to is the bottom of this damn bed. I have to get the hell out of here."

"Maybe he is in another county and they will send someone else. They have to have several camera crews at the station."

"Fat chance, Lover Boy. The way my luck runs, he will be here any minute."

Three rounds came flying through the window and glass was flying everywhere. It sounded like the third world war had started. "We are going to die right here," Jeff said.

"I'm not ready to check out just yet. These son-of-a-bitches are getting it on."

The shooting stopped and Jeff eased out from under the bed. He walked over and lifted the blind. "Damn, there are thirty cops in fifteen squad cars. Two fire trucks and three ambulances are here."

Sarah walked over and peeped out. "Oh Lord, they have roped off the parking lot. They are starting to go door to door, Jeff. I have got to get my ass out of here quick."

"The cops are writing down all the license plate numbers. My ass is staring at a big divorce."

Sarah's mind was racing now but panic had not set in. She picked up her cell phone and called Scooter. He almost didn't answer thinking it might be his wife.

"Hello," Scooter said.

"Scooter, this is Sarah. I got my ass trapped with a guy in the motel over here in Eastville. A drug deal must have gone bad and they shot up the place. The cops are everywhere and I know damn well the Channel Four film crew is going to be here any minute now. Henry will kill me when he gets here. You have to help me out of this mess."

"What room are you in?"

"327," she said.

"You ain't going to believe this Sarah. I'm in 331 with Nancy Thomas. Get your ass over here and take Nancy with you to the car. I'll tell Henry you and Nancy got together to plan a surprise party for his birthday."

"In a damn motel room late at night, Scooter? My God, you must think the man is completely brain dead."

"Give me a minute to think. You caught me off guard. I got it, Nancy was going to take her life and you rushed over to talk her out of it."

"I'm coming over right now."

"Where are you going?" Jeff asked.

"I'm headed two doors down and out of here before I buy the farm."

"What about me?"

"It's every dog for himself baby. You're a grown man and it is past time to be creative."

She grabbed her purse and out the door she went. Nancy heard the knock on the door and came out. "Come on, Sarah. Let's hit the road."

"This crap could only happen to me. Scooter, how the hell are you planning on getting out of here?"

"I'm walking out of here and driving Nancy's car to her house. I gave the desk clerk Jimmy's name and address."

"Jesus Christ, the man is in the hospital fighting for his life, Scooter."

"Why are you so uptight? He ain't going to mind. We always use each other for an alibi."

They got in the cars and hauled ass out of the parking lot. A mile and a half down the road, the Channel Four news team was flying by them. Helicopters were everywhere as the girls made their way home.

"I'm getting too old for this crap," Sarah said.

"Hell, I just needed a good lay. Your brother can go like a Boeing for hours. He can definitely take you across the country. Bobby Jack is the worst and Doctor Wind is right beside him."

"Be quiet, Nancy. I have to call Henry."

She dialed his cell phone and he answered. "Henry, Nancy and I are at the hospital with Jimmy. I will be home in ten minutes."

"I'm working on a story in Eastville. The Minden cartel from Tamaqua had a gunfight with a rival gang tonight. There are nine people dead and we have a national story."

"Nine people are dead, Henry?"

"Yes and four more are not expected to live. The state police have all the license plates and are running them as we speak. These guys were some bad actors and they were determined to end it all tonight."

"Henry, Nancy tried to take her life tonight. I had to go to the hotel in Eastville and get her before it was too late. She thinks she is pregnant with my brother's child and couldn't bear the thought."

"Jesus Christ, you could have been killed. The gang war was at the Eastville motel. That's where I am now."

"I understand fully that I could have been killed. Be careful and I'll see you when you get home."

"Can you even believe it?" Henry said.

"Did the idiot buy the story?" Nancy asked when they hung up.

"I think so, Nancy. God, what you don't have to go through to get a piece of ass."

The next morning, Jimmy sat up and said hello to the family. R.E. launched into the story of Bobby Jack with his usual flair. Florence was raising nine kinds of hell about missing the trip to gamble. Howard was telling Jimmy that he felt Bobby Jack was looking at three years in prison and that poor R.E. was going to go back to work, running the car wash. Vicki told everyone Beverly was at C Jacob Cattleman's office filing for divorce. Shirley filled him in on the mayoral race, which was heating up. Both the ex wives filled him in on Billy's status from the drug overdose. Sarah gave him the story of the drug deal going bad and the nine dead people.

"I heard the ambulances coming late last night. I thought the hospital must have been on fire," Jimmy said.

"It was terrible," Nurse Morgan said as she changed Jimmy's IV. "They were using assault rifles. One of the men had thirty bullets holes in him."

"You think Bobby Jack will really do prison time?"

"I'm afraid so, Jimmy. Ben will not take the case. Faith will not let us speak to Don and Beverly is long gone," R.E. said.

"The judge set bail at five hundred thousand dollars," Florence said.

"That's the craziest thing I've ever heard of," Jimmy said.

"Jimmy, we are going this weekend and gamble. I'm going to put down five bucks on the roulette table for you," Joan said.

"I'll put five dollars in the high stakes slot machine for you. Keep your fingers crossed I hit," Renee said.

Doctor Wind came in and checked on Jimmy. He was very pleased with the surgery and told them Jimmy would be going home in a few days. They all looked as a well dressed man came in the room. The fellow didn't waste much time introducing himself.

"I am F.B.I. agent, Bill James." The man showed his badge and walked over to Jimmy. "Sir, were you at the Eastville Hotel last night?"

"Man, I just had open heart surgery and I've been right here in this hospital. I've never been in the Eastville Motel in my life."

"I performed his surgery and I can assure you the man was here," Doctor Wind said.

Sarah stood with her mouth open and didn't say a word. R.E. chose not to keep his mouth shut and so did Florence.

"What the hell is wrong with you asking if the man was in Eastville last night?" R.E. asked.

"Someone signed the register at the Eastville Motel as Jimmy Martin with his address."

"Well, it damn sure wasn't Jimmy so you need to carry your ass back where you came from," Florence said.

The man ignored Florence and went right on with his questions. "Do you have any idea who might have used your name and address, Jimmy?"

"No sir. I don't have a clue."

"I'm sorry to have bothered you, Jimmy. Good luck on your recovery."

The man left and they all chatted for a few more minutes. A nurse came in and told them it was time to leave. They all left peacefully and headed for the city jail.

G. Jackson Warrington was one of the world's richest men. Warrington was a loner and protected his privacy with an army of security people. The financial press said he was the third wealthiest man in America. He lived in New York City and was by far the largest property owner in the state. Don was sitting with his tax attorney in the conference room when his secretary came in and handed him a note. He looked at her and the client sitting across from him.

"Please excuse me for a moment. I must take this call."

He went in the next room and closed the door. "Mr. Warrington, this is Don Hudson, how may I help you?"

"Don, I need to secure your services."

"Mr. Warrington, I only practice criminal law."

"I'm well aware of that Don. I have a grandson who, it seems, has created quite a mess for himself. I disowned his father years ago and he does not know I exist. The boys parents are both dead now and you and I are going to save his stupid ass from going to the state pen."

"What is the man being charged with?"

"Well, the good news is he didn't shoot anyone or rob a bank. The bad news is the damn fool was speeding and got caught by the state police. He then proceeded to drive himself home in the state policeman's car. Are you familiar with the case?"

"Yes, I guess it's a small world. Bobby Jack is married to my wife's sister's daughter."

"He was until she filed for divorce today. Beverly hired some buffoon named C Jacob Cattleman. I want you to take this case for me, Don. The boy should not go to prison for one night of stupidity."

"Why don't you call Ben Rollins? The case is going to be tried in his back yard. The man is a great attorney and wired to the wall politically."

"I spoke to Ben four hours ago, Don. He can't get the boy off and he told me only one man could. I am now talking to that man. Don, I am blessed to be a very wealthy man and money is no obstacle. I am prepared to offer you ten million dollars to represent Bobby Jack. I will have a cashier's check delivered to your office in one hour."

Don was stunned at the offer and didn't hesitate when he spoke. It's amazing how ten million dollars will open your mind up and let you see the way clear to go to Littleville. "You got yourself a deal Mr. Warrington. I will clear my schedule and be up there today."

"The check is waiting on you when you walk out. There is a dark skin man in a three piece suit waiting in your lobby. No one can ever know I hired you. Don, from this moment on you call me Jack."

"Jack, let me get to work and send his crazy ass home."

"There is one more thing, Don. I don't care for that pompous ass Mayor running his mouth about my grandson. I believe it is past time we rid that community of his red neck, illiterate ass. Find me something on C. Jacob. I'm going to put him out of his misery as well."

"It will be my pleasure, Jack."

Now, there are private detectives and then there are Don's private detectives. The former F.B.I. agents descended on Littleville over the next few days. Huey had run things his way for a long time. He had always dealt with the locals. He had never dealt with real professionals, but the game had changed. Man, it was like going from high school to the major leagues. If you look real close, you can see it all very clearly. Huey and C. Jacob are standing in their yards just as the tornado comes out of the sky and carries them both away. Being as C. Jacob weighed over three hundred pounds; you have to know it was a mighty tornado.

The story of Bobby Jack leaving in the state police car had captured the attention of the entire country. The family arrived to find television cameras were set up everywhere. Court T.V., CNN, FOX, MSMBC, CBS, NBC and ABC were all on hand. They had been tipped that the great Don Hudson was on his way to represent Bobby Jack Cullen. The Martin clan came and went in the city jail. Their eyes widened as they looked at all the reporters.

"Good Lord, we are on national television R.E. I feel right at home in front of the cameras," Florence said.

"I don't have enough lip stick on. I'm going to look terrible on television," Renee said.

"I know the reporter over there. I watch Court TV all the time. Damn, I had a feeling I should have gone to my hair stylist today. Florence, the camera adds ten pounds," Vicki said.

"I wear the extra weight just fine."

"Come on, Florence. Let me see if the damn boy is still alive. The bastards may have killed his ass by now," R.E. said.

"They ain't killed nobody's ass. Kate is standing inside the police station giving five of the cops a piece of her mind," Vicki said.

Don was on the phone with the District Attorney of Littleville County. Jackie Simpson had been the DA for thirty years and he was stunned when his secretary told him Don Hudson was on the phone. He almost died when she told him Don was representing Bobby Jack Cullen. She put the call through and Jackie answered.

"Hello," Jackie said.

"Mr. Simpson, this is Don Hudson. Thank you for taking my call."

"Don, my secretary just told me you are representing Bobby Jack Cullen."

"I am his attorney, Mr. Simpson. I will be up to see him in three hours. I am putting you on notice. He is not allowed to speak to any one in your department. If I catch a policeman getting within ten feet of him, I will bring the full force of the law down on their ass. You can tell that idiot, Judge Harrison, that I'll have him removed from the bench if he keeps up this nonsense of a half million dollar bail. I shall look forward to seeing you at trial."

The line went dead and Simpson sat staring at the four walls. He called his buddy, Ben Rollins. Ben's secretary passed him through to Ben. Jackie was breathing hard and sweating profusely. Ben answered and Jackie started talking.

"Ben, I just got a call from Don Hudson and he was not very nice. He told me he was on his way up here and would be in Littleville in three hours. Bobby Jack has caught a big break getting Hudson. The man charges millions to represent a client. The damn Martin family doesn't have any money."

"Jackie, you better figure a way out of this mess. If that man gets you in a courtroom, it will be hell to pay. I know Don very well and he is a very nice man until he represents a client. The man turns into a cold blooded killer in a courtroom and he will leave your ass on the side of the road to die. Someone big wants this boy to walk and you can take it to the bank."

"We have Bobby Jack dead to right. There is no way Hudson can win the case. The man was drunk, speeding, and stole the police car. I can win this case against anyone, Ben."

"How long have we known each other?"

"Thirty five years, Ben."

"Do you think I'm a good trial lawyer?"

"You are the best lawyer in the state. There is no one even close to you. Hell, you're a legend in your own time."

"You bet your sweet ass I am, Jackie. Hudson is ten times better than me on my best day. You cannot imagine, in your wildest dreams, how good the man is in a courtroom."

"Damn, you can't be serious."

"I'm damn serious and you better listen to me. You'll think a damn bobcat jumped your ass without a gun."

"He threatened Judge Harrison. The man flat told me Harrison would drop the bail or he would run him off the bench."

"Harrison better wake up and smell the roses. Jackie, I hate to be the one to tell you, but this isn't Littleville anymore. The national media covers every one of his trials. Hudson will put the Governor on the stand and turn his world upside down."

"What do you mean, Ben? He can't put the Governor on the witness stand. You can't call Governor Jones on a case he is not involved in."

"The hell he can't, Jackie. Governor Jones ran his mouth on every television station in the damn state. I am going to tell you one last time my friend. Jones will be foaming at the mouth like a drug addict going through withdrawals when Hudson finishes with him."

"Ben, there is no one I respect more than you. I'm telling you I can and will win this case."

"Jackie, get something heavy on your balls. Don Hudson is going to kick them right out of your body. You better not have a skeleton in your closet because Hudson's people are damn sure going to find it."

The word spread like wildfire threw the courthouse and police station. The family expected a hostile environment and was shocked to find Bobby all alone in his cell. The entire family was allowed to visit the man. The cops all looked like they had seen a ghost and said nothing. Huey was in the office with Chief Thomas and two of the assistant District Attorneys. R.E. looked over and Huey was red as a beat and sweating profusely.

"Bobby, we are trying to help you," R.E. said.

"R.E., I'm getting very nervous. The cops were harassing me until about an hour ago. Judge Harrison and the D.A. were down here twice telling me to cop a plea and I would get four years. Something has happened and I don't have a clue. Simpson came in here white as a ghost and told me he and Harrison never spoke to me. The cops are acting like someone is coming to kill all of them."

"Son, Ben Rollins turned us down. You are going to get stuck with a court appointed attorney. We called Tom Agee over in Cloverville and he is scared to take the case," Howard said.

"I caught one of the cops saying my attorney was coming this afternoon. I guess the worst case has unfolded for me."

"Beverly filed for divorce, Bobby," Renee said.

"Hell, how could I blame her? I'm looking at serious jail time if I even make it out of here alive. I still can't believe I drove off in the damn cop's car."

"Son, no one else can believe it either. You better prepare yourself for the worst," R.E. said.

"Maybe I should cop a plea and take the four years. Simpson told me with good behavior, I could be out in thirty months."

"All the televisions networks are outside. I'd sit tight if I were you. Those people wouldn't be here unless they knew something big was going to happen," Renee said.

"Listen to Renee, Bobby Jack. I guarantee you some shit is getting ready to come down. I've been around these cops all my life and something has all of them scared shitless. They damn sure ain't worried about any of us," Kate said.

The wheels were up and Don was on his way to Littleville. You don't get to be the best criminal defense attorney in the country without being smart and ruthless. The man had acquired a richly deserved reputation of being brilliant and tenacious. He picked up the phone and called Faith.

"Where are you, baby?" Faith asked

"I'm in the jet on my way to Littleville. I've taken on a high profile case with national coverage."

"You can't be serious, Don."

"I decided to represent Bobby Jack Cullen."

"Have you lost your mind? Who called you?"

"I can't discuss it with you. I hope you understand I have to observe the attorney-client privilege."

"I am watching these fools right now on national television. You are going to walk into five news networks when you arrive at the jail."

"I'll be home late tonight. Trust me, baby. I am going to take these boys to school. I love you, Faith."

"I love you, Don."

Faith was stunned as she sat watching the family leave the jail. She called Renee in an uproar. Renee heard her voice and smiled.

"Faith, did you decide to speak to me?

"Which one of you called Don?"

"Faith wants to know who called Don."

They all looked at each other and shook their heads from side to side. "No one called the man," R.E. said.

"No one claims to have called Don."

"One of you called my husband. He is on his way to Littleville to represent that damn fool."

The Fox cameraman was standing next to Renee and heard her reaction. He rushed over to his producer and declared in no uncertain terms the second coming of Jesus was on his way.

"Don is on his way to represent Bobby Jack," Renee kept shouting.

"The damn boy has a chance now," Florence said.

"These dumb suckers are going to get their worthless butts steamrolled. Don will skin their ass alive. I knew damn well something was happening," Kate said.

The family went wild jumping in each other's arms. After all the bad breaks, they were going to catch a good one. They had no earthly idea just how big it was going to be, but they were all ecstatic.

The CNN anchor was live on the air two minutes later breathlessly reporting the news. "We have a breaking exclusive from Littleville. The countries top criminal defense attorney, Don Hudson, will be arriving any minute to represent the state police car bandit."

The camera cut to another story and the show's executive producer, Mitt Haley, placed a call. "Call Wesley Arnold and thank him for the tip. I don't know how in the hell he knows so much about Hudson," Mitt told his boss, Ralph Coffee, in Atlanta.

"I'll call him when we hang up. He has never steered us wrong when it comes to Don Hudson."

G. Jackson sat at his country club with four of his wealthy friends and smiled. His buddies were watching a clip of the story in Littleville. They were carrying on about what an idiot Bobby Jack must be.

"I say this Hudson fellow is going to walk that boy who stole the state police car. It doesn't matter that he was drunk and driving a hundred and twenty miles an hour. I'd bet big money he walks."

"There is no way, Jack. Hudson is the best lawyer money can buy, but this one is hopeless," Gordon Moss said.

"Gordon is right, Jack. That boy is going to serve time in the state pen," Randy Clinton said.

"What about you two boys?" Jack asked.

"I'd bet anything he goes down for the count. The crazy fool stole a state police car," Derek said.

"He goes to jail for sure. That man must have been totally wasted and out of his mind," Boyd said.

"I have ten million that says he walks with no deal cut."

"Are you serious, Jack?" Boyd asked.

"You bet your ass I'm serious."

The four men talked for a brief moment before they responded. Gordon stood and spoke for the four men. "You got a bet, Jack. We will each take two and a half million."

"The bet is on my friends."

"Hudson is getting ready to lose his first case. Someone dropped big money on Hudson to take this case," Gordon said.

"You got the second part right. You my friend are getting ready to lose your ass on the first part."

Faith was madder than a wet hen. Renee looked up and saw the jet come from out of the sky. The Judge and D.A. were watching as well. Twenty minutes later, Don and three of his assistants arrived. The car hadn't stopped ten seconds when another car full of his detectives arrived. The assistants headed for the courthouse to file bail reduction motions. Don stood in front of the cameras and smiled.

"I'll be happy to speak with all of you a little later. I need to see my client and get this ludicrous bail removed. I'm counting on this still being a part of the United States of America."

"This case could prove to be quite a challenge for you, Mr. Hudson," Nancy Morgan said.

"I'm looking forward to trying the case. You are looking wonderful today Nancy," Don said.

"I have one quick question, Mr. Hudson. Do you really think you can win this case?" the CNN reporter asked.

"I'm certain we will win. There is absolutely no doubt in my mind Bobby Jack Cullen will be acquitted."

Over at the courthouse things were a little stirred up. The Judge was sitting behind his desk having a smoke when his clerk came in.

"What are you going to do, Judge Harrison? They are all over the courthouse with motions to reduce the bail. The damn television people are filming everything."

"Ben told me to be real careful with Hudson. He said the bastard is ruthless and would humiliate me in front of the national press. My old law school buddy, Judge Warren down in Florida told me the bastard had his best friend run off the bench. I already told the D.A. I'm dropping the bail to ten thousand. I should never have set the damn bond so high. The Governor wanted to make an example out of Cullen. It will be the last time I listen to his ass."

Don walked in the jail and announced himself. "I am Don Hudson and I wish to see my client now. His name is Bobby Jack Cullen."

Frank Jordan was in charge of the jail and a nice fellow. He shook hands with Don and escorted him to Bobby Jack's cell. The jailer was a fat ass jerk and leaned against the wall. He stood staring at Bobby with a smirk on his face. The cold hard truth was that all the Mayor's nephews were fat ass jerks. Anyway, the old boy stood with the keys in his hand and made no effort to unlock the door. Well, what happened next is often called a reality check and he was about to get a full dose of it.

"Open the damn door and put us in a room, you moron!" Don snapped.

The jailer almost wet his pants. "Who do you think you are, telling me what to do? This is my jail and I make the rules," Wayne Gray said.

"You creep. I'll tell your stupid ass exactly who I am. I'm the son-of–a–bitch you dream about ruining your worthless ass life. You'll open the door or I'll have your badge. You dip-shit! If I even think you are bugging that office, I'll put you in a federal pen for the rest of your chicken-shit life. You tell your idiot uncle I'll put his stupid, redneck ass away for good if he doesn't shut the hell up about my client."

Don was less than a foot from Wayne's face when the chief deputy rushed and grabbed Wayne. "Give me the keys, you crazy fool! The man has a right to see his client," he shouted.

Wayne was so shook up; he dropped the keys on the floor. Bobby Jack's eyes were about to pop out of his head as the jailer pushed Wayne aside and opened the cell. Don followed the man down the hall to a private office and walked in.

"Thank you, we would like some privacy."

"Yes sir," Frank said.

Don put his briefcase on the table and looked at Bobby Jack. "Bobby, you don't open your mouth except to drink, eat, and breathe. You have one chance and you will do exactly what I tell you."

"Yes sir."

"Did the cop give you a sobriety test?"

"No."

"Were you drug tested?"

"No."

"Do you take any medication?"

"Yes sir. Doctor Hillman has me on medication. I get disoriented when I haven't gotten enough sleep and I freak out when I get scared."

"Bobby, I'm going to make you out to be an idiot. It will be embarrassing, but you will walk at the end of the trial. Has anyone talked to you about a plea bargain or threatened you?"

"Yes sir. The D.A. and Judge Harrison offered me four years. The cops have been threatening to kill me since I got here."

"Are you telling me the Judge and D.A. came to your jail cell and offered you a deal?"

"Yes sir. I almost took it because eight cops were standing right beside them. Every hour on the hour for the last two days, the cops have taken turns threatening to kill me. That fat ass brought Huey back here twice."

"No one is going to touch you. Keep your mouth shut and I'll have you out of here before the end of the day."

Don stood and called the jailer. "Take my client back to his cell and you and none of your officers are allowed to speak with him."

"Yes sir," Frank said.

Don looked at Wayne and pointed his finger directly at him. "If that piece of shit walks by my client's cell, I'll put him in prison along with the Mayor for the rest of his worthless life."

"I understand completely, Mr. Hudson."

Don walked outside and gave the news organizations thirty minutes before leaving. Trust me when I tell you all the locals were watching.

Now in Littleville, things are done a certain way. The Judges, District Attorney, Mayor, Senators, and State boys run things their own way. It's kind of like a third world country, only they do have an election every four years and people actually get to vote. They don't take kindly to city slickers coming in and they damn sure stick together. The problem was the damn national press was here and so was Don Hudson. The Sheriff sent word that everyone needed to be on their best behavior. He also sent word that Don was no one to mess around with. Lastly, they were told the story of Don saving the under cover officer in Florida years ago.

Mayor Huey Cox was brain dead and continued to run his mouth nonstop. The man was a complete egomaniac and red neck to the bone. In fourteen years as Mayor of Littleville, Huey had pissed off everyone at least once. He was a liar with no peer. Along with that, how he had escaped a federal indictment, was a question for the ages. Huey was a flat out crook. He was very upset with Hudson for threatening his nephew. When he was told of the threat to put him in prison, he burst out laughing. Like I said, the man was completely brain dead.

C. Jacob Cattleman ran his mouth as well, until he ran into Ben at the Rotary Club luncheon. He had a few drinks and was his usual obnoxious self, constantly running his mouth.

"That smart ass, big city lawyer is going to get his cocky ass handed to him, Ben."

"How much money have you got, that you feel like pissing away today?"

"On what," C. Jacob asked?

"I have ten thousand that says Hudson walks that fool out a free man. Jackie is going to lose."

"God couldn't walk Bobby Jack Cullen. If I was the District Attorney, I would crush Hudson. I love the fact his big city ass is going to get taken down right here in my town."

"Then put your money where your mouth is, C. Jacob."

"Your serious aren't you, Ben? Are you telling me if I shut up, I'll be the next Mayor?"

"No, I'm telling you he is going to make a fool out of you and Huey. I am telling you Huey is going to keep right on talking."

"How the hell could he possibly win, Ben?"

"C. Jacob, he is going to walk up Jackie's ass with steel cleats on. Then he is going to firmly plant them in you and Huey's face. You are going to look like you have been in a fight and had the living hell beat out of you. Your Mother won't be able to recognize you."

"I still can't see Hudson winning, Ben."

"You better buy a thick pair of glasses."

Every once in a while the sun comes through the blinds. That, my good friend, was the very last time C. Jacob opened his big, fat mouth about Bobby Jack Cullen. Unfortunately, for C. Jacob he had already talked too much. The wrong fellow was listening and he was not a happy camper. Which once again proves the old adage: It is better to remain silent and be thought a fool, than to speak up and be proven one. Huey and C. Jacob were both on a short leash with a rope around their necks. Both the boys were standing on top of a damn mountain cliff. Maybe it was better they didn't know that an elephant was getting ready to pull the rope.

In case you were wondering, Jeff didn't fare nearly as well as Sarah. The cops not only got his license plates, they cornered him as well. There he stood, like a fool, on statewide television describing the shootout. His cold ass wife sat watching along with everyone else. Beverly had no sooner left C. Jacob's office filing for divorce when Jeff's wife came through the door. The boy just didn't have enough experience at this sort of thing. It turned out to be a very expensive fling for poor Jeff. The only good thing was the boy couldn't eat and damn if he didn't lose fifty pounds. He had gotten over the trauma and called Sarah with the good news of his weight loss. But, bad luck covered him up once again. It seems Sarah had a new boyfriend and gently blew the boy off.

CHAPTER SEVEN

The family was euphoric as Bobby Jack's bail was dropped to ten thousand dollars. Someone posted the bail and they assumed it was Don. Don flew back to Florida to prepare for the trial and take care of his other clients. He took Bobby with him and put the boy up in a nice hotel with room service. The national press headed off to cover other stories around the country. The trial was scheduled to begin in a month and the Martin clan headed off in the Winnebago to gamble. Emily and Jake didn't approve and stayed home. Jimmy was still recovering and couldn't go, but everyone else crawled in for the ride. R.E. had borrowed the vehicle from his best friend, Possum Wainwright, and Renee's boyfriend, Paul drove. Old Florence was drinking her Jack Daniels and having a fine time as they made their way to the casino. Joan sat with her boyfriend, Elmer Benson playing her guitar.

"We are going to take all their money. They will be closing the place down when I finish," Florence said.

"Florence, I'm giving you five hundred and no more. Don't you come to me begging for more money. The last three times we went, you blew your money the first day."

"You ain't my damn Daddy! I better not catch you spending more than five hundred. Don't you try and hold it over my head that I never worked. I gave you two fine upstanding kids you can be proud of. You old tightwad! You need to loosen up and enjoy life."

"Damn you, Florence, I'm not Bill Gates. I'm living off my little retirement check and social security."

"No shit, R.E."

"Woman, you have been beating me up for money since I said, 'I do.'"

"I only have four hundred to gamble with," Joan said.

"I got seventy dollars," Elmer said.

"Paul, how much are you giving me to gamble with?" Renee asked.

"I brought my own money to gamble. You are on your own, Renee. I'm a working man and I watch my money."

"Paul, you are so cheap it's unbelievable. You are going to up some money if you want any of this action."

"I don't gamble anymore and I don't miss it a lick. The Lord is my Shepard and I'm in the flock. I've wanted to see Metropolis for a long time. R.E., you want to be real careful. You're not in the flock and you may get sheared."

"Howard, I don't need to be in the flock to get taken. How the hell do you think they build these casinos and never close?"

"I just want to play Wheel of Fortune. I've always just loved the girl so much," Vicki said.

"What girl do you love?" Elmer asked.

"The one who puts all the letters up on the board."

"Is Vicki bi-sexual, Joan?" Elmer asked.

"Hell no, she isn't into another woman."

They were all wound up after a five hour drive to Metropolis. R.E. and Florence hit the ground with Howard and Vicki on their heels. Joan and her boyfriend followed with Renee and Paul. Elmer had a hearing aid the size of a silver dollar hanging out of each ear. The old fellow could barely hear a shotgun going off two feet from him. Joan had insisted Elmer come along for the ride.

"Superman lives here, R.E. I want to see the house where he grew up. I bet his parents still live here," Howard said.

"Howard, the man does not exist. That was a movie and comic book for God sakes. An actor was playing the role of a fictional character. Please tell me you don't believe Superman exists," Renee said.

"What are you talking about, Renee. Superman was from Metropolis, you fool. I know for a fact Superman exists. Don't you remember how fast he changed clothes and got his cape on."

"I'm ready to gamble. Howard you check in and go find Superman and his parents. Take your cell phone and call me when you find Clark and Lois," Florence said.

"Florence, I don't know anybody named Clark. The only Lois I know lives in Horseville."

"Hell, she might be here this weekend. Your best bet is to run by the local newspaper."

"Did Howard say a bunch of horses were here?" Elmer asked.

"He was talking about Lois Lane from Horseville," Joan said.

"Trent Milder started that rumor back in high school. I never had sex with Lois."

"No one said you had sex with Lois."

"I don't want her boyfriend hearing I was fooling around with her. He is liable to come over here and beat me up."

"No one is going to beat you up, Elmer."

"I can't fight anymore, Joan. I'm eighty four years old and my fighting days are over."

When Florence was drinking, she was a happy camper. They checked in and went straight to the casino. No one was having much luck, as you might imagine. R.E. had been sitting at a fifty cent progressive slot machine for two hours. Florence walked up and sat down next to him.

"I'm hungry, R.E. Come take me to eat."

"I'm not hungry, Florence."

"Come on, R.E. I'm starving. Get your old ass up and feed me."

"I feel real lucky. Go eat by yourself. I know this slot is going to pay off any second."

"That damn slot machine ain't going to pay you a dime. You have been sitting at the damn thing since we got here. Come on and feed me."

"Give me ten more minutes, Florence. I just know I'm going to win big."

She was not going to let it slide and keep right on badgering him to eat. Finally, he gave up and stood to take her to dinner. A woman sat in his seat and smiled as she put a dollar bill in the machine.

"You got this seat all warmed up for me, Sugar?"

"You damn right the seat is warmed up. I'd still be sitting in the seat if it were not for my wife."

"I need to win big, Sugar. I cashed my welfare check and I'm down to nothing but a hope and prayer."

Elmer stood listening to the exchange between R.E. and the woman. "Is Big Sugar the name of that new fighter we saw on the T.V., Joan?"

"No, Elmer, he is not a fighter."

R.E. was bitching non stop as he started to walk away. He hadn't taken six steps when the woman started screaming at the top of her voice. The light went off and the sirens started blaring as the jackpot flashed. R.E. turned and saw the woman jumping up and down. The casino employees came running and he looked to see she had won sixteen thousand dollars. Elmer wasn't quite sure what happened. He saw how mad R.E. was and backed up from the scene. R.E. glared at Florence and could not contain himself. He started to jump up and down like a crazy man. Two casino employees were watching him closely as he let loose on Florence.

"Damn, if you want to eat stay home. You just cost me sixteen thousand dollars, you old bat!" he screamed.

"Watch your mouth, you little son of a bitch!"

"This little son of a bitch can still kick your fat ass, Big Mouth!"

"I never should have married you, Shit Head! Floyd Murray was crazy about me and his family had money. Why I married you,

I'll never know. I should kick my own ass for being such a fool. Daddy told me I would regret marrying your no good ass."

"I wish you had married the son-of-a-bitch, Florence. I'd be a hell of a lot better off than I am now. I've been trying to take their money for ten years. Your fat ass has cost me my chance and I will never get over it."

"You no-good jackass! I ought to leave you right now."

"Be my guest and carry your fat ass home!"

Elmer was taking in the whole scene with a wary eye. "Why are they so upset about a fat jackass?"

"Elmer, R.E. just missed winning sixteen thousand," Joan said.

"Where was he going to put sixteen thousand donkeys?"

"Elmer, when we get back home you have to change your hearing aids. They are doing more harm than good."

Poor Howard had to jump between them with Vicki. Across the floor, Renee had started to warm up. Joan walked over and sat down to play. An hour later, she was completely wiped out. She walked across the casino floor and spotted Renee.

"I lost all my money. What am I supposed to do, go sit in my room and watch Days of Our Lives?"

"Has Elmer got any money?" Renee asked.

"Elmer has his hearing aids and they don't work."

"I'm so sorry you lost all your money. Sit here and play this machine for me, Joan."

"Thanks, I think I will."

Joan sat down and saw Renee was up three hundred on her machine and two hundred on the machine she told her to play. There is nothing like money to separate family and friends. Joan started pushing the button and ran the money down to a hundred and twenty dollars. Twenty minutes later, she was back up to two hundred. She kept right on pushing the button and boom; she hit the jackpot for over a thousand.

"I won the money," Joan shouted.

"That's great, Joan."

Renee was happy as a pig in shit until she turned and Joan was gone with the ticket. Ten minutes later Joan came back and handed Renee two hundred dollars. "What the hell is this for Joan?"

"There was two hundred in the machine when you asked me to play. I'm giving you your money back."

"That was my damn money, you bitch! Give me all the money, you crap ass old fool."

"I won the money and it is mine. You should have played the machine yourself. I told you I was going to watch Days of Our Lives.

You asked me to play. Did you think I was dumb enough to sit here and do all the work for you, and not get paid?"

"You old fool. I told you to pull the lever for me. You came over here crying your old ass off. I felt sorry for you and told you to sit down and play my machine. Do you think the machines play for nothing? Give me my money before I whip your old ass right here in front of God and everybody else."

"What are you going to do, Renee? Are you going to beat up an eighty year old woman living on social security?"

Joan took off across the casino floor as Renee tried to cash out. Florence was fuming at R.E. and went up to her room. She had bought a quick pick and wanted to watch the ten o'clock news to see if a miracle had occurred. She barely made it out of the bathroom to see the numbers. Her glasses were dirty and she wrote the numbers down in bold letters. When she placed her glasses on her face, she looked down at the numbers and screamed. She was beside herself as she hit the elevator button to the ground floor. She tried to call R.E., but his cell phone was off.

"I just won seventy five thousand dollars," she said to the man and woman on the elevator.

"Isn't that wonderful," Lucy said.

"What did you win it on?" Martin asked.

"I won the quick pick. Can you believe I finally won after all these years? My husband is going to have a fit. We ain't been getting along too good if you know what I mean. I married the wrong man and he knows it."

"Oh my, that must be awful," Lucy said.

"You get used to it after fifty two years. Still, you always wonder what life would have been like."

"Martin was my high school sweetheart. We have a wonderful life together. I am so thankful to have him."

"Well, count you're lucky stars, dear. The little ass I'm married to is tight as a tick and runs women constantly."

She had her ticket in her purse when they hit the ground floor and stepped off. Florence took two steps when a man came running by and grabbed her purse. She was holding on for dear life, but when she hit the floor, he pulled it away and ran out the door.

"Robbery!" Florence screamed.

"Robbery!" the couple screamed.

Security came running down to the elevator. "What happened lady?" the security officer asked.

"He stole my purse and my lottery ticket is in it. It is worth seventy five thousand dollars!" she screamed.

"What did he look like?" the second security officer asked.

"He looked like a rabbit running for his life."

"Ma'am, was he black, white, Asian, tall or short?"

"I want my money," Florence screamed.

"The man was about five ten and two hundred pounds. He was white with tattoos on both arms," Martin said.

The security officers took off running out the door. Renee was hot on Joan's heels as they rounded the corner and saw Florence screaming.

"What happened, Florence?"

"Some cock-sucker stole my winning lottery ticket, Renee. I won seventy five thousand and now it's gone!"

"Go get R.E., Paul," Renee hollered.

"Leave me alone, Renee!" Joan screamed.

"Joan, give me my damn money before I kill you!"

"I won the lottery and he stole my ticket," Florence bellowed.

Paul rushed back in the casino and saw R.E. shooting the shit with another man. He ran over to R.E., who was playing the slots. Elmer was sitting across from him playing Wheel of Fortune.

"Florence has been robbed. You better come quickly before we have a murder. Renee is threatening to kill Joan."

"Damn, did Joan steal the money?" R.E. asked.

"Did Joan get caught stealing money? Who murdered poor Joan?" Elmer asked.

"Joan stole the money from Renee. Someone else stole the money from Florence. No one is dead yet, Elmer."

R.E. jumped up and followed Paul. Security was swarming the place now. Elmer decided to stay and play the slot machine.

Panic was spreading through the casino. The hotel's head of security was taking no chances. "I need every available man at the elevator bank. We have an armed robbery and a woman threatening to kill another woman!" Justin said.

The hotel manager was getting very nervous and called in the local police. R.E. found Florence screaming and Renee with a headlock on Joan. Three security officers were frantically trying to pull Renee off Joan. Four more were trying their best to settle Florence down.

"What's going on, Florence?"

"I've been robbed. We won the lottery and the man robbed me."

"What lottery, Florence?"

"We won the quick pick for seventy five thousand, R.E! The man stole my purse with the ticket."

"Son of a bitch!" R.E. shouted.

R.E. and Florence were about to lose their minds over losing seventy five thousand dollars. Renee was more than ready to kick Joan's ass over taking her money. Security finally got Renee off

Joan and kept them apart. It was about as much excitement as they could stand. They all wandered off and went to their rooms.

The next morning, they sat in the restaurant having breakfast. Everyone was in a deep depressed state of mind. "I don't know what else can go wrong. We have to be the most snake bit people on the face of the earth," R.E. said.

"We lose when we win," Florence said.

"Well, at least the hotel gave us our rooms and meals free."

"Seventy five thousand is going to take a lot of free rooms and meals," Florence said.

"I'd be up eighteen hundred if Joan had not stolen my money. The bitch will be walking her ass back to Littleville if she doesn't up my money. What the hell else can happen to me?"

Paul looked up and shook his head. "Carol can show up with a drug dealer," Paul said.

"Son-of-a-bitch," Renee said.

They all looked up and Carol stood outside the café with Richard Wall, Billy and Sammy Joe. Richard was the known drug king in a ten county area.

"They're higher than the space shuttle," Florence said.

"They're standing right on the ground, Florence," Howard said.

"I hope to God they don't see us," Renee said.

"Billy couldn't see us if we were standing a foot in front of him," R.E. said.

"Shit, Joan is walking right up to them," Paul said.

They watched as Joan stopped and started talking to them. She pointed in the café and Carol looked in to see her Mother. A second later Carol walked in arm and arm with Richard. Billy and Sammy Joe were a step behind.

"Damn, the feds are going to be all over our ass," R.E. said.

"What did we do to get them on us," Howard said.

"Be quiet, Howard, this man is a big time drug dealer," Vicki said.

"Imagine running into you down here. Howard, what are you up to old timer. Have you started gambling?" Carol asked.

"I've just been looking for Superman."

"I've been looking for Superman myself. I need some of that kryptonite to put on the cops ass," Richard said.

"Mrs. Florence, I'm sorry about falling on you at the hospital," Billy said.

"You can buy me a couple of drinks and we'll call it even."

"Mother, how long are you staying here?" Sammy Joe asked.

"We are leaving after we eat, son."

"What are you driving?" Richard asked.

"We borrowed Possum's Winnebago," R.E said.

"I got some heavy suitcases that won't fit in my car. I'll pay you good money if you will carry them back home."

"What are you calling good money?" Florence asked.

"Hell, I just won fifty thousand on the craps table. I'll give you a grand for your trouble, since you're so nice."

"Show me the money and pack your bags in the back."

Joan walked in and caught the conversation. "I have to go and find Elmer," Joan said.

"Are you talking about Elmer Benson?" Carol asked.

"Yes, have you seen him?"

"He is standing at the cashier's window having his picture taken. He just won the big jackpot for three hundred twenty three thousand."

"I've lost a seventy five thousand dollar lottery ticket," Florence said.

"I lost sixteen thousand when Florence made me leave my machine. Elmer brings seventy dollars and walks out rich," R.E. said.

Elmer came around the corner and walked in. "Rufus, I won a lot of money. I'll help you buy a farm to put your donkeys on."

"Elmer, have you lost your mind? I don't own any donkeys."

"Who did you sell all those donkeys too?"

"I sold my donkeys to Fudge Moran years ago."

"Where is Fudge going to put sixteen thousand donkeys?"

"Elmer, why don't you let me take care of your winnings?" Florence said.

"No thank you, Florence. I'm going to see if Fudge wants to sell me all those donkeys."

They checked out of the hotel and Richard put his four suitcases in the back of the Winnebago. He walked off after giving Florence ten one hundred dollar bills.

"Damn, have you lost your mind, Florence? You don't know what is in those suitcases. That damn boy is a known drug dealer," R.E. said.

"Do you see my fingerprints on those suitcases? I'm just lending a helping hand to a boy in need, you old fool."

"You better hope to hell we don't get stopped by the cops. We'll see who the old fool is then."

"You never did have a set of balls."

"How the hell would you know? You haven't seen them in twenty years you old refrigerator."

"Your penis is too small. I couldn't get any satisfaction. It wasn't worth the effort anymore."

"I've seen his penis and it don't look small to me," Howard said.

"Howard, stay out of their business," Vicki said.

Off they went down the highway, on the way back to Littleville. They had been traveling for a little over an hour when they came to the top of a hill. Paul looked and ten police cars came off the side of the road and fell in behind him. Twenty seconds later, the flashing lights went on and he pulled over to the side of the road. The cops swarmed around the van and one of them opened the door on the drivers' side.

"Everyone steps out of the vehicle right now," the D.E.A. officer said.

"Florence, did you look and see what was in those suitcases?" R.E. asked.

"They're locked up tight as a tick."

"I'm stepping out right now," Paul said.

They made their way out one by one. They were all now standing outside the Winnebago and reality was setting in fast. Paul was shaking like a leaf as he handed the state trooper his license.

"We have probable cause to search your vehicle. Is there anything you wish to tell us?" Trooper Jackson asked.

"Richard Wall gave me a grand to bring four suitcases back. He didn't have any room in his car," Florence said.

"The man gave you a thousand dollars to carry four suitcases? Show me the suitcases right now."

"Show him the suitcases, R.E.," Florence said.

"You show him the damn suitcases, Florence. You took the damn money from the bastard."

"I got a wimp for a husband, Officer. Come on and we will find the damn suitcases. Richard put them in the back of the damn vehicle. His fingerprints will be all over them."

"None of your fingerprints better be on them," Jackson said.

"My fingers prints are damn sure not on them," Renee said.

Renee, Paul, Howard, Elmer, and Vicki watched as the police pulled the suitcases from the Winnebago. They pried one open and it was full of cocaine. The rest were opened and all were full of the white powder. Joan walked over and stared at the coke.

"You are transporting three million dollars of cocaine. You better start talking because you all could be looking at long prison sentences. You better spill your guts while you can," Jackson said.

"I swear to God, we didn't know what was in the suitcases. My damn daughter came in with Richard and he offered Florence a grand to bring his suitcases home," Renee said.

"What's your story, Mister?" he asked Paul.

"I never saw the man in my life. I swear. I'm just driving us home. I'm nothing but a boyfriend caught in a bad situation. I've never done drugs in my life."

"What have you got to say for yourself, Mr. Cage?"

"My stupid ass wife let the boy pull one over on her. I hope you haven't gotten your ass in trouble."

"We'll of all the damn nerve! I think you have gotten a little too big for your britches, Rufus Cage."

"What's your story, old timer?" Jackson asked Elmer.

"I won the jackpot at the casino. I'm on my way home to buy sixteen thousand donkeys."

"Are you smoking a banned substance or taking pills, Elmer?"

"I ain't taking anything but my Viagra."

"You just told me you were buying sixteen thousand donkeys. You are either stoned or full of shit."

"Elmer has bad ears and he misunderstood. It's a long story, but it is true," Joan said.

"What about you, Mr. Minter?"

"I've been on the right side of the fence for years. I don't even know what that stuff is, Officer. Vicki and I walk the line for the Lord. Son, I hope you have made the decision to get on the right side of the fence."

"You and the Lord are going to follow us to the police station," the D.E.A. agent said.

"I hope you're satisfied, Big Mouth! We have to follow these men to the police station."

"Stick it up you're ass, R.E."

"You took the damn money, Florence. None of us had a thing to do with the drugs. Don't you get down to the police station and try to involve the rest of us. I swear woman, I just don't understand how your mind works."

"Rufus, if you open your mouth one more time, I'm going to close it for you. I didn't hear you refuse to let me take the money."

"Kate is not going to believe this has happened to us," Renee said.

"Why do you always have to run your big mouth to Kate? One of these days it's going to get you in trouble," Florence said.

"If I have to call my father, I will be dropped from his will. This is my last trip with any of you."

"What the hell do I see in you, Paul?" Renee asked.

"Did she say we were all going to hell, Joan?" Elmer said.

"Elmer, you are not going to hell."

"I heard the man say it was his last trip."

"Elmer, no one is going to die and go to hell."

They had to go to the state police station and fill out sworn affidavits and agree to testify against Richard Wall. Seven hours later, they were cleared to go home, but only after Richard was brought in and they identified him. He denied he had ever seen any of them and was being framed. Florence gave him a good piece of her mind, but the others were just glad to be able to leave.

Long story short, they didn't catch the thief. The seventy five thousand looked like it was long gone. Renee never got her money from Joan. They never spoke again the rest of their lives. She called Kate when she got home and gave her a blow by blow account. It was a decision she would live to regret. Paul was so upset he nearly wrecked the Winnebago twice on the way back. Howard and Vicki decided it would be their last gambling trip. Howard never found Superman's house and was greatly disappointed. R.E. never got over losing the sixteen thousand at the slot machine. There was some justice, but none of then ever knew about it. The man who stole the lottery ticket brought the purse home and removed the thirty dollars in cash. He went to the bathroom to relieve himself and his girlfriend spotted the lottery ticket. The next day, she cashed it and the man always wondered why she left without so much as taking her clothes. The Martin's staggered back to Littleville and prepared for the event of the century. The national press and Don Hudson were coming to town. Most folks thought Bobby Jack Cullen was going away for quite a while. The locals just couldn't see how poor Bobby Jack could get his ass out of the trap. Tickets to get in the courthouse were hard to come by, as people lined up to see the show. It wasn't long before the big jet flew in from Florida with Faith, Don, Bobby, and a boat load of lawyers.

CHAPTER EIGHT

The District Attorney was making his opening statement to the jury. Jackie Simpson was a kindly old fellow who talked the local folk's language. He knew the people in his community and he rarely lost a case. Jackie was a frequent patron of the local Pancake House. Jackie topped out at three hundred and five pounds. Everyone liked Jackie and he was affectionately called, Killer. He had been reelected time after time. Despite the warning from Ben, he was totally confident of securing a conviction.

"What we have here is a man intoxicated and driving one hundred and twenty miles an hour. High on drugs, he leaves the scene of a major accident and steals a state police car. Such arrogance and disrespect for the law cannot be tolerated. The state will show, through eye witnesses, that every crime we allege was indeed committed. My friends, this is an open and shut case. I'm sure all of you will agree, Mr. Cullen, is a menace to society and should be incarcerated in the state penitentiary. No one in his right mind would dare steal a police car. Anything less than a maximum sentence would send a terrible message to the citizens of our fine state.

The family sat in two rows and watched as Simpson sat down. The Judge informed Don he could begin with his opening statement to the jury. Don stood and walked directly to the jury box without even acknowledging Judge Harrison. He looked like something right off a Hollywood screen with his stunning good looks. Trust me when I tell you, it was no accident that all twelve jurors were young women.

Simpson had wondered aloud to his staff why Don had beaten him up seating the jury. "Twelve people from outer space would convict this fool," Jackie had told them. He looked at the jury and whispered to his assistant. "I didn't know we had twelve good looking women in Littleville County."

Don walked slowly and made eye contact with each of the jurors. The smile never left his face as his eyes moved across the jury box. He made a point of addressing each one of them as he started to speak.

"Ladies, thank you for taking your valuable time to serve your community. You are being asked to determine the fate of a man. His future will rest in your hands. Bobby Jack Cullen is a real character. He drinks too much. He drives too fast. He ran around on his wife. He even has a smart mouth." He paused and winked at the women. "The state wants you to believe this is an open and shut case. When we are done, I'm sure you will all agree. The open and shut case is Bobby Jack Cullen should not be sitting in this courtroom. We will show you in graphic detail why each allegation the state charges is false. We will further show why you would never want to find yourselves in his position."

Don cut the billion dollar smile and each woman thought he was winking at them. He walked back and sat down next to Bobby. The women on the jury started talking to each other in hush tones.

"Damn, can you believe this gorgeous sex machine was standing a foot away from me," Denise whispered.

"I'm soaking wet," Donna said.

"The deputies are watching every thing we are doing. I'm calling my sister on the next break. I have to let him know I want him. I'll have Peggy slip him a note outside the courtroom," Denise said.

"Be careful. We are not supposed to talk in the jury box. Please don't get us kicked off the jury," Donna said.

The Martin bunch was sitting together watching the proceedings. Howard was getting very uneasy watching Don.

"I got to see this boy operate with my own eyes," R.E. said.

"Old Timer, you are in for the best show you have ever seen," Anne said.

"Why is Don always looking at the women? Faith is going to ream him a new ass if he don't stop flirting in front of her. I think that boy is trying his best to get a piece of ass while he's here. Vicki would try and kill me if I was carrying on like that in front of her."

"You old fool! He is playing to the jury. He is taking all their asses to bed," Carol said.

"That's what I said, Carol. That boy is carrying on right in front of all of us. He is being blatant over there. He better hope none of those women are married and their husband's come in here. I swear I thought I saw him reach over and hand one of those girls his phone number."

"Damn Howard, go outside and smoke a joint. He's not giving the damn woman his phone number," Anne said.

The Judge looked at the packed courtroom, filled with members of the national press. "Call your first witness," Judge Harrison said.

"Your Honor, we call Trooper Brian Watkins," Simpson said.

Watkins took the stand and was sworn in. Simpson took him through the night of the arrest and documented all the facts. Watkins was glaring at Bobby Jack as he recounted the story. The trooper was totally at ease and spoke with great confidence. Simpson sat down and smiled at Judge Harrison.

"Your witness, Mr. Hudson," Judge Harrison said.

Don stood and walked across the courtroom. He stopped directly in front of Watkins and looked him dead in the eye. "Did you have a stroke, Mr. Watkins?"

"I haven't had a stroke."

"What is that smirk on your face?"

"I don't care for your client."

"That would be obvious to anyone who is not blind. How long have you been a state policeman?"

"I have been on the force for twelve years."

"Did you administer a sobriety test on Mr. Cullen the night of his arrest?"

"No, I did not."

"Did you administer a drug test?"

"No, I did not."

"Why did you write on your report Mr. Cullen was intoxicated and high on drugs. Are you some kind of psychic? You obviously didn't do your job that night. You violated his rights and made a fool out of yourself and your department. You just told the court you had been an officer of the law for twelve years."

"I didn't need to give him a test. He was about to fall down and his eyes were blood shot red."

"Do you have a medical degree?"

"Oh shit, here we go. Watch this cocky son-of-a-bitch. Don will cut him into a million pieces," Carol whispered.

"You can take it to the bank," Anne whispered.

"That boy can't bring a knife in here."

"Howard, it's a figure of speech for God sakes," R.E. said.

"No, I don't have a medical degree, Mr. Hudson."

"Mr Watkins, do you know what a prescription drug is?"

"Of course, I know what a prescription drug is."

"Are you aware that prescription drugs have side effects?"

"Yes."

"What qualified you to decide Mr. Cullen was not on prescription medication. How would you know that, Mr. Watkins? What right did you have to make a determination of my client's state of being? I'm going to show you a bottle of medicine that Doctor James Hillman prescribed for Mr. Cullen."

Don walked up and handed the Judge the bottle. "Your Honor, please mark this bottle as Exhibit A."

Don walked to the witness stand and stared at Watkins. "Can you read?" Don said coldly.

"Of course, I can read. For your information, I have a university degree in criminal justice."

"I'm sure we are all very impressed, Mr. Watkins. Why don't you show the court your reading skills? Read the warning label to the court."

Watkins started to read and turned bright red. "Lack of sleep can cause the patient to become disoriented. The patient may exhibit symptoms synonymous with drunkenness and disorientation. The patient may feel helpless and exhibit great anxiety under stress leading to irrational decisions."

Watkins was sweating profusely as he handed the bottle back to Hudson. The family was taking it all in from the front of the courtroom.

"That man just shit in his own dinner bucket," Florence said.

"It will get a hell of a lot worse. You haven't seen anything yet. Don will not stop until he destroys the man," Carol said.

"Believe it or not, you will feel sorry for the piece of shit when Don finishes with him," Anne said.

"I don't give a damn if that asshole has a stroke on the stand. Let Don bury the mother six feet under," Kate said.

Don was starting to bear down and Watkins was shifting from side to side in the witness chair. "Did you remove the keys from Mr. Cullen's car, Mr. Watkins?"

"Yes," Watkins almost whispered.

"Speak up, Mr. Watkins, we can't hear you."

"Okay, I'm nervous," Watkins said.

"You removed the keys and went across the freeway to administer help to dying people. You left a man standing on the side of the freeway to witness a catastrophic scene. A man who was certainly going to experience a dramatic degree of stress. Mr. Watkins, you and the other policemen did something else didn't you?"

Don walked over to the jury box and leaned against the rail. He slid his hand over the side of the rail and looked directly at Denise. Denise thought he was going to touch her hand.

"Those girls on the front row are all hard of hearing. Their leaning forward so they can hear Don."

"Howard, trust me they can hear just fine. That ain't why their leaning forward," Florence said.

Don never took his eyes off Denise and the other eleven women when he spoke. "Mr. Watkins, I assume you know what perjury is and the sentence that goes with a conviction. I want you to know that if you lie to this court, I will contact the United States Attorney and present him with the evidence. I will not hesitate to bring every policeman in this county in this courtroom and put them under oath."

"I understand, Mr. Hudson."

Don turned around and walked over to the witness stand. His voice suddenly became harsh and threatening. "Did you and your fellow officers threaten to kill Mr. Cullen?"

"It was just a figure of speech. No one was going to kill your client."

"You mean, if you tell me you're going to kill me I should take it as a joke? You have a loaded gun strapped on your side and the right to use it. What kind of fool would think you are kidding?"

"I admit I was very angry. The other officers were angry as well. No one laid a hand on your client."

"Excuse me, Mr. Watkins. How the hell do you think he got a pair of handcuffs on his wrist if nobody touched him?"

"I mean outside of the handcuffs being put on him, no one touched him."

"Were you one of the eight officers standing in front of his cell when he was offered a plea bargain and his life was threatened?"

Watkins thought he was going to throw up. The man turned white as a sheet and couldn't even speak.

Don glared at him and looked at the jurors. "Never mind, we know exactly what happened in that jail."

Harrison and Simpson both turned red as an apple in spring. Sheriff Holley looked across the courtroom and shook his head.

"We are going to lose the Judge and District Attorney," R.E. said.

"Where are they going, R.E.?" Howard asked.

"Where ever Don wants to send their ass."

"Jesus Christ, he is going to have me disbarred along with Harrison," Jackie whispered to the assistant District Attorney.

Don turned and looked at the twelve women. He walked over and looked each one of the women in the eye. He put his hand on the rail and walked the full length of the jury box without ever lifting it. "I think we have heard all we need to hear from you, Mr. Watkins."

"I'm going to die right now," Donna whispered.

"I can't breathe," Denise said.

The Martin clan was quietly sharing their two cents worth with each other. "Mercy, the man just got himself destroyed right before our eyes. Is that legal what Don did to that boy," Vicki said.

"The poor bastard just realized he was an idiot. That boy cranked up a chain saw and put the policeman on the ground. Man, I'm sure glad I didn't get me one of those criminal justice things," Howard said.

"That boy ain't playing with a full deck. Someone stole half the cards and I know who stole them," Joan said. "Jesus Christ, if he puts my poor son on the stand, I'm going to die right here in this courtroom."

"Herb better get down on his knees and pray he doesn't get called," Anne said.

"Jackie's done fooled around and pissed in his pants over there. I always thought he was smart and educated. Don's done come in here and made the boy look real bad in front of everyone. I voted for that man a bunch of times," R.E. said.

"The son of a bitch won't have any pants left when Don finishes, Mother," Anne said.

"Girls, please be on your best behavior. I don't think Don needs anyone's help."

"He damn sure doesn't need anyone's help. The man whipped the trooper's ass with a sharp stick. That no good sucker has fifty thorns stuck three inches up his rotten ass," Kate said.

The Judge told Watkins to step down and called for a one hour recess. The jurors walked out and into the jury room. They were ready to make their feeling known.

"Jesus, I've never seen anything look that good in my life. Where in the hell is he from," Peggy said.

"He ain't from around here. I can't believe my rotten luck getting stuck on the back row," Susan said.

"What I wouldn't give for one night with Don. I haven't heard a damn word. All I can think about is taking his beautiful ass to bed. God, can you imagine a night of love making with him," Mary said.

"He can park his shoes under my bed anytime he wants. I'd drop my husband like a bad habit if I thought I had a chance of having Don," Connie said.

"Did you see him when he winked at me? I had to make myself not reach out and touch his hand. Lord, I can't even breathe when he is standing right in front of me," Sharon said.

"He was making eye contact with me. I'm wearing something tomorrow to show him my body. I think I might get lucky and score," Lynn said.

"God, I hope this trial lasts for weeks. Every time he looks at me, I almost die," Donna said.

"I cursed for a week when I found out I had jury duty. Wallace tried to get me out of serving. I would have shot myself, if I'd walked in and seen him," Diane said.

"I didn't hear a word he said. I was between his legs in bed. I can't begin to tell you how good he is," Kathy whispered.

"Don't any of you fools do something stupid and cause a mistrial. Keep your damn hands off of him, Sharon," Patsy said.

"God, I am going to dream about him at night. How could anyone be that handsome," Toni asked.

"I'm going to sleep with him if it's the last thing I ever do. My husband went from okay, to the ugliest man on the planet," Denise said.

The girls looked at the woman deputy standing on the other side of the room. She was doing her best to keep a straight face. "What about you, Gertrude?" Denise asked.

"I'm not allowed to talk with you about the case. I have a professional code of conduct I am required to maintain."

"What planet are you from, Chick? Who the hell is talking about the case, girl?" Toni said.

Gertrude shook her head and stepped outside the jury room. She spotted Sheriff Holley talking to another deputy and walked over. They were discussing the fist fight that had broken out earlier in front of the courthouse.

"Gertrude, how are you today?" Sheriff Holley asked.

"I'm fine, Sheriff."

"What do you think so far about the trial?"

"Sheriff, can I be blunt with you?"

"Of course, you can speak to whatever is on your mind."

"I don't think we are having a trial. I think we are having a love fest between the jury and Mr. Hudson. I think we are going through the formality of Mr. Cullen being acquitted."

"Don sure made Watkins look like a fool."

"They don't even know Watkins was on the witness stand. A damn bomb could go off and they wouldn't take their eyes off of him."

"It sounds like Jackie has his work cut out for him."

"Sheriff, Jackie doesn't have a chance in hell of getting a conviction. I'd bet my badge and life on it."

"Did you know Don has never lost a case?"

"I didn't need to know, Sheriff. I know his record will stay intact."

The family was gathered outside the courthouse. They stood smoking and shooting the bull with each other. The destruction of Trooper Watkins was complete and they were feeling much better about Bobby Jack's chances. Carol and Anne were watching as Faith and Renee visited.

"Every one of those bitches will come dressed to the nines tomorrow. I think Mary has a vibrator under her dress. She keeps closing her eyes and taking a deep breath," Carol said.

"This trial is already over. Your right, Carol; the bitches will come tomorrow showing off their bodies for Don. That damn Denise is ready to jump over the rail and grab him. Those two bitches in New York would have raped him if we hadn't been there."

"He only has eyes for Faith, but he sure knows how to turn a woman on. You should have been with us in Miami. I told this bitch to take a walk when she started hitting on him. We were on the dance floor and she tried to grab his dick. I swear to God on my life I had to grab her hand, Anne."

Ben's phone was ringing off the wall. "The bastard subpoenaed the Governor, Ben," Simpson said.

"I told you he would."

"Harrison is scared shitless! He will have both of us disbarred for going to the jail."

"He will have you disbarred. Both of you must have lost your minds going to the jail. He has a loaded gun pointed right between both of your eyes. He will bring so much heat on the Governor; the man's enemies will start a recall. I told you Jackie; you better find a way to make this case go away."

"We will be the laughingstock of the country. Ray Tipton told me he threatened to put Huey and all the cops in prison. Huey's nephew, who is the jailer, got busted last night and hauled off by the feds. How the hell can you lose a case like this, Ben?"

"Jackie, when you walk in the courtroom tomorrow, do me a favor. Take a good look at the jury box. They will all be decked out and showing every inch of cleavage they can. If I am wrong, and they dress plain and conservative, you might have a slight chance. If I'm right, your ass is fried."

"The women are all married. I made sure he didn't seat any single women."

"Jesus Christ, Jackie, have you lost your mind? Do you think they give a shit if they are married? In their minds, Tom Cruise is taking their ass to bed. How old would you say Don is, Jackie?"

"I'd say about thirty four maybe thirty six."

"How old are the women?"

"Six are thirty three, two are thirty four, one is thirty five and three are thirty six."

"Have you ever seen a better looking man in your life?"

"No. I have to be honest about it. Don is one handsome man."

"Jackie, what the hell were you doing when jury selection was going on?"

"Hell, I was there the whole damn time. Harrison is so scared of Don, every time he flipped a juror, Harrison went along. That son-of-a-bitch fought for those women like they were all going to screw him. The man is tenacious, Ben. He went through two hundred and twelve people to seat the damn jury. He had every male admit they were prejudiced against Bobby Jack. The word spread like wildfire and none of them wanted to serve. Hudson may as well have been sitting in Harrison's seat."

"You can bet your damn life they all want to sleep with him. How the hell do you think he has never lost a case? Do you think it is a miracle he has never lost? Jackie, you did a hell of a job seating this jury. You have about as much chance of winning with that jury as I do of being the next President of the United States. They will never convict Bobby Jack of anything."

"What the hell am I supposed to do about bringing this to a close?"

"Any damn thing you have to. I have to go Jackie. Governor Jones is on the phone and he's mad as hell."

"Shit," Jackie said.

The Governor had high political aspirations. He fancied himself to be a man of the people. His political antenna had rarely let him down. When he ran his mouth to the press about Bobby Jack, he thought he was on solid ground. Suddenly, the ground had shifted under his feet. He wanted to be grilled by Hudson about as much as jumping off the high diving board into an empty pool.

"Governor, it is a pleasure to hear from you."

"Ben, I'm about to get my balls squeezed in a vise by Don Hudson. The man is a verbal killer. I don't want any part of him chewing on me. I just hung up with my good friend, Governor

Graham, down in Florida. He told me in no uncertain terms Hudson can and will destroy me."

"I know Governor. How can I help?"

"You get that damn Harrison and Simpson to drop the case. You can tell the damn fool Mayor to shut up. The stupid bastard is going to get every cop in Littleville put in the pen along with him. Hudson filed a formal complaint with the Attorney General and the U.S. Attorney over the way his client was being treated. The damn Attorney General has been raising money for months to run against me. The no good prick has six of his people down there wearing the cop's asses out. Two of them have already rolled over and admitted they threatened to kill Cullen. The Sheriff is the only one over there with any damn sense."

"Can I speak for you when I approach these men?"

"You sure as hell can. Ben, we have to stop this case from moving forward. You tell Simpson and Harrison if they get indicted, I'll let them rot in jail. A pardon is out of the question."

"Let me get to work right now."

"I'm counting on you, Ben."

Court was set to resume at one o'clock. Ben looked at his watch and headed out the door. He went straight to Judge Harrison's chamber. The good Judge looked up and was surprised to see Ben.

"Hell Ben, what brings you here?" Harrison asked.

"The Governor wants me to speak to you off the record."

"I have court starting in five minutes."

"Judge, you need to get sick the rest of the day. We have to stop this trial before everyone gets indicted. Hudson knows you and Jackie went to the jail. He is going to drop the hammer on both of you. Dismiss the jurors and let me cut a deal with Hudson before he blows you up."

"Are you sure, Ben?"

"You better damn well believe I'm sure. We need to get that man on a plane back to Florida before it is too late."

"Okay Ben, I'll dismiss the jury for the day."

Don sat at the defense table smiling non stop at the twelve women. Trust me, when I tell you, they were all smiling back. More winks and suggestive looks were going back and forth than cars in rush hour traffic. I mean, Gertrude had nailed it right on the head. Simpson had about as much chance of winning the case as he did of dropping a hundred pounds in a week.

"I've got to get him my phone number. I know he wants me," Donna whispered to Lynn.

"Bitch, you will never see the day. There is no doubt in my mind he will be making passionate love to me."

"I'm going to pop two uppers before I get in bed with Don. I want to make damn sure I can go all night," Denise whispered.

"God, he has undressed me ten times. No one could have convinced me I could have an orgasm in a jury box," Donna said.

Judge Harrison was announced and came in and took his seat on the bench. "Court is adjourned for the rest of the day," Judge Harrison said. He looked at the jurors and told them they were dismissed. "I'm sorry, but I am not feeling well." He stood and walked out of the courtroom. Don smiled at the twelve women as they filed out of the jury box.

"There will not be a tomorrow, Howard. The boys are getting ready to cut a deal. Don has them by the balls and he's squeezing hard. Harrison and Simpson's nuts have shrunk to nothing."

"How do you know that, R.E.?" Florence asked.

"I saw Ben leave Harrison's chamber when I came in the back. Sure as the sun comes up, that boy is going to walk."

"I'll have to see it with my own eyes," Howard said.

"The only way you won't see it is if you go blind. Bobby Jack is going to walk out of here a free man," Anne said.

"Damn, I really like that boy. He just brought his ass up here and kicked Simpson and Harrison right in the balls. Joan's son is standing over there shaking like a leaf in a damn hurricane," Kate said.

Across town, Ben was looking the Mayor in the eye. "Huey, you have to shut your damn mouth. Your redneck ass is going to get fried."

"That city slicker don't scare me one bit. He threatened me and my jailer. I will not stand for it. This is my town and I call the shots. I have been running this place for fourteen years. I'm the king of the hill. I don't put up with any sucker like Don Hudson."

"You're going to be calling the shots from the state pen if you don't shut up. You have more corruption in your administration than the rest of the state combined. I've kept your dumb ass out of jail for years. Hudson has this town full of private detectives digging up dirt on your ass. Do you think it was an accident your nephew was busted and taken away? My sources tell me the fat ass is under the lights and singing like a canary. Governor Jones has laid down the law, Huey. Shut up or he is going to turn the dogs loose on you."

"C. Jacob, will use it against me."

"C. Jacob is the least of your worries."

"I completely outclassed him in the last election. I'll completely outclass him again. You can't sling mud in the Mayor's race. It don't work around here. People won't stand for it."

"Huey, let me try one last time and paint you a picture. You are watching the news on national television with your wife. Here you come in handcuffs and chains followed by a dozen police officers.

Six of your in laws and a dozen members of your administration are all dragging chains and moving real slow. C. Jacob's fat, ugly ass is standing and applauding as you come by. Don Hudson is shooting you the bird and laughing his ass off. You have posted your bond and you're looking at six years in the pen."

"I don't like it, but I get your point."

"Huey, take a week off and go somewhere warm. It is as much heat as you want. You are living on borrowed time."

Ben showed Huey the door and placed the call. Don looked at his cell phone and smiled. "Hey buddy, I thought I might hear from you this afternoon."

"Can you come by my office?"

"I'll be there in thirty minutes."

"I'll see you in thirty minutes."

Don hung up and looked at Faith. She was visiting with Renee and Emily. "Have you arranged for the photographer, Faith?"

"Yes baby. The man will be in the courtroom all day tomorrow."

"It will be over before noon. I'll see you at the hotel in a couple of hours." They kissed and Don got in the car for the ride over to Ben's law office.

"Why was he asking about you having a photographer?" Renee asked.

"The women will all want their pictures taken with him. He always arranges for every one to have a picture as a group and individually."

"The trial won't be over tomorrow," Emily said.

"It's already over, Aunt Emily," Anne said.

"What's she talking about?"

"She's talking about the twelve chicks on the jury. They would free a mass murderer if they thought they could have one night with Don," Carol said.

"They haven't made up their minds."

"Jesus, what kind of water are you drinking in Lilleyville. Those bitches are star struck, you damn fool! They can't even breathe they are so shook up. Tell her, Aunt Faith," Anne said.

"Emily, it always happens this way. His office is full of the pictures with the jurors. He always fights to seat the women. Once it took a week and over eight hundred potential jurors. He wears the D.A. down and the Judges are scared of him getting on television. It started years ago when he got a District Judge removed in Tampa. The man kept fighting with Don over seating the jurors. Don keeps four former F.B.I. men on his payroll and they found out the Judge smoked pot. It was terribly embarrassing to the man and his wife divorced him. He was removed from the bench and disbarred from the practice of law."

"Well, I've never heard of such a thing. I'm sure you are all blowing smoke."

"You will bite your tongue when you see the jurors tomorrow. Of that, I am absolutely sure. If you still think they haven't made up their minds tomorrow, we will all get you some mental help," Anne said.

"I'd never cast my vote against him. I'm telling you, Faith did real good," Florence said.

"That boy is breathtaking. I've been kicking my ass for six years over making a fool out of myself," Vicki said.

Don walked in and Ben greeted him at the door. "Come in my office, Councilor. The boys want to cut a deal and have asked me to make the offer."

"I'm all ears."

"We need a graceful way out, Don. We rest our case without calling another witness. You call Doctor Hillman and have him explain that the medication caused Bobby Jack to do the things he did. You step forward and ask for a dismissal. You don't call the Governor, and you don't expose Harrison and Simpson."

"Fair enough, you got yourself a deal, Ben."

They stood and shook hands. "Did that boy really take his medication and it messed him up?"

"Hell no, that script expired two years ago. I had to get the Doctor to write another one. Bobby Jack is a living, breathing disaster."

"I spoke to G. Jackson Warrington before you came over. The old man is happy as hell."

"Why didn't you take the case?"

"I couldn't win. I have to live with these fools every day."

"Thanks for the referral, Ben. Jack really wanted to see Bobby Jack walk."

"The man hates Huey and C. Jacob. Are you going to drop the hammer on them?"

"It's going to be a lot worse than a hammer, Ben. It will be more in line with a two thousand pound cluster bomb."

The next morning, all the women were up early. Mary's husband looked up to see her as she came in. "Damn Mary, you look like your going to a party. I haven't seen you ever look like this."

"I want to look my best in court."

"Damn Honey, you are leaving nothing to the imagination. Is that a see through blouse you're wearing?"

"I have a jacket over it, Buford."

"I didn't know you had a skirt that short."

"I bought it with the money you gave me for my birthday, Sweetie."

Out at Twelve Trees, Connie and Sharon were decked out and ready to make a splash. Sharon's husband did a double take when she walked out. "Where are you going looking like that?" Wallace asked.

"I'm on my way to court, Honey."

"Damn, Sharon you look like a hooker."

"Don't be silly. I have to pick up Connie. She bounded out the door as he watched with his mouth open.

Connie was putting the finishing touches on her lipstick when her husband, Frank, walked in. He stood staring at his wife. "Damn, you ain't going no where looking like that."

"I'm late for court," she said as she rushed out the door.

"Son of a bitch! What the hell is going on in that court?"

He called his best friend, Victor Bowen, who was an assistant D.A. Victor came on the line and said hello.

"Is Connie on the jury in that Bobby Jack Cullen trial?"

"Yes. Why are you asking?"

"The bitch walked out half dressed with a skirt up to her ass and half her breasts hanging out, Victor."

"Well, she is definitely on the jury, Frank."

Lynn was through dressing and slipping out the door. She had timed her exit to miss her husband. Donna's husband had already left as had Kathy's. Denise was putting the finishing touches on when her husband, Brian, came in.

"Where the hell are you going? I've been to a whore house and seen more clothes than you have on."

"You're too damn possessive. I'm going to court to serve on the damn jury. Where the hell do you think I'm going? You think I'm going to get laid in the courthouse?"

"Damn it, Denise, I know you are up to no good."

The doorbell rang and Brian opened the door. He almost passed out as Toni stood with nothing on but a smile. Well, almost nothing on but a smile. Denise came in and headed for the door.

"Come on, Toni. We are going to be late for court."

Brian watched as the girls took off like a bat out of hell. He climbed in his pickup and followed them to the courthouse. He sat watching from the red light as they got out and walked in. When the light turned green, he started to pull off and head for the parking lot. He almost went through the windshield when the car plowed into him from the rear. He looked back and saw it was Homer Ruston. He was mad as hell when he got out of his truck.

"What the hell is wrong with you, Homer?"

"I'm sorry, Brian. My insurance will pay for everything."

"What the hell were you thinking about?"

"Man, I think they must have busted a bunch of good-looking hookers and they are going to court. My eyeballs almost popped out of my head. I didn't read anything about this shit."

"That's my wife, you son-of-a-bitch. I ought to kick your ass from one end of the street to the next."

"You let your wife dress like that, Brian?"

"I'm going to kick your ass all the way to the Littleville hospital, Homer!" Brian screamed.

Across town Patsy, Susan, Peggy, and Diane were all going through the same ritual. They started to arrive at the courthouse and walked in. Chief Thomas was at the station when the calls started coming in.

"Damn, there are four wrecks in front of the courthouse. A fist fight has broken out and the deputies are trying to break it up. Get three squad cars over there, Frank."

"The roads must be slick or something, Chief. We have never had a wreck in front of the courthouse," Frank said.

Florence, Vicki, Renee, Joan, Shirley, Carol, and Anne sat watching as the women filed in and took their seats in the jury box.

"Mother of God, they look like a hooker's convention. What on earth are those women up to?" Florence asked.

"Those girls are all going to be getting a divorce. I've never seen anything like this in my life," Vicki said.

"I've never seen that much skin in the women's room at the pool. Faith and the girls are right. Bobby is going to walk. They don't give a shit about Bobby Jack or Jackie Simpson," Renee said.

"My God, they look like they are trying to go to work for Victoria Secret. The bitches are doing a damn good job of it," Shirley said.

"Bobby Jack could have killed a dozen people and walked. This is a damn instant replay of what happened in Florida," Anne said.

"Renee, you got it dead right. Those bitches have one thing on their minds and it ain't the trial. There all in heat and looking for some Don Hudson action. I'm going to hang around and see if one of them jumps the rail," Kate said.

Emily came in with Faith and the photographer and sat down. She looked at the women and almost fainted. "Faith, are we going to see an xxx movie. My God, Jake is going to make me leave."

"My baby is going to win again," Faith said.

Don sat smiling at each and every one of the women. Simpson took his glasses off and put them back on. "Ben was right as usual, Sam. My dick hasn't been this hard in thirty years."

"Everybody calls me a slut. I'm a damn angel compared to these bitches. They all think they're going to win the lottery. They all have a damn vibrator and there getting ready to use it," Carol said.

R.E., Howard, Jake, Morris, and Paul sat with their tongues hanging out. "I saw one of them x-rated movies one time. It wasn't nearly as good as this, R.E.," Howard said.

"I'm going to have to slip over to Myrtle's later and get me some. That old gal can still strap some loving on you. You have to be careful how you position yourself. She farts like a mule in heat," R.E. said.

"Jesus, what has the world come to?" Jake asked.

"I don't know, but I sure like it," Morris mumbled.

"We have to get Faith out of town and give Don some breathing room. I think our boy Don is going to get him some Littleville women," Howard said.

Paul looked over to see Renee staring at him. He raised both hands in the air and gave her a shit eating grim.

Kate sat with Chuck taking in the scene. "It's all over but the shouting, Chuck."

"I've never seen anything like this in my life. Bobby is minutes away from walking out of this courtroom. The damn man is magic. Every woman on the jury is ready to leave their husband."

"Faith told me they will all be crawling all over Don the minute their dismissed," Kate said.

"Order in the court, please rise for the Honorable Judge," the man nearly shouted.

Harrison walked in and sat down. He looked at the attorneys and then the jurors. He couldn't talk and grabbed a glass of water. "The court will now come to order. Mr. Hudson, the state has rested. You may call your first witness."

"Your Honor, the defense calls Doctor John Hillman."

Doctor Hillman was sworn in and Don approached him. "Good morning, Doctor Hillman. We are going to make this very brief. Are you a licensed physician?"

"Yes sir."

"How long have you practiced medicine?"

"Thirty two years."

"Do you have a patient named Bobby Jack Cullen?"

"Yes."

"Have you prescribed any medication for Mr. Cullen?"

"Yes. I have on several occasions."

Don walked over and showed Simpson an empty bottle. He approached Doctor Hillman and handed him the bottle. "Doctor, explain to the court the side effects of this medicine."

"The side effects can be quite bad. The patient can experience high anxiety and fear of dying. One can appear to the non trained eye to be drunk or on drugs when in fact they are having a violent reaction to the medication. Trauma can be brought on by being exposed to any kind of violence."

"Would an explosion, involving several automobiles, twenty feet away fall into that category?"

"Absolutely. It would be devastating."

"Would the sound of sirens blaring and helicopters descending from the sky further that reaction?"

"It would in all likelihood cause the person to fear for their lives. They would at that point do anything to escape the violence."

"I assume someone threatening to kill that person would cause even a more drastic reaction?"

"Mr. Hudson, it would be a minor miracle if that human being could survive."

"Thank you, Doctor, I have no further questions."

"Your witness, Mr. Simpson," Judge Harrison said.

"I have no questions for the witness," Jackie said.

"You may step down, Doctor," the Judge said.

Doctor Hillman walked back to his seat and Don stood. "Your Honor, I move that this case be dismissed immediately."

Harrison motioned for Simpson to approach the bench with Don. They walked up and Harrison looked at Jackie. "What is your position Mr. Simpson?"

"Judge, in light of these facts we move to dismiss."

Harrison looked across the room. "The court orders this case be dismissed. Mr. Cullen, you are free to go." He looked at the jurors. "Ladies, thank you for your service."

Don walked back to the defense table and shook Bobby Jack's hand. "Don't even think about pulling this crap again."

"I'm walking the straight and narrow from this moment forward. I owe you my life, Don."

"Watch these bitches, Mother," Carol said.

"They're all reaching for their purses to pull out their phone numbers," Anne said.

"You can go to work now," Faith said to the photographer.

"Those women have no shame," Florence said.

"How can you tolerate Don carrying on with these women? Howard wasn't this blatant in his wildest days."

"It is his job, Vicki. Don only has eyes for me. He plays these women like a violin."

The girls took their pictures as a group with Don. Each one had their own taken with him. If you think they were whispering in his ear about the weather, you think you live on Mars.

"Lord, Don is hugging and kissing every one of those women on the cheek," Howard said.

"Come on, Howard. It's time to go home," Vicki said.

Kate stood and looked at the women. "I would never have believed this if I hadn't seen it with my own eyes. The man just flat out buried these fools without a grave marker. I got to get my butt home and have lunch."

"Things ain't ever going to be the same around here," R.E. said.

"Look at Ben standing over there smiling like a cat who ate the goldfish. I bet he was up to his eyeballs in this with Don," Florence said.

Don and Faith got in the limo for the ride back to the airport. He reached in his coat pocket and handed her all the cards with the phone numbers. "How many does that make baby?"

"Seven hundred and sixty two."

"Baby, we are still undefeated."

"You have blown my family's mind. They will never get over watching you in action. I love you with all my heart."

"I love you more than life, Faith."

The five men sat at their country club watching as the news of Bobby Jack's acquittal flashed across the screen. "It's time to pay the piper," Warrington said.

"How the hell could this have happened? That damn prosecutor must be the dumbest bastard on earth," Gordon said.

"Hudson must be magic. I'll tell you one damn thing. If my ass ever gets in a jam, I'm hiring Hudson," Derek said.

"You better be ready to reach deep in your back pocket. Trust me when I tell you, 'He doesn't come cheap!'"

"I can't believe I lost the bet. How did Hudson convince the jury to vote not guilty? He must have used an insanity plea and the damn fools bought it. I'm going to order the transcript of the damn trial," Randy said.

"Jack, I guess there is a reason you are the wealthiest man in New York. You must be able to see things no one else can. How the hell could a jury of twelve of your peers vote to acquit?" Boyd asked.

The men all reached for their check books and made out the checks to Warrington. Randy looked at the television and there stood Don with the twelve women.

"There is your answer, Boyd. Jack, you are a son-of-a-bitch. Who paid Hudson, he costs a fortune?" Randy asked.

"You did my friends. But, all is not lost."

Don's cell rang and he picked up. "Thank you, Don, for saving my grandson's stupid ass."

"It didn't turn out to be as hard as I expected. I hope I get to meet you someday, Jack."

"How about we make it tonight in the city? I took the liberty of hiring your favorite band and booked the Rainbow Room. I want you to meet some of my friends and their wives."

"You got yourself a deal."

"Bring your beautiful wife, but leave her family in Littleville."

"We will see you at nine o'clock."

The four men sat in stunned silence. "You are my guests tonight. You will get to meet Don along with myself."

"Did you know he was going to pack that jury with young women?" Randy asked.

"Randy, you need to broaden your reading material. He always packs the jury with women."

"How the hell does he manage to do that?"

"How the hell did you get rich? You know every damn thing about software. He is the best trial lawyer in the damn country. He knows how to seat his jury, you fool!"

"Why the hell didn't the District Attorney stop him from seating all the women?

"Do I really have to answer that, Randy? No one is good enough to stop him."

Don reached over and popped in a Bruce Springsteen CD. Pink Cadillac came blasting away. "Let's party, Princess!"

"Where are we going?"

"New York City."

"Who was that man and where are we going in the city?"

"Mr. Warrington, one of my clients, Faith. He booked a band for a party tonight. Are you ready to let your hair down?"

"I'll never understand why you took this case."

"Someday, when we are old and I'm through practicing law, I'll tell you. In the meantime, trust me when I tell you, 'We did very well."'

CHAPTER NINE

Everyone was in an upbeat mood as they prepared for the family reunion Saturday night. Once a year, they got together and came from all over the state. Hell, some of them came from around the country. They rented the Elks Lodge on West Avenue and hired a local country band. Everybody pitched in with a hundred dollars. Scooter was assigned the task of securing the liquor and soft drinks. Scooter was a little shook up over a recent incident at his tanning bed business. He was talking over drinks with two of his buddies and recounting the story.

"I can't believe my damn bad luck," Scooter said.

"I heard on the radio about the cops busting the hooker," David said.

"Man that had to be embarrassing as hell. My sister was over at the center shopping and saw four police cars," Ducky said.

"I thought it was a good idea to offer massages for my customers. The damn girl came by and seemed like a nice person. She convinced me she could increase my business. I rented her a room for three hundred a month."

"You didn't know she was a hooker, Scooter?" Ducky said.

"I guess looking back, I should have known. She was busy as a bee all the time. One day, I went in her room thinking it was empty. She was giving Sarah's husband a massage and had practically nothing on. I thought it was just the way she worked."

"Damn, it's the middle of the winter, Scooter," David said.

"Yeah, that's what the cops said when they came. It turned out she was a pro."

"Did you have a lot of customers in your place when the cops raided it?" Ducky asked.

"That was the worst part of all. I had four old ladies in the beds when they came barreling their ass in. They freaked out and started screaming and falling down. One poor woman lost her towel and was trying to tell the cops she didn't work here."

"Who did they catch the hooker with?" David asked.

"C. Jacob's ugly ass son, Buck, was caught red handed. The Mayor just happened to be here with Chief Thomas and half the department. The old, crooked bastard was carrying on to the newspaper about some people's lack of moral values."

"Huey is a damn joke," Ducky said.

"You will land on your feet, Scooter," David said.

"They say bad press is better than no press."

"Scooter, did you get any from her?" Ducky asked.

"Hell no, that's the worst part of all. My wife swears I was banging her every day. I never get in trouble when I'm running around. I always catch hell when I'm not doing anything. Amanda is giving me a steady dose of hell and both her parents hate me. The bitch has all the money."

"Life is just not fair, Scooter. What's the story on the tanning bed that messed up?" David asked.

"The damn thing was a new product from the distributor. He gave it to me to use for three months at no charge. The thing has a vibrator that moves from one part of your body to the next. There is a button that moves it around your body and adjusts the speed. Helen Forrest came in for a tan and I told her about it."

"What went so wrong?" Ducky asked.

"The distributor said it was a faulty switch. Helen said she couldn't get out and it beat her to death. It kept getting faster and faster. She told me and the insurance guy if she wanted it in the ass; she damn sure didn't have to pay for it. I've never seen anyone as mad as that lady was."

"She was probably telling the truth. She will be gone for good, Scooter," David said.

"Well, crap always happens to the Martin's. The thing I really hated was the interview with the Littleville Times. I thought for sure no men or women would ever come. It turned out; we got a lot of gay men and women who love it in the ass. I'd love to get that damn Huey Cox in there, just one time. I'd bolt the damn top shut and crank up the volume to the max."

"Huey is going to keep screwing with people and someone is going to stick it up his ass, big time," Ducky said.

The boys split up and Scooter headed for the liquor store. For the next thirty minutes, he was busy buying all the liquor and drinks.

Over in Lilleyville, Jake and Emily sat discussing whether they should attend with their family. Their three sons were all married and two were straight arrows.

"Jake, we haven't been in three years. It's the only chance I get to see all my relatives."

"I don't like your family. There is always a scene between them. They will be smoking dope and drinking like fish."

"Moose loves to go and see everyone. Freddie and Jane always look forward to getting away for a weekend. Tyler and Becky never get to go anywhere."

"Sue Ellen hates being around your family."

"Moose will talk her in to going. Jake, I really want to go this year and see everyone."

"Alright Emily, I'll go but I know it will wind up being a scene. We will have to drive back late. I have a sermon to preach Sunday morning."

"We won't be drinking and neither will the kids. All of us will be home a little after midnight."

Carol and Morris were both stoned as they sat passing a joint back and forth. "Are we going to the family reunion, Carol?"

"Hell yes, we're going. Scooter is going to spike the punch and get all of them drunk. I hope Emily and Jake come with their kids. Moose is a hoot when he gets wasted."

"Are Mr. Hudson and Mrs. Faith coming?"

"If the moon falls and hits the earth, Don will be here."

"Why are you so crazy about Don?"

"Oh, I don't know Morris. Could it be that he is rich, handsome and treats me like a doll. He takes me to fabulous places and parties in the finest clubs. Maybe it's the five star restaurants."

"Bobby Jack sold the car wash and moved away."

"Morris, if you had every cop in the state wanting a piece of your ass, you would be long gone too."

"My momma needs some false teeth."

"You're momma needs a brain. She ran right through the front of the Dollar Store last week. Sarah told me she almost ran over six people. People were running for their lives when the glass started to shatter. Nell told me she thought a tornado was coming through and it was over for her and little Spunky."

"Momma said she thought she hit the brakes. She lost control and ran into the garbage bin outside. It hung on the front of her car and she couldn't see where she was going. The damn accelerator is right next to the brakes."

"No shit, Morris."

"Are you going over to Anne's today?"

"Morris, I'm going to bed. It is eleven at night, honey. Are you coming to bed?"

"I don't want to bother you."

"You ain't bothering me, Morris."

Friday afternoon, Florence, Vicki, and Joan were grocery shopping at Elmer's Market. Old habits are hard to break. They had shopped with Elmer Jenkins for fifty years. The store was in a rough part of town. Security cameras were mounted inside and outside the store. A security guard was always stationed at the front exit.

"Get some more chips for tomorrow night, Florence. Jake and Emily are coming with their crew. That damn Moose can eat three bags by himself. Those boys all tip the scales north of three hundred pounds," Joan said.

"Howard wants some pork and beans. I hate buying the damn crap. The old coot farts all night when he eats them."

"R.E. won a hundred and seventy dollars on the football games last weekend. The tight wad gave me twenty bucks."

"Who is he betting with?" Vicki asked.

"We met a bookie in Tunica, at the casino. R.E., Renee, and I bet every week. R.E. and me are both still losing, but I'm about to figure it out."

"How do you do that?" Joan asked.

"The bookie's name is Lum Badino. He sends us the betting line every week. We call him and place our bets. Renee is up over a thousand dollars."

"Is that legal?" Vicki asked.

"No. But who is ever going to know? Nobody gives a damn about people betting on ball games."

The women heard loud noises coming from the next isle and they all peeked around the corner. They were shocked to see a young couple going at it full speed ahead.

"You cheating, low life son of a bitch," Hillary Grisham shouted.

"Lower your voice, Hillary," her husband Foster said.

"I'll lower my voice when you're dead, Foster."

"If you were not frigid, I wouldn't have to chase strange women. Do you think I can live with only getting a piece of your ass once a month?"

"You dirty rotten bastard! I'm going to put your lights out!" Hillary shouted.

"Oh my Lord, they're going to kill each other right here. Call 9-1-1 Joan. Tell them there is trouble at Elmer's," Florence said.

"Damn, you can't even go the grocery store anymore without running into trouble," Joan said.

"It is getting really bad over there," Vicki said.

"Who the hell do you think you are threatening me?" Foster shouted.

"I'll kill you!"

"I'm getting the hell out of here," Vicki said.

"What are we going to do about all these groceries? We have two shopping carts filled to the top," Joan said.

"The hell with the groceries, woman, we can get groceries anytime. If Hillary has a gun, she is going to shoot Foster. I don't want to be in this store if she misses. Her Momma shot her Daddy in the ass twelve years ago. He was caught red handed in Katie Sims back seat at the drive in theater and started running. They were pulling bullets out of his ass for a week," Florence said.

"My Herb said the place emptied in two minutes."

The purse snatcher was looking for the right opportunity to make his move. The man had been casing the store looking for a victim. He stood and watched the woman as she placed her purse in the top of the basket. She walked over and picked up some rolls of toilet paper. Two isles over from the Martin women, the purse snatcher went for her purse. He grabbed the woman's purse and took off running.

The woman looked up as he ran for the door. "Robbery, I've been robbed," the woman screamed.

"Shit!" Florence screamed.

"Where is the robber?" Vicki said.

The security guard blocked off the front of the store and drew his gun. The thief came running past the Martin women and pushed Florence. Across on the next isle, Hillary had picked up a can of beans and was ready to drop the dime on Foster. The thief rounded the next isle where Hillary stood.

"Lord, save us from death," Joan said.

"Run Florence," Vicki said.

Florence got tangled up and fell backwards into the rack of cans. She screamed as the rack started to fall.

"You die right now, you cheating bastard," Hillary screamed.

Foster ducked in the nick of time as the cans went flying from Hillary's hands. The thief caught it flush on his temple and crumbled to the floor. Less than a second later, Florence came crashing down with six hundred cans on top of him. Pandemonium broke out as the security guard rushed over and the store emptied.

"Lord, is she dead?" Vicki asked.

"I think she is starting to move," Joan said.

"Shit always happens to Florence. The woman has been a dark cloud since birth."

The security guard had handcuffed the thief when the police arrived. Florence was helped off the floor and Joan retrieved her wig. Hillary was still screaming at Foster and the police pulled them apart. Elmer Jenkins had been called and rushed over to his store. Charlotte Mims, the lady who was robbed, retrieved her purse and vowed never to come back.

"I have a two thousand dollar reward," Elmer proudly announced.

"Give me the damn money, Elmer. I almost got killed."

"I busted that mother. Give me the money, Mr. Jenkins. I'm leaving this piece of shit," Hillary said.

"What are you talking about?" Florence asked.

"I threw a can and popped the no good bastard in the head."

"There is nothing to debate ladies. We have cameras mounted and we will go take a look and see who got this punk."

They all went in the back and watched the video tape. Sure as hell, it was Hillary by a split second. Elmer had a big smile on his face as he handed Hillary the check.

"What kind of place are you running here, Elmer?"

"This can happen anywhere, Florence."

"I never thought I'd get nipped at the wire for two grand. Why don't you keep your dick in your pants?" Florence shouted at Foster.

"I'll buy you two fifths of Jack Daniels, Florence."

"Well, I don't usually drink, but I'll take them anyway."

"Mother of God, you are the biggest liar on the planet," Vicki said.

Hillary got her check and left. Florence, Vicki, and Joan, headed home with yet another story for the Martin legacy. Foster called his mistress for a ride and explained in vivid detail the events that had occurred. He was shocked when the woman told him to walk home. It was even worse when she told him she wasn't talking about her home.

Saturday night came and the Martin's showed up in force. All the local Martin families were there. Wild Buck came from a big family himself. One of his brother's grandsons was coming with his family. A granddaughter from a sister was coming. By eight o'clock, the band had started playing and the drinks were flowing. Scooter and Carol were busy giving all the non drinkers a big glass of punch.

"Give me another glass of that punch, Scooter," Moose said.

"Sure, I'm glad you like it Moose. I made it myself."

"Mother, have another glass of the punch. It is really good," Moose said.

"I'll have another glass myself," Jake said.

Freddie, Tyler, and their wives were drinking the punch with Sue Ellen. Howard and Vicki were partaking as well. Morris was stoned and walked up to Renee and Paul. "Are you having a good time?"

"We just got here, Morris," Paul said.

"I'm having a real good time myself."

"I said we just got here."

"Well, I think I'll have a beer. I hope both of you keep having a good time. Carol says the band is really good." Morris turned and walked across the floor to the bar.

"The boy is brain dead," Paul said.

"I knew Carol had walked off a cliff when she married that boy. The poor bastard is nothing but a meal ticket to Carol. She runs around on the poor boy nonstop."

"I've never seen Jake so animated. He must be real comfortable with his children here."

"He is acting like he's had a few."

"Jake has never touched a drop of liquor in his life."

"Howard is dancing up a storm. He used to dance that way five years ago before Vicki made him stop drinking."

The family was really starting to get loose and let their hair down. Jimmy had come in with Shirley. Everyone was thrilled to see him up and about. Raymond Chambers had come down from Boston. Raymond was one of Wild Buck's brother's sons and everyone called him Frog. The man was a big time investment banker and was responsible for selling pools of mortgage loans to investors around the world. R.E. and Florence were visiting with Frog and his son Jack.

"Frog, are you still in the stock market?" R.E. asked.

"I'm taking the fools' money every day we are open. We are bundling up a boat load of crap mortgages and selling them all over the world."

"Did Hampton ever get Wayne out of prison?" Florence asked.

"Don't you watch the news, Florence? Wayne got life without parole for killing those two women. There is a nationwide manhunt for him as we speak. He escaped from the state prison two days ago in Louisiana."

"He was spotted stealing a car less than a hundred miles from Littleville. I heard it on the radio on my way over here," Jack said.

"Lord, I can't believe Beverly went out with that boy," Florence said.

"Is that Jake dancing with Sarah? That boy ain't ever been to a dance in his life," R.E. said.

"I can't believe my lying eyes," Florence said.

"Emily is check to check with Anne's guy on the dance floor. I don't think Jake had a clue about the girls past when he married her," R.E. said.

"Their both trying to score a different sex partner tonight," Florence said.

"Scooter turned out to be a nice young man. He hasn't stopped bringing people punch since I got here," Frog said.

"Carol is doing the same thing," Florence said.

"Renee and Vicki must have had a good talk with both of them," R.E. said.

"Is Jimmy still banging every girl in town, R.E.?" Frog asked.

"The boy has been under the weather with a bad heart for the last little while. He'll have two in his bed again real soon."

"Faith hit the jackpot."

"Frog, I know you will think I'm lying when I tell you this story. I swear on my life it is the gospel truth. Bobby Jack got busted doing a hundred miles an hour. He was drunk, stoned, and stole a state police car. Faith's husband came to town and the damn boy walked free as a bird. The jurors were all good looking women and me and Howard thought they were going to strip naked for him."

"I read the story in the Boston Globe. He did the same damn thing in Houston, except the women were older. The young ones want to take him to bed and the old ones want to be his mother. The man is a rock star in women's eyes. My granddaughter has a picture of him that covers the whole damn wall. I shit you not. There is Don, Brad Pitt, and Tom Cruise. She got the picture of him on the cover of Time and had it blown up. Am I telling the truth, Jack?"

"Marty is crazy about him. She must have printed a hundred stories of Don off the internet. The damn girl has a book thicker than the Boston phone book."

"The man blows my mind," R.E. said.

"My best friend's father got indicted for securities fraud in New York. Teresa told me Don was flipping men for having a filling in their mouth. He caught a woman Judge and the U.S. Attorney was screaming bloody murder every time he flipped another man," Jack said.

"Did the man have to serve time?" Florence asked.

"Hell no! He is right back at work. Don has never lost a case, Mrs. Florence."

Moose was feeling his oats. He didn't have a clue he had downed half a dozen mixed drinks. Sue Ellen looked over and he was draped all over Anne. "Moose, what the hell do you think you're going?"

"Having fun for a change," Moose said.

"Get your hands off Anne."

"You are one boring ass bitch."

"I'll show you how boring I am, meat head." She started unbuttoning her blouse and dancing by herself.

"You better get your ass on the dance floor with your wife," Anne said.

Freddie and Jane were both drunk and had passed out cold. Tyler and Becky were about to have sex on the dance floor.

Jake and Emily were both totally wasted now. Vicki looked up and saw Howard dancing on the stage with the band.

"Scooter, get your ass over here."

"What is it Momma? Are you having a good time?"

"Jimmy Ray, did you spike the punch?"

"I most certainly did not, Momma."

"Son, something is wrong when Florence is the straightest person at the party. Your father is up on the stage dancing his butt off."

"Relax and have a good time. I have to take Aunt Renee some punch."

Across the dance floor Renee was knocking down another glass of punch and smoking nonstop. "I haven't felt this good in twenty years, Paul."

"Something funny is going on here," Paul said.

"Here is some punch, Aunt Renee. I brought you another beer, Mr. Paul."

"Thanks Scooter," Paul said.

"Enjoy," Scooter said.

"I thought you told me Jake's church didn't approve of music and dancing," Paul said.

"I guess they all decided to lighten up tonight."

"Renee, I'm telling you they are all drunk. Jake just pinched Sarah on her ass."

Jimmy was taking it all in with a smile on his face. "Everybody's drunk, Shirley."

"Jake is shit faced, Jimmy. I'd bet you anything Scooter spiked the punch. It is going to be a sight to see in a couple of hours."

"Daddy would love being here tonight. Jake is going to stand up his congregation tomorrow morning."

"Jesus, Emily is rubbing her body all over that boy."

"Go out to the car and get the video recorder. Jake will pay me a grand to destroy the film."

Kate and Chuck were making their way around the room talking to everyone. They walked over and started to visit with Joan. Herb was standing with Joan and her boyfriend, Elmer, when his beeper went off. He called the station and his face turned bright red.

"Mother, Wayne was spotted ten minutes ago at Harvey Kessler's gas station by Judy Morris. Every police officer in the county has been called to duty."

"Damn, don't leave us here. Go out to the car and get your gun."

"I'm making an announcement and locking down this building."

"I hope they shoot that son of a bitch right between the eyes," Joan said.

"I'll put that creep's lights out for good if he screws with me. I have my gun in my purse," Kate said.

Herb ran to his car and secured his weapon. He came back in and spoke to the lead singer. The band stopped playing and started grabbing their instruments. Herb grabbed the microphone and looked at everyone.

"Wayne has escaped from prison and is in Littleville. I'm ordering the building to be locked down until further notice. He is considered armed and dangerous."

"You didn't have to tell us that, Herb," R.E. shouted.

"Son-of-a-bitch," Carol said.

"Who has a gun?" Howard screamed.

"Scooter, please tell me you have your gun," Vicki said.

"I don't carry a gun around with me."

"I got my damn gun," R.E. said.

"Anyone who has a gun, please get it now," Herb said.

"Wayne doesn't know we're here," Jake said.

"Oh Lord! That is not true, Jake. I sent the boy a letter two weeks ago telling him we were praying for him. I told him I sure wished he could be here for the reunion at the Lodge."

"I ought to kick your stupid ass, Emily. Have you lost your mind, sending a murderer a letter?" Kate shouted.

"That bastard has been writing me for years. I'm getting my ass out of here right now," Beverly said.

Herb walked to the back of the stage. He felt the hard steel against his back and his heart sank. "Shut your mouth and walk back on the damn stage," Wayne said.

"Don't do something stupid and kill someone."

They walked out on the stage and Wayne screamed at the top of his voice. "None of you suckers are going anywhere."

Everyone froze as Wayne made his way to the front of the stage. Florence had passed out and Renee was about to do the same. R.E. looked at Howard and shook his head. Man, you could have heard a pen drop it was so quiet.

"Play, you dick heads!" Wayne screamed at the band. "Beverly, where are you?" he shouted.

"We are all dead mothers," R.E. said.

"I wish you had made your peace with the Lord, R.E. I've been trying my best to get you to cross the fence."

"Go to hell, Howard."

Beverly crawled under a table with a blanket in the back of the room and started praying non stop. No one moved an inch as Wayne waved his gun at the band.

"We're in a bad position here," Howard said.

"Where are the damn cops when you need them?" Anne said.

"If I somehow get out of here alive, I swear I will never set foot around the Martin's again. These idiots are a magnet for trouble. Faith is the only one not screwed up," Paul said.

"Paul, kiss my ass. On second thought, say goodbye to the best piece of ass you ever got your ugly hands on," Renee shouted.

"Who's raising all that hell back there?" Wayne said.

"You are going to get me killed."

"I got a foul mouth boyfriend, Wayne."

"You want me to shut him up for you, doll?"

"I can handle his fat ass."

"If that bastard kills me, I'll come back and haunt you until the day you die, Renee."

"You pricks better not get any ideas about collecting the hundred thousand dollar reward. I'll shoot every one of you Martin bastards' right between the eyes. Give me some whiskey, Scooter."

"We should have stayed in Boston," Frog whispered.

"Wayne has tattoos on every inch of his body," Moose said.

"Shut up, Moose before you get us killed," Sue Ellen said.

"Where's Emily?" Wayne screamed.

"I'm right here, Wayne."

"Thanks for the letters. I may kill all these rotten bastards but I'll give you a pass. Are you still married to that dip shit preacher?"

"Yes, I'm still married to Jake."

"What on earth did you ever see in that ugly mother?"

"I was just ready to get away from Daddy."

"Well, that's perfectly understandable. Step forward, Preacher Jake and let me see your ass."

Jake was so drunk he could barely walk. "I'm right here on the sofa."

"Did I tell you to sit on the sofa? Get your ass in front of me or I'll shoot your long lanky ass right now."

Jake came off the sofa and walked in front of the stage. He was shaking like a leaf on a tree with hurricane winds blowing. The three sons didn't know whether to shit or go blind.

"You are a drunken ass hypocrite and I ought to waste your worthless ass. You ain't good enough for Emily." He raised his gun and everyone gasped.

"Wayne, don't shoot him. I spiked the punch. The idiot didn't know he was getting wasted," Scooter said.

"I ain't going back to prison. I'm going down right here with guns blazing. Damn, where are you Beverly? I know you're here I saw your car out front."

"I think this is the end, Joan," Vicki said.

"Daddy was in tighter spots than this on several occasions. Hang in there, Vicki. I got a feeling someone is going to waste his ass."

"Where's those old women chasers. R.E., you and Howard get your ass up here. You're both going to tell the family every piece of ass you ever got. My daddy told me every name. If either one of you forget a single one, your ass goes down right here."

Florence had come back from passing out. Vicki was all ears as R.E. and Howard walked slowly to the stage.

"Are you going to tell everything?" Howard whispered.

"You better believe I am. His father ran women with both of us for thirty years."

"Man, we are both going to be looking at a divorce, R.E."

"You crazy son of a bitch, the last thing I'm worried about is a divorce. This maniac is going to kill us."

Howard and R.E. made it up to the stage and Wayne looked at them. "Here's how we are going to do this, old boys. You name one Howard and then R.E. names one. You take turns until you have named every single one. You can start by telling everyone the best piece of ass you ever got. I got my list right here in my hand. The first one that stops before he names the last one, I pop a cap in your head. You both better have a damn good memory."

God, it was just awful as they went on and on for five minutes naming women they had bedded. Florence and Vicki were both fit to be tied. Kate had quietly made her way to the side of the stage. After two dozen each, Florence had heard enough. "Bust a cap on the bastard right now, Wayne," Florence screamed at the top of her lungs.

"Damn you, Florence!" R.E. screamed.

Wayne smiled for the first time since the siege began. Some people claim they know what would have happened next. The truth is no one could ever be completely sure. Wayne pointed his gun at R.E. and told Jake he was the next one to die. The shot rang out and Wayne dropped like a pickup truck from the sky.

"You ain't so bad," the voice shouted. "You ain't so bad."

"Jesus, Rocky has saved our ass, R.E.," Howard said.

"That ain't Rocky, you stupid fool! I'm going to kill Florence when we leave here."

Beverly looked up to see what the hell happened. Moose couldn't talk and Jake was pretty sure life as he knew it was over. He looked down and his pants were soaking wet. Morris sipped on his beer and made the best of a bad situation. Anne and Carol swore on their lives they were leaving Littleville. Freddie and Tyler along with their better halves were never leaving Lilleyville again.

"Damn, daddy would have just had a ball tonight," Jimmy said.

"I need a drink now," Scooter said.

No one moved and R.E. and Howard looked down at Wayne, deader than Kelsey's nuts. From the back of the room, the man came walking slowly towards the stage with the gun in his hand. He reached over and helped Beverly up. He handed her something and kept walking. Her eyes were big as saucers and she couldn't speak.

"Carol, how are you?"

"I'm fine now, thanks to you."

"Renee, it's good to see you again."

"Thank you," she whispered.

"Anne, you are beautiful as always."

"I miss you."

"Florence, thanks for everything."

"God bless you, son."

"Mrs. Vicki."

"We will always think of you," Vicki said.

"Jimmy, you look real good. I'm sorry I couldn't come see you in the hospital. I got myself in a tight spot."

"You look really good yourself. I knew you would have come if you were able too."

"R.E., I'm sorry I let you down."

"Son, don't you ever give it a second thought."

"Kate, are you still kicking ass and taking names?"

"Slick, I was getting ready to put a bullet right between the cock-suckers eyes. You beat me to the punch."

"How do I get the reward, Herb?"

"Just come with me to the station and fill out the paperwork. I'm sure everyone at the station will welcome you with open arms. You just saved a lot of people from being murdered."

"Okay, but first I'd like to call Don and make sure it is alright."

"Take as long as you like."

You guessed it good folks. Bobby Jack Cullen was on the front page again. The police came and interviewed everyone. Old Wayne was hauled off to be prepared for his final resting place.

Jake and his family sat down at the Cracker Barrel drinking coffee nonstop. They had a four hour drive across the state back to

Lilleyville. Church services started at eleven and Jake was desperate to sober up. Moose and Emily were beyond repair and slept the entire way home. They arrived in time to change clothes and rush on down to the church. Jake was shaky as he entered the pulpit to deliver his sermon. Emily sat on the front row with her first hangover, feeling like warmed over coffee.

Jake looked out at the people and began speaking. "Life is short and can be over in a second. Death can come when you least expect it and we need to be prepared. You can be having a nice evening with friends and family, when an escaped convict shows up and tries to kill you."

Jake carried on about dying the entire sermon. The congregation had never seen the emotion before and was quite impressed. Jake was rocking back and forth and nearly screaming.

"Brother Jake must have experienced a near death experience. He is running his mouth like a D.J. on the radio," Deacon Miller said.

"I was thinking the same thing, Deacon Miller. Jake is always quiet as a church mouse," Deacon Autry said.

"Maybe he has been watching those televangelist and been inspired. Emily looks really sick today," Deacon Brown whispered.

Jake finished his sermon and all the church members shook his hand and congratulated him on a fine sermon. Jake and Emily drove home and sat on the sofa looking at each other.

"Wayne was going to shoot me. I never would have believed Bobby Jack Cullen would save my life."

"I'll never go to another Martin reunion. I could just choke Scooter for getting us all drunk."

"I thought about what Scooter did, Emily. The truth is if we had been sober it may have ended far worse than it did."

"Jake, I have to get some rest. My head is just about to shoot off my shoulders."

The good news was, of course, that nobody died and life went on. In case you might be wondering, the collection plate broke all the previous records by a mile. Jake was now a firebrand preacher and word spread through out the state.

CHAPTER TEN

The sun came up and it was a beautiful day in Littleville. R.E. and Florence had just finished having breakfast. He was just getting ready to take his morning walk. The doorbell rang and R.E. went to the front door. He looked through the window and saw two well dressed men in suits. They didn't have a lot of visitors and he was quite pleased someone was coming over. He opened the door and greeted them.

"What are you boys up to on this fine morning?"

"Are you Rufus Edgar Cage?"

"The last time I checked."

"Is your wife Florence Maxine Cage?"

"She sure is, Mister. Are you two boy's salesmen?"

"Mr. Cage, we are not salesmen. Sir, is your wife home?"

"She is standing right behind me. You'll have to deal with Florence if you boys are selling something."

"You will probably wish we were selling something. Sir, we have a subpoena to serve Rufus Edgar Cage and Florence Maxine Cage."

"Damn, do we both have jury duty?"

"Sir, I am United States Marshal Bill Martin. This is Marshal Bret Jackson. We are here to serve both you and your wife. You are commanded to appear before a Federal Grand Jury in Jackson, Mississippi three weeks from today. Failure to appear will cause a warrant to be issued for your arrest."

R.E. couldn't speak as the Marshal handed he and Florence their papers. The two Marshals walked back to their car and drove off. They sat down and stared at the subpoena for five minutes.

"We have got our ass in a bind, Florence."

"Tell them you were making the bets and just used my name. I never wrote a check to the damn bookie. You have to take the heat, R.E."

"Why should I have to lie for you?"

"You dirty bastard, you have been a liar for over fifty years. I should have been out screwing around all those years like you and Howard."

"Damn Florence, they probably recorded every bet we made. I don't sound like you on the phone."

"Well you big coward, R.E. Cage. What kind of man takes his wife down for the count? I've given you fifty years of my life and this is how you reward me. I never gambled a day in my life before I met you."

"Get off my ass, Florence. You are the one that introduced me to the bookie at the damn casino."

"Oh, so it's me you want to take the fall. Well, let me tell you, Mister, it ain't going to happen. If I go down for the count, I'm taking your little shinny ass with me. My daddy told me not to marry you."

"I wish to hell you had listened to your daddy."

"Not nearly as much as I wish I had."

Across town, Renee was drinking coffee and smoking as she watched Good Morning America. She had her drapes open and saw a car drive up and two nice looking men get out. They walked to the door and knocked. She got up from her rocking chair and opened her door.

"Good morning, can I help you?"

"Are you Renee Louise Watkins?"

"Yes, is something wrong?"

"Miss Watkins, we are serving you with a subpoena commanding you to appear in Federal District Court in Jackson, Mississippi. Failure to appear will cause a warrant for your arrest to be issued." He handed Renee the papers and both the men left.

Now, if you think two United States Marshals showing up on your doorstep at daybreak won't ruin your day, you are sadly wrong. Especially, if they have a summons to appear before a federal grand jury in another state, five hundred miles away, no less! You better have a damn good heart to withstand the shock. Renee was trembling when R.E. called to tell his story.

"Me and Florence just got served by two federal marshals."

"I just got served R.E."

"The bookie got busted and cops are going to drag us into it."

"What the hell are we going to do, R.E.?"

"Florence is on the verge of a heart attack. I think I'm having one right now."

"My damn hands are shaking."

"Call Faith and have her talk to Don."

"I'll call Paul at the airport. His Father is a criminal defense attorney. He can tell us how much trouble we are in."

"Paul's Daddy ain't who we need, Renee. That old rascal is scared to death of the feds. We need someone with a set of balls."

They hung up and Renee called Paul at the airport. He came to the phone and she started talking like a convict cutting a deal to save her life.

"Paul, you have to help me. I just got served with a subpoena to testify before a federal grand jury in Mississippi. Please call your Father and see if he will help us."

"Good God, what the hell did you do, Renee?"

"I bet on football games across the state line."

"Listen, you are nothing but a girlfriend. Don't even think about dragging me into this mess. I'm not calling my Father at the law office. I gave you the money to bet on one damn game. It is not us, Renee."

"You dirty bastard!" she screamed.

"I won't be coming over tonight. Don't be calling me here or at home. They may be recording your calls."

"You won't be coming over tomorrow night either. You have seen the last piece of this ass you are ever going to see. Go get you a hamburger and eat it by yourself you cheap ass."

Well, surprise, surprise, in two hours every Martin knew the plight of Renee, R.E., and Florence. The worst case seemed inevitable as family members discussed the situation. Kate announced she had gone to the internet and betting across state lines was indeed a federal crime. Conviction carried a sentence of five years in a federal pen. She gave Chuck the bad news and called her sister.

Renee didn't get hello out of her mouth before Kate sprang into action. "Your only hope is if Don can save you, Renee. You are looking at a five year prison sentence. You will probably get eighteen months since it is your first conviction."

"I'm not going to prison."

"Then sell everything and get the hell out of the country. I'll look up on the internet and see which countries don't have an extradition treaty with the United States. Give me an hour and I'll call you back."

"I'm not going to flee the country. Save yourself the time."

"Suite yourself, Renee, it's your ass on the line. I don't have time for all this bullshit anyway."

"I didn't ask you to waste your precious time. I can take care of myself."

Kate hung up and looked at her husband. "The stupid asses are all going to wind up in the pen."

Across town, Vicki and Howard were digesting the bad news. Despite Vicki and Florence's occasional spats, they were always close. Well, that is an exaggeration, but they did like to share news. I'm not sure how being served with a subpoena to testify translates into being indicted. But, somehow Vicki and Howard had certainly come to that conclusion.

"You better call R.E. and see how he is taking being indicted. I'm sure the man is a wreck."

"I can't believe Florence and R.E. are going to do hard time. They are both going to be eighty three when they get out. They are probably going to be sent to one of those bad prisons."

He put on his glasses and dialed the number over at R.E. and Florence's house. Howard had already decided in his feeble mind to tell it the way he saw it. "You sure have crossed the line. You have all crossed the wrong line and will have to pay the price," Howard said, the second R.E. answered.

"If you were standing in front of me, I'd make you think Superman got a hold of your stupid ass," R.E. bellowed.

"R.E., I've been reading about the men in prison being sexually assaulted. You better design something to protect the back of your ass. You ain't much to look at, but those boys might not care."

"Howard, if you ever call me again I will come over there and shoot you right between the eyes."

"R.E., I know you are a little upset at the thought of going to prison. I'm going to forgive you. I'm going over to my church and pray for your survival, but I can't promise you anything. I'll do the best I can, but you are on the wrong side of the fence."

"I may be on the wrong side of the fence, but I damn sure know how to find your ass."

Jake read the stories and told Emily she better get up to Littleville and see Renee before she was sent away. Jimmy offered to store all their belongings in his warehouse while they served their time. Renee's drugged out son offered to stay in her house while she served her time. Tough times was staring them in the face, according to the Martin family.

Don and Faith had been out partying with his lawyer friends. She turned on Headline News and watched the story of the bookie network across the country being busted.

"Don, are you representing Frank Lombardy Junior?"

"No, he can't win."

"Why does the government care about people betting?"

"They are dumb and have nothing better to do with their time."

She walked over and checked her messages. Faith came back in with a look of worry on her beautiful face. "Renee, R.E., and Florence got served to appear before the Jackson grand jury. Their bookie got busted and the cops have his records."

"The cops just want the bookies. All they have to do is show up and tell the truth."

"Will you talk to them, baby?"

"Jesus Faith, just tell them to go down and testify truthfully. The government does not have enough jails to put all the people in who gamble."

They went to bed and the next morning Don left for a trial in Dallas. Faith called Renee when she woke up and had her coffee. Renee answered and Faith heard the fear in her voice.

"Renee, Don said you have nothing to worry about testifying. Just tell the truth and you will be on your way."

"Faith, I am scared to death something is going to go wrong. I've always been able to sense real trouble. I keep having dreams that all three of us are going to die. We are going to die a violent death. It will come out of the clear blue sky. I couldn't sleep last night."

"Renee, no one is going to die. How are you going to get to Jackson?"

"Old man Smokey told R.E. he would fly us down at no charge. I hope it is safe, Faith."

"That old man is still flying an airplane? He has to be at least eighty years old."

"Yeah, he still has his license. R.E. has flown with him for forty years. He flew for the company R.E. worked for. He has his own plane and it was sure nice of him to make the offer. I don't think I could take a nine hour drive."

"Tell Florence and R.E. to just relax. Nothing is going to happen to any of you."

"I'll tell them and thanks for the call."

Well, the big day came and they got aboard with Smokey. It was a nice, clear day and Smokey had assured them it would be a smooth flight. Renee had found them a hotel to stay at that night. R.E. had promised Smokey he would pay for the meals and hotel. Most of the family was at the airport in Littleville to see them off and wish them well. The plane was a light twin engine. Jimmy and Scooter hitched a ride down to Jackson with them. They had never flown and thought it would be fun.

"Smokey, I really appreciate you doing this for me," R.E. said.

"Hell, I owe you one R.E. You got me laid more times than I can remember."

"I bet he did. How do you feel, Smokey?" Florence asked.

"I woke up with a damn ear ache, Florence. I think I have a sinus infection."

"Are you going to be alright?" Jimmy asked.

"Jimmy, I've been cheating death for eighty years. I've flown these buzzards longer than you have been alive. Climb your ass in and let's be on our way to Jackson."

Florence was very nervous as she had never been in a small plane. The takeoff was smooth and the plane climbed up to ten thousand feet and leveled off. She was talking to Smokey as they made their way to Jackson.

"Smokey, I'm as nervous as a whore in church."

"Flying is the safest means of transportation, Florence. You got an old pro that has seen and done it all. I've landed in ice storms, flown on one engine, and never bought the farm. Do any of you know how to fly?"

"I've never had a lesson," Jimmy said.

"This is my first time to fly and I'm really enjoying myself. I should have been traveling this way all my life," Scooter said.

"How about you, Renee? Have you ever flown a plane?"

"Lord, I wouldn't have a clue. My former boyfriend flies, but I never went with him."

"I know R.E. and Florence can't fly. We will be there in two hours with any luck. Sit back and enjoy the trip."

Now Smokey had felt a sharp pain in his right ear climbing out, but he didn't want to worry anyone. They were flying along at ten thousand feet and were now twenty minutes out of Jackson. Smokey started to descend and the pain was terrible. He started to feel himself blacking out and decided it was past time to make everyone aware of his predicament. The old fellow turned and looked at everyone.

"Folks, I'm afraid I've got some terrible news. I'm just about to black out completely."

"Damn Smokey, you have to hold on man. I don't want to die this way," R.E. said.

"Mother of God, I knew it was going to end this way," Renee said.

"What the hell are you doing, Renee?" Florence asked.

"I'm taking a hand full of these pain pills. I hope I die before we crash."

"Give me some of those pills. I'm going to kill the damn bookie if I ever get to see him."

Scooter and Jimmy looked at each other and shook their heads. The plane started to rock back and forth. "Nothing in life comes free, Scooter. We never should have taken the free trip to Mississippi."

"Man, I'm not even ready to die. We have to figure a way out of this mess."

Smokey was screaming in pain and fell on the wheel. The plane headed straight down out of the sky. All of them were looking at the earth below closing in fast. R.E. was seated next to Smokey and let out a blood curdling scream. Scooter unbuckled his seat belt and grabbed Smokey off the wheel.

"Grab the wheel and pull back, R.E.," Jimmy yelled.

Rufus was white as a sheet as he took the wheel and pulled back. Now, for those of you who have never flown an airplane, you may never want to get in one after hearing this story. R.E. pulled back way too far and the damn plane shot straight up and rolled to the left. Florence was staring out the window and the plane was almost on its side. He kept pulling and the plane rolled upside down. You never heard such commotion in all your life. Smokey came to again and grabbed the wheel just as it spun out. The plane was going round and round in a tight spiral on the way to the earth below.

"Damn you, Rufus!" Florence screamed.

"Save us, Smokey," Scooter yelled.

"I'm trying; I have to get us out of this spin before we die."

"Fight Smokey, we don't want to die!" Jimmy screamed.

Florence's eyes were about to pop out of her head. Finally, after thirty seconds of shear hell Smokey saved the day. Florence couldn't open her mouth for the first time in her life. Things got better for a while when Smokey blacked out again. The plane had descended to four thousand feet and Smokey was able to recover when Jimmy slapped him on the back of the head. He called approach control and declared an emergency.

"Jackson approach control, Cessna 487 Charley. I'm eight miles from your airport and I'm blacking out. I have a severe inner ear infection and a plane load of people who can't fly. You have to help us, because there is no way I'm going to last."

"Roger Cessna 487, we copy and understand your situation. We will clear the active and give you a direct approach to the airport."

"Jimmy, get in the front seat with me. I see ten runways side by side. You have to tell me which one I'm lined up on."

R.E. climbed out of the front seat and Jimmy climbed in. Scooter's heart was in his throat as he watched the men change seats.

"If I can hold on, you have to ride the brakes when we land."

"Do they work like a car?"

"Yeah, except there's two of them son. I'm dying!" Smokey screamed as he grabbed his ears. The plane was starting to wobble as poor Smokey blacked out again.

"R.E., get off your ass and do something!" Florence screamed.

"What the hell do you want me to do, Florence? I can't fly the damn plane."

"Try and stay calm," Scooter said.

The air traffic controllers were all watching through their binoculars. "Cessna 487, I'm giving you to the tower on 102.6," Mike Martin, the air traffic controller said.

"Smokey, wake up, their talking to you," Jimmy shouted.

Smokey came to again for a split second and grabbed the mike. Jimmy told him the frequency to turn to.

"Jackson Tower this is Cessna 487. Help us, we are going to die."

"Cessna 487, hold on. You are a half mile from the runway," Mike said.

Smokey rolled his eyes and grabbed his ear. He managed to line up and descend to a thousand feet when he fell over the wheel.

"Pull him off the wheel, Scooter," Jimmy shouted.

Renee and Florence were now both passed out, which if you think about it was a good thing. Who the hell wants to watch themselves die? Smokey had dropped the landing gear and Jimmy was on his own.

"Wake up, Smokey. We are all going to die!" R.E. screamed.

Scooter was white as a ghost and prepared for the worst. "Please don't let it end this way," he said.

Mike Martin looked at his fellow controller, Dave Meyers. Cessna 487, if you can hear me slap the pilot. The next thirty seconds are critical," Mike shouted.

R. E. was slapping Smokey from the back seat while Jimmy held on for dear life. Smokey came back and saw the runway. They were coming in sideways and he managed to get the plane lined back up with the runway. He cut the power and the plane hit the runway twenty seconds later. Poor Smokey collapsed on the wheel again. Jimmy was riding the brakes as the Cessna nosed dived into the runway. They were going way too fast and the propellers were grinding into the runway. Sparks were flying everywhere and smoke started pouring into the cabin.

"Hang on, Jimmy!" Scooter yelled.

"Fight for your life, son!" Rufus screamed.

"I hope to God they make it," Mike said.

"The plane is leaving the runway!" Dave shouted.

Off the runway they went, as Jimmy headed straight for the Delta Airlines hangers. The Delta employees took off running like a bat out of hell. People in the terminal were screaming like they were in the damn plane. They finally hit a patch of soggy ground and came to a sudden stop. Fire trucks came racing with three ambulances and a half dozen police cars. Jimmy opened the door and pulled Smokey out of the plane. Scooter and R.E. were scrambling to get the women out. It took two cops to help them get Florence out. They finally made it out and were a good two hundred feet away when the plane exploded. Damn if they didn't have to start running again. The plane went up in flames as they quit running and looked back.

"Holy shit, we came that close to being killed, Scooter."

"I can't even talk right now, Jimmy."

"At least neither one of you is looking at going to prison. My little ass might have just bought some time," R.E. said.

Smokey and the women were loaded in the ambulances and the men got in one of the police cars. "Damn, that had to be a harrowing experience," the cop said.

"Officer, we thought the end was here," Scooter said.

"We are just plain snake bit," R.E. said.

"I'm sure my heart operation worked," Jimmy said.

They arrived at the hospital and Smokey was in bad shape. The girls came around and three hours later they were at the hotel. Smokey wasn't going anywhere, but his hospital room. Florence got her a bottle of Jack Daniels and Renee bought a bottle of Scotch. They proceeded to get very drunk that evening.

The next day Renee, R.E., and Florence walked in the Federal Court House and were shown where to go for the grand jury appearance. There had to be two hundred people standing in the hall waiting their turn to testify. Florence had downed half a pint of Jack Daniels to calm her nerves. A man was standing next to R.E. and they started to speak to each other.

"R.E. Cage, from Littleville."

"Robert Bush, Mr. Cage. I'm an attorney here with my client."

"Are all these people here to testify?"

"I'd say about half will need to testify. The rest of the people are attorneys and press people. We may be here three days."

"God, I sure hope not, mister. What is it like in there?"

"It is not a pretty sight and the U.S. Attorney is a real prick. He got one of my clients indicted for perjury. He is always trying to trick someone into lying and nailing them to the cross. It was really very distasteful, Mr. Cage. The poor man had to serve sixteen months."

"My God, I'm scared to death."

"It was horrible, Mr. Cage. The man was raped the third day he was in prison. His life was ruined as a result of the U.S. Attorney. Be very careful how you answer his questions."

"Damn, I knew it was going to be bad."

"Mr. Cage, don't let that man ruin your life."

R.E. was shaking when Bush walked off. He came over to where Florence and Renee were seated. His voice was quivering as he looked at the girls. "Remember girls, you can't speak to anyone about the case. We will just sit here and wait our turn. Nothing scares me after yesterday."

"Faith said whatever we do don't lie. If you're not sure of the question, just say you don't know," Renee said.

"I'm never betting on another ballgame the rest of my life. If I can just get back to Littleville in one piece, I'll be so happy," Rufus said.

Florence looked at her husband with a frown on her face. "If you're not scared, how come you are shaking?"

"You don't even want to know, Florence."

"I damn sure do want to know, R.E. Cage."

He looked at the two women. "If I screw up, I'll be raped."

"Rufus, you need to calm down," Renee said.

"He's a damn coward," Florence said.

A federal man stood and shouted down the hallway. "The grand jury session has begun. Your name will be called and you come to this door."

"We'll probably be one of the last to be called. Maybe Lum will cop a plea and we won't have to testify. The lawyer told me we might be here three days."

The man hadn't gotten the words out of his mouth when the guy yelled. "Rufus Cage, step forward."

R.E. was starting to shake and had real bad thoughts racing through his mind. He walked over to the man standing outside the grand jury room. "I'm R.E. Cage, mister."

"Follow me, Mr. Cage."

R.E. walked in and did a double take. It looked like there were thirty people on the grand jury. The Judge was behind the bench and the U.S. Attorney sat behind a table. A court reporter sat waiting to work. The man escorted R.E. to the witness chair and told him to raise his right hand.

"Do you swear, under oath, to tell the truth and nothing but the truth so help you God?"

"Yes sir."

"You may be seated, Mr. Cage."

The U.S. Attorney, Stafford Bone, never got out of his seat. He looked at R.E. and took a drink of water. The tone of his voice was harsh. "State your name for the court."

"R.E. Cage."

"State your full name, Mr. Cage."

"Oh, I'm sorry. People have always called me R.E. for years. My full name is Rufus Edgar Cage."

"Do you bet on football games, Rufus?"

"Yes, I have made bets on ball games."

"Where do you live, Rufus?"

"512 Fox Circle, in Littleville."

"Mr. Cage, you don't live in Mississippi. Are you aware it is a felony to place a wager across state lines?"

"Damn, I'm going to be indicted," R.E. thought. "No sir. I thought it was okay to bet on games. I didn't know anything about a law."

"Do you know a man named Frank Lombardy Junior?"

R.E. thought for a moment before he answered. "I don't think I know nobody by that name."

"You don't know Frank Lombardy Junior?"

"Does he live in Littleville?"

The U.S. Attorney's voice hardened. "Are you aware the crime of perjury carries a five year jail term? You are under oath, Mr. Cage."

"What does the man do for a living?"

"You know very well what Mr. Lombardy does for a living."

Suddenly, it hit him and he could barely speak. "I know a bookie named Lum Badino. He is the bookie I placed my bets with."

The grand Jurors, Judge, and U.S. Attorney started laughing. R.E. thought they were laughing because he had lied and was going to be indicted. All he could think of was being raped in a prison.

"The man's name is Frank Lombardy Junior, Mr Cage."

"I'm sorry. I knew him as Lum Badino. I swear I didn't lie."

"Have you declared your winnings to the I.R.S.?"

"I ain't got any winnings to declare, Mister. My wife and I both lost our ass betting with the fellow."

"What is the largest bet you placed with Mr. Lombardy?"

"I can't rightly say for sure. I believe it was two hundred dollars."

"I'm going to remind you again that you have sworn to tell the truth. The punishment for committing perjury is five years on each count."

"Hell, I'm pretty damn sure it was two hundred, Mister. I'm pretty shook up with the thought of going to prison."

"Yes, the thought of spending time in prison is a sobering thought. I'm finished with you for now. You are excused Mr. Cage. You will receive a summons to testify in the event the grand jury chooses to indict."

R.E. almost passed out and he blurted out. "Indict me? How many counts am I looking at here?"

The U.S. Attorney kept a straight face. "I can't comment on any possible indictment that may come out of this grand jury. Rest assured you will be notified by a United States Marshall."

"When will I know, Mister?"

"It will be sooner than you think, Mr. Cage. It could come very soon and it would be wise for you to prepare yourself to testify."

R.E. rose and almost fell coming down the steps. He was so shook up he didn't realize he had ripped a huge hole in his pants. Stafford saw the big rip and addressed him as he made his way to the door.

"Mr. Cage, you may want to get something over your butt. It could be quite embarrassing."

R.E. turned and looked at Stafford with a frown on his face. "I've already been warned by an attorney and my brother in law."

When he got to the door and walked outside, he almost fainted. His whole life raced before him as he sat down and looked at Renee and Florence.

"How did it go, R. E.?" Florence asked.

"I think I'm going to be indicted on three separate counts. Each count means you get five years. Faith didn't know what the hell she was talking about. We are all in deep shit. Howard was right, they rape you in prison. That cocky ass attorney just told me to get something on my ass."

"What did you do to get indicted?" Renee asked.

"They think I committed perjury three different times. The damn bookie is Frank Lombardy Junior. I told them his name was Lum Badino. The man told me I committed a felony betting across state lines. He thinks I lied about the biggest bet I ever made. I told him two hundred, but he reminded me again I was committing perjury. I'm going to be charged with three separate felonies. If I have to get down on my knees and beg, I'm getting Don to represent me."

"Rufus, I know this is a terrible time to tell you, but they already know. You bet three hundred two times on the Cowboys. You did bet two hundred for yourself, but you bet a hundred for Scooter one time and a hundred for Jimmy another time. If they get you for fifteen years, you will be a dead mother before you get out."

"Scooter called to tell us Smokey will be okay, but his eardrums burst. The poor man has an eighty percent hearing loss in one ear and sixty in the other. He is in really bad shape," Renee said.

"I wish I had a total hearing loss. Damn, I'm looking at prison staring me in the face."

Now, for those of you fortunate enough to have never been before a grand jury, it is a serious place. Nobody smiles and it is real formal and full of tension. Inside the grand jury room, everyone was howling including the Judge.

"Florence Cage," the man yelled.

"R.E., I just want you to know no matter how this goes down, I always liked you a lot. You sure as hell ain't been the best husband, but you were better than most."

"Thanks a lot, Florence. I might get lucky and live to be ninety. I never thought I'd spent my golden years in prison."

The old girl walked down to the entrance to the grand jury room with a heavy heart. She was not going to make the same mistake her husband made. The Marshal showed her in and took her to the witness stand. Florence was sworn in and the U.S. Attorney started asking her questions. He walked over next to the witness stand.

"Mrs. Cage, I'm Stafford Bone. How are you today?"

"I'm about to have a fit. I almost died in a plane crash yesterday and I just found out my husband is being indicted. The stupid bastard is looking at fifteen years. I never worked a day in my life and I don't know how I'm going to survive."

"I'm sorry to hear that, Mrs. Cage. Do you know a man named Frank Lombardy Junior?"

"You bet your ass I know the son-of-a-bitch. He rolled over big time on all of us, Mr. Bone."

"He did?"

"That no good bastard gave our names to the cops to save his worthless ass. The bastard beat me out of three hundred dollars and had the gall to roll over on me. He lied about his name and got my husband indicted."

"Is your husband a bookie?"

"Hell no, R.E. can barely add numbers. That damn Lombardy hung around the casino looking for easy prey. It just irks my ass raw."

The Judge made a gesture to Bone and looked at Florence. "Let's take a break," the Judge said. "Mrs. Cage, don't you worry about him rolling over on you. You are dismissed and may go home now."

Florence looked around at the Judge. "My sister told me you were a nice man and her husband has practiced before you. She told me to just come in here and tell the truth."

The Judge was a kind man and thought it appropriate to placate Florence. He smiled at her and spoke in a kind voice. "Wonderful. I have no doubt you did just that, Mrs. Cage. By the way, who is your sisters' husband?"

"Don Hudson."

"You can't be serious."

"You bet your sweet ass I'm serious. That boy is so damn good looking it's a sin and he is smoother than melted butter."

"He certainly is that and more."

"Did all the women jurors come to court half naked? Don represented my son-in-law in court in Littleville. Me and my family went to watch the trial and show our support for the boy. The women all came to court the second day looking like under dressed hookers. Judge, there ain't no damn telling how many orgasms those women had sitting in that jury box. They were cooing like a bird in heat."

"I think we need to discuss that at another time. You have a safe trip back to Littleville. Good day, Mrs. Cage."

"Good day to you too, Judge. If you ever get up to Littleville give me a call. I'll cook you some supper."

Florence gathered her purse and left the courtroom. The Judge went in his chambers and started laughing. "Jesus, that woman is a real character," he told his clerk.

"She definitely tells it the way she sees it," Betty said.

"Tell the U.S. Attorney to step in here for a moment, Betty."

Betty went out in the courtroom and found Bone visiting with a marshal. "The Judge wants a minute with you."

Bone came in the Judge's chamber. "You wanted to see me, Your Honor?"

"Can you believe that woman? Could Hudson really be married to her sister?"

"I seriously doubt it, Judge. Hudson's wife came to court in the Smith trial. The woman is drop dead gorgeous and at least thirty years younger. I think old Florence was trying to impress, Your Honor."

"I think she is telling us the truth. Will you ever forget those women coming to serve? I've been on the bench for thirty years and I have never seen anything like it. I knew he was going to beat your ass like a drum."

"We didn't have a snow ball's chance in hell. Did you think he was ever going to stop flipping jurors? He wouldn't stop until he seated all twelve and the alternates. He was grilling all the men like they were on trial. I felt sorry for the man who wanted to serve. He just would not stop until he broke the man."

"Lombardy wants to cop a plea. Are you willing to accept two years and a three hundred thousand dollar fine?"

"Sure, he is just a bookmaker."

"Okay, send word to everyone they can go home."

Outside in the hallway Florence was happy as hell. "They gave me a pass," Florence boasted.

"Why did I have to walk in the trap?"

"You were too damn nervous and freaked out."

"I guess I'm next," Renee said.

"How the hell are we going to get home?" Florence asked.

"Jimmy rented a big suburban and will drive us home. He wants to stop in Tunica and let us gamble."

"Jimmy doesn't gamble," Renee said.

"Yeah, but he screws. He has a twosome he has had for years in Memphis. They will drive over and we won't see Jimmy. He will have them bring a set for Scooter as well."

They looked up as the Marshall walked by. "Everyone is dismissed. Your subpoenas are no longer valid," the Marshal shouted as he walked up and down the hallway.

"I'm free," Renee said.

"Ain't but one fool going to jail out of this group," R.E. moaned. "I have to be the unluckiest bastard on the planet."

"I'll put in a good word for you with the Judge. He has a crush on me that a blind man could see. I'll tell him you ain't very bright and you got all shook up. I'll tell him you made a fool of yourself."

"Florence, you can tell the son-of-a-bitch I'm the dumbest bastard on the planet. I just don't want to go to jail."

The next morning, they picked up Smokey and headed back to Littleville. Old Smokey felt terrible about putting them through such an ordeal.

"Rufus, I'm really sorry about putting all of you in a pinch. I don't know how we are all not dead."

"I wouldn't have even worried about it if I knew then what I know now. Smokey, I've found myself looking at a long stay in a federal prison. I'm glad everyone made it and I'm sorry about your airplane."

"Rufus, what did they catch you doing old friend?"

"I bet on some damn football games and didn't know the name of my bookie. I just got tricked by this slick federal man and I'm going down for the count. Florence was smart and sailed right through without a scratch."

"I'm so sorry to hear you are going to jail, Rufus."

They made a quick stop in Tunica and sure enough Jimmy and Scooter disappeared for the night. R.E. explained to the women how Jimmy and Scooter had always preferred two women at a time. Renee and Florence each won five hundred, but R.E. lost his ass. The next morning they made their way back home. The big news was Mayor Cox had been indicted on sixty separate counts by a federal grand jury. Small towns being what they are, everyone was talking about Huey. C. Jacob was unable to take advantage of the situation. He had carried on a little too much himself and got caught screwing the Mayor's secretary. Someone had put the pictures in every mail box in town. People claimed to be outraged, but for some strange reason they kept the pictures. One went up on a billboard on the interstate before it got taken down. Huey was on four billboards being hauled off in handcuffs. Some committee, called Clean up the Scum, filed the financial disclosure forms with the state. Some fellow named John Hogan cruised to victory. Hogan worked as a teller at Littleville Bank and Trust. He didn't earn a whole lot of money and people wondered where all the money came from to oust Huey. People also wondered aloud how the federal boys suddenly had an open and shut case. One man who had no doubt was Ben Rollins. Ben had flown over to the capital to have dinner with the Governor at the mansion. They sat together having dinner and afterwards Governor Jones wife excused herself. The men went in the study and the Governor closed the door.

"Ben, you did a hell of a job for me on that damn Bobby Jack Cullen crap. Huey is looking at four to six years. C. Jacob is looking at over half his money being taken by his soon to be ex wife. This Hogan boy you picked seems to have something between his ears."

"Governor, we have everything under control. The boy is honest as the day is long and will clean up Huey's mess."

"Damn, I was shocked to see how much money Hogan spent."

"The boy outspent C. Jacob and Huey ten to one. Someone with a lot of money got really pissed off and sent some big money in. A lot of power was brought to bear. Huey and C. Jacob are both destroyed."

"You think Hudson dropped the dime on both of them, Ben?"

"No, I think Hudson gave someone the information and they destroyed them."

"I saw where Cullen killed the escaped convict and saved some lives. Where is he now?"

"He moved to New York City of all places. His wife divorced him."

"That certainly should come as no surprise. I'm amazed the woman stayed with him as long as she did."

"You never know Governor. Someday she may look back and regret it."

"I suppose you may be right. I'll tell you something off the record, Ben. If I ever get indicted I'm flying to West Palm and hiring Hudson."

"I'll tell you on the record Governor. I'd hire him so fast it would make your head spin."

CHAPTER ELEVEN

Howard and Vicki were planning their fifty fifth wedding anniversary. It was considered by most folks in Littleville to be nothing short of a minor miracle the marriage has lasted this long. Invitations had been sent to everyone they knew. They were hoping for a big turnout. They had let it be known that a money tree would be set up for everyone's gift. The bank president at The Littleville Trust was surprised when he received an invitation. Tim Marksman had run the bank for over twenty years and knew almost everyone in the community. He sat down with his senior vice president over a cup of coffee.

"How long has it been since Howard Minter has banked with us?"

"It has been at least fifteen years," Dusty Rhodes said.

"I guess old Howard and Vicki are going for a score. They want everyone to bring money in an envelope with their name on the outside. It takes some kind of nerve to pull a stunt like this."

"If Mr. Jackson hears about this, he is going to have a stroke. I can't believe Howard would have the nerve to send an invitation to the bank. He caught his wife and Howard naked in bed at his house."

"I remember that very well. I had just gone to work for the bank a week before it happened. Everybody in town was talking about them for weeks. The story I heard was Howard jumped the rail from the balcony with Jay shooting at him. He ran for a while and came up on a bunch of gay guys having sex in the park."

"I think that is a true story. R.E. Cage told one of the bank's directors Howard was soaking wet and looked like he had seen a ghost. He ran over a mile to get to Mr. Cage and his wife's house."

Jay Jackson was the founder and Chairman of the Board of Directors of the bank. The divorce had cost him a ton of money and he hated old Howard with a passion. The men looked up and in walked Jay with an ugly look on his face. He sat down and threw the invitation on the conference table.

"That son-of-a-bitch, Howard Minter, had the nerve to send me an invitation to his wedding anniversary. I'd like to shoot that bastard and leave him for the buzzards to pick on."

"I think he and Vicki sent one to everybody in Littleville. The Martin family has no shame," Tim said.

"Howard and R.E. got shot at over at the golf course several years ago. One of my customers saw them running for their lives," Dusty said.

"I should have killed the bastard when I caught him with Martha. I carried my gun with me for months, but the sleazy bastard was staying out of sight. I can't believe Vicki stayed with his sorry ass."

The story was being repeated all over the county by a dozen men. It seems before his conversion to becoming a man of God, Howard tried his best to service every married woman in Littleville. He was crossing the wrong fence for years. He was definitely ignoring the Posted-Keep Out signs. I guess the man thought no trespassing meant come on in. Just as remarkable were the invitations to many other people. Amber Wallace and her sister, Candy Johnson, were having their garage sale. Their mother was sitting in her rocker on the front porch chewing tobacco and drinking a Bloody Mary. She had a few items to dispose of and had put her girls in charge of the merchandise.

"Amber, do you know Howard and Vicki Minter?" Candy asked.

"I met Mrs. Minter one time at the pharmacy. It is strange you asked that question. I got an invitation to attend their wedding anniversary. They want you to bring money and put it on a tree," Amber said.

"I got the same invitation. I can't recall ever meeting either of them. All my neighbors got an invitation."

"There was no stamp on the envelope. I guess they drove all over town and put the envelopes in the mailboxes."

It seems everyone in the town was getting an invite to the big event. Emily and Jake had driven over for the event. Renee and Emily left Jake to watch the soaps and headed out for their favorite pastime. In Littleville, there were always twenty garage sales a day. Renee and Emily tried their best to make all of them. They parked the car and strolled across the lawn.

"Good morning," Amber said.

"Good morning," Renee said.

The girls started to look around and Emily found an old jewelry box. It was a big box and Emily thought it would be perfect for her bathroom. It was marked at two dollars. She picked it up and took it over to the table where the girls stood. Renee couldn't find anything and walked over with Emily.

"I'll buy this jewelry box."

Amber took the two dollars and handed Emily the box. The girls walked back to the car and Emily opened the box. She lifted the bottom up and could not believe her eyes.

"Renee, there must be a thousand dollars in the bottom of this box. Hundred dollar bills are stacked on top of one another."

"Hurry up and let's get out of here before they realize we have the money."

"That is not the Christian thing to do, Renee. I have to give it back."

"Don't be a fool, Emily. You bought the box and everything in it. Put it in the back seat and drive away."

"Well, I like money just as much as the next person, but I have to give it back."

"Give me the damn box and drive away. I'll buy it from you for four dollars and you can say you doubled your money, Emily."

"You must think I'm a complete fool. I didn't drive in from Mars. Why would I give you the money?"

"I'm broke, Emily. Show some of your Christian compassion and lend me a helping hand."

"You don't need to start in on me, Sissy. All you do is poor mouth and run to the casino and gamble. You are always carrying on about how broke you are. Where is the money coming from to gamble?"

"Is anything wrong over there?" Amber asked.

"No," Renee said. "Emily, back your stupid ass out of this driveway before I kill you."

They drove off with the money and the promise to put most of it on the money tree. Jake was waiting when the girls drove up. "I'm starving; we need to go get some supper."

"Let us have a little while to freshen up," Emily said.

"Hurry up; I've been sitting here all day watching television."

The next afternoon, everyone headed over to Howard and Vicki's house for the big event. Everyone in the family was there, along with several dozen people from the church. Howard and Vicki were busy shaking everyone's hands. Scooter stood guard on the money tree and put a clothes pin on every envelope handed to him. The Martin family was loaded with outlaws and drug users. Howard and Vicki were taking no chance of being robbed.

Danny Minter was Howard and Vicki's oldest son. Danny was now the minister of the church they attended and a reformed sinner himself. Danny still held the record for fights in Littleville. He was one bad ass dude growing up and had caused Howard and Vicki a lot of grief. He dealt drugs and pain as a young fellow. Danny was expelled four times in one year alone. He had gone to three different high schools before finally giving up. The last straw came when he broke the principal's jaw at lunch one day.

Danny walked right up to a group of visitors and started talking. "Praise the Lord for you good people. I'm a reformed sinner and praise the Lord for saving me. I was the worst man in the county. I beat people up every day, drank whiskey, and smoked dope. Yes, I even sold drugs and spent the money on prostitutes all over the state."

"Jesus, spare us the sermon, Danny. I had to commit to going into rehab to stay out of jail," Carol said.

"You better get off that junk. You're going to lose all your teeth and it won't look worth a dang. How much money did you give Howard and Vicki?" Jimmy asked.

"I didn't give them a dime. There is nothing wrong with my teeth."

"How much money did you give them?" R.E. asked.

"Twenty-five dollars," Florence said.

Renee had met Johnny Kirk and brought him with her to the party. Johnny was new to town and Renee had instantly taken to him. Paul was long gone and a bad memory. Johnny was the polar opposite of Paul. He was a nice looking fellow and not a pound over weight. Paul never bought her anything and was tight as a tick. Johnny, on the other hand, always had money and spent it on her. She thought it a little strange he always paid in cash and had a wad of bills on him.

The party went as well as you could expect for Howard and Vicki. They were able to collect fifteen hundred and keep it.

No one tried to steal the money and no one got drunk. Emily and Renee went back on their promise and kept the money. Renee finally shamed her into giving her a hundred. Emily pocketed the rest and swore it was for the church. Howard and Vicki sat opening all the envelopes and came to the one from Don and Faith.

"I bet Faith and Don gave us at least a hundred," Vicki said.

"I think you are right. It should be the biggest gift by far."

"I wonder why the envelope is so big. I sure didn't think anyone would need one this big."

She opened the package and couldn't believe her eyes. There were four first class tickets on American Airlines to New York. The note from Faith explained the hotel was paid for and a limousine would take them everywhere for the weekend. Their meals would be paid for and Howard and Vicki would each have a thousand dollars to spend on shopping and seeing the Broadway shows. They could invite anyone they wanted with the extra tickets. The rooms and meals would be paid for as well. Lastly, a limousine would pick them up at their home in Littleville and take them to the international airport.

"I just love that man. I'd still to this day would like to choke my damn fool self thinking Don was a murderer. I don't know what the hell was wrong with my head. I've never been so embarrassed in my life. If I live to be a hundred, I'm never going to get over it."

"He is the finest man I have ever met. Faith won the Powerball Jackpot when she married that boy."

"I guess we should invite R.E. and Florence."

"I'm not sure if Florence will get back on an airplane after Smokey nearly cost them their lives."

"I'll invite them over for supper tomorrow night. Two weeks from now, we will be in New York City. I never thought we would ever get to see a big city. I'm going to call Frog and see if he wants to meet us."

"I'd like to see old Frog myself."

Now Paul was the jealous kind. He had not taken kindly to Renee showing him the door. He started trying to follow Johnny Kirk to see what was happening. His best friend was Ray Crouch. Ray was a private detective in Littleville, and he was on the case as well. Paul was sitting at home when the phone rang.

"Paul, they just pulled in Renee's driveway. They are going in her house now," Ray said.

"Stay with them and tell me what their doing."

"Alright, but prepare yourself for the worst."

"She better not be sleeping with that guy."

Ray had seen this movie before and he dreaded having to call Paul with the description of the show. Sure as the sun rises in the morning, it wasn't thirty minutes later when the lights went off in the bedroom. He turned on his night lens and looked through the thin drapes. Ray started shooting pictures and stopped after ten. He picked up his cell phone and hit the speed dial to Paul.

"Paul, can I be blunt with you?"

"Just tell me what she is up too."

"She is up to being on top of the man, naked in her bed."

"The dirty rotten whore never got on top of me. I want to know how long he stays."

"I'll call you when he leaves, good buddy."

"Did she give him a blow job?"

"It lasted a good twenty minutes."

"I can't believe it, Ray."

"No one ever can, my friend."

"All the bitch ever wanted from me was money. I had to beg to have sex with her for four years."

"Are you sure you want these pictures? They are going to give you a bad case of heartburn."

"I want the damn pictures, Ray. I'm starting to understand the two men shooting at each other."

Ray settled in for a long wait. He had been a cop in Littleville and knew everyone on the police force. At three in the morning, a squad car eased in behind him. Charley Holcomb recognized Ray and walked up to his car and got in.

"Who's screwing who tonight, Ray?"

"Renee is entertaining Johnny Kirk."

"You have the best gig in town. I wish I could get paid to watch people have sex all the time. I can't believe that tight wad, Paul, is paying you to make him sick at the stomach."

"You don't miss your water till the well runs dry. Paul is going to have a very bad day tomorrow. The chances of Johnny leaving tonight are slim and none. Would you mind going down to Wendy's and picking me up the number six? I'll buy you anything you want."

"I'll be back in fifteen minutes."

The next morning at six, Ray placed the call to his buddy with the bad news. Paul was not a happy camper as he left for work. On the other hand, Renee and Johnny were asleep in blissful peace. Ray went on home to get some sleep himself.

Vicki called Florence and invited her and R.E. to supper. She told her about the trip to New York and Florence was beside herself. She called everyone in the family and Vicki did the same. Faith listened as Vicki went on and on thanking them for the wonderful present. She told Don of the call when he came in that night.

"I would love to have a video with sound of their trip. The big apple will never be the same after they leave."

"Renee has fallen in love. I spoke to her for an hour today. She is on cloud nine over this fellow, Johnny Kirk."

"Do you know the man?"

"He just moved to town recently. No one in the family knows him."

"How did they meet?"

"They met at the bank on Main Street. They were both making a deposit and struck up a conversation."

"That's a strange place to meet someone and start dating."

Jimmy and Scooter were on their way to Littleville Bank and Trust to make a deposit. When they arrived, the parking lot was swarming with police. They looked at each other as they got out of Scooters' pickup.

"This doesn't look right, Jimmy."

"Stay here by the truck. I see Boyd walking over here now."

"Scooter, the bank has been robbed. We're looking for a lone gunman," Detective Boyd Bounds said.

"No shit! How long ago did he rob the bank?" Jimmy asked.

"Ten minutes ago and he was a pro. He walked in the bank president's office and made him empty all the cash drawers and open the safe. The power to the alarms and cameras was cut seconds before he walked in."

"Was anyone hurt?" Scooter asked.

"Nope, he walked them all in the vault and closed the door. The guy was dressed like an old man and the description is probably worthless. The bastard wore gloves so we don't expect to find fingerprints. He got over two hundred thousand in bills."

"Damn, for once we didn't get caught in the middle of trouble. The way my luck has been running, he would have shot me and Scooter."

"The bank employees are all shook up. Tim and Dusty both look like they saw a ghost. I have to get back to work boys. Y'all be careful. The bastard may still be in the area."

"Come on, Jimmy, and let's get out of here. We almost lost our damn money, sure as hell."

"Hold on a minute. I see Violet over there."

"I don't know the girl, Jimmy. Is she one of your girls?"

"Yeah, and she is hot as hell. She works in the store next to the bank. I need to walk over and say hello."

"Jimmy, if you're not back in ten minutes, I'll know you scored and I'm leaving."

"Fair enough, Scooter."

Scooter sat in his truck and watched Jimmy go to work. He gave Jimmy the benefit of a doubt and waited fifteen minutes before he drove off. He wasn't the least bit surprised, as he had seen this movie before many times.

R.E. and Florence arrived at Howard and Vicki's home for supper that evening. The big bank robbery was the talk of Littleville, but these four were only interested in New York City. Both the gals had spent the day picking out clothes for the trip. They sat in the living room and visited.

"Me and Howard called Frog and he is coming over to the hotel Saturday. He has us some tickets to see a show," R.E. said.

"I've never seen one of them Broadway shows. Dang, this is going to be something else," Florence said.

"I'm cooking that boy a meal for the ages when he and Faith come back."

"I don't like to cook worth a damn, but I'll sure as hell help you, Vicki. That boy just flat out hung the moon."

"The man from the limousine company called me. He said someone will be here next Friday morning at eight o'clock to take us over to the airport. R.E., are you coming over here?" Howard asked.

"We'll be at your house by seven thirty, Howard. I always wanted to see New York. Beverly told me Bobby Jack lives there now. I think he went to work for his grandfather doing something."

"That boy ought to put a statue of Don in his front yard. I didn't think nobody could save his ass. Howard, you and R.E. have to wear your suits. I called Faith and she said you need to have a suit to get in the restaurants and shows," Florence said.

"What kind of restaurants and theaters make you wear a suit?" Howard asked.

"We are going to fancy places. I saw them on television, Howard. Those city slickers get all dressed up. Just put on your Sunday go to meeting clothes and you'll be fine," R.E. said.

"Faith told me they are having their own driver take us around. She said he is a fine fellow and don't have no airs about him. She said the boy will show us a fine time and everything was taken care of. He will be waiting for us at the airport in New York," Vicki said.

"I'm going to get him to take us to see the lady out in the water. I've been watching her for years," Howard said.

"I'm going to shop up a storm," Florence said.

"Florence, don't you go crazy and run up the credit cards."

"You get off my ass, Rufus Cage. You and Jake need to learn you can't take it with you."

"Maybe we will run into Bobby Jack," Howard said.

"Howard, seven million people live in New York City. I don't think we are going to see the boy," R.E. said.

"I'm so excited I can't sit down," Vicki said.

They visited for hours before R.E. and Florence made their way back home. They were surprised to see Beverly sitting in the driveway. She opened the door and Florence could see she was very upset.

"Beverly, what on earth are you doing here in the middle of the night?" Florence asked.

"It is not the middle of the night, Mother. Since when did nine o'clock become the middle of the night?"

"Don't get cute with me young lady. We go to bed at nine thirty every night. You would be wise to starting going to bed earlier yourself. You better listen to me."

"What is troubling you?" R.E. asked.

"Daddy, I have made a colossal mistake divorcing Bobby Jack. I can't believe I let him go out the door."

"Honey, I always liked the boy. You said he was drinking and running around on you. Why have you had a change of heart?"

"Thirty one billion dollars," she wailed.

"Beverly, have you lost your damn mind. Have you been hanging around popping those pills with Carol?" Florence asked.

"Hell no, I haven't, but I'm about ready to! Bobby Jack went to work for his grandfather. The old man has fallen in love with him and he's going to leave him everything."

"Hell, you ought to feel happy for the boy. I wish someone had left me a few dollars. It will help him pay the child support."

"Daddy, are you deft? His grandfather is the third richest man in America. He is worth thirty one billion dollars. Who the hell do you think paid Don to represent him? Don gets millions to represent a client. Bobby Jack is picking up the kids this weekend in the old man's private jet. There going to New York while I sit at home all weekend alone."

"My Lord in heaven! What are we going to do now? This could only happen to us," Florence said.

"You better hope to hell Bobby Jack has not met someone. The damn boy has one bad night and you run him off. Hell, he saved all our lives at the reunion. The poor boy was heartbroken when he came to give you the final divorce papers that night. Florence, you better have a good talk with your daughter. Damn, I can't believe you have blown it."

Florence gave Beverly a hard look. "Honey, you need to go buy yourself some sexy clothes like those girls at Bobby Jack's trial wore. You have to get your ass to New York and strap some loving on that boy he won't soon forget. When those women in New York find out, it will be too late for your ass."

"I didn't go to the trial. What were they wearing, Mother?"

"They had a smile and little else, my dear. Find something that covers about twenty percent of your body. Are you getting the picture, Beverly?"

"The stores in Littleville don't sell sexy clothes."

"You better haul your ass to somewhere that does."

Johnny and Renee were having dinner at Center Cut on Watkins Avenue. The police cars were everywhere looking for the bank robber. Johnny looked out the window and back at Renee.

"I heard someone robbed the bank today. Did you hear if they caught anyone?"

"Scooter and Jimmy just missed walking right into the middle of the robbery. Scooter said the cop told him the guy was dressed like an old man. The cop told them the guy was a real professional. Did you hear about the woman leaving the club at Twelve Trees?"

"What happened out at Twelve Trees?"

"Joyce Dillard left the club drunk. She drove into Mae and Jack Jones bedroom at one in the morning."

"Was anyone hurt or killed?"

"Everyone survived without a scratch. Joyce has three DUI arrests in a year."

"How is she staying out of jail?"

"She is banging Judge Porter and Chief Thomas is covering it up."

"Well, I suppose that's one way to take care of it."

"My daughter, Carol, called me just before you came over. She and Morris got into a spat and she drove off in the convertible with the top down."

"Where was Morris, Renee?"

"He was standing in the back of the car. He flew out the back and hit the concrete on his head. The bitch kept right on going and left him. The cops have a warrant out for her arrest."

"I think your old boyfriend is having us followed. I've seen him three different times in front of my place. The prick's name is Ray Crouch. If he keeps it up, I'm going to nail him along with fat Paul."

"I don't know what I ever saw in that piece of shit," Renee said.

It is not the easiest thing trying to service multiple women. Jimmy had his hands full trying to keep everyone happy. One of the girls in particular was a jealous type, prone to throwing things. Her name was Mona and she lived on the second floor of an apartment complex. Mona had seen Jimmy two days before with a woman she didn't know. Mona sure as hell knew Jimmy wasn't showing real estate. The hussy was almost sitting in his lap when they passed the Sonic. Mona had left several messages and Jimmy finally returned her calls.

"Hi baby, its Jimmy."

"I saw you two days ago with a blond sitting in your lap. Don't start lying, because I saw you with my own eyes," Mona said.

"Hell, I was giving that woman a ride home. I sold her a bunch of stuff from the warehouse. Her car broke down and we pilled everything in the car."

"I bet you were giving her ass a ride. Are you coming over tonight, Jimmy?"

"I can't make it tonight, doll. Shirley has me on a short leach and I have to stay home."

"What about tomorrow night, Jimmy. I'm horny and I need some good old fashion love making for a couple of hours."

"Hey, I'll be there at eight o'clock sharp. I have to go now and pick up Shirley. I'm taking her to dinner."

"I'll see you tomorrow night, Jimmy."

"I'll be there with bells on."

Mona hung up and looked at her watch. She went down and got in her car. Ten minutes later, she sat outside the Shady Inn Motel. Like a church bell ringing on Sunday morning, Jimmy came in with Violet Blue. They checked in the motel and she watched them go in a room. Mona drove back home steaming at the thought of Jimmy lying to her. The next evening at eight o'clock sharp, Jimmy was ringing the doorbell.

"Come on in, lover boy, and give me some of your action."

"Damn, you are the hottest piece of ass in Littleville County. I should leave my girlfriend and have you moved in."

"Which girlfriend are you talking about, Jimmy?"

"I'm talking about Shirley."

Mona decided to put the conversation on hold and get some sexual gratification. Jimmy was busy taking care of business and thinking life was good. Wild Buck was smiling up from his seat in hell as Jimmy carried on. After a good two hour romp, it was time to call it a night and get on home. He got dressed and started for the front door.

"Baby, you were great, but I have to be going. We can hook up again next Monday at the same time, if that works for you."

"What are we going to do about Violet Blue? I thought Monday and Thursdays were her nights."

Jimmy started to feel real uneasy and opened the door. When you have run women as long as Jimmy, you get a "sixth" sense when trouble is brewing. He turned and Mona stood with nothing on but a smile and steel skillet in her hand.

"You lying Martin bastard," she screamed.

"Mona, don't throw the skillet!"

Jimmy ducked as the skillet came flying six inches over his head. He took off running down the stairs looking over his shoulder. The skillet hit the windshield of the police car and the glass shattered. The police officer hit his brakes and jumped from the car with his pistol drawn. He looked up and saw Mona screaming at Jimmy. Jimmy was moving like an Olympic sprinter trying to get away from the scene.

"Don't you move, you crazy bitch," Officer Cowden shouted.

Mona was now on the porch shaking her fist and shouting obscenities at Jimmy. He could see Cowden running up the stairs and Mona in the rear view mirror as he hauled ass out of the parking lot. He grabbed his cell and called Scooter.

"Scooter, don't go over to the Marion apartments and see Georgia tonight. Mona went crazy and the cops are over there."

"It's too late Jimmy, I'm already over here. I wondered what the racket was about. Are you okay?"

"I am now, Scooter. She must have followed me last night and seen me with Violet. That bitch threw a skillet at me after I gave her twenty orgasms."

"You must be losing your touch. Maybe she was faking the orgasms and setting you up for the kill."

"Scooter, kiss my ass. I know when a woman is having a good time. I have to get my ass home before she calls Shirley."

"Okay, if you need to use me for an alibi, I'm right here." He hung up and looked at his girlfriend.

"Scooter, am I still the only girl you ever loved?" Georgia asked.

"You bet your sweet ass, baby."

"Why don't you leave Amanda and marry me. You don't have any children and her parents hate you."

"Baby, Amanda is holding the note on my business. The house and cars are all in her name. She had me sign away my life when we got married. If I walk, it will be with the shirt on my back."

"Scooter, I'm crazy about you, but there is no future. You will never leave Amanda and I need to move on with my life. I don't understand how you can be married to a woman who won't even acknowledge your family."

"Honey, if you knew my family, you would understand. Damn, I sure hate to lose you, baby."

"Mona told me you are just like Jimmy. She said all you both want is strange pussy and you will never be faithful to any woman."

"Honey, if I ever become a rich man I'll leave Amanda and marry you in a minute. I sure wish you could see fit to give me a little more time. I swear to you on my life Mona is full of bull."

CHAPTER TWELVE

The big day had arrived and the limousine pulled up to the house. The whole family had come over to see them off. They were trying to be cool, but the thought of flying on the plane was a little unsettling.

"The limo is here, Daddy," Beverly shouted.

"Come on, Howard, the limo is here to take us to the airport," R.E. said.

"Mercy, we are going to New York," Vicki said.

The stretch limo looked unlike anything they had seen. It just kept going and going. "It that thing legal, R.E.? I don't want to get in no trouble," Florence said.

"Of course it is legal, Florence."

"Y'all have a wonderful time. I'm so jealous," Renee said.

"Mother, call me and tell me what you are doing," Sarah said.

Everyone had given their request for a souvenir to be brought back from the trip. Jimmy wanted a Yankee baseball cap. He handed Howard a twenty dollar bill. Renee wanted a fake Rolex and the other women wanted a fake Gucci bag. Scooter wanted a hockey shirt.

"Hurry up, Daddy! You will miss your flight," Scooter said.

The group picture was taken in front of the limo and they were off to the airport. The drive was an hour and a half from Littleville. The driver, Sam Coffee, introduced himself as he opened the door for them.

"Mr. Hudson has a bottle of champagne iced for you."

"That boy makes all the right moves. Rufus, you need to take lessons from Don."

"Woman, that boy can buy and sell me out of petty cash. You can't take the bottle on the plane. I read where they made new rules after the crazy people flew the planes into the buildings."

"I'm not leaving Don's gift in the limo. What kind of person would do such a thing?"

She opened the bottle and poured them all a glass. Thirty minutes later it was long gone and they were all feeling good. Florence was checking everything out and spotted a bottle of Crown Royal.

"Sam, you mind if I fix myself a drink of this Crown Royal?"

"No ma'am, Mr. Hudson said you are to have anything you wish."

Well, needless to say, Florence helped herself all the way to the airport. Sam pulled up to the departure stand for American and they got out of the car. He made sure their baggage got checked and the claim checks stapled to the tickets.

"Have a wonderful trip," Sam said.

"Son, I'm well on my way," Florence said.

"You leave out of concourse C, gate 24," the American agent said.

"What is a concourse?" Howard asked.

"That is a part of the terminal, sir."

"I don't know anything about a terminal or a concourse."

"I know how to find it, Howard," R.E. said.

"Lead the way, big spender," Florence said.

"I'm about to have a fit I'm so excited," Vicki said.

The good news was the gate was nearby and they checked in with no trouble. First class was called and they walked on the plane. A stewardess seated them and asked if she could bring them something to drink.

"Honey, what do you have in the way of liquor?" Florence asked.

"What would you like ma'am?"

"Jack Daniels, no water or ice."

"I'll be right back with your drink."

"You better slow down, Florence," R.E. said.

"There you go trying to be my damn daddy again."

The flight took off and the trip was smooth as silk. Florence had three Jack Daniels on the way and was happier than she could ever remember. They started the decent into the city and they all looked out the window.

"Oh my Lord, can you believe it?" Vicki asked.

"I didn't know there was this much concrete in the world. I always wanted to see a high rise," R.E. said.

"Some boy did really good selling all this concrete," Howard said.

The plane was now at one thousand feet and dropping, as the pilot made his way to the LaGuardia Airport. All Florence could see was the skyscrapers and she grabbed R.E. by the arm. "Don't hit the buildings for God sakes."

"He ain't going to hit the damn buildings, Florence."

The big jet circled and started in on the final approach. Florence looked out and saw they were coming in over water. The jet dropped down to less than fifty feet over the water and Florence lost it. "We're going to crash in the water and drown!" she yelled.

"Woman, the boy has to land the damn plane. Hush, before you scare the hell out of everyone."

The jet landed and taxied to the gate. They got off and were shown how to get to the baggage area. People were everywhere as they made their way to baggage claim. A big man stood holding a sign with Howard Minter on it.

"Look at that man R.E.," Howard said. "He thinks he knows me."

"That's the limo driver, you fool," Vicki said.

"R.E. Cage and Howard Minter," R.E. said as he walked over to the man. "This is my wife, Florence and this is Howard's wife, Vicki."

"Welcome to New York, Mr. Cage, I am Don and Faith's driver. My name is Pedro Gonzales."

"Where are you from, Pedro?" Howard asked.

"I'm from Queens, Mr. Minter."

"Is that in Latin America or Central America?"

"Mr. Minter, you are standing in Queens."

"Son-of-a-bitch, we are supposed to be in New York. How did you know we would be landing in Queens?" Florence said.

"Mr. Hudson called and gave me your flight information. Mrs. Cage, you are in New York. The airport is in Queens."

"Well shit, I've managed to make a fool out of myself and I haven't been here ten minutes. Damn, I thought as big as New York was; they could afford their own airport."

"They probably ran out of money and made a deal with Queens to use their airport," Howard said.

They retrieved the luggage and headed into the city. They were all in awe of the skyscrapers and the size of Manhattan. Don had forewarned Pedro about R.E., Howard, Vicki, and Florence. He had sent Pedro a tape recorder so he could take it all in after the trip. Don had done the same with the manager of the restaurant at the Palace.

"I'm really surprised Don makes Pedro live at the airport," Howard said.

"How do you know Don makes the man live at the airport?" Vicki demanded to know.

"He said the airport was in Queens, Vicki."

"Howard, do you think the only thing in Queens is the airport?"

Pedro looked in the rear view mirror and spoke. "You will be staying in Manhattan at the Palace."

"Good God! Don arranged for us to stay in a palace. I hope Manhattan is close to New York. I want to see the Statue of Liberty," R.E. said.

"I'm sure Don wouldn't stick us out in the boon docks. I believe Faith told me they stayed in a palace," Florence said.

Pedro smiled but said nothing as they drove on. Vicki and Florence were talking nonstop. R.E. and Howard were taking in the sights. They pulled up to a toll booth and Pedro drove through. Now the men had never seen a toll booth on anything but television and the movies. They sure as hell didn't know you could buy a toll sticker.

"I hope Pedro doesn't get caught, Howard. He just drove through without paying," R.E said.

"How much was the toll?"

"It was three dollars and Pedro said the hell with it."

Damn, if they didn't come to another one and he did the same thing. Pedro kept driving and Howard spotted the Empire State Building. He pointed at the building and shook his head.

"That's where that big gorilla was knocking down the airplanes. I watched it in the movie. Thank goodness he wasn't up there today."

"They finally killed his ass, Howard," Florence said.

They were a block from the United Nations now and protesters and police were everywhere. Pedro saw they were all looking out the windows. "Hugo Chavez is in town raising hell and the protesters are out in force. Please don't be concerned, the police will keep order. I have to pass by the U.N. to get to the Palace. The damn thing sits right in the middle of Manhattan. I don't know why they didn't put it in lower Manhattan."

"Oh Lord, it looks like all of Littleville is here. Those people are very upset about something," Florence said.

"We had an asshole for fourteen years ourselves. The bastard finally got his ass indicted," R.E. said.

"They can't indict Chavez, Mr. Cage. Maybe, someone will kill the sorry dictator."

"I know what you mean, Pedro. I figured someone would take Huey down for the count."

"Where is Yankee Stadium," Howard asked.

"It is in the Bronx and you don't want any part of the Bronx or Harlem. They are both infested with very high crime and it is not safe for any of you. Thirteen murders last night alone in those two boroughs. They stand on the side of the road and put needles in their arms. You want to stay in upper Manhattan. Midtown and lower Manhattan are fine as well. You must be very careful even in Manhattan. Mr. Hudson always brings two bodyguards when he and Mrs. Faith come."

"Oh hell, I didn't know that," Florence said.

"Mr. Hudson must be very careful. He is a very high profile person as you well know."

"Where is the Palace?" Vicki asked.

"It is in Midtown right across the street from St. Patrick."

"Y'all get saints living in New York?" Howard asked.

"The Arch Bishop lives here. You should walk across the street one day and look at it. It is magnificent and Saks is right across the street."

"What is Saks?" Vicki asked.

"It is a famous department store."

"Can you buy fake watches and purses there?" Florence asked.

"No ma'am, the street vendors sell those. They are on every street corner in the city. You can find them across the street from the Plaza and General Motors, next to Central Park."

"Does General Motors have a car dealership on a plaza?" Howard asked.

"Sir, General Motors has an office tower and the Plaza is a New York landmark."

"Can you go see the Plaza and sit down?" R.E. asked.

"Yes, you can watch the horses take people for a ride in Central Park. Be prepared to pay twelve dollars for a beer or bottle of water. The Plaza is very expensive and Mr. Hudson never stays there. It is old and the rooms are quite small. He says they are living off their reputation."

"Screw them. I can watch a damn horse out at Howard and Vicki's for nothing. Don is right as usual, R.E. Can you believe the nerve to try and charge twelve dollars for a bottle of water?" Florence said.

"Everyone is going broke drinking the water," Vicki said.

The limo pulled up to the Palace Hotel and Pedro opened the door. The bellman stood watching as they got out of the car. He approached them and started to speak.

"Are you staying with us?" the man asked.

"Hell no, we want our own room. Howard and Vicki want their own room too," Florence said

"Of course, have you stayed with us before?"

"Are you hard of hearing? We never stayed with you before and we're not going to start now. Pedro, tell this crazy bastard we're from Littleville as the guest of Don," R.E. said.

Pedro took the man to the side and they chatted for a minute. He came back over and spoke to them. "You will be taken to your own rooms. Please follow this man and he will take your luggage up. What time do you wish me to come back for you?"

"Don has arranged for them to cook our supper here at the hotel. Pick us up at seven in the morning and we will go see New York," R.E. said.

"I will be here at seven in the morning, Mr. Cage."

They followed the bellman to the elevator and went up to the rooms. The man brought their suitcases in and sat them on the floor. They had adjoining rooms and all four stood looking at the man. He put his right hand out with the palm facing up.

"Is there anything else I can do for you?"

"What restaurant serves supper?" Howard asked.

"Dinner is served starting at seven in the Madison."

"I have never had supper later than five thirty," Vicki said.

"There is a snack bar in each of your rooms. Room service is available twenty four hours a day. Coat and tie are required for the Madison."

"I saw a hot dog stand on the corner when we drove up," Florence said.

The man continued to stand with his palm extended upward. He seemed to be quite agitated as another minute passed. "Is something wrong with your hand?" Howard asked.

"Sir, I am waiting for my tip."

"I'll give you a good tip," R.E. said.

"I was beginning to wonder if you were ever going to give me one."

"Hell, you should have opened your mouth and said something. I ain't a mind reader. Son, don't even think about betting on a football game. Under no circumstances, place the bet across state lines. You will find your ass sitting in front of a grand jury if you are lucky enough to even get there."

"Is that my tip?"

"Yeah, and it is a damn good one son. Rufus nearly went down for fifteen years," Florence said.

The bellman was furious as he came back down. He saw his supervisor standing and laughing when he approached. "Those two bastards stiffed me."

"Don said they would, Philip. He handed him a twenty. Here is your tip. Mr. Hudson said they are to be treated with respect. Don't let me catch you getting cute. Those people are his wife's family and he wants them to have a good time."

Florence liked to eat and she was getting very hungry. "Go down and get us some hot dogs, R.E."

"Alright, I'll go get you a hot dog."

"I want two big hot dogs."

"I'll go with you," Howard said.

"We will unpack while you are gone," Vicki said.

The boys went down and walked outside the building. The problem was they were on the wrong side of the building. The thought never occurred for them to walk around the building. They started walking looking for the hot dog stand. Thousands of people were walking past them. It was a typical New York day with horns blowing nonstop. The ground was littered with drunken people lying in the grass along the streets.

"These people must be plum worn out, R.E."

"Howard, these are a bunch of drunks."

"It must have been a big party."

"Man, these people must all be in a hurry. I never heard so many horns blowing in my life."

"They must be having some kind of contest, Rufus. All those cars can't be in a hurry."

"Everybody must be looking for a hot dog, Howard. I hope they don't sell out before we get there."

"Hell, it can't be very far, R.E., Pedro said they were on every corner."

"He said the vendors were on every corner. The hot dogs are going to be hard to find. Pay attention to where we are. I don't want to get lost. Damn, I've never seen this many people in my life. There must be trouble brewing on every corner. I see policemen everywhere I look. One of the cops was riding a horse."

"Them girls over there look like the ones at Bobby Jack's trial. Maybe they can tell us where the hot dogs are, R.E."

"I'm getting turned around, Howard. These buildings are all starting to look the same. Let's ask these girls where you can find a hot dog."

They walked up to the hookers. They had been warned the folks in the city were not very friendly. They were quite surprised when the girls started talking. One of the girls even put her arm around Howard.

"Are you boys looking for a little action?" Maria asked.

"You look like a hot little number," Joyce said to Howard.

"We're looking for some hot dogs," R.E. said.

"You're on the wrong street baby. The hot dogs are two blocks over. I bet if we strapped some of this tight little ass on you wouldn't want a hot dog again," Maria said.

"Our wives are waiting at the Palace for some food. That's all they want to do is eat," Howard said.

"Let those bitches wait, cutie. You won't ever forget New York if you come with us. You like your women and your hot dogs," Joyce said.

"Damn, I wish you had found me five years ago. Jimmy and Scooter need to be here. They would take you up on your offer in a second. We just need to find the hot dogs girls," Howard said.

"Suite yourself boys, to each his own," Joyce said.

"Walk two blocks down and tell Frank he owes me a favor," Maria said.

"I'll sure tell him," R.E. said. Are they good hot dogs?"

"I wouldn't know, Sweetie. You have to come back and tell us. Frank swears he has the biggest one in the city," Maria said.

"I love great big hot dogs," Howard said.

"What made you quit liking tight pussy?" Joyce asked.

"They get so old you have to settle for less. Believe me, as a man you don't like it worth a damn," R.E. said.

"Well, I hope you enjoy the big hot dog," Maria said.

R.E. and Howard took off down the street looking for the damn hot dog stand. They looked back and waved at the hookers.

"I wouldn't have thought those two were queers," Maria said.

"Hell, you never know until you ask. I wonder what made them turn into gays," Joyce said.

"I don't know why straight men turn into gays. They said their wives were at the hotel wanting food."

R.E. and Howard were pounding the New York pavement looking for the damn hot dogs. "Howard, I'm about to walk my fool self to death. We have to find the damn hot dogs."

"We have to be getting close. Look, there is the Plaza Hotel. I'm getting thirsty as hell."

"You can just get it out of your mind. I can't believe someone would pay twelve dollars for a drink of water."

"There it is, R.E."

"Where do you see the hot dogs?"

"There right across the street next to the park."

They walked up to the man and ordered eight hot dogs. He was busy getting them ready and put them in a bag. "Are you Frank?" R.E. asked.

"Frank is off today I'm filling in for his lazy ass. That prick called in and my boss sent me over. All Frank does is chase pussy. My name is James."

"Tell him Maria and Joyce sent us over. They said to tell him he owes them a favor. How do we get back to the Palace?" Howard asked.

"Man, you are ten blocks from the Palace. You better hail a taxi unless you're planning on eating those dogs right here. Did you walk up here from the Palace?"

"Hell yes, my fat ass wife is always wanting to eat. I thought there was one downstairs, but they must have moved," R.E. said.

"That's Frank's lazy ass brother that runs the stand. Their both going to get their ass fired."

"A man is supposed to take his job seriously. I'd fire the shit head after making me walk a mile," R.E. said.

"Their day is coming for sure, old timer. What did you say those girls' names were?"

"The girls were Maria and Joyce. They said Frank told them he had the biggest hot dog in the city," Howard said.

"That lazy dickhead only wishes he had the biggest one in the city."

They walked to the side of the street and flagged a cab. They got in the back seat and told the driver they needed to get to the Palace. The idiot couldn't speak a word of English. He took them to the stock exchange in lower Manhattan. Being the idiots they were, out of the taxi they went. Florence and Vicki were getting very concerned as over an hour had passed. Florence called R.E. on his cell phone.

"Where the hell are you? I'm starving."

"The damn cabbie dropped us off in the wrong place. We are down here at the stock building."

"What were you doing in a cab? The hot dog stand is downstairs. You better not be blowing my money on stocks."

"They must have moved it, Florence. It wasn't there when we went down. We have walked our ass off trying to find a damn hot dog."

"R.E. Cage, you get your butt back to this hotel right now. You and Howard are up to no good."

"Damn you, Florence, if you were not always eating like a cow I wouldn't be out on the streets."

"Have you been with a hooker, you no good bastard?"

"I damn sure got propositioned, Florence. Howard did too, thanks to you."

"I've heard it all now. You and Howard are out chasing women and blaming me for wanting a damn hot dog."

Florence hung up and was fit to be tied. She walked in the next room and Vicki saw the fire in her eyes.

"Where the hell are they?"

"Both the sorry bastards are out chasing pussy."

"I knew I had no business letting Howard get in the liquor. I'm not going to stand for him starting all over again."

"The bastard I'm married to had the nerve to tell me he was propositioned because of me. The little prick is down at the stock place now blowing my money."

The men finally found a cabbie that could speak English and got back to the hotel. It was now six thirty and they scrambled to get upstairs. They told their story and the girls bought it and settled down. At seven, they went down and announced themselves at The Madison. Roberto Hernandez was the manager and had been expecting them. He had placed the recorder under the table and put a mike on their server. Of course, he also had one in his pocket.

"Good evening, welcome to The Madison. I am Roberto Hernandez. Don and Faith has instructed that you be treated royally tonight."

"Thank you, Roberto," Vicki said.

"Let me show you to your table. Please do not hesitate to let me know if you need anything. Congratulations on your fifty fifth wedding anniversary."

"That boy seems like a fine fellow," R.E. said when Roberto left.

"Lord God in heaven! There is Bobby Jack sitting over in the corner with a woman," Florence said.

"I told you we would run into the boy," Howard said.

"Don't you even think about going over there and embarrassing the boy, Florence," R.E. said.

Vicki put her glasses on and looked across the room. Bobby and the woman were holding hands and she was beautiful. "I'm afraid Beverly's ass is grass."

"It ain't looking good for damn sure," Florence said.

The waiter came over and handed them all a menu. The bus boy poured them a glass of water. Another waiter brought a basket of bread and crackers.

"Good evening, I am Walter Marks. It will be my pleasure to serve you tonight. I understand we are celebrating a special occasion tonight."

"I don't know what your celebrating, Walter. We are here for Howard and Vicki," R.E. said.

"Where are you from, Walter?" Florence asked.

"I am from Brooklyn."

"Where is Brooklyn, Walter?" Howard asked.

"It is one of the Boroughs. You cross over the Brooklyn Bridge and you are there. We used to have the Dodgers, but California stole them away. We have the Yankees and the Mets, but they stole our Dodgers. I just want to cry every time I pass where Ebbets Field was located. My father never got over losing his Dodgers. Mr. O'Malley wanted the money and he took the Dodgers to the West Coast."

"We got some sorry thieving bastards in Littleville ourselves. Not a day goes by without one of them stealing something. Your father probably didn't have insurance," Florence said.

Walter looked at Florence like she had lost her mind. He reached over and took the women's napkins and placed them in their laps. Walter did the same with R.E. The man jumped up from the table and grabbed Walter's hand.

"Whoa Walter, this boy is straight as a string. Howard is the same way. You came to the wrong place looking for action."

"I'm sorry about that, sir."

"Well, you should be. I didn't give you any reason to think I was gay and looking for action. You and your father need to get over losing the Dodgers."

"I made a mistake, sir. Please forgive me and enjoy your evening."

Walter left the table and walked over to Roberto. He was seating a four top and came back over to his stand. "Are you sure Mr. Hudson isn't playing a joke on us? These people can't be real."

"They are very real, Walter. Just wait until they try to read the menu."

"Walter must be adopted," Howard said.

"Why on earth would you say such a thing?" Vicki asked.

"The boy is gay, Vicki. His father was obviously gay, too. The Dodgers must have been a gay club. When this guy O'Malley stole them and took off for California, it broke the old man's heart."

"The Dodgers were a baseball team, Howard. Something else happened to make the boy gay. What are you having for dinner, Florence?" R.E. asked.

"I don't have a clue. I've never seen any of these things before."

"What is escargot?" Vicki asked.

"I think that's Italian food. Do you think you look like a queer, R.E.?" Howard said.

"Hell no! I don't look like a queer. These New Yorkers are just bold as hell."

"I'm starving. Walter will explain everything when he comes back," Florence said.

Walter came over and took them through the specials. He might as well have been speaking French. Just when all hope appeared lost, R.E. spoke. "I wish Frog was here to pick something."

"The frog legs are wonderful. Mrs. Faith orders them all the time and Mr. Hudson has tried them as well."

"Do y'all frog gig around here? I saw a lot of water when the plane was flying in," Howard said.

"I'm not certain where the frog legs come from."

"Me and R.E. used to go frog gigging. One night, we hung a big snake and that was it. R.E. damn near killed me trying to get away from the snake. That's what got me into coon hunting."

"You were running from the damn snake yourself. Quit trying to make me look bad in front of Walter."

Bobby Jack excused himself to use the restroom. He was coming back to his table when he looked across the room and saw them. He could not believe his eyes as he walked over to their table. Florence looked up as he reached their table.

"I can't believe you are in New York."

"We're here for Howard and Vicki. It's their fifty fifth wedding anniversary," Florence said.

"Don and Faith gave us the trip as a present," Vicki said.

"My grandfather believes Don is the best attorney in America. He sure saved my life."

"Son, I understand you hit the Powerball Jackpot. We are all very happy for you," R.E. said.

"Life is full of strange twists and turns. I went from looking at going to prison to being free and a rich man. I need to get back to my date. I trust you will have a wonderful experience. It was good to see all of you and congratulations."

They watched Bobby as he joined his date. "Damn, that is one good looking woman with Bobby," Howard said.

"Beverly may as well write it off as a lost cause, Florence. I hate to say it, but poor Beverly ain't ever looked like that woman a day in her life," R.E. said.

"She ain't got anyone to blame but herself. The damn boy is rich and has taken to wearing suits. Hell, he even talks different," Florence said.

They got through the meal and called it a night. Well, they thought they were calling it a night.

CHAPTER THIRTEEN

Folks, I don't know how many of you have spent a night in New York City. Let me just say "loud" would be the understatement of the century. Florence and R.E. got ready for bed and Howard and Vicki did the same. Their heads had barely hit the pillow when the hell started. The garbage trucks and work crews got it started. The sirens from the police and fire trucks picked up the pace.

"Rufus, there is bad trouble in the city tonight."

"There must be a bad wreck close to the hotel."

"I can't sleep with all this noise and I need my rest."

"What the hell do you want me to do, Florence? The police and firemen have to take care of their business."

Vicki and Howard were next door having the same conversation. Florence heard the knock on the door and got up. Howard and Vicki stood in the doorway with a bewildered look on their faces.

"Vicki thinks something terrible has happened. The sirens are going nonstop."

"I'm afraid the terrorists are back tonight and we are caught in the crossfire. I called the front desk and they laughed at me," Vicki said.

"I'm getting hungry again. I think I'll try the room service," Florence said.

"Don't order the damn water," R.E. said.

The noise never stopped and they all ordered a hamburger and fries. The man brought the food and Florence signed the check. They sat and ate while the sirens continued. R.E. picked up the bill and almost fell on the floor.

"The damn burgers cost ninety dollars. The damn boy put an eighteen dollar tip for himself. The bill with the cokes is a hundred and thirty dollars."

"My Lord, there must be a mistake," Vicki said.

"There ain't any mistake, Vicki. These blood suckers are out to break the bank."

"Relax. Don is picking up the tab, Rufus. You old coot! You have half of every dollar you ever made," Florence said.

"What the hell is Don going to say when he sees this bill? The boy was nice enough to pay for the trip and we don't need to be abusing his friendship."

They finished eating and didn't get a wink of sleep all night. The next morning, Pedro was waiting at seven when they came out of the hotel. He looked up and saw them moving slowly towards the limo.

"Did you have a nice evening?" Pedro asked.

"Pedro, we were up all night looking at the walls. There must have been a disaster in the city last night," Howard said.

"It was just a typical night in the city."

"I don't know how you get any rest here," Vicki said.

"I guess you get used to it over time."

"Pedro, we want to see the Statue of Liberty and the girls want to go shopping," R.E. said.

"I'll take you and Mr. Minter down to the docks and drop you off. I'll take the ladies shopping and come back for you in three hours."

"Why are you going to drop us off at the docks? We want to see the Statue of Liberty," Howard said.

"You have to ride the ferry over to the statue. I can't drive across water. It is perfectly safe. You will be in lower Manhattan. Did any of your family come through Ellis Island?"

"How close to Littleville is Ellis Island?" Howard asked.

"I would say eight to nine hundred miles, but I'm not sure."

"I think my daddy might have gone fishing there, Pedro," Florence said.

"What nationality are you, if I might ask?"

"Church of Christ," Vicki said.

"I used to be a Baptist. I pretty much just read the bible ever so often now. What nationality are you, Pedro?" R.E. asked.

"I am a Mexican American."

"We don't have any of them in Littleville," Howard said.

Pedro dropped the men off and showed them where to buy their ticket. He made sure their watches were in sync and told them he would pick them up at eleven. The women were excited as Pedro took them to go shopping. It was a hot, muggy day and the men were dressed in shorts and short sleeve shirts. They bought the tickets and boarded the boat for the ride over.

"Who are all these funny looking people," Howard said.

"Those suckers are the ones who bombed Pearl Harbor, Howard."

"When did they bomb the place?"

"In World War Two, you idiot. Howard, you drank way too much whiskey. I hate to be the one to have to tell you. I'm afraid you have lost your mind."

"Hell, if anyone had to tell me, I would want it to be you. Is Pearl Harbor in our state?"

"Hell no, it's not in our state. The place is clear on the other side of the ocean. It's where the people wear the little straw skirts and cook the food under the ground. They dance around in a circle like the Indians did in the old movies and grow pineapples and sugar cane. Beverly said they love to sing songs, but you can't always understand them. I never been there, but I was told the folks are real nice and pretty."

The boat made its way over to the island and they fell in line to begin the tour. They made it to the statue, only to be informed by the Park Ranger the elevators were broken and they had to climb the steps. R.E. wasn't very excited about the thought of climbing, but Howard was adamant they go see the top. They were about half way up and feeling the walk.

"This is killing my ass," R.E. said.

"My ass is fine, but my feet are killing me."

"Howard, I'm turning around and going back down. I'll never make it to the top where the torch is," R.E. said.

"Okay, I'll see you in a little while. I need to go on up and say hello to the lady."

"I'll wait downstairs for you."

"Okay. Maybe you can find some Preparation H for your ass. I saw a gift shop close to where we started."

R.E. just shook his head and started back down the steps. The Japanese tourists were talking nonstop and the old boy felt like he was in a foreign country. He made it to the bottom and damn if the Japanese didn't start asking him to take their picture. He couldn't understand a word they were saying, but he finally got the hand signals. He wound up taking pictures of six different couples. Every time he finished, they would smile and bow their heads to him.

The girls were out of the car and shopping hard on the street corner. Pedro knew better than to take them anywhere else. Florence had spotted the bags and the Rolex display. The vendor was hawking his merchandise and Florence looked him in the eye.

"How much do you want for the Rolex?" Florence asked.

"How many are you buying lady?"

"I think I'll buy four, if the price is right."

"I'll sell you four for a hundred dollars."

"How much do you want for the Gucci bags?"

"I'll take twenty five for the bag."

"I'll take eight of the bags and four of the Rolex watches."

Florence paid the man. She and Vicki headed back to the limo. She gave Vicki a watch and bag. "How come you didn't buy a bunch of stuff? Them Rolex's cost three to five grand at the jewelry store."

"I want to save my money and go to that fancy place."

"You ain't going to find a better deal than I got."

They headed out to have a bite to eat when her phone rang. She looked and saw it was Beverly. The moment she said hello, Beverly started ranting.

"Bobby Jack doesn't want anything to do with me, Mother. He told me it was over and he has a new life."

"Hell, I could have saved you a dime. Bobby Jack is now a stud horse in heat. I bought you a Gucci bag and I'll give it to you when I get home. I'm shopping now. I'll call you when we get home Sunday."

"The hell with a Gucci bag, Mother. Bobby has left me high and dry."

"Watch your mouth with your mother. You ran the damn boy off and you have to pay the price. I don't have time to listen to you cry all day. Vicki and I are doing our shopping."

"You told me to get rid of him for years."

"Dammit girl, I can't always be perfect. I ain't the one who told the boy to hit the road. If you work it right, the boy will give you more child support. I can assure you he is a different economic category now. I'll call you later."

"I feel really bad for the girl," Vicki said when they hung up.

"The damn girl ain't ever going to get over running the boy off. Hell, I'd like to choke myself for letting her."

Pedro pulled up next to Saks and told the girls he would be back for them in an hour. They went in and starting checking out the store. They stood in front of the store directory looking at the different floors with the merchandise. They decided to try the third floor and rode the elevator up. They came off and started to shop.

"Look at these stretch pants. I think they are Casmir. They are real nice and they are only twenty dollars," Vicki said.

"I guess I could buy Beverly a pair."

The sales lady walked over and smiled. "May I help you, Ladies?"

"We are looking at the britches," Florence said.

"I'm sorry, what are you looking at?"

Florence and Vicki pointed at the pants. "We are thinking about buying a bunch of the britches," Vicki said.

The sales lady quickly regained her composure. "This is one of our best lines. It is a good value, Ladies."

"Do y'all offer a discount if we buy a dozen?" Florence asked.

"No ma'am, I'm so sorry but unless it is on sale, I can't help you. Still, it is a great buy for twenty four thousand."

"Did you say twenty four thousand?" Vicki asked.

"Yes, they are two thousand each."

"Mother of God, we need to get out of here," Vicki said.

Florence looked at the sales lady. "Honey, I'd have to go naked and quit drinking water if I lived here."

The sales lady stood with her mouth open as Florence and Vicki headed for the elevator.

Another sales lady walked up to her. "Why is your mouth open, Peggy?"

"I think I just waited on two crazy women."

The men had completed the tour and were heading back across the water. They were taking in the sights on the second deck when all hell broke loose. The boat served ice cream and the people on the top deck were licking away. The wind was blowing and the ice cream was flying down on the people on the lower decks. The man standing next to them was madder than hell. He looked up to see a bunch of Japanese tourists enjoying their ice cream. R.E. and Howard both jumped as the man exploded in rage.

"You son-of-a-bitching Jap bastards! Do you think you are back at Pearl Harbor?" the men screamed.

About the same time, three other men took a direct hit in the face. The wind and the boat movement had the ice cream flying everywhere on the second deck. When the entire scoop nailed a big fellow, they all took off for the top deck.

"Howard, we have a bad situation here. This is probably how the damn war got started."

"I hope no one starts a war. Vicki will never let me come back."

The Japanese tourists didn't have a clue they were raining down ice cream on everyone down below. Bedlam broke loose as the men went running up the steps to confront the ice cream droppers. People on the top floor saw the fights break out and ran for the lower floors. The boat captain was telling everyone to calm down. The police had been alerted and they stood ready onshore. As fate would have it, a coast guard boat was in the area and called in to help.

"Man, this is a rough place. We better stick close together, Howard. The boat is starting to rock."

"I can't swim. R.E., you may have to save me."

"Look out, Howard! They are coming right at us."

"Jump behind the bar, R.E., before we get hit. These fellows are really mad at each other."

They sat side by side on the floor as the fighting continued. "Rufus, your cell phone is ringing."

R.E. picked up his cell phone. "Hello, this is R.E. Cage."

"R.E., how is your trip going?" Jimmy asked.

"Son, we are on the boat coming back from the Statue of Liberty. All hell has broken loose. Howard and I are hiding behind a bar. There must be two hundred people fighting like hell."

"Jesus Christ, what the hell happened?"

"The damn Japanese started some shit and the Americans crawled right up their ass. We were just minding our own business when the man standing next to us started screaming. The next thing we knew, World War II was being reenacted."

"Scooter wants to speak to his father."

Rufus handed his buddy the phone. "Howard, your son wants to have a word with you."

Howard took the phone and looked at the hell going on around him. "Scooter, we have stumbled upon a massive fist fight."

"Dad, are you and Rufus going to make it?"

"Son, I think the Good Lord will come to our rescue. This ain't the first time I've found myself in a tight spot."

"How has the rest of your trip been?"

"It has been just fine. I told two girls I wished you and Jimmy had been here. They were hotter than the Fourth of July and looking for some action. Son, Rufus has another call coming in so I'll say goodbye."

"Dad, you better be careful."

The fights were going on everywhere and two police helicopters were now overhead. Pedro pulled up and could not believe his eyes. Florence had grabbed her cell phone and called R.E.

"Hello, R.E. Cage."

"I know who the hell you are. R.E., what the hell is happening on that boat?"

"People are trying to kill each other and we are right in the middle of it."

"Ask Mr. Cage if two gangs are fighting?" Pedro said.

"Pedro wants to know if it is two different gangs."

"Tell Pedro it is the Americans fighting the Japanese. The Americans were on the bottom and they ran up to the top and attacked the Japanese. I think the Americans are going to win, but the Japanese are fighting like hell. I see why the war lasted so long, Florence."

"R.E. Cage, don't you dare make me a widow. Jump off that boat right now and swim to shore. The damn war is over and it is no time to try and be a hero. I'd rather have a live coward than a dead hero."

"Damn Florence, Howard can't swim a lick. I can't leave him to die at the hands of the Japanese."

"I swear I can't leave you alone long enough to go shopping. I better not find out you started the trouble."

"I better not find out you ran up a bunch of credit card debts."

Man, it was some anxious moments, but the boat finally made it to shore and the cops swarmed the boat. R.E. and Howard were all shook up as Pedro opened the door and drove back to the Palace.

"Mr. Cage, how did the fight start?" Pedro asked.

"I think the Japanese started making fun of the Americans. The next thing we knew, at least a hundred men on our side ran upstairs. Before you could say coon, all hell had broken loose. I felt bad not helping, but I'm too damn old now. Hell, I went from taking their pictures to running for my life."

"What the hell do you mean by taking their pictures?" Florence said.

"The Japanese asked me to take their pictures."

"You don't speak Japanese and you don't have a camera. I knew you started something with those people."

"Woman, they had the camera and they asked me in sign language."

"Well, I'll be damn, Rufus. Now you're telling me you understand sign language."

"I guess bitter feelings still persist to this day," Pedro said.

"Pedro, that's the understatement of the year. Those fellows were mad as hell and really getting it on. Those little fellows were fighting like hell. We had to jump behind the bar to keep from getting our ass kicked," Howard said.

"I'm just glad neither one of you was hurt. I've never heard of this happening before."

"Pedro, bad luck follows us everywhere we go," R.E. said.

Back on the home front, Jimmy stood looking at Scooter. "Why does shit like this always happen to our family?" Jimmy asked.

"I've thought about it a lot and there is no answer. I mean, how many times can you be at the wrong place at the wrong time?"

"Well, it will be one more story to add to the book. I sure wish we had been there when the hookers showed up."

"Isn't that the truth? I bet they could have gotten two more girls. I love two at a time."

"Man, I know exactly what you mean. The first time I ever got any was two girls on the back of the school bus. Hell, I thought that was the way it was supposed to be."

"Let's go get some girls and have some fun."

"What are we waiting for, Scooter?"

The mortgage crisis had kept Frog busy all morning, but he came over late that afternoon and bought them supper. They sat having their meal and discussing the day. They were all exhausted from no sleep the previous night.

"I wish I could go to the show with you tonight. I have to be back in Boston for a meeting at my firm. The sub prime lenders are going under and we have an emergency on our hands. The Japanese banks in our syndicate are backing up on us."

"Frog, I wouldn't be counting on the Japanese to help you. The Americans kicked the shit out of them today, and I saw it coming. They are in no mood to be giving you a damn thing."

"By God, that's exactly what we have run into today. I never realized how smart you were, R.E."

"My best guess is it will be quite a while before they settle down. They lost big time today."

"R.E., you need to be trading the currency markets. Did you really see it coming today?"

"I saw it in no uncertain terms, Frog. If the authorities hadn't shut it down, Lord only knows how bad it would have been."

"R.E., you are right as rain! The Japanese told us they were sick and tired of seeing their blood running on the floor. They said we tried to screw them by selling them crap mortgages. One man told my boss we were trying to wipe them out."

"Well, you know damn well we sold them crap. The thing is they should have known better than to buy it. I knew when they started raising hell it was going to be bad. They thought just because they were on top they had an advantage. They found out the hard way they were sadly mistaken."

"They are madder than hell. On top of everything else, we just found out the damn Attorney General in New York is starting an investigation."

"I hope to hell Howard and me don't get called to testify. I'm telling you. I saw exactly when it all started. You would be mad as hell if you got the living hell beat out of you."

"Well, they certainly lost their ass."

"Frog, Faith and Don had already bought us tickets to a show. I feel bad not using them," Vicki said.

"I know what kind of show you all like. Trust me when I tell you, this show was made for the four of you. Don will not be offended I can assure you. Give me the tickets and I will have someone cash them in."

"Are you sure, Frog?" R.E. asked.

"Hell yes, I'm sure." He handed them the four tickets to the show.

"I guess by now, you have heard the story of my former son in law. Beverly is going to be kicking her ass until the day she dies," Florence said.

"Man, she should have held her horses," Howard said.

"We do a lot of business with Mr. Warrington. Bobby Jack was in Boston last week and I had the chance to meet him. He thinks the stock market is ready to crash. I have to leave now. Everything is taken care of here. Have some desert and don't be late for the show. I have you seats on the front row. I'll send you the money from the tickets."

Frog shook the men's hand and hugged the women. He left and they all had a piece of apple pie and vanilla ice cream. It was getting close to show time and they walked out to the car.

"Where would you like to spend your evening?" Pedro asked.

"We are going to see our first Broadway show, Pedro. We need to go to the Majestic Theatre," Vicki said.

Pedro almost burst out laughing, but caught himself. He headed for the theater and parked on the street. "I have to let you off here. There is no place to park in the district. I will be back to pick you up after the show. Please don't leave early, as this is a bad area and you could be mugged. There is a game next door at the Garden and those hockey fans are a rough bunch."

"Don't you worry, Pedro? After what Howard and I went through today the last thing we're looking for is trouble."

"I thought they played hockey on ice. I never heard of any game being played in a garden," Howard said.

"They play basketball and hockey in the Garden. They have live concerts with many famous entertainers. The Garden is a New York landmark. I'm sure you have seen it on television many times. You know it as Madison Square Garden."

"We have a square ourselves," Howard said.

They got out of the car and saw everyone looking at them. The people were lined up to get in and they were all very young. The men looked to be in their thirties and all had beards. The women were dressed like hippies from another era. They went in and handed the usher their tickets. The usher took them down to their front row seats just as Frog had promised.

"I can't believe we are sitting down to watch a real Broadway show. I can't wait for it to start," Vicki said.

"That was awful nice of Frog to give us the tickets. I'm glad that boy has done so well for himself. I hope I can stay awake to see the show," Howard said.

"I'm not even ready to go back home tomorrow. I'm really like this fine dining and life in the city. I feel like a big shot, Rufus. Frog has us sitting on the front row," Florence said.

The light dimmed and a voice instructed everyone that no cameras were allowed, and to please hold their applause until intermission.

"Well, here comes the show," R.E. said.

"We are going to watch a Broadway show," Florence said.

The curtains came up and the cast stood in the dark on stage. The lights slowly came up and the cast stood totally naked ten feet in front of them. They were each introduced and made their bows. The four of them sat with their eyes about to pop out and unable to speak. The show began and R.E. looked at Florence.

"What are we going to do, Florence?"

"I don't know, R.E. We can't leave. We will be mugged for sure. That one boy is hung like a horse."

"All those boys have big dicks."

"Howard, if anyone finds out we were here, the church will kick us out. Did Frog tell you this was an all nude show?"

"I thought the girls at the trial were showing everything. These girls are really showing everything."

"That's not what I asked you."

"I swear he never told me anything."

The show had been on for fifteen minutes. The cast was really getting it on now. The acts of having live sex were getting very real. Florence started shifting around in her chair.

"God, no one is going to believe this when I tell them. They will all swear I was drunk. R.E., we need to go on and leave."

"Dammit, didn't you hear Pedro tell us we would be robbed if we left. This can't get any worse than it already is, woman. Just sit here and it will be over before you know it."

Time moved along and they thought the worst might be over. Suddenly, and without warning, a man started screaming. "Give it to her," the man screamed in the back of the showroom.

"Shut up, you asshole!" a woman yelled.

"Man, that guy is all shook up," Howard said.

"Shut up, Howard," Vicki said.

The house lights came up, and security pulled the man from his seat screaming and yelling. The lights went down and the show continued.

"We have to take a chance on being mugged. Vicki is about to have a cow," Howard said.

"That damn Frog set us up for the kill," Florence said.

"I knew better than to not use Don's tickets. We got exactly what we deserved for being rude," R.E. said.

"I think I'm going to pass out," Vicki said.

The man sitting next to them looked at the four of them and spoke sternly. "Shut up and be quiet. I'm a New York vice officer. We are getting ready to bust these people. None of you are going a damn place." He flashed his badge and put it away quickly.

"Oh, my goodness, we are going to be on national television when they break up a porno ring," Florence said.

"Man, we have found ourselves in a bad spot," R.E. said.

The cast were all now in the act of having sex. Suddenly the lights went up and the vice officers were swarming the stage.

"Get us out of here, Howard," Vicki screamed.

"I'm right on your heels, sister. Screw it if I get robbed. It's the price I have to pay."

"Make a run for the door," R.E. shouted.

They came running out the door and there sat Pedro bigger than life. They almost trampled themselves getting to the limo.

"God, I've never been so glad to see someone in my life," R.E. said.

"What happened in there, Mr. Cage?"

"Pedro, we almost got caught in the middle of the biggest porno bust in the country," Florence said.

"You don't ever want to go to that place," Howard said.

"I happened to be making the block and was quite concerned when the police pulled a man out in handcuffs. I took a chance on getting a ticket and came back around and parked."

"Pedro, you are a good man. We better get the hell out of here fast. I know damn well the cops are going to be hitting the door with a dozen people in handcuffs any second now," Florence said.

"Damn, Vicki has passed out," R.E. said.

"I will get you back to the Palace right away."

They made it back to the hotel. Vicki had come back from passing out. They finally made it to bed and the noise never stopped all night. The men walked behind their wives to the elevator the next morning. They all looked like hell as they checked out. R.E. led them out the door and there stood Pedro.

"Good morning," Pedro said, as he held the door open.

"Pedro, good morning to you," R.E. said.

"What did you think of New York?" Pedro asked as they drove to the airport.

"Pedro, Don must be paying you a shit load of money. They sell britches for two grand and a bottle of water for twelve bucks," Florence said.

"I don't think we will be back. If you ever find yourself in Littleville, just give us a call. I'll be more than happy to give you a lift. We have some places to stay away from our self," R.E. said.

They pulled into the airport and Pedro parked. He opened the door and smiled. "It has been my pleasure serving you."

"Pedro, you are a real gentleman. Don't you go out on that damn boat? I got a feeling those people are going to fight again at the drop of a hat. We have some bad asses in our neck of the woods, but they ain't nothing compared to these New Yorkers," Howard said.

"I will take your advice and stay away from the boat. I still cannot believe those men got into a fight. Please give my best to Mr. and Mrs. Hudson."

"We will call them as soon as we get home," Vicki said.

All of them thanked him for everything. They went inside to board the flight back home. They were all worn out and slept the entire way back. The flight got in right on time and the limo was waiting to take them to Littleville. The driver loaded their bags and they all got in the back. They left the airport and were on the freeway when the driver looked back.

"How was your trip?" Sam asked.

"It was just your typical Martin trip," Florence said.

"I'm sure you missed the story of the porno bust right in the middle of the show district."

"Son, we were right in the middle of it. The vice cops were sitting right next to us. I'm going to whip me a frog's ass when I see him."

"Jesus, you were there, Mr. Cage?"

"I was right up to my eyeballs in the shit. The naked bastards weren't ten feet from us."

They drove for an hour and the driver kept looking in the rear view mirror. Finally, he got up the nerve to ask the question. "Mr. Cage, what were you doing at a place like that?"

"It's like I told you an hour ago. That damn frog tricked us into going. We got exactly what we had coming to us for being so rude. I should have told that damn frog we were going to the other show."

Sam looked directly at R.E. and realized he was serious. Naturally he told everyone he knew the story and it spread across the county. R.E. and the Frog were known by all in forty eight hours.

CHAPTER FOURTEEN

The F.B.I. had been on the scene of the bank robbery immediately. They quickly recognized they had a serial bank robber on their hands. This was now the sixth robbery in two years, all with the identical description of the suspect. The robber had hit banks in small rural areas. Each one had occurred ten minutes before closing time. The story of the robber had spread throughout the state. No one was coming in the banks at closing time. The Martin clan was all discussing the chain of robberies when another one took place in Littleville that afternoon.

"Maybe I should take our money out of the bank, Vicki."

"Your money is insured by the F.D.I.C. You don't have to worry about losing your money," Sarah said.

"I don't know anybody by that name. Our insurance is with State Farm. It has been for years."

"Daddy, the government is the F.D.I.C. They insure your deposits up to a certain amount. Unless you and Mother have won the lottery and not shared the news with us, your money is safe," Scooter said.

"Son, we ain't ever been lucky enough to win the lottery. The last thing I won was the cake walk at the church."

"Howard, you won the buck dancing contest two months ago."

"They just gave me a trophy, Vicki. I have never won any money."

"Scooter is right, Howard. That boy ain't stealing our money. He's stealing it from the government. He is damn good at what he does. The boy has probably been studying for a long time," R.E. said.

"What the hell do you know about bank robbers?" Florence said.

"They ain't caught his ass yet, Florence."

"Well, they are going to catch his ass and send him away for a long time. He is probably one of Wayne's friends that got out. Did you ever send Bobby Jack a thank you note for saving our lives?"

"I thanked the boy to his face, Florence. You don't send a thank you note to someone who saved your life."

"Well, ain't you an expert on doing things proper?"

"We need to leave. We are going to be late for the movie. Renee and Johnny are meeting us there with Jimmy and Shirley," Beverly said.

"We haven't been to the movies in months. Tightwad always wants to stay home. I've about figured it out. Jake and Rufus are brothers," Florence said.

"Florence, if I didn't rein you in, we would be street people by now."

"I hope none of Jimmy's girlfriends show up tonight. The women are starting to get really aggressive about him," Sarah said.

The police were everywhere and had finally caught a break. A woman had seen a man taking off his disguise. She thought he left in a gray Range Rover. The interstate had been shut down and the police found no trace of the disguise in the Shell restroom. Chief Thomas was proud as punch as he relayed the news to the F.B.I. agents. It would have been helpful if he had shared the woman was eighty seven and half blind. But, hell this was Littleville, and you never want to let the truth get in the way of a good story.

The family had all arrived and been seated. Johnny left and came back with two hands full of popcorn and drinks. Everyone was visiting and having a good time. The movie began and they sat looking at the big screen. The manager looked up to see squad cars all over his parking lot. The F.B.I. agents had spotted a gray

Range Rover and the engine was warm. After checking the car, they descended on the theater. The agent flashed his badge and instructed the manager to lock down the theater. Agents went into the restrooms looking for any clothing or disguises that may have been dumped.

"I have it," the agent whispered to the other agents when he came out of the men's restroom.

"The bastard is in the theater," Agent Bowen said.

"I'll run the registration on the car," Chief Thomas said.

"I want two men on every exit immediately. We have to consider him armed and dangerous. I don't want any hostage situation developing with the people in there. Get every officer in the city over here," Agent Murphy said.

R.E. and Howard excused themselves to go to the restroom. They came through the doors and froze in their tracks. A dozen policemen stood staring at them.

"We didn't do anything," Howard said.

"How many people are in the theater, R.E.?" Herb asked.

"I don't know, Herb. What the hell is going on?"

"We think we have the bank robber cornered in the theater. Is my mother in there?"

"She had enough sense not to come," Howard said.

"Go back in and don't say a word to anyone," Agent Bowen said.

"Damn, do we have to go back in there?" R.E. asked.

"Please Mr. Cage, we think the man may be with you," Chief Thomas said.

"Damn, are you crazy? I don't know any bank robbers and neither does Howard."

"We just ran the tags and the gray Range Rover belongs to Johnny Kirk. Mrs. Scott saw a man taking off his disguise at the Shell station. He got in a gray Range Rover and drove off."

"Mrs. Scott can't see two feet in front of her, Chief," R.E. said.

"She is adamant she saw the man get in a gray Range Rover."

"Oh shit! What do you want me and Howard to do, Chief?"

"Just go back and sit down."

"I don't know that boy, Chief. I don't want to go back in there. I'm too old to be getting shot," Howard said.

"Please just go back in and nothing will happen. Whatever you do, don't speak to anyone," Bowen said.

R.E. and Howard went back in, white as ghosts, and sat down. Florence looked over and saw both of them shaking. "What the hell is wrong with you, R.E.?"

"Be quiet, I can't say anything. Leave me the hell alone."

"Did you run into one of your whores? I bet Myrtle Lee is out in the lobby."

"Good God, I ran into something much worse. Be quiet before you get us all killed."

"You're not fooling me, you old coot. I'm going to find out what is going on."

She started to get up and R.E. grabbed her arm. He leaned over and whispered in her ear. "Florence, there is a bank robber in here. He is sitting right behind us. The cops are everywhere."

Florence bolted out of her chair with a wild look in her eyes. "Bank robber!" she screamed at the top of her lungs.

"Damn you, Florence."

"Where is he, Florence?" Jimmy yelled.

"He's right behind me," Florence screamed.

"Good God, she has lost her mind," Renee said.

"This shit could only happen to the Martin's," Sarah said.

The lights came up and police were everywhere. Johnny was cool as an ice cube in January. The police walked up and asked him to stand. The man sitting in the back row got up and quietly left the theater with two of his friends.

"What is the problem, officer?"

"Sir, please step out and come with us. You are a person of interest in the bank robberies," Chief Thomas said.

"What the hell are you talking about?" Renee asked.

"Its okay baby I haven't robbed a bank."

The family watched as the police took Johnny from the theater. R.E. was all shook up and Florence had to be taken to the emergency room. Renee couldn't speak as they took her home.

"You may be his alibi, Renee," Jimmy said.

"What does Johnny do for a living?" Sarah asked.

"He buys and sells music equipment," Renee said.

The word was on the street. Carol and Anne came rushing over to Renee's house with Morris. Paul got the news and was ecstatic at the thought of getting Renee back. He called his buddy with the good news.

"Ray, they caught the bank robber. It is Johnny Kirk."

"Don't get your hopes up, Sport. They got the wrong man. The old woman is blind as a bat and dumber than hell. Your boy was stretched out at Renee's."

"Are you sure?"

"I'm sure, and I just told the cops."

"Damn, I'm never going to get back in the saddle again."

Over at Renee's house the girls were busy putting their two cents worth in. "Don't ever say a word to me again. You are living with a bank robber," Carol said.

"Mother, have you completely lost your mind. They are going to name you as an accomplice to the crime," Anne said.

"He didn't rob a bank. Get off my ass."

"Mother, the cops found the disguise in the men's restroom. You are in denial," Carol said.

"What time was the bank robbery?"

"It was at three fifty," Beverly said.

"You can't be two places at one time. Johnny was between my legs at three fifty. The cops have the wrong man."

The phone rang and Anne answered. "Paul is on the phone, Mother."

"Tell that fat, ugly prick that I hope he chokes to death."

"Do you really want me to tell him that?"

"You bet your ass you can tell him exactly what I said."

"Paul, Mother said she hopes you choke to death. She called you fat and ugly. I hate to be the one to tell you, but I feel the same way. I could never understand what she saw in you. That about sums it up."

"Your mother is a whore and you can go to hell."

"Paul says you are a whore Mother and I can go to hell."

"Hang up on the piece of shit."

"Paul, I have really wanted to tell you this for a long time. You really are the ugliest man I have ever seen. Kiss our ass and don't even think about calling here again."

The cops were running fingerprints and interrogating Johnny. It turned out the fingerprints were not his. Ray, of all people, had given him an alibi. He was released and headed over to Renee's house. He walked in and started laughing.

"Did y'all really think I robbed the bank?"

"I knew you didn't rob a bank," Renee said.

"Florence scared the shit out of me," Jimmy said.

"Hell, I didn't know what the hell to think," Scooter said.

"I think my mother is losing it over Bobby Jack. There has been too much excitement in her life lately," Beverly said.

"You ought to sue those assholes. I know a lawyer who will take your case on contingency. Those suckers are always trying to plant dope on me. They follow me everywhere I go," Carol said.

"Man, I'm just glad the nightmare is over. I almost had a heart attack when all those cops showed up. Some old woman that can't see gave them a description of my car. What's really scary is the bank robber was really in the theater. The cops found his disguise in the restroom."

"Hell, Florence was right after all. The robber was right behind her," Jimmy said.

"I've got to get my mother off the booze," Beverly said.

They say curiosity kills the cat. Over in Lilleyville, Emily and her best friend sat discussing movies over sweet tea. Sally Lott was a wild child as a young woman, as was Emily. Wild Buck had once taken a shot at one of Emily's boyfriends. The story goes that the boy was from the wrong side of the tracks and stayed in trouble with the law. One night he came driving by on his motorcycle, driving up and down the street calling out for Emily. Wild Buck was no fool and didn't want Emily within a mile of the boy.

"I want my baby," he screamed as he drove by the house.

"I'll give you your damn baby," Wild Buck yelled.

"I want my baby," he yelled as he came by the second time.

The boy circled and was headed back when Buck hit the front porch with his shotgun. It seems Buck unloaded the sixteen gauge in the boy's rear end and he went flying through the fence. That turned out to be the last time he came courting. The same night, Sally came in very late and her date took a bad ass whipping from her father. The women had both found religion and were married to preachers. However, their wild side kept trying to creep back up on them.

"I always wanted to watch an xxx movie," Sally said.

"Do they rent them at the new video store?" Emily asked.

"I was down there yesterday and stuck my head in behind the curtains. They have three shelves full of them."

"Jake is going on one of his missionary trips tomorrow. Let's go down there and get one."

"My husband is flying to Los Angeles for a convention. No on will ever know we rented the movie. We'll pick it up and grab a burger. We'll come over here and watch it."

The next morning, Jake took off on his missionary work and Sally's husband headed for the airport. Emily picked up Sally and off they went to the video store. They walked in like two thieves in the night. Both of them looked around to make sure no one was in the store. Sally grabbed a video and they headed for the checkout counter.

"We have to fill out a new customer card," Sally said.

"I'll fill it out," Emily said.

The young man behind the counter handed her the card and she filled it out. Emily paid cash and they hauled ass out of the store and stopped at the Burger King. Ten minutes later, they were sitting in Emily's living room eating their burger. Sally put in the DVD and they started to watch the show.

"My Lord, Jake doesn't do any of this stuff."

"This is great, Emily. We might learn something new. I've never had two men at one time."

"Sally, another woman is joining them. Have you ever had sex outside in the yard?"

"The closest I came was at the drive in movie."

"I never even thought of getting it on outside. Well, that's not really true."

"Look at the size of that penis on the tall one. My Lord, she is taking the whole thing."

"I can't believe what I'm seeing," Emily said.

Suddenly, and with no warning, they looked up to see Kay Jones. "Is anybody home?" Deacon Jones wife asked.

Emily tried to turn off the video but was too nervous and it kept playing. "My Lord, is that on regular television?" Kay asked.

"Yes ma'am, we just turned it on," Emily said.

"What is the world coming too? I am going to call the television station and file a complaint. Can you believe they have the gall to put this on the air right in the middle of the day?"

"We must have gotten some kind of cross over feed from a porn site on pay for view," Sally said.

"That must be what they call an orgy. My husband will not believe this when I tell him. The Deacons and Brother Jake need to go over to that station and demand they quit showing this filth. I'm calling the Sheriff the minute I get home. Mr. Smith down at the paper needs to know about this himself."

Emily had finally managed to get the television turned off. Kay walked over to see what channel it was on. Thank God she didn't have her glasses on. The old gal tipped the scales at two hundred and eighty pounds. She finally waddled back to the kitchen. Finally, after a good thirty minutes, she left. The girls were beside themselves at the thought of what had happened.

"We have to take this video back tonight," Emily said.

"They close at ten o'clock. We will drive by and put it in the overnight drop," Sally said.

"Everyone in town is going to know when Kay finishes talking."

"That woman has a mouth the size of her ass."

Now that was good solid thinking on their part. However, no one was planning on the store being busted. The girls drove up to find the place covered with cops.

"What are we going to do now? Jake is going to divorce me sure as hell, if he doesn't kill me first."

"They have the record of you renting the video."

"I have to get someone in my family to take the fall."

"Offer Renee five hundred and I'll split it with you."

"That's a great idea, Sally. I'll call her right now. If Renee will stand up for us, we are home free."

Renee and Johnny were watching the ten o'clock news. The F.B.I. had caught the bank robber and everyone was relieved. The phone rang and Renee saw Emily was calling.

"I can't believe Emily is calling this late."

"It must be important, you better take the call."

She looked at Johnny and picked up the phone. "Emily, why are you calling so late?"

"Renee, I'm in a terrible bind and I need your help. I rented an xxx video and the store got busted. I'm staring a divorce in the face and public humiliation. I'll give you five hundred dollars if you will just say you rented it. You were over here visiting and went to the video store. You wrote down my name since I live here."

"Since when did you start watching porno movies?"

"I swear to God it was the first time. Sally and I got a wild hair and rented the darn thing. Please Renee I'm begging you to bail me out of this mess. I'll do anything to make it up to you."

"It will cost you a thousand."

"You are taking advantage of me."

"Take it or leave it, Emily."

"Alright, I'll pay you the thousand."

Emily was fuming when she hung up. Renee put the phone down and laid her head on Johnny's shoulder. "The bitch got caught with an xxx video and freaked out. The cops busted the video store. That's the easiest grand I ever made. I always knew she regretted marrying Jake."

"The preacher's wife is watching porno movies? What kind of church do they have?"

"It's one of those where they scream and shout and hit each other, but they don't drink or cuss."

"Renee, has anyone ever told you your family is messed up?"

Emily hung up and was beside herself. "That damn Renee nailed us for a grand."

"She nailed you for seven fifty and me for two fifty."

"You said you would pay half."

"I said I'd pay two fifty. It's your name and address on the paperwork at the store. I can't help it if Renee is shaking you down."

"Where is your Christian spirit, Sally? Five minutes ago, you were as scared as I was and in the same boat. Now you are on an ocean liner and I'm in a canoe. Why didn't you fill out the paperwork?"

"I guess I was smarter than you, Emily."

"Well, of all the nerve. You are up to your eyeballs in this mess with me. You better stop using me. If I go down I'm rolling over on your big ass."

"Honey, there ain't but one big ass in this car and it damn sure isn't mine. Pay the damn money and shut the hell up, Emily."

Two days passed and Emily was starting to feel a little better. Jake had called to check in and let her know he would be home in three days. She was about to call Renee and try to get her down to five hundred when the doorbell rang. The Sheriff and one of his deputies stood at the door.

"Sheriff Monroe, what brings you out here?"

"Emily, we busted the video store two nights ago. They have you down renting an xxx movie."

"Well, that was my sister, Renee. She was spending the night and asked if she could use my name and address to rent a video. I can't believe she rented an xxx video. There must be a mistake."

"We will be calling on her to testify when the case goes to trial. There is no mistake, Emily. I will need her name and phone number."

"I'll let her know, Sheriff. Please let me call her first. I promise I'll get you the information. This is terribly embarrassing. I hope you can keep this between us. Jake is on a mission to Central America and he won't understand."

"We are not going to allow this kind of business in our community. We need to be on our way. Your sister has a lot of nerve coming over here and putting you and Jake in a situation like this. I want you to call me in two hours with the woman's name, address, and phone number."

"I promise, I'll get you all the information. Thank you so much for your understanding. I'd like to ring her neck."

"I wouldn't do it for anyone, but you and Jake."

Emily watched as they drove off and sat down. Her nerves were shot as she picked up the phone and called her sister. Renee answered and Emily sprang into action. "Renee, we need to talk."

"Emily, I haven't gotten my money."

"I'm sending it today."

"I better not have to go to court. If I do, it will cost you another grand and a plane ticket to Las Vegas."

"I had to give the sheriff your number. He just left and I told him it was you who rented the movie."

"You better get me the money, Emily. If he calls and I don't have the money, I'm telling him you rented the movie."

"I swear I'm sending the money today."

"I better have it tomorrow. Goodbye, Emily."

Johnny was listening and the man was a little taken aback. "You are sure being hard on your sister. I can't believe you are shaking her down for money."

"Johnny, those two cheap asses have stayed here a hundred times. They have never offered me a dime. I'm going to get my money for all those years of them free loading off me."

"Why do you let them stay at your house?"

"I would feel bad making them get a motel."

Kate was grocery shopping and checking out the pork chops at Kroger. She was having a hard time choosing. A man walked up next to her and started looking at the pork chops himself. Kate was not paying any attention to the man. She never saw the ear piece or speaker on the side of his mouth. The man had his hand over the left side of his face. She was looking down when the man started talking.

"I'm having a hard time finding what type of pork chops to buy."

"I have the same problem myself," Kate said.

"What type of pork chops do you usually buy?"

"I usually buy the boneless pork chops. The selection is pitiful today."

"Are you getting ready to leave now? I could meet you for drinks and follow you home. I'm horny as hell. It has been four days now."

Kate's head flew up and she almost popped the man in the mouth. "I'm married, you sorry bastard! I'll stick this pork chop right up your ass. I should beat the shit out of you. If you even think about following me, I'll kill your ass. Are you blind? Can't you see this wedding ring on my finger?" Kate screamed.

The man stood flabbergasted as he explained to his wife what had occurred. "The woman next to me thought I was talking to her, Sharon."

Kate was mad as hell and thought about going back in and kicking his ass. She drove home and told Chuck the story of being propositioned. Hours passed and she was still fuming over the man pulling a stunt like that on her. Chuck drove for U.P.S. and left at eleven to make his nightly run across the state. Kate had shared the story with all the Martin's and was ready to call it a night. She turned off the lights and heard a noise outside. A woman was screaming at the top of her lungs. A man was screaming back at her. Kate lifted a slat on her blinds and saw a man running down the street and a woman in a van following him.

"I'll get you, Sammy Joe!" Melanie screamed.

"Stop trying to kill me. I told you, that woman was nothing but an old friend," Sammy Joe yelled.

"It's that no good kid of Renee's," Kate said.

The van came back and this time the woman was running. Sammy Joe was in the van screaming at her. Kate picked up a baseball bat and continued to watch. Damn if the van didn't come back by again with the woman driving and Sammy Joe running. Five minutes later, it came back and they were both in the van. The neighbors had heard all the commotion and were watching as well. Kate's eyes widened as the van swerved off the street and ran across her yard. The crash was loud as the van plowed right into the side of her house. She came running out of her house with her two dogs, with the baseball bat in her hand and her hair in rollers.

Now, you probably have figured out by now everyone in Littleville had a dog. Matter of fact, most folks had several dogs. They were the first line of defense when trouble came to the neighborhood. The dogs started barking and the doors flew open. Out came the dogs making a bee line for the action.

"Sick him, Spike," Old Lady Moon screamed as she opened her screen door.

"Eat him alive, Bones," Homer Jacobs hollered to his German Shepard from across the street.

"Tear the bastard apart," Mrs. Hastings shouted as her pit bulls went running for the van.

No less than thirty dogs descended on the van and Kate. Sammy Joe knew he was in big trouble and locked the doors. The policeman came running from his house six doors down with his gun drawn. The 9-1-1 calls were going nonstop and the officers on night duty headed for the scene with flashing lights and sirens blaring. Kate was ready to start knocking the windows out. The good news for Sammy Joe was the dogs cut her off and got in a big fight. The brown nosier was sniffing under her dress and she dropped the dime on his ass with the baseball bat. There was more noise than a home run being hit in Yankee Stadium.

"My momma is going to kill me. We have run dead ass into my Aunt Kate's house."

"I'm going to kill you first, before she has the chance. You are a drug crazed fool, Sammy Joe. You are so dumb you don't know come here from sick him!" Melanie shouted.

All the neighbors had now rushed to the scene to pull their dogs off one another. "Get your dog off mine," Hooter shouted.

"My dog is tearing your dog's ass up. Keep the damn wimp inside if he can't fight," Wallace said.

It wasn't twenty seconds later and the two men were in a fight along with their dogs. The cop started firing rounds into the air to separate the dogs. Four squad cars arrived and the dogs and home owners were finally separated. Two cops held Kate back as they arrested Sammy Joe and Melanie.

"I'll get you, Sammy Joe! You no good bastard, I'm going to put this baseball bat upside every tattoo on your ugly ass body. If you were my son, I'd kill you right now," Kate screamed.

"I'll come fix your house, Aunt Kate."

"Sammy Joe, I swear to God, if I see you on this street I'll shoot you dead on the spot."

The reporter from the newspaper, Janice Rice, was on the scene interviewing people and taking pictures. When she found Kate, the action got lively. You have to understand that the Martin family had no secrets and Kate spoke her mind.

"I understand it was your house the van ran in to. What is your name?" Janice asked.

"My name is Kate Manley and I mind my own business. The piece of shit that ran into my house is my sister's son. I was going to kill the bastard, but the damn dogs got between us."

"Was the boy coming over to visit?"

"That sucker knows better than to come to my house. He is a drug crazed idiot who stays in trouble with the law. The little bastard doesn't have a spot on his body that's not covered with tattoos."

"I'm sure this has been a shocking experience."

"Listen, I mind my own business. This damn town has gotten so bad; you can't go to the store or be safe in your own home. Do you realize today I've been propositioned in the grocery store, had a brown nosier try to smell my ass, and a fool run into my house? My damn sister raised three criminals and turned them loose on society."

"Is your family from Littleville?"

"Every one of the son-of-a–bitches was raised here. The old bastards married to my older sisters have run women for years. One of them has been shot at a dozen times for messing with married women. The crazy bastards sent wedding anniversary invitations to every living soul in town. The invite said 'Bring money only, we have a money tree.' The family is so screwed up; they had their son guard the tree. The other fool damn near got indicted by a federal grand jury and sleeps with his dead friend's wife. His wife is a full fledged drunk who looks like she walked out of the damn zoo. The cops thought this boy's mother's boyfriend was a bank robber. They hauled his ass right out of the movie theater. I got a sister married to a preacher over in Lilleyville and she got popped for renting an xxx video. She had to pay off this boy's mother to take the rap. Every one of the damn kids is a drug addict and my brother runs women like it's a sport. He had surgery at the hospital and his son showed up and overdosed in his bed. I have one sane sister who lives in Florida. My oldest sister damn near got killed for stealing money from this boy's mother at the casino. The crazy ass that used to run women now goes to some church where they whack people on the head with tambourines. The preacher is his son and the man was the original bully bad ass of Littleville. The S.O.B. broke so many peoples jaws, the orthopedic doctor send him a case of whiskey at Christmas. Now, he thinks he is the second coming of Jesus. See why I keep to myself, Janice."

"Well, I'm so sorry about your horrible day. I don't think I could take a day like this."

"I'm telling you, Janice. It ain't easy being a Martin. My father was worse than all of the living ones put together. Can you imagine being the father of forty three kids?"

"Surely, you are not serious about the man having forty three kids."

"Listen, I wish I was bullshitting you, but it is the gospel truth. The older sisters remember when men would come in the middle of the night and take him. He had gotten another woman pregnant and she would be having his baby."

"My Lord, how do you manage to keep your sanity?"

"I keep to myself with my dogs and music. I got a good man and he takes care of me."

"Kate, thank you so much for your time. I better be on my way now."

"Janice, you take care of yourself."

Janice took off for the newspaper office like a bat out of hell. She knew damn well she had the front page story. The editor, Smiley Adams, was waiting when she came in. He had listened to the police scanner and rushed back to the office. Janice came in and showed him the quotes from Kate.

"Are you sure this woman really said these things? We could get our butts sued for printing this kind of slander."

"I'm absolutely sure. I recorded every word. I have my notes and the tape. Believe me; I did nothing to provoke the woman. She was just ready to get it off her chest."

"Jesus, I can't believe we could get this lucky. She must be ready to take Huey's place."

"Huey is nothing compared to Kate Manley. The woman is a real life person and she says exactly what's on her mind. I'm telling you, 'She is a hell cat with sharp claws!' I'd like to write it verbatim, if it's okay with you."

"Go right ahead and be my guest. We are going to sell the hell out of the paper. You can take it to the bank. This is going to bump Huey's trial off the front page. We might get lucky and have one of the wire services pick up the story. This is just unbelievable stuff."

Man, let me tell you Smiley had no earthly idea how right he was going to be.

CHAPTER FIFTEEN

The next morning's headline was Kate's story and all hell broke loose. Everyone read The Littleville Times from cover to cover. A big story normally ran a half a page. This was no normal story and it ran two full pages. The family was madder than hell and speaking their mind. Sammy Joe had sobered up the next morning and posted bail for he and Melanie. He went into hiding in another county and didn't even call Renee. Everyone in town was talking about the story. Smiley was dead right and every paper printed was sold. In fact, the requests were so strong, they printed a thousand more. People were buying two and sending them across the country. Sure as hell, the big newspapers grabbed the story and ran with it the next day. By six o'clock the following evening, the local network stations were carrying Kate's story on the evening news.

Chuck had raced home when he got the call from Kate. He stood outside with Kate and the insurance adjuster, Mike Henry, the next morning. The van had done some serious damage and the adjuster had a crew out boarding the room up.

"Kate, you were lucky you were not in the room when the van hit. The fool ran through the walls and stopped right on top of the bed," Mike said.

"I was up and saw the boy going back and forth down the street."

"Mike, what do we need to settle the claim and have our home put back together?" Chuck asked.

"I have three builders coming out today to give us a bid. I'll do my best to have one of them started next week."

People were driving by looking at the damage. The cars were stopping and the people were pointing at the house. Kate was fit to be tied and Chuck knew the fallout was coming from the family. Mike left and they went in the house. Kate was cussing up a storm.

"Kate, I hope you are prepared for the shit to hit the fan."

"If one of the pricks dares come over here, I'll kick their ass."

"Honey, Channel Four wants to come interview you. Could you just talk about the boy running into our house?"

"Chuck, I'm going to say what's on my mind. If they don't like it, they can kiss my redneck ass."

"Kate, they are all going to hate you."

"I should be so lucky, Chuck."

The phones were being put to use all over Littleville. Vicki and Florence were going at it with each other.

"I'll never speak to Kate again. Howard has turned his life over to the Lord and she is digging up the past. I can't believe the nerve of that bitch to publicly humiliate my poor husband and me. Pedro will be reading about this in New York."

"Who told the bitch R.E. almost got indicted? I'd bet my last dollar Renee ran her mouth. She is worse than a water hose running wide open. Emily is going to kill her. She must have lost her mind calling me a drunk. I have a drink once in a blue moon when I'm in the mood."

"I never liked the big mouth bitch. She thinks she is better than the rest of us. Her damn son is living in a trailer with two women. She ain't got a pot to piss in or a window to throw it out of. I wish she had been in the room when Sammy Joe ran into it."

"Did Emily really get busted with an xxx movie?"

"I never heard anything about it. Renee talks to Kate everyday. I guess Renee told her the story. Old Jake is going to have a cow when he finds out. I always thought that girl had a wild hair. Daddy always had to run boys off from over there. She has probably been cheating on Jake for years. If the school sex scene ever comes up, Jake is going to realize what he married," Vicki said.

"I don't, for the life of me, know why that girl wanted to put us all on the front page of the paper. This is going to cause real trouble for poor Jimmy. Emily is staring a divorce dead in the eye. She won't even let Daddy rest in peace for God sakes."

Renee was spitting mad as she sat having breakfast with Johnny at the Cracker Barrel. Johnny knew she was upset and said nothing.

"I'll never speak to that woman again. She called my kids criminals and may have blown Emily's cover. If she costs me a thousand dollars, I'm going to blow her damn house up. I could choke myself for telling her about the damn video. R.E. is going to be furious at me for telling her about the grand jury ordeal."

"She definitely spoke her mind. I'd be more worried about Emily choking you."

"I know plenty of dirt on her ass and I'm going to tell it all. She slept with half the managers at Hook Motors. That goofy ass son of hers pops pills with Morris every week."

"Are you going to call Emily?"

"Hell no! I'm waiting on the damn check. It should be here today and I'm going straight to the bank."

"Don't you think someone is going to call her and spill the beans? These people talk about everything and everybody."

"They are too pissed off to call anyone today. By tomorrow, they will get their nerve up and start talking."

"It's your call and your family. I'd hate it for Emily if Jake hears it first. The man is going to take it badly, being a preacher and all."

"Johnny, if Kate tells everything she knows on Emily, it's going to be horrible. Jake will never be able to preach anywhere again."

Shirley had gone to the store to pick up some groceries when she spotted the headline. She went out to her car and read the story. She was not pleased when she came in. Jimmy sat drinking coffee and looked up to see her face red as an apple.

"Jimmy, Kate said you chase women like it's a sport. I'm reading it right here in black and white."

"She must have gone off in the deep end of the pool and lost the oxygen to her brain. You know I don't run around on you. All I ever do anymore is work all the time. Hell, I do good to get home by ten o'clock every night."

"Everything else she said was the truth."

"Honey, the woman has never liked you and is trying to run you off. Kate is always saying bad things about you and I never told you. I didn't want to upset you and hurt your feelings."

"I'm going to call Kate and give her a piece of my mind."

"I wouldn't do that if I were you. She is mad enough to kill someone right now."

"I always thought the two of you were close. Are you trying to tell me she dreamed this stuff up?"

"Baby, I did chase women before I met you. She must be talking about the old days."

"Kate was not speaking in the past tense, Jimmy."

R.E. and Howard had gone fishing over at Possum Lake. They always left well before sunrise, so they could get to their favorite fishing hole. They had no idea Kate had dropped a bomb on the family. They made it out on the lake and were about to settle in for a morning of their favorite past time.

"Damn. Sonny and Witt beat us out here and got our fishing hole," R.E. said.

"We'll have to find another place," Howard said.

"We'll go over by the duck blind. I caught a bunch of brim there two months ago."

"I hope we catch a mess of fish today."

Well, the boys did their best to catch a mess of fish for the next hour to no avail. Every time they threw the line out nothing but their bait came back to the boat. "The damn fish decided to take a vacation. Sonny is catching them left and right and we can't get a bite. That no good rascal saw us catching all the fish and stole our hole," R.E. said.

"The only thing moving is that damn goose. He keeps flying back and forth across the lake."

"If I had my gun, I would shoot the loud mouth son-of-a-bitch."

"The goose is coming back again."

"We're wasting our time, Howard. We may as well go home."

They cranked up the motor and started back to the bank when it happened. R.E. was driving and Howard was on the lookout for stumps. He looked over and the goose had dumped a big load on R.E. in two places. "R.E., the goose has shit on your head and the back of your shirt. Your hat is covered in shit."

R.E. looked to see the mess all over him and was madder than hell. "I'm going home and get my gun, Howard. That goose has shit on the last person he is ever going to."

"You can't shoot the goose. The season is closed and the game warden will get you."

"The man will just have to catch me. I'm going to put the lights out on that goose."

They stopped on their way back at the country store to get a Coke and let R.E. clean up. They walked in and four of the old timers were sitting at the table playing a game of dominos. The men looked up and started to give the boys a piece of their minds.

"You boys made the front page of the paper," Harold said.

"We knew you chased women, Howard, but none of us knew you almost got your ass indicted, R.E.," Jack said.

R.E. bowed up like a monkey in his cage and walked over to the table. Howard was right on his heels. "Don't be starting any crap with me," R.E. said.

"Read the story yourself, smart ass," Jack said.

The newspaper was on the chair and both of them looked and saw the headline. They took turns reading it and both turned red as a beet. "That damn woman has lost her mind. I've never been indicted by anybody."

"The woman said you almost got indicted. What did you do to almost get yourself indicted?" Harold asked.

"I got tricked by a bookie in Mississippi."

"The preacher's wife likes xxx movies. We need to get us a church like that here in Littleville. I would start going with my wife again," Jack said.

"A goose shit on R.E. He was a big one and almost got him right between the eyes. The goose nailed his head and back from fifty feet."

"Kate shit on all of you right between the eyes and she didn't miss. Man, she must have woke up on the wrong side of the bed," Harold said.

"She ain't going to have a bed to wake up on when Florence gets on her ass."

"You boys better get on home and start putting out the fires before the house burns down," Jack said.

"Come on, Howard. We need to get back and find out what the hell happened."

Renee got home and the check from Emily was in the mailbox. She rushed down to the bank and cashed it on the spot. She had just walked back in when the phone rang and it was Emily.

"Emily, I got the check and cashed it. I'll stand up for you and Sally, but we may have a little problem."

"What kind of problem are you talking about?"

"Kate ran her mouth about the xxx video and the story hit the local paper."

"I didn't tell anyone about the video. How would Kate have found out?"

"I must have let it slip."

"Where was it in the paper? Jake is coming back tomorrow."

"Emily, it was on the front page with a lot of other trash on the family. She called my kids criminals and Florence a drunk. She blasted Howard, R.E., and Jimmy, for chasing women as well. She said Daddy had forty three kids. Sammy Joe ran into her house and she went crazy."

"Jake is going to find out about everything. I'm going to have to tell him before he get's hit right between the eyes. I must have lost my mind renting that damn video."

"Emily, get your self together and quit whining. I told you I would stand up and say I rented the video. Johnny will stand right beside us. Tell Jake you went to bed and never knew we were watching the damn thing."

"Why can't you keep your mouth shut, Renee?"

"I told you, I must have let it slip. How the hell was I supposed to know Kate was going to lose it? You are not going to get kicked out of the damn church. Just relax and go get your vibrator, Emily."

Emily was fit to be tied. "I don't need a vibrator smart mouth. You and Johnny better get your story straight. I paid big money to you, Renee."

"I've got my story straight, Emily."

Faith loved watching the television talk shows. Her best friend, Nancy Cleve, sat with her watching and having a glass of wine. Don was on his way home from a case in Atlanta and was due in any minute. The story came over cable news and Faith almost passed out.

"Damn, did the woman say what was on her mind? I thought I was raised in a dysfunctional family," Nancy said.

"I can't believe it."

"That woman better get her some protection. Where in the hell is Littleville?"

"I'll be damn if I know."

"Faith, there may be a killing in that family. Kate must be one bad ass broad. I mean the woman just unloaded on her family. Can you believe any man could father forty three children?"

"I'm in a state of shock."

"I cannot fathom any woman on earth saying all these things. The woman didn't pull any punches. She just flat told it like it was."

Faith got up and looked at the ceiling. "She certainly did, Nancy."

Florence had a birthday coming up the next day. R.E. had decided to give her a present. He had called a temp firm and paid to have the house cleaned. He told Florence and she was quite pleased someone was coming to clean the house. R.E. promised to take her to dinner that evening and invite Howard and Vicki. They were all furious about Kate. They thought the worst was over, but they couldn't have been more wrong. Florence was steamed about not getting a thank you note. A friend had passed away and Florence had gone in with Renee and Emily on a flower arrangement. It turned out the daughter of the deceased had not sent a thank you card. Florence called Renee to get it off her chest and express her feeling. Florence had a voice every bit as loud as Emily. If you were on the other end of the phone, it was not close to your ear.

Renee was having a cup of coffee and saw her caller I D. "Good morning, Florence."

"Did you get a thank you card from Mary Lou?"

"Florence, we sent the flowers two days ago. How the hell could the girl have sent us a thank you note?"

"How much were the damn flowers?"

"I told you, they were forty five dollars plus tax."

"Did you put my name on the card with you and Emily?"

"Hell yes, I put your name on the card."

"I think we got screwed. The woman charged us too much for the flowers. Since you picked her to do the arrangement, I'm putting up ten dollars. R.E. is busy, so it may be a couple of weeks before he can run me over there."

"I tell you what you can do with the ten dollars, Florence. Stick it up your ass." The phone went dead in Florence's hand and R.E. stood staring at her.

"Woman, you have as much class as a herd of elephants. You have a lot of nerve calling me cheap."

Wesley Arnold had made millions in the radio business and he was launching a new television network. Wesley was a marketing genius and had a real sense about what people wanted to see. He sat in his office in Hollywood and read the story of Kate and the Martin family. He hit the intercom and told his secretary to have his programming director come to his office. Wesley was a hell of a salesman and he had an idea. Carl McGill came in and had a seat.

"Carl, did you see the story about the woman in Littleville?"

"Linda showed it to me an hour ago. The girls are back there laughing their butts off," Mr. Arnold.

"I've got an idea for a show. This woman may be perfect. I want you to send some one down there and get me an interview. Take as much time as you like with her and fly the tape back to me."

"You think she is real, Mr. Arnold?"

"I have a hunch she is very real and the answer to my prayers. If she is what I think she is, I'll go make the offer myself."

"I'll call our connection as soon as I leave."

"Make it a priority," Wesley said.

By the next morning word had spread throughout the family. Kate was going to be on Channel Four at six o'clock. Renee called

Faith to give her the news and was shocked to hear it was on the cable news channels. Emily found out herself and was in full blown panic. Sally had left the ocean liner and climbed back in the canoe. Sarah thought about sending flowers she was so grateful to be left out. Jake was sitting in the Dallas airport waiting for his connection. The poor man almost died when he saw the news and called Emily.

"Emily, you are on national television renting a porno movie. How could you do this to me?"

"Jake, Renee rented the movie and I didn't know. She came over with her boyfriend. She asked if they could use my name and address to rent a movie. I had no idea the woman rented an xxx movie."

"You have to show a driver's license."

"I let her use mine. I never dreamed she would rent an xxx video."

"Everyone in town is going to know about it. The church will fire me and we will be disgraced."

"No one is going to fire you. I can explain everything. They don't know if Kate is even telling the truth. I'll pick you up at the airport tonight."

"When did Renee start watching porno movies?"

"I think, between me and you, Johnny is into watching them."

They hung up and poor Jake was so shook up he almost missed his flight being called. He was as nervous as a cat on a hot tin roof the whole flight back.

The Channel Four reporter, Jim Hunt, and his crew were set up in Kate's living room. They had filmed the damage from the van. The interview was set to begin in ten minutes. The dogs were going crazy and Kate locked them in the bathroom. She came back and took a seat.

"Mrs. Manley, is it alright for me to call you Kate?" Jim asked.

"You can call me, 'Kate.' I don't have a high fluting attitude."

"Okay, just relax and we will start in a few minutes. I'm not going to ask you any trick questions. I thought we would go over what happened last night and some of the comments you made in the newspaper."

"Kate was chewing her tobacco and spit it in her can. I'm just going to tell it like it is, Jim."

"That's exactly what I want you to do, Kate."

Chuck looked at his wife with a worried look on his face. "Kate, please just talk about the boy running into our house."

"Why don't you take the dogs for a walk? I'll say any damn thing I'm a mind to say."

Emily was out of the viewing area for Channel Four, but everyone else was glued to their television set. R.E. had run over and picked up barbeque for dinner. After finding out about Kate being on T.V., dinner at the restaurant went out the window. The news came on and the anchor ran through the program. Kate's interview was the second story of the evening. Her time came and the station switched to their reporter in Littleville.

"Good evening, this is Jim Hunt coming to you tonight from the home of Chuck and Kate Manley in Littleville. Most of you know a van rammed into the bedroom of their home around eleven o'clock at night."

Footage of the van sitting on top of the bed was being shown as Jim spoke. The camera switched to a live shot of Jim sitting with Kate. "We are joined by Kate Manley at what's left of her home. Have you gotten over the shock yet?"

"I'm never going to get over it."

"Tell us what exactly happened."

"One of my sisters' stoned out kids ran into my home. The fool kept driving up and down my street chasing some woman. The next thing I knew, she was chasing him. When I looked out again they were both in the van heading right into my house."

"What happened next?"

"The dogs were let out and they came running for the van. Fist fights broke out among the neighbors and the cops came. I tried to get to the boy with my baseball bat, but the dogs were blocking me."

"Kate, we read in the local paper where you had some things to say about your family. Did your father really have forty three children?"

"He had eight legit ones with my mother. The rest were with seven other women. He was a womanizer and passed it down to his son and my brother in laws."

"I understand one of the men was shot at a dozen times after being caught with men's wives."

"The old coot is brain dead. Can you imagine anyone being dumb enough to get caught a dozen different times? My sister damn near killed him one night in a pay phone booth. She caught him red handed and ran over the phone booth with her car. The bank president almost nailed him in bed with his wife. He jumped over the balcony with the man firing away. The old fool ran up on a bunch of gay men having sex in the park. He took off running for his worthless ass life again."

"Is it true another brother in law almost got indicted by a federal grand jury?"

"He is almost as stupid as Howard. They call him R.E., but his real name is Rufus. He looks like a Rufus. He thought he committed perjury. The fool didn't even know his bookie's name. He is a little bigger than a midget, so he probably couldn't even see the man."

"One of your sisters' is married to a preacher and got caught renting a porno movie?"

"Yes, she had to spring for a grand to one of my sisters to take the fall. It was the same sister whose boy ran into my house. Renee has one kid who likes to shoot the bird to the cameras. The other girl writes more false scripts than the pharmacist. Emily has always been a wild ass and hides it."

"I understand one of your sisters is a drunk?"

"Jack Daniels would go busted if she croaked. She is big as a house and looks like an oversized Jersey cow. She and Emily have a set of lungs that would reach your entire viewing area. Emily scared the hell out of my neighbor's little boys one night over at the Outback. Some fool tried to hit on her and she put the jerk out of commission for life."

"Are all the children really drug addicts?"

"Every single one of them is dopers. Hell, Jerry Springer wouldn't believe the Martin's were for real. My damn brother is doing his best to catch my father. I got a cousin who runs right beside him twenty four seven. He got caught in a shootout over in Eastville with one of his women. The sucker has no shame and used my brother's name and address at the motel. My brother was in the hospital trying to cheat death from open heart surgery. All the bitches think they are supposed to sleep with every man in town. One goofy ex boyfriend is having Renee followed by a stupid ex cop. They all have a gambling problem and their always running off to some casino."

"I believe you were quoted as saying you have one sane sister."

"She lives in Florida and the girl is a real sweetheart. I'm sure you know her husband. He walked the state police car bandit. The man has never lost a case."

"Really, who is her husband?"

"Don Hudson."

"Are you serious, Kate?"

"You bet your ass I'm serious. Listen to this one, Jim. The family all thought he was a murderer and made a complete fool of themselves. The old coots and one of the kids ran and got their guns. The idiots put them under the chairs and the boy's gun went off. The Sheriff and everyone else hit the floor. I don't have enough time to tell you the whole story."

"Kate, thank you so much for taking the time to speak with us. This is Jim Hunt reporting from Littleville."

Jim stood and shook hands with Kate. He thanked her again for the interview. He started out the door and his phone rang. Kate stood waiting for him to finish his call. He hung up and looked at Kate. "Thank you again for your time, Kate."

"I hope you got what you came for."

"I certainly did, Kate. That was my station manager and he told me Wesley Arnold had requested we send your interview to him in Hollywood."

"Who is Wesley Arnold, Jim?"

"He is a millionaire. He is starting his own network."

"Good for Wesley. The damn shows on T.V. are not worth watching. I need to get in the kitchen and make my husband some supper, Jim."

Well, needless to say, most folks were laughing their ass off. Over at R.E. and Florence's house, no one was laughing. The entire clan had watched the interview and there were a lot of red faces.

"Which one of us is going to kill the bitch?" Florence asked.

"You can't kill her, Mother," Beverly said.

"Man, what did I do to piss her off?" Jimmy asked.

"Emily is as good as divorced. Carol may try to kill her. I'm really worried about Anne taking a shot at her," Renee said.

"She just can't get enough, Florence. First, she humiliates me about Howard and then tonight, she does it again about Don. She has no soul! I'm here to tell you. What kind of person makes fun of your church?" Vicki said.

"She ain't ever liked me, Howard. Out there on T.V. making fun of me and my name," R.E. said.

"Who told her I was shot at by twelve men? What are you going to do about her saying you were a drunk, Florence?" Howard asked.

"I'm going to sue her ass off," Florence said.

They sat running their mouths nonstop. Scooter saw his cell phone ring and took off without saying a word.

"Where is Scooter going, Vicki?" Howard asked.

"He is going to try and save his marriage. You can bet your ass that was Amanda calling. Sarah, was your husband over there filming the bitch?"

"Yes ma'am. He was there last night as well. This damn woman has stirred up a hornet's nest."

Shirley walked over and got right in Jimmy's face. "Jimmy, some girl named Mona called me. She said you were sleeping with her and Violet Blue," Shirley said.

"Lord, I don't know a Mona or Violet. Kate probably put some girl up to calling you."

"We will get through it alright. I'm just worried about Emily surviving the storm. At least this will be the last we hear of it," Renee said.

They all left and Renee made a bee line home to call Emily. She was on her way to the airport to pick up Jake. She looked and saw Renee was calling. Emily grabbed her cell and cut loose.

"Jake is furious and he is going to divorce me. I told him you rented the video, but he thinks he is going to be fired and run out of town."

"Kate just did an interview with Channel Four. She blew our story to hell, Emily. She said you paid me a grand to take the heat."

"I'm about to wreck the car. Can you keep your big mouth shut about anything? What am I going to do, Renee?"

"Stay cool and don't change your story. Kate will never be called to testify in a silly video bust six counties away. No one will ever hear from her again. She got her five minutes of glory."

"What else did she say, Renee?"

"It would be easier to tell you what she didn't say. It was worse than the newspaper story."

"I'm at the airport and Jake is standing on the sidewalk. I'll call you tomorrow."

"You better stay cool, Emily."

"I'm hanging up, big mouth!" Emily shouted.

"Emily, I can't breathe," Jake said when he got in.

"Everything is going to be fine, Jake."

"Deacon Brown just called me on my cell phone. He saw the story on Channel Four. He was in Rainville and watched the whole interview. Kate said you paid Renee a thousand dollars to take the fall for you."

"She is a liar and always has been. Renee and Johnny are going to testify they rented the video. She also said daddy had forty three kids. No one is going to believe her."

"Emily, the deacons want to sit down with me tomorrow. Deacon Brown told me they were very upset. They believed every word out of the woman's mouth."

"Jake, I told you not to worry about Kate. The truth will set us free."

Faith got the scoop from Renee and put her glass of wine down. She lit a cigarette and took a deep drag. Don walked in and looked at her. "Faith, you get more beautiful every day."

"Baby, I need to speak to you. I'm afraid Kate gave a television interview tonight and exposed my family. She even mentioned you in the piece."

"I already know about it and I don't care. Ben called me a few minutes ago laughing his ass off. He said Kate dropped the hammer on the whole family. You always told me she was a hell cat. Did your father really have forty three kids?"

"Don, I have no idea how many kids he fathered."

"I bet Howard and R.E. have their hands full tonight. Emily must be into porno movies."

"Renee thinks she is looking at a divorce. Jake can't take the heat."

"Faith, this is the Martin family. Your sister is not going to be divorced. I need to take a shower and change clothes. Give me twenty minutes and we will go to the club and have dinner."

"I can't believe you are not upset."

"You never know, Faith. Something good may come from Kate telling it like it is."

"What good could possibly come out of her exposing my family?"

"Just give it some time, Faith. I have a good feeling about Kate."

Faith watched him go in the bathroom and shook her head. Every time she had seen the look on his face, they had made big money.

Huey's trial was set to begin. Ben had succeeded in having the trial moved to the state capital. Hudson had given the feds so much dirt on Huey; he was looking at spending the rest of his worthless life in the pen. Ben had been working on a plea deal, but Huey was determined to go forward at all costs. They sat together in the law offices of one of Ben's friends.

"I'm going to beat this rap and walk."

"Huey, this is a sixty count indictment. The government has eye witnesses to each crime."

"Hell, it's my word against theirs, Ben."

"Huey, you need to accept four years and take your medicine. They have you dead to right."

"I need to win and make a comeback. I know I can win back my job. That damn boy outspent me ten to one."

"Huey, we are now up to ten of your cops going to jail. Thirteen people in your administration are going down. Do you even have a clue as to who nailed your butt to the cross?"

"It had to be C. Jacob, but he got his ass ruined."

"Huey, Hudson dropped the dime on you. I told you a hundred times to shut up about the Cullen boy."

"Hudson ain't got any power in Littleville. He got lucky and won one case with the Cullen boy."

"Huey, I just don't know quite how to say this to you. If you had a brain, you would take it out and play with it. When the Governor hears the man's name, he gets the shakes and can't move. The man is taking your ass down for the count. He is not going to back off until you are behind bars."

"Governor Jones will give me a pardon if I somehow lose. I went on a trip to China with him and he likes me."

"The Governor will let you rot in prison until you die. You need to take the deal for four years. If we go to trial the deal is off. You are looking at three hundred years."

Well, Huey never saw the light and the train ran over him head on. He was convicted on every single count and got the three hundred year sentence. The press had a field day and C. Jacob was happy as hell. The only problem was suddenly, and without warning, C. Jacob's world fell completely apart. He lost half his money to his former wife and then the damn things started to happen. The Sheriff nailed him on a D.U.I. to start the ball rolling. He swore he never cursed the deputy much less took a swing at him. One of his new clients sued him and turned him in to the state bar. Damn if a week later another new client didn't nail his ass with the same charges. The state bar looked at the situation and removed his license to practice. The Judge hearing his D.U.I. and assault charge threw the book at him. The next thing he knew he was on his way to jail with Huey.

Don took the call from Mr. Warrington and was told in no uncertain terms how pleased he was. It seemed like things were going to settle back down in Littleville for the Martin family. Jake and Emily caught a big break when the video store owner agreed to shut the store and pay a fine. Jimmy survived the scare with Shirley and she decided to stay. Scooter, being the smooth talker he was, convinced Amanda that Kate was crazy. He insisted he was not the cousin Kate was talking about. It was some cousin in another state and he didn't even know the boy. The church had long ago forgiven Howard. Don called Vicki to say things would be just fine. R.E. got ragged for a while, but it all died down. Florence assured everyone the only Jack Daniels she knew lived in Texas. The kids all knew better than to say or do anything. Yes, life was going to be right back to normal. How could anyone have possibly known some Hollywood millionaire was going to change their world forever? Well, how could anyone except one smooth operator on the inside.

CHAPTER SIXTEEN

Wesley Arnold sat watching the interview Jim Hunt had done with Kate for the third time. The smile on his face said it all. Carl McGill had rarely seen it in the twelve years he had worked for the man. He thought he knew exactly what was coming next, but he was very wrong.

Wesley stood and looked at Carl. "I have to get down there and cut a deal with Kate. This woman is a natural born star. I'll bet my net worth she will be the biggest thing to hit television."

"We have to change her look and talk her into moving to Hollywood."

"Carl, there is a reason you work for me. We are not going to change a damn thing about the woman. She will never come out here. My parents have lived in the same little town for forty years. They wouldn't move if I bought them a mansion in Beverly Hills and neither will Kate. You lived your whole life in the city. You don't know country people."

"What are your thoughts on how to get her? Where are we going to film the show?"

"I'm going to find the biggest house in Littleville and set the studio up inside it. Kate is going to do her show right in her home."

"What are you going to do about zoning? You can't run a studio out of a residential house."

"My partner has it taken care of, Carl."

"How in the hell do you get these things done? She made it plain in the interview she is a private person. You are going to have a hell of a time convincing her to do the show, Wesley."

"Carl, I built a little radio station into an empire. You can bet your ass, that whatever it takes, I'm going to get that woman."

"You're not going to use a studio audience?"

"No. I don't need a studio audience. I just need Kate to be Kate. I'll take the world by storm."

"What are you going to name the show?"

"I'm going to name it, 'Straight Talk with Kate in Littleville."'

"What afternoon time slot are you thinking about placing it?"

"I'm going to put her on in prime time for two hours."

"You are going to bet the network on Kate Manley?"

"Relax. She is money in the bank, Carl. I have dreamed about doing this show forever."

"Wesley, Oprah is not on in prime time."

"Kate Manley is damn sure going to be on in prime time. You just get everyone ready to kick ass."

"Yes sir."

Carl left and went to a meeting with his staff. He was all shook up at the prospect of a one hundred million dollar bet on Kate. Everyone was in shock when he gave them the news. Most of you probably figured by now that Kate was going to be a hard sell. The woman kept to herself and cherished her privacy. But, Wesley Arnold was one slick talking son of a gun and he had spoken to Kate. The next afternoon, he was on his way to meet the straight talker from Littleville. His people had already retained the real estate agent and she had her instructions.

Anita Johnson let nothing stand in her way of a big commission. She had no sooner hung up with her instructions from Wesley when she immediately placed a call to Doctor Robert Browning and set up a meeting that evening at his home. The Doctor and his wife had the finest home in the county. Anita knew they wanted to build a home at Twelve Trees. Anita arrived and the good Doctor showed her in.

"Anita, you said you have a buyer for our home. We need to build our new home before we sell," Doctor Browning said.

"The buyer is motivated and needs the home now. I can find you something in Twelve Trees while you build your home."

"I'll sell for two million, but I need to build first."

"That's not going to work, Robert. Give me a price to sell tomorrow and I'll put you in a fine home."

"The only way I'm going to sell tomorrow is if the buyer pays me three million."

Anita smiled and put the paperwork in front of him. He looked and sure enough, there sat the contract at three million cash. A check from Anita's firm was made out for three million dollars.

"Jesus Christ, the people must love our house, Anita."

"There's a fool born every minute, Robert. This one has money and he wants your and Susan's house."

Well, the good Doctor didn't get through medical school by being a fool. The contract was signed and Anita was on her way. Little did any of them know, the house would become more famous than South Fork. Anita was looking at a one hundred eighty thousand dollar commission. She put the petal to the metal and headed for Twelve Trees to celebrate.

Kate and Chuck sat in their living room waiting for Wesley to arrive. "The man was so nice; I told him he was welcome to come see us."

"What is he trying to offer you, Kate?"

"He said the world needed some straight talk and he wanted to offer me a job. He said he paid good money and I didn't have to leave my house. I don't mind watching shows for him, but I don't want to call anybody."

"I can't imagine what he is going to offer you. My back is absolutely killing me. I wish to God I was able to retire."

"You better let me put some cream on your back. He ain't going to be offering me enough for you to retire."

"Make him pay you at least ten bucks an hour."

"Alright, I'll hang tough and get at least ten bucks. The damn dogs are barking. The man must be here."

The doorbell rang and Kate went to the door. She was shocked to see Wesley playing with the dogs. They were wagging their tails and having a large time. Wesley stood in his jeans and cotton shirt and extended his hand. They shook hands and Kate liked what she saw.

"Come on in, Wesley, and take a load off. We ain't got much, but I'll fix you a ham sandwich if you are hungry. We were just getting ready to have a sandwich ourselves."

"Thanks for inviting me over. I'd love to have a ham sandwich with you."

"Wesley, this is my husband, Chuck. He has a bad back and he's moving a little slow."

"It's nice to meet you, Chuck. I'm sorry to hear your back went out on you. My mother has been having a terrible time with her back."

"Come on in the kitchen, Wesley. We can talk while I put us a sandwich together. You like mayo or mustard?"

"I'll have the mayo, Kate."

"You said you were in the television business. I don't have any background with T.V., Wesley. I ain't much into calling folks to see what their watching. I just stick to myself, if you know what I mean."

"Kate, I like the way you tell it like it is. I think people need to hear someone being honest for a change."

"Wesley, I've seen so much crap coming down from all these fools in my life. I made my mind up years ago. I wasn't going to take no shit from any of them. I got the most messed up family in America. You got to keep their ass at arms length. There ain't a day goes by without some kind of drama."

"You might be surprised at how many families are screwed up. Do you and Chuck have any kids?"

"Wesley, I ain't going to bull shit you. We got them and they are a bunch of sorry asses too. My boy called me yesterday to tell me he was living with two girls. The little dip shit tried to tell me he was just living with them. No sex or anything like that. I asked him what track he thought I was on when the freight train ran over me. The little bastard takes after my damn brother. If they find themselves with one woman, they think something is wrong."

"Kate, you think you might like to have a T.V. show. Just be yourself and talk about what went on in town that day. Hell, around the country for that matter. I'd be willing to pay you and Chuck good money. You could do it in your own home."

"Wesley, we ain't got enough room to walk in here." The dogs started barking and Kate torn into them. "Shut up, you assholes, before I come in there and put a stick on you. I'm sorry about the damn dogs, Wesley. They are still all stirred up from the other night."

"That's okay. I've got dogs myself. I'll tell you what I'll do, Kate. If you will do the show for me, I'll buy you and Chuck a big house and set up a big room just to do your show. I was thinking we could do it five nights a week for a couple of hours. I'd have someone with you and they could talk with you. People could call and ask a question. You could even invite folks if you wanted to."

"How big of a house are you talking about, Wesley?"

"I'll buy you and Chuck a real big house, Kate. I'd even be willing to pay for furnishing it."

"Damn, that's mighty nice of you, Wesley. How much are you paying an hour?"

"I got more money than sense Kate when I see something I like. I believe we owe it to the country to help them see the light. I'd be willing to buy that house and pay you and Chuck a million dollars a year. That comes to a little over nineteen hundred dollars an hour. All I ask for is you agree to do the show for five years."

"Wesley, did you have a wreck on your way over here? You seem like a fine young man, but a rock must have flown up from the road and got you."

Wesley pulled out a contract and a cashier's check made to Kate Manley for one million dollars. He handed it to Kate and her mouth fell open. Chuck looked at the check and back at Kate.

"Kate, I ain't going to blow smoke at you. There is good money in the T.V. business and I'll do just fine. I don't want you to hear from someone that I cut you short."

"Don't you worry about some S.O.B. bad mouthing you. I'll kick their ass from can to can't, Wesley. I got to be straight with you. I have never had a job in my life. Chuck married me right out of high school and he provides for us."

"That doesn't give me any cause for concern."

"When do you want to start?"

"Well, we will get you and Chuck moved in and the room built for the show. My folks will come down here and get everything ready for the show. I need to advertise it for a month. I'd say two months from tonight we could get started."

"Do I have to get all dressed up and wear makeup?"

"You don't have to do a damn thing, but wear what you have on. We are going to give America the real deal."

"Wesley, you got yourself a deal. I hope to hell you know what you're doing, because I damn sure don't have a clue."

"I sure enjoyed the ham sandwich and Coke, Kate."

"Let us get moved and I'll fix you a real supper when you come back, Wesley."

"One last thing and I'll be on my way. If anyone of my people is not nice to you, just let me know. I'll fire them on the spot. I try my best to hire nice people, but you never know what's going to happen when your back is turned."

"Wesley, me and you are going to get along like two peas in a pod. Don't you worry yourself for one second. If anyone gets in my face, I'll kick their ass. I ain't going to be bothering you with any of that crap. We got plenty of smart ass pricks around here. I won't be seeing anything I haven't seen a thousand times. I damn sure appreciate your trust. I'll be pinching my ass for the next five years."

Wesley headed out the door and drove three miles to the Shell station. He got out and handed his man the keys to the rent a car. He walked over to the limousine and looked at his people.

"I expect all of you to move heaven and hell to get the studio built. Sam, you see that Kate and Chuck get moved. Nancy, you help her furnish her home. I've got to get back to L.A. and get moving on our end. Let me tell you one last thing before I leave people. If she ever tells me you were rude to her or her husband, I will fire you on the spot. This is your horse and we are going to ride it to the finish line. I've got the triple-crown winner and nothing is going to stand in my way."

Wesley got in the limo and placed the call to his partner. He answered his cell and Wesley started talking. "I got her signed and she is ready to go."

"I'll be damn, Wesley. You are one smooth operator, buddy. I really thought she would be a hard sell."

"We are going to make a killing."

"Let me know if you need anything."

"Don, I'll call you if anything comes up."

Anita was holding court at Twelve Trees and the place was buzzing. Bankers, lawyers, doctors, and businessmen were flabbergasted. Doctor Browning had sold his house for three million dollars. The cell phones were going off as the news spread all over the county. Jim Kelly owned and developed Twelve Trees. He made it over to Anita's table the minute he heard the story.

"Anita, Justin just told me the Browning house sold for three million. Who was the buyer?"

"Kate Manley. She is moving in next week. My decorator has been hired to help furnish the home."

"My God, that's the woman who blew up her family in the press. They must have won the lottery."

"I signed a confidentiality agreement. I'm not at liberty to disclose anything, but the person taking title."

"I don't give a damn how it got paid for. This is going to blow the comps out the roof."

"Jim, you are right as rain. Let me buy you a drink and celebrate the new Littleville real estate market."

"Hell, let me buy you a bottle of champagne," Jim said.

Scooter was at his tanning business when he heard the news from a customer. After being assured there was no mistake, he called his mother in a panic.

"Mother, before you ask, I have not been drinking. Doctor Browning sold his house to Kate for three million dollars."

"The lucky bitch won the damn lottery, sure as hell. The first thing she does is run out and spends the money."

"Mother, she didn't win the lottery. The man who won the lottery is in today's paper."

"Where the hell would she get three million dollars?"

"She got more than that, Mother. The lady told me she gave the decorator a budget of five hundred thousand to furnish the house."

"The woman is pulling your leg, Scooter."

"The woman was told by the agent who sold the damn house. I have to run and meet Amanda."

"What the hell is going on, Scooter?"

"Someone dropped a boat load of money on Kate, Mother."

Florence was at the liquor store picking up some Jack Daniels. Doctor Browning and his wife, Susan, walked in to pick up a case of Crown Royal. Florence was standing behind them waiting to pay her bill. She had two fifths in one arm and her purse in the other. The owner, Hank Dooley, came out and greeted Doctor Browning and Susan.

"I heard you hit a home run, Robert."

"We have to be the luckiest people in the county. Anita came over and I told her I wanted two million, but wasn't ready to sell. She told us the buyer wanted in right away. I threw out a crazy price of three million and she took it. I had no idea Kate Manley had this kind of money."

Florence was taking in the conversation and boldly confronted the good Doctor. "Excuse me, Doctor Browning. Did you say Kate Manley paid you three million for your home?"

"Yes, do you know Kate?"

"I know a Kate Manley from Littleville. She couldn't buy a three million dollar house in ten lifetimes."

"It must be a different Manley. Kate and her husband Chuck live out on Waller Pike. They gave us a cashier's check for the three million. I told Anita we would sell for two million, but needed to build our new home first. They wanted it immediately and paid another million like it was a hundred dollars. Anita is bringing them over tomorrow to see the house. I have a moving company coming next week. Anita found us a house to live in until we build our new one."

Florence felt her knees buckle and when she came to Doctor Browning was kneeling over her. The Jack Daniels had splattered all over her.

"Are you alright?" Doctor Browning asked.

"I think I went into shock. I'll be okay now."

She gathered herself and left the store in a daze. Renee lived three blocks over. Florence pulled in the driveway and rushed to the front door. Renee opened the door and saw Florence, wild eyed and reeking with the smell of liquor.

"Are you on a drinking binge, Florence?"

"I need a drink in the worst way. I think I'm going to die, Renee."

"What the hell is going on, Florence? You can't come over here reeking of whiskey. Did you catch R.E. with another woman?"

"Renee, I wouldn't even care if I saw the old fool in bed with Myrtle Lee. I'm telling you, some hell is coming down. I don't know where it is coming from or how to get out of the way."

"Florence, you are scaring the hell out of me. I think you have gone overboard and drowned."

"Where did the bitch get three million dollars? Just tell me that and I'll calm down. Ain't any damn T.V. station pays you three million dollars for an interview!"

"Florence, I'm taking you to the emergency room. I don't know what they can do for you. You have lost your mind. Carol is not this messed up when she goes on a binge."

"Kate bought Doctor Browning's house for three million dollars. Where the hell did she get three million dollars?"

"Who told you that bullshit, Florence?"

"Doctor Browning and his wife, Susan, told me in the liquor store. I passed out cold. The bottles of Jack Daniels splattered all over me."

"She must have won the lottery. Let me look in the paper."

The phone was ringing and Florence answered. Renee had gone in the back to find the paper. Vicki had patched Emily in and they were both going crazy. Renee came out and looked at Florence.

"No. Some old man won the damn thing."

"Kate paid three million cash for a house. She sold the story to one of those trash magazines. We are going to be on every check out isle in America. Jake and I are finished!" Emily shouted.

"Pick up the other phone, Renee. Emily and Vicki are on the line. Emily said Kate sold our family story to the National Enquirer."

"Jesus, I think she has no shame," Renee said.

"Howard just came in. Let me ask him if he has heard anything."

Remember the story about the bad ears or lack of a brain? The sun had set and Howard had been looking at the stars. Vicki asked him if he had seen anything.

"I been looking up and seeing it in the stars. I've been asking the Lord to forgive me for all my sins. Everywhere I went; people were making fun of me."

"The story is in the Star Magazine. Howard said people have been making fun of him all day."

"They don't pay that kind of money. She must have sold the damn story to all of them," Renee said.

R.E. had just left Myrtle Lee and looked over as he passed Renee's house. He saw Florence's car and decided to pull in the driveway. He walked to the door and saw it was slightly open. He walked in and jumped when Florence yelled.

"Kate has nailed our ass again! She has our family on the front of the Star and Enquirer. People are going to be coming forward claiming to be our step sisters and brothers. Kate got all the damn money. We got nothing but an ass kicking. I should have told the story and got the money."

"Woman, have you lost your damn mind? You smell like a distillery, Florence!"

"Someone paid Kate three and a half million dollars, according to Scooter. Florence knows of three million for sure," Renee said.

"Luke Smith's boy works for the company that owns those rag sheets. I'm calling his ass right now. I think y'all are crazy," R.E. said. He went out on the front porch and placed his call.

"Sally just called on my other line. It isn't on the newsstands over here."

"I never should have told that girl she needed braces years ago. Kate has hated me ever since," Vicki said.

R.E. came back in with a big smile on his face. "They ain't paid her a dime. Luke said they don't give a damn about a bunch of Martin trash. They like them movie stars and their trash."

"Where did she get all that money? I wonder if Chuck may have stole some money from U.P.S.," Florence said.

"Damn, Florence, that boy carries packages to people's homes. They don't deliver money to anybody. We need to go get you a shower and me some food."

Renee was on the phone with Emily. "Emily, you are going to kill me. I told Kate the story of the ghost trying to play with you in the hotel room."

"I can't believe you have the nerve to call me a loudmouth. You have the biggest mouth in the whole damn state."

"I told her about Moose getting drunk and running the car through the fence. She swore she would never repeat it."

"You need to get a life, Renee. All you ever do is sit at home and gossip about other people. Jake is driving up. I have to go now."

"What have you told her about me?" Florence asked.

"I have not told her anything about you."

Well, with great anxiety, they all left and went their separate ways. Let me be the first to tell you. They had every right to be concerned. The Martin bunch had more skeletons in their closets than sand on a big beach. A time bomb was ticking and they all knew it.

The next morning, Anita drove over to pick up Kate. The dogs were barking and she called to say she was outside.

"I would have come to the door, but two dogs are trying to eat my car. I hope you don't mind, Kate."

"Stay right where you are and I'll be right out."

Anita looked and saw Kate open the screen door. "Get your sorry asses in this house right now," Kate screamed. The two dogs tucked their tails and went in the house. Anita could hear them howling as Kate gave them justice. Two minutes later, Kate walked out as though nothing had occurred.

"It is a pleasure to meet you, Kate."

"I'm glad to make your acquaintance, Anita."

"Are you looking forward to seeing your new house?"

"I hope it is bigger than this one."

"That's funny," Anita said.

Well, they drove over and came up the long driveway. Anita parked and started to get out. She noticed Kate was still sitting in the car. "Are you coming, Kate?"

"I'll just wait while you see these people. I ain't much for meeting new people."

"Kate, this is your new home."

"Jesus Christ, Wesley has gone and outdone himself. I didn't know they built houses this big."

"Mr. Arnold wanted you and Chuck to have the best home in town. That man doesn't let anything stand in his way."

They went in and the decorator, Doris Delaney, stood with Susan Browning. Everyone was introduced. Susan and Anita showed her every room in the house. Doris showed Kate what her thoughts were on furnishings.

"What do you think about the house?" Anita asked.

"It is more than I imagined in my wildest dream. I think I'm going to bust my ass for that boy. I'm going to talk more than a parrot on the loose. That Wesley doesn't have an ounce of bullshit about him. I told Chuck that boy was the real deal."

"Well, he certainly is the real deal. He dropped three million on me so fast, it made my head swim. Are you excited about having your own television show?"

"Anita, I don't know what the hell to think to be real honest with you. I told Wesley he better know what he has gotten himself in to. I don't know a damn thing about television."

"He has made quite an investment in you. He has given us a budget of five hundred thousand to furnish your home," Doris said.

"When does the show start? I can't wait to watch your show," Susan said.

"It is starting two months from yesterday, Susan. By the way, does your husband fix bad backs? Chuck has been walking around for weeks moaning and groaning. I need to get the man some relief."

"Kate, Robert doesn't operate on backs. He will be happy to recommend someone and set up an appointment for your husband."

"Chuck has been trying to see a doctor for three weeks, but can't get in. We don't know any doctors."

"I assure you, we will have Chuck in to see a Doctor tomorrow morning. I'll call Robert right now and have him set up an appointment."

"That's very nice of you, Susan. Listen, I don't want to be rude, but I need to get back home and feed my dogs."

"What kind of dogs do you have?"

"They used to be Dalmatians, but I've about whipped the spots off the hard headed fools."

Anita drove Kate home and Susan called her husband to arrange a visit for Chuck. The three women proceeded to inform everyone they knew Kate was going on national television. She had her own show and it was going to be filmed live from Littleville. Everybody pretty much knows each other in Littleville. It didn't take long for word to reach the Martin family. You would have thought someone had driven up with a hand full of rattlesnakes. Florence, R.E., Howard, and Vicki were at their favorite restaurant when the owner came over and gave them the news. Phillip Waters and his wife were excited about the prospect for new business coming from the show.

"Florence, I bet you and Vicki are excited as hell about your sister having her own show on television."

"Phillip, I'm in no mood to hear jokes about Kate. She had her five minutes of fame at our expense," Florence said.

"I can't believe none of you has heard the news. Wesley Arnold hired Kate to do her own show. It airs nationally in less than two months. I hope it is a huge success and people from all over the country come to our little town."

"Tell me you are pulling our leg, Phillip," Vicki said.

"I am dead serious, Vicki. The show is going to run in prime time for two hours a night. Anita said it will be on five nights a week. A crew is at the house building the studio. Doctor Browning and his wife are scrambling to get out."

"That's where she got all the money," R.E. said.

"Mr. Arnold paid three million for the house. He gave Kate another five hundred thousand to furnish it. He deeded it over to Kate free and clear. I was told on the Q.T. she is being paid millions. Your sister is a multi millionaire. I can't wait to see the show."

"Do she and her husband ever come in here?" Florence asked.

"No. However, I am making it my business to have her come in. I sent her word the food and drinks are on me."

R.E. and Howard got up and went in the men's room. Howard hadn't quite got the picture, but R.E. knew the shit was going to hit the fan. They stood at two separate urinals taking care of business when Howard started talking.

"Oh no! This is terrible," Howard said.

"You can bet your last dime it's terrible."

"This is just awful."

"It will be hell to pay, Howard."

"Someone has marked his spot and he didn't miss anything."

R.E. looked at the floor and shook his head. "Some ass came in here and was three sheets to the wind. Howard, get your fly closed and let's get back to the girls."

Florence and Vicki were talking nonstop about the fallout from Kate's show. "The damn woman is going to tell it all," Vicki said.

"Renee has a mouth bigger than a hippo. We have to assume anything we ever told her got to Kate."

"I'll be ruined if she talks about Fred."

"Fred is dead, Vicki. A dead man can't talk. You better be worried about Rory. He is liable to come back when he hears about the show. The man has always sworn Sarah was his daughter."

"How could this have possibly happened to us? Are you worried about Floyd Murray?"

"The man is a Congressman, Vicki. He ain't going to open his mouth. Emily is the one who's going to be in deep shit. Old Jake can kiss his shinny ass goodbye. When she starts telling the stories on Emily our windows will be shaking. Hush, the men are coming back. Maybe I can shame Phillip into giving us a free meal and desert."

Jimmy and Scooter were having a beer at Treetop Hill Bar when they heard the news. They looked at each other and shook their heads.

"I may as well start stealing all the money from the tanning business. Amanda is going to show my ass the door."

"I know what you mean, Scooter. Shirley is about ready to pack her bags. I can live with her leaving. I'm worried about kids popping up everywhere. The women will think I have money and start talking."

"I don't know why you would worry about that business. You got clipped years ago."

"It hasn't been that many years ago."

"Man, Kate is going to drop the dime on us."

"I know Renee has some trash on Kate. We need to get over to her house and get the scoop. Maybe we can drop the dime on her ass and she will leave us out of the show."

"Jimmy, who is Renee going to tell? Kate has the damn show and we have nothing but the short end of the stick."

They decided to give it a shot and headed over to see Renee. Carol and Anne were already there with the bad news. Sarah was driving up when Scooter pulled in with Jimmy. She got of her car and looked at her brother.

"Scooter, I just got the news."

"Why does this kind of shit always come to our doorstep?" Scooter asked.

"Henry told me it is all the talk at Channel Four. Wesley Arnold is telling the trade journals he is spending a hundred million dollars to promote the show."

"Kate is going to tell every family secret. I don't know whether to shit or go blind," Jimmy said.

They all went to the door and Carol answered. She was so messed up on drugs her eyes were crossed. Renee sounded like a cow being branded inside.

"Come on in," Carol mumbled.

They came in as Anne was holding court. "I just passed by Kate's house and there must be ten cars over there. There has to be thirty cars and trucks at the Browning house. The workers are building a huge brick fence around the property."

"Morris told me his boss said Arnold has rented two thousand billboards from his company. They are going up in three weeks across the country," Carol said.

"They probably have a picture of Kate shooting us the bird," Renee said.

"Arnold has blocked commercial time on every network. Henry told me he has never seen anything like it except for the super bowl."

"Sarah, Kate knows about the shootout at the motel. She told me you were in the room romping with some married shit head named Jeff. I swear to God I didn't tell her."

"I'm getting the hell out of this place before the show starts. Her goofy ass son knows every man I've ever been with. The damn hockey player from New York will come looking for me," Anne said.

"Emily just found out and she is coming over tomorrow morning. She is going to give Kate a piece of her mind. Emily can whip her ass and she is ready to do just that," Renee said.

"Emily better keep her loud mouth away from Kate. She is going to find herself drinking through a straw. I saw Kate kick the living hell out of a two hundred pound woman in Kroger's one day," Jimmy said.

"That's not such a bad idea, Jimmy. I'm hauling my little ass down to West Palm and staying with Aunt Faith and Don," Carol said.

"You are in your dreams. Johnny is going to leave me when he hears all these terrible things about me."

"Howard's stories are going to have old men all over the county getting divorces at eighty," Jimmy said.

"I'm more worried about the stories on my mother coming out in the open. Renee, don't you have some trash on Kate?" Scooter asked.

"You bet your ass I know plenty on her big mouth. The problem is I can't use it, Scooter. She knows five times more on me."

They all left and headed back to their homes and businesses. Depression would have been much to light a term too describe their feelings. The clock was ticking and they all knew the bombs were going to start falling. The Martin kids knew their mother was smiling down from Heaven. Wild Buck was taking it all in from the place down below. He had an even bigger smile as he waited for the show to unfold.

CHAPTER SEVENTEEN

Wesley Arnold and his staff were working around the clock. He had cut a deal with every cable operator in the world. He was betting the farm, giving every cable operator ninety days at no charge to air his network. The Wes-Star network was the talk of the industry. The buildup to the launch of the network was unprecedented in the history of television. A month before the launch, the billboards went up. Two weeks prior, the spots started airing on television with clips of the Channel Four interview. The late night talk shows were having a field day running the clips. Wesley was back in Littleville with Kate.

Wesley had hired Tom Kerry, a veteran of twenty years as her sidekick. The show was set to air Monday night and everything was set to go. It was Friday afternoon and Wesley and Kate sat down for a visit.

"Kate, we are rounding up guests for the show. Are you getting on with Tommy okay?"

"That boy is nice as he can be, Wesley. He has been explaining everything to me about how all this is going to work. All of your people are really nice."

"I'm really pumped up about the show. Everyone loves you, Kate."

"Wesley, I assure you not everyone loves me. I been getting word my so called family is mad as hell. I could do the whole damn show talking about their screwed up asses."

"I'm sure you could, Kate. You just be yourself and say what's on your mind. I'll be right here with you for the first week."

"My sister Faith and her husband called to wish us good luck. Don told me the show is going to be a smash hit."

"Man, I'd sure like to see that dude in a courtroom. I've been told he will blow your mind."

"Wesley, we would have to slip you in the courtroom. I never saw so many half dressed women in my life. These women fight and claw for a seat in court when he's there. The men haul ass for another state when he shows up."

"Is he a ladies man, Kate?"

"The boy is straight as an arrow, Wesley. He is crazy in love with Faith. Let me tell you that don't stop those bitches from wishing.

There ain't enough hours in a day for that boy to service all the women after his ass. If you want to blow your numbers up, just get Don in here one night. Every damn woman in the country will be glued to the show."

"That's a damn good idea. Is anything exciting happening with your family these days?"

"It's just the same old shit, Wesley. The girls are cheating on the husbands. The whole bunch is popping pills and smoking dope. The cops have a warrant out for Carol. Anne met a bank robber and knocked him through the wall when she found him cheating with some gal. They're all scared shitless about the show."

"Well, I have to fly down to New Orleans to promote the show. I'll be back Monday morning and I'll see you and Chuck then."

"I'll make us up a mess of turnip greens and peas with a roast."

"That sounds great, Kate. I'll see you at noon on Monday."

"Wesley, I sure hope this works out for you."

"Thanks for saying that, Kate. I have no doubt we will have the number one show on television in no time flat."

Wesley left and got in the limo for the ride to the airport. Don was in his jet on the way to Boston to try a case. The cell phone rang and Wesley answered. "Don't you ever get tired of flying around the country in your jet?"

"I get tired of trying cases. Do you still feel we have a home run with Kate?"

"This woman is going to make us more money than we can count."

"Have a safe trip to New Orleans, buddy. I'll talk to you tomorrow."

Don hung up and placed a call to Ben in Littleville. Ben's secretary passed him through immediately. "Don, how are you my friend?"

"I'm fine, Ben. I wanted to thank you for taking care of the zoning for the show. Wesley and I are both indebted to you."

"It was my pleasure, Don. I hope the show is a big success."

"I'm holding my breath, but Wesley says it will be a huge success. Thanks again, Ben."

"Don, don't hesitate to call if you need anything."

Well, I hate to be the smart ass that said I told you. But, if you thought the new rules at Littleville City Hall applied to Ben, you think rocks grow. The chances of the house not getting the required zoning were about the same as Hillary Clinton becoming a conservative republican.

Emily had driven over and she and Renee sat discussing the future. Johnny was in the back room making phone calls with the door closed. They were both in full blown panic mode.

"Johnny is going to walk out of my life when Kate tells the stories on me. I have no one to blame but myself. Why did I have to open my mouth and tell her everything?"

"If I weren't a good Christian, I would shoot her right between the eyes. If it hadn't been for that dang Scooter getting me drunk and talking at the reunion, Kate might have never known."

"Did you tell her about being caught naked at the drive in?"

"Yes, and I told her about daddy catching me and Billy Ray in the bedroom when we lived on Nothing Lane. Billy Ray is in prison now for fifty years to life. My Lord, if she tells that story I'm a cooked goose."

"I told her things that were even worse about me. Do you remember when Harry Freed shot Blake at the intersection?"

"What has that got to do with you, Renee?"

"I was having a fling with Blake and Harry at the same time. Harry found out and went gunning for poor Blake."

"Harry shot Blake over you?"

"Yes and all the cops in town know about it. I know that damn Joan is still feeding Kate all the trash."

"We just didn't have a chance, Renee. We inherited the sex genes from daddy and took off looking for action."

Emily looked over and almost fell out of her chair. A man was standing buck naked and hunching the wall. He had a towel over his head and was going to town. She started kicking Renee under the table.

"Emily, stop kicking me."

"Look over my right shoulder," Emily whispered.

Renee looked up and saw the man. She thought it was Johnny and jumped up from the chair. "Johnny, what in the hell do you think your doing?"

The man took off through the back door with nothing on, but the towel over his head. Johnny came in from the back room and looked at Renee. "Why are you screaming my name?"

Emily and Renee were both pointing to the back door. "A naked man was standing there hunching the wall," Renee said.

Johnny took off after the man and caught him trying to get in his car a block from the house. He knocked him to the ground and called the police. Within less than two minutes, they arrived and arrested the fool. Joan was listening to the police scanner and called Kate with the story.

"Kate, here's a good one for your show. Renee's old boyfriend decided to pay her and Emily an unannounced visit today. The fool showed up naked and Johnny ran him down. He is in the county jail booked on indecent exposure."

"Which one was it?"

"It was Paul Grisham, of all people. His old man is going to shoot his fat ass."

"He must have walked into one of those propellers at the airport. I got to go and fix Chuck something to eat."

"I heard Wesley hired Herb and five off duty policemen to guard your house. Do you feel like a big shot?"

"I feel like the luckiest mother on earth. I'm telling you that damn Wesley is hot as a pepper."

"Lord, don't tell me you got a thing for the boy."

"Bite your tongue, you old fool."

Time just flies when you don't want it to. The family felt like the mortgage payment was coming due every five days. Monday's prime time show was starting in ten minutes. Wesley was not happy with the results of the earlier shows on Wes-Star. He was a nervous wreck looking at a hundred million dollars going down the tube. The Martin clan was just as nervous for a different reason. Florence was drunk as a skunk as she sat with R.E., Vicki, and Howard. Amanda and her family sat down with Scooter. Sarah was grateful Henry was at the station. Emily and Jake sat with their family in Lilleyville.

Carol and Anne had come over to Renee's. Jimmy and Shirley were joined by Jimmy's former wives. Joan and Elmer had Herb and his wife over for the show. Beverly couldn't get over tossing Bobby Jack and didn't give a damn what Kate had to say. Her brother was a straight arrow and wasn't the least bit worried about any trash coming his way.

Wesley was no fool and had the callers loaded with the right questions to turn Kate loose. Tom Kerry was on the set with Kate keeping everyone loose. The cameras were rolling now as Kate sat with Tom.

The music came blasting as the lights went on. The announcer came over the air. "Live from Littleville, it's the show the world's been waiting on. 'Straight Talk with Kate in Littleville' is on the air."

"Good evening from Littleville. I'm Tom Kerry and I have the pleasure of being Kate's sidekick. This is the show you have all been waiting for. Straight Talk with Kate in Littleville is on the air. Kate Manley, say hello to our audience."

"Hi everybody, I'm sure glad y'all have chosen to tune in tonight. Listen, I hope y'all like the show. I'm a plain spoken woman and I call it like I see it. You call me on our dime and I'll tell you what I think. There ain't nothing to be ashamed of with your family. I got the most messed up bunch of fools in the country. Your family couldn't be more messed up than mine."

"We are ready for our first caller. Call toll free 1-800-444-4444. Our first caller is on the line from Bowling Green, Kentucky," Tom said.

"Honey, fire away with your question," Kate said.

"Kate, this is Harold Ford. Did your father really have forty-three children?"

"Harold, he had forty-three that I know about. The old drunk traveled for a record company and he might have had even more. There are eight of us that are legit in the purest sense."

"How on earth did he manage to keep the other women from knowing?"

"Harold, like I said a minute ago, the old fool was a drunk. He didn't give a shit if the sun came up. From everything I know, the women all knew about each other. I guess they were all brain dead like him. I can't tell you how many times he almost bought the farm. The son-of-a-bitch invented the word alcoholic. Three different times, he came home all beat to shit. One of the women's brothers tossed him through a window at a bar one night. He was a bootlegger of some renown. The way I heard it, he out ran a dozen state policemen one night up in your neck of the woods."

"Man, your daddy was unbelievable. He must hold the record for fathering the most kids."

"He damn sure holds the record for the most drunks, Harold."

"Thanks Harold, our next call comes from Baton Rouge, Louisiana. Wanda Franklin, you are live with Kate," Tom said.

"Kate, I just got kicked out of my country club. I don't think I did anything to deserve it."

"What the hell did you do, Wanda?"

"I was playing with three women in the club championship. They were all big fat bitches and had no sense of humor. One of them hit a good shot down the middle of the fairway. I told her, 'Good shot, Pork Chop.' They started glaring at me like I slapped them with a wet towel. I told them I was paying her a compliment. You know, right down the middle is called a center cut. They told the management I called her a pig and they kicked me out."

"Honey, how big are you?"

"I'm five foot five and weight one hundred and seven pounds."

"Honey, I don't know anything about golf. I see where you are coming from, but fat asses are real sensitive. I called a woman a lard ass one day in the grocery store and had to whip her ass. If I were you, I'd find me another club where the bitches don't live. Wanda, they probably haven't gotten any in twenty years and you know how that goes. You might want to start saying good shot and leave it at that. A little thing like you needs to be careful around those hogs."

"My husband said the same thing. He said all the men at the club loved the story. Women are just bitches."

"I hate to admit this to the audience because I'm a woman. You are right as rain when it comes to women. I just think they need more sex. You know what I mean? It's like Toby says in his song; 'A little less talk and a lot more action.' I got to take the next call."

"Our next call comes from Portland, Oregon. Emmett Welch, you are live with Kate," Tom said.

"Thanks for taking my call. I have a real bad complex from the way I grew up. My daddy was a former Special Forces man. He was just meaner than hell and always kicking our ass. My big brother thought he could take him on one night. He got right in the old man's face and told him he was going to kick his ass. It was just awful and I'm still carrying the scars."

"Damn, Emmett! What the hell happened?"

"My father put down his paper and looked my brother in the eye. My brother was standing there all bowed up and ready to get it on. I'll never forget what he said to my brother.

"What the hell did he say, Emmett?"

He said, "Boy, I'm gonna fuck you up."

"Who got the ass whipping, Emmett?"

"My poor brother got his ass hauled off to the hospital. I ain't been the same since I saw it. I was too scared to move an inch."

"Emmett, if you can't run with the big dogs, you have to stay on the porch. There ain't anything wrong with staying on the porch. Hell, look at it this way, Emmett. Millions of people pay to watch the fights on pay per view. They don't feel bad at all watching the action. You don't have anything to feel bad about, son. Your ass would have been in the ambulance too, if you opened your mouth."

"Kate, my poor brother walked around drinking through a straw for three months. His jaw was wired shut."

"I bet his ass was wired shut too. Emmett, there ain't nothing quite like a bad ass whipping to give a person religion. You get those negative thoughts out of your head. Just be glad you had enough sense to stay on the porch."

The show broke for commercials and Wesley was beaming. The Martin's were holding their breath. Across the world, people were dumbfounded. The phones were lighting up as friends called each other. In Orlando, Sue Martin called her best friend Julie Washington, in Kansas City.

"Julie, turn on channel 229 right now. It's the new Wes-Star channel and you will not believe this chick. I'll call you back after the show. This is the best shit I've ever seen in my life," Sue said.

"Frank is watching some damn sports show. I'll watch it in the bedroom."

The show came back on and Tom took the call. "From New York City, we have Kenny Arthur."

"Kate, I love the hell out of your show. I experienced something similar to Emmett as a youngster. My brother was a piece of work and full of himself. One morning at breakfast, he plopped his smart ass down at the table. He looked my father in the eye and told him if he ever opened his mouth again, he would call child services. He told him if he dared lay a hand on him, he would put his big ass in jail."

"That was a very bad move on your brother's part."

"Kate, I'll never get over what happened next. The old wall phone was next to my dad with the cord hanging down. The man didn't seem especially upset at first. The next thing we knew, he reached over and took the phone off the wall. He threw the damn thing and hit my brother square on the temple. My brother was out cold and slid down the chair."

"What did your father say to him?"

He said, "Don't wait. Call the mother fuckers right now, dip shit."

"That boy wasn't in any shape to call anybody."

"Kate, he looked at me and my other brother. He just calmly said, 'I think it would be a good idea for you boys to eat your breakfast now.' No one ever threatened to call anyone again. I assure you, we were eating like we hadn't had a meal in a week. It was almost surreal to eat watching someone knocked out and slid down in a chair. I didn't stop eating until there wasn't a crum left."

"Thanks for sharing your story, Kenny. I think it's pretty safe to say your brother got religion that morning. If he didn't, I'm sure he is in a graveyard somewhere. My boy popped off to me one time. The next pop was me upside his stupid head. He ain't run his big mouth again to his mother in fifteen years."

Our next caller comes to us from Big D, Dallas, Texas. Hoyt Robbins, you are on the air with Kate Manley," Tom said.

"What have you got cooking, Hoyt?"

"Kate, have you ever seen a stone cold drunk go instantly sober?"

"Hoyt, I can't say that I ever have."

"My best friend was a bad drunk. He was on drugs as well. Bottom line was, his children were being neglected. His mother was not happy about the situation. One night, we were in a bowling alley and his momma came in after finding the children alone."

"I bet I know where you're going with this story."

"Well, she walked right up to Larry and they exchanged words. The next thing we knew, she reached in her purse and pulled out a pistol. She proceeded to stick the gun in his mouth. She told him if she ever found those kids not being taken care of, his ass was grass. I swear on my life, the man was instantly dead sober. His teeth kept hitting the barrel of the gun and he was shaking from head to toe."

"Good for her and everyone like her. If I found my grandkids left alone, there wouldn't be a second chance. I'd smoke my kid's ass on the spot. Hoyt, we need to stop with all the bullshit. If I was the person in charge, I'd cut the nuts off every child molester in the world before I beat the sorry perverts to death. These chicken shit judges and politicians ought to be run out of the country. We need to treat these bastards like we would a mad dog. I say, 'put their sorry asses to sleep for good.'"

"I couldn't agree more."

"Our next caller joins us all the way from London. Sandra Roberts, you are up late tonight."

"I saw your film clips for the show. I wasn't going to miss this for anything. Kate, I want to hear the story of the boy running into your house."

"Sandra, it was not an enjoyable evening. My husband left for work and I was calling it a night. I heard a lot of racket and looked out to see a woman chasing a man on foot. She was driving an old van and screaming at the top of her lungs. The next thing I knew, the man was chasing the woman. She was running and he was in the van. Long story short, the next time I looked, they were both in the van and heading straight for my house. It was my damn sister's son and the boy was wasted on drugs. I got my baseball bat and went outside but every dog in town was on the scene."

"Did the fool run into your house on purpose?"

"Sandra, the boy didn't even know a house was in Littleville. He's a drug addict like the rest of her kids. You don't even want to get me started on those freaks."

"Oh, but I do want to hear about the woman and her kids."

"Honey, I don't know if we have enough time tonight. Let me just put it this way and we can move on. One of her kids shot the bird to the cameras on statewide T.V. after being busted. She thinks she is a bad ass and is always busting some man upside the head. Another one writes more false scripts than the druggist. The boy thinks he lives on Mars and the mother runs her mouth about the whole family. My brother in law has more clout than the U.S. Army and keeps their asses out of jail."

"Wow, which one is the brother in law with the clout?"

"He is the one and only Don Hudson, Sandra. Have you ever heard of the boy?"

"Of course, I've heard of him. He has never lost a case. God, is he as good looking in person as he is on television?"

"Honey, the damn boy ought to be declared illegal he is so handsome. Women go crazy when he is around them. You have to see the shit to believe it."

The show cut to more commercials and the people tracking the viewers were all talking. It seems every fifteen minutes the audience was growing larger.

Renee, Carol, and Anne were having a fit. "I should call that bitch on live television and give her a piece of my mind," Renee said.

"I don't think that is a good idea," Johnny said.

"Aunt Kate is having a field day at my expense," Anne said.

"That bitch is going to get me put in prison. Everyone knows who she is talking about. I ought to shoot my brother for running into her house," Carol said.

"I can't believe you can't trust your own damn sister. If I ever get on that show, I'm telling her off."

"Renee, you don't ever want to find yourself on Kate's show," Johnny said.

The older ones sat in the living room watching and hoping for the best. The men were expecting the worse and the women were holding their breath.

"I wish Daddy was here to kick her ass. Imagine telling a tale that my dead father has forty three children," Florence said.

"Where in the name of God does she come up with this trash? I know for a fact he only had thirty six," Vicki said.

"Do you know about Ginger Rangel?" R.E. asked.

"Buck had four with her, Vicki," Howard said.

"How would you know that, Howard?"

"Her daughter told me to my face back when I was a sinner."

"That old bitch used to run me to death at school. I always wondered why she hated me," Florence said.

The show was back on the air with a caller from Jackson, Mississippi. "Larry Toms, you are live with Kate from Littleville," Tom said.

"Kate, I just got off a jury hearing an armed robbery case. I thought you would get a kick out of the story."

"I was called for jury duty once myself, Larry. I told the man with the government I was going to hang the defendant. I was home cooking supper an hour later. Go ahead and lay the story on us."

"Two men were planning on robbing the Seven-Eleven store. The cops were tipped off and laid waiting behind the door. Sure enough, the two men came in and went into high gear. The cops shot one and arrested the second. It was a pretty open and shut case and we had all made our minds up. The officers testified they raised their guns and told the men to halt in the name of the law. When the defendant took the stand it was just so funny you had to laugh. His attorney took him through the night of the robbery. The robbery occurred on Christmas night. The man was incredibly honest and admitted everything. Then, he got to the officers statements about halt in the name of the law. He looked all of us in the eye and started to speak. "I pretty much have to say everything the officers said was the truth. They did rise up and point their guns at Herbert and me. They damn sure started shooting and killed poor Herbert. But, I remember them both saying; Merry Christmas mother-fuckers."

"You know damn well that S.O.B. was telling the truth, Larry. Did y'all cut the man any slack?"

"No. We gave him the maximum sentence. But, I'll tell you one thing, Kate. If it had come down to what the officers shouted we would have walked his ass. Even the District Attorney buried his head in his hands."

"I would have come to the same conclusion myself. Well, at least the old boy can tell the story to everyone in the state pen."

"Our next called comes to us from Clovis, New Mexico. Samantha Welch say hello to Kate Manley."

"Kate, I almost got my ass kicked out of my damn country club. What the hell is wrong with these damn stiff ass bitches?"

"Honey, what the hell did you do to almost find the door?"

"I was playing golf with three women I didn't know and made a joke. The club has a bad ass hole, and I hated to play it. All I said was I'd rather give a blow job than play the hole."

"Honey, I told the lady earlier I have never played golf. You must have been hooked up with a bunch of right wing Christians. I got a damn sister married to a preacher and they are the worst. They don't fool old Kate for one second. Can you believe the woman rode down the interstate naked as a jay bird one night? The preacher didn't know whether to shit or go blind, the way she told it. Different strokes for different folks I guess. They almost got their ass caught by the cops. Now, wouldn't have that little story have goosed the locals."

"My husband said the same thing, Kate. The next time we played, he told me to pick up my ball and not to worry about it. He said to get in the cart and he would be thrilled to give me a hole in one."

"No shit. The man ought to buy you the damn golf cart. Take some advice from old Kate. Don't ever sell yourself short when it comes to a blow job, baby. Men will give away anything they have for a damn good blow job. Tell your man to keep the hole in one and toss you the keys to a new convertible. Watch how fast he carries his ass to the car dealership."

"I'll give it a shot and let you know what happens."

"Save your dime, baby. I already know what is going to happen. Tell your friends about the show if it's not too much trouble. Wesley has dropped a boat load trying to make this work."

"Kate, I'm calling everyone I know."

Emily looked over at Jake and he was white as a sheet. The grown kids didn't say a word and Emily was about to spit. The show came to an end and the Wes-Star phones lit up in New York.

The next morning, Wesley and Kate were having breakfast. Wesley was one happy man as he looked at the ratings. "Kate, we got off to a great start last night. The audience doubled the second hour of your show. I couldn't be happier."

"I've been really worried about you losing your money, Wesley."

"Everything is coming along better than I thought it would. It takes a while for people to tune in. You were great last night."

"Hell, I have to tell you I enjoyed it myself. I thought this was going to be a little scary."

"It will be a walk in the park for you."

"I never knew so many women played golf. I'm going to buy me a book and study up on it. I got two calls last night about golf. I don't like sitting here telling the people I don't know anything about it."

"Kate, people love your straight talk. You don't have to know a thing about golf. The office in New York is telling me the folks out there want to hear all about the Martin family. Are you comfortable spending a couple of nights talking about them?"

"Wesley, they talk about me everyday. You bet your ass I'll tell the truth about them."

"Okay, I'll run the commercials starting tonight. We will do Friday night's show on the family."

Well, when the Martin bunch saw the commercial, they fell into sheer panic. R.E. was even willing to spend his hard earned money. He called Ben and tried to hire him to stop the show. Ben got a good laugh and told him to save his money. He gently as possible tried to explain you could not stop the truth from being told. It took less than thirty minutes for every Martin to hear the story. Needless to say, everyone in Littleville was watching the show. It was come to Jesus time and they all had to fess up to the past. Jimmy decided to let the chips fall where they landed and told Shirley nothing. Scooter and Sarah came to the same conclusion. Renee and Emily decided it was best to come clean. The older generation came to a mixed conclusion. Emily asked Jake to sit down and started with the bad news.

"Jake, I've been told Kate is going to spill the beans on the whole family. I want you to know that I've never cheated on you in all our years of marriage. However, I did in fact, have a wild side before we met."

"Emily, what are you trying to say?"

"I had a bad habit of getting caught naked. It happened three different times and I fear Kate is going to talk about it."

"Are you telling me you were caught naked with three different men?"

"I was caught with two different boys, Jake. The cops got me at the drive-in movie once. Daddy caught me in my bedroom once. The worst was in the parking lot at school one night after the game."

"The deacons are going to kick us both out of the church. I will be publicly humiliated all over the world. My life as a preacher is over, Emily."

"Sally and I rented the xxx video, Jake. I'm sorry I lied to you about it."

"Emily, you had sex in front of the whole high school. Everyone in town has to know about it."

"Well, if it is any consolation to you, the boy is in prison for life."

Well, needless to say, Jake was not having a good day. He got up and left the room. Renee was having her truth session with Johnny at the same time.

"Johnny, I guess you know by now Kate is going to drop the hammer on all of us Friday night. I hate to have to tell you all the bad things I've done. I can't bear the thought of you hearing my past on national television."

"You haven't done anything that I haven't done. I don't care if you had other men before me. Frankly, Kate is the least of my worries."

Renee was greatly relieved and called Florence when Johnny left. It seems R.E. had spilled the beans about his past. Howard had nothing left to tell and Vicki clammed up. Florence was way too smart to tell about her dark past.

"Florence, Johnny didn't want to hear anything about my past. I'm still a wreck thinking of all the things Kate could say about me."

"The little son-of-a-bitch I'm married too has been screwing half the women in town. I got the bastard right where I want him,

Renee. The sleazy little devil was running wide open with Howard all these years."

"Florence, I never wanted to tell you about the affairs. You are my sister and I couldn't stand the thought of hurting you. He claims the reason he ran women was he couldn't get any from you."

"The no good liar is full of shit. Where does he think Morgan and Beverly came from? Are you telling me he has been running his mouth all these years about other women?"

"I'm afraid that is exactly what I'm telling you."

"I'm going to bleed that tight wad dry."

"Are you going to leave him?"

"He ain't got any money, Renee. Like I said, I'm going to bleed his ass dry. The first thing I'm going to do is get me a new car."

Howard was out in the back yard playing with his two coon dogs. The phone rang and Vicki answered. The man's voice sounded very familiar.

"Vicki, I just wanted you to know, I told Kate about Sarah. I left my wife and you should have left Howard," Rory said.

"Rory, have you lost your damn mind. Kate is doing a show on national television now."

"I know, all my friends in Chicago are watching it. It is past time for Sarah to know the truth about which man her real father is, Vicki."

"Rory, you are not Sarah's father. I was having an affair with Miles Lane and he is her real father."

"You can't fool me, woman. I slipped a DNA sample from Sarah and I am her father. I've done quite well financially, I'm happy to say. It is past time Sarah enjoyed a better life."

"Rory, why the hell are you doing this after forty two years? My God, we are seventy five years old."

"I needed to step up and make it right before I kick the bucket. I saw what happened with Bobby Jack and I'm not going to stand by for another day. Sarah deserves to be wealthy and enjoy the rest of her life."

"I am hanging up, Rory. My husband is coming in the house. Please don't call here again."

"I'm calling Sarah when we hang up," Rory said.

Vicki hung up and took off like a bat out of hell for Florence's house. Howard looked up and she was long gone. Florence looked out the window and saw Vicki as she came in the driveway. She nearly jumped out of the car and made a mad dash for the front door. Florence opened the door and Vicki stood white as a ghost.

"I have big trouble, Florence."

"That damn Rufus has admitted to all his women. It turns out Wayne didn't come close to getting all the names."

"Rory called Kate and told her Sarah was his child. The son-of-a-bitch called me and told me he had proof she was his child. He claims he is rich and wants Sarah to have a better life."

"I always thought that boy was going to do well. Beverly blew her chance with Bobby Jack and now Sarah is going to be rich. You should leave Howard and run to Rory."

"I'm having a fit, Florence. How the hell am I supposed to tell Sarah? Kate is coming from one direction and Rory from the other."

"Have a drink and calm down woman. If that damn Rufus had money I'd fly my big ass out the door."

"What am I going to do, Florence?"

"I told you what to do, woman. Take the money and haul ass with Rory."

"I can't leave Howard after fifty five years. The man has turned his life around."

The old gals proceeded to get drunker than hell. When old Rufus came home, he found them both passed out and called Howard. Howard took the news very well as R.E. explained he had confessed.

"I'm at fault for breaking the news to Florence. She must have called Vicki for support and they got into the Jack Daniels."

"I didn't have anything left to tell. I'll drive over and bring her home. Let me feed my dogs and I'll be over."

"Let them both sleep it off, Howard. I'll come over and we can play a game of cards and talk about the old times."

Don and Faith sat down for dinner at the country club. Faith was uptight and felt all the people staring at them. The local newspaper had carried an article about Kate's show and mentioned Faith as being a sister. The first nights had been a huge success and the press was all over the story.

Finally, after fifteen minutes, four women approached the table. "Please excuse our rudeness, Mr. and Mrs. Hudson. We are all huge fans of your sister. May we please ask if it would be possible for you to get her autograph for us? We would all be most happy to make a donation to the charity of your choice," Tracy Lewis said.

"You like Kate's show?" Faith asked.

"Like it? We love it," Martha said.

"I'm sure Kate would be pleased to sign an autograph for all of you. I will call her tomorrow."

They left their names and apologized once again. Don looked at Faith and smiled. "Your sister is going to have the number one show on television."

"Are you ever wrong about anything? I thought you were crazy when you told me she was going to be bigger than anything on television."

"Faith, what do you know about the man that founded Wes-Star?"

"I know he is rich and made his fortune in radio."

"Yes, he certainly did. He started with the shirt on his back. Wesley is the smartest executive I've ever met."

"How do you know the man?"

"We went to law school together. The man worked two jobs putting himself through school. I always told Wesley I wanted to be his first investor."

"What are you telling me, Don?"

"I was Wesley's first investor in the radio station in Nashville. I never took a penny out of the deal. We were doing great with the law practice and I just let it ride. Everybody else cashed out along the way. Wesley told me I would always have first shot with anything he did. We have been close friends for sixteen years."

"You never cease to amaze me, Don Hudson. I guess the next thing you are going to tell me is you own part of Wes-Star."

"Yes, my dear, we most certainly do. A very nice piece of the company, thanks to Wesley."

"I knew something was going on when you were not upset with Kate's interview. You always have that look on your face when you smell money. How long have you known about Wesley doing the show?"

"Let me answer the question this way, Faith. We talk every day."

CHAPTER EIGHTEEN

A lot of strange things were starting to happen in Littleville and the surrounding counties. The Friday show on the family was tonight and Carol was at her wits end. The girl liked her drugs and suddenly, you couldn't buy anything. Morris had just returned empty handed after trying to find his drug dealers. He broke the news to Carol, but she already knew.

"Every drug dealer I ever bought from has disappeared off the planet. I can't even get a joint for God sakes. Kate's damn T.V. show has all of them scared to death," Carol said.

"Why are they scared of Kate?"

"The damn bitch is going to talk about me tonight."

"Hell, she doesn't know the names of our drug dealers."

"Morris, you pop pills with her damn son every week. Do you think he doesn't know the names of the dealers? When she starts in on me, all hell is going to break loose, you fool."

"My momma said she never misses the show, Carol."

"Your momma and every one in the damn country are watching the show. She is going to fry the entire family's ass. Morris, I may be checking out of town permanently."

"What does that mean, Carol?"

"It means my little ass is long gone, Morris."

I can assure you the sentiment was shared by everyone in the family. Sarah had gotten a strange phone call at work. The man told her she needed to know the truth about something very important. She stood to inherit a large sum of money and he needed to meet face to face. He told her to come alone, but to feel free to name the time and place. He even told her it was okay to have Herb and another policeman at the next table. It was kind of like the old T.V. show, with Mr. Tipton. You were going to get a lot of money, but you couldn't tell anybody. If you told anyone, you had to give the money back. Anyway, she didn't tell anyone and arranged to meet the man on Saturday. Vicki was on the verge of mental breakdown thinking about Rory exposing her. Jake had pretty much resigned himself to being humiliated and kicked out of the church. Emily and Renee were prepared for the worst. Jimmy couldn't figure out why Kate was on his ass. They had always been close, and suddenly without warning she wanted to talk about all his women.

It was show time as the clock hit eight o'clock Friday night in Littleville. Kate sat with Tom as the show was announced. The cameras were on and Tom started his usual routine.

"Welcome back for two hours of fun with the one and only Kate Manley. Tonight, we will focus on the Martin family. Kate, as you all know, is a full fledged Martin herself. The phone lines are open and we have our first guest of the evening. "Gordon Harris, from Denver, Colorado you are live with Kate in Littleville."

"Kate, I want to know the scoop on the niece that writes more false scripts than the druggist who writes the legit ones. My brother has his hands full with one of his daughters doing drugs."

"Gordon, the girl has spent time in jail. She runs in and out of rehab on a regular basis. I guess she ran out of pills and got the bright idea to become a pharmacist. The trouble was, she ain't got a degree and got her some pads made up. She finally got caught when the druggist called the doctor to verify he was writing the scripts. The doctor didn't even know the girl. She had him writing thirty one scripts. The cops busted her ass and off to jail she went. I'll be damn if she didn't turn right around and do it again three days after she got out."

"Did she have to do hard time, Kate?"

"Gordon, she's out walking the streets. Around here, it is all about who you know. I ain't any fool, Gordon. I'm not calling names because I really like living, if you know what I mean. I got a crazy ass boy who does that shit himself. He never comes around me when he is on the crap. He learned his lesson the hard way one night years ago. I kicked his ass from one end of the block to the other. Chuck, my husband, took his beat up ass down to the emergency room."

"Wow, she walked on two separate felony counts?"

"Gordon, they never even indicted her ass. She got her ass hauled down to the jail and the next thing we knew she was free as a bird."

"Maybe she rolled over on the drug dealers."

"Gordon, you can buy a joint at a drive thru window in this town. All these crazy asses smoke pot non stop. I keep my ass at home. If you go to a restaurant, every server is messed up on dope. The damn former Mayor is serving a three hundred year sentence. Carol wouldn't have anyone to roll over on. The cops know every drug dealer in the county."

Carol watched with Morris at their house. She stood up and walked to the television set. She turned it off and headed for the bedroom to pack. "That's it; my ass is out of here."

"Where are you going, Carol?"

"Morris, I will not be seeing your ass again. It's been nice knowing you, but I need to move on to greener pastures."

"Are you leaving me?"

"I think you are getting the picture."

"I don't want to miss the rest of the show, Carol."

"Hell, turn it back on and enjoy yourself."

The show was moving ahead at full speed. "Thanks for the call, Gordon," Tom said. "Our next call comes to us from Boston. Please welcome Barbara Johnson."

"Barbara, how the hell are you doing tonight?"

"Kate, I'm so happy I got through. I was raised with a bunch of outlaws myself. My mother started her career as a porno star in California."

"All the women in my family gave it away, Barbara. Faith was the exception to the rule."

"What's the story on your sister who is married to the man who has been shot at a dozen times? Was she out there on the make herself?"

"She was a little more discreet, but she had her men. One of the men is claiming to be the father of her daughter. He claims he has the DNA to prove it. It damn sure wouldn't surprise me. She was a hot little number for a long time. Hell, the woman is in her seventies now and still don't look half bad."

"My God, how old is the daughter?"

"The girl is in her early forties. Can you even believe the man is showing up after forty plus years? What the hell? He says he is rich and wants the girl to have the money."

"Your older sister and her husband are going to have a fit, Kate. I'm not sure how the girl will take it."

"Hell, if some dude came out of nowhere and dropped a boat load of money on my ass, I'd be happy as hell. I wouldn't even bother with a damn DNA test. The old man could tell anyone he wanted he was my daddy."

"Thanks for your call, Barbara. We will take a short commercial break and be right back," Tom said.

Well, now how would you feel if you heard that little piece of news on world wide television. Carol drove straight to the airport and boarded a flight to West Palm. She called Anne and gave her the news. Sarah's mouth fell open and Vicki just passed out right in front of God and everybody. Howard looked at Florence and R.E. and dropped his head.

"R.E., do you know who Sarah's daddy is?"

"I always thought you were her daddy."

"Florence, I want to know who the girl's daddy is."

"You are the girl's daddy, Howard. You raised the child from birth. Vicki might have had a weak moment when you were out running women. You can't hold her in bad faith after all the shit you pulled. There is no telling how many of those married women delivered your child."

Emily and Jake had come in and sat watching with Renee and Johnny. The tension in the air was thick as smoke. "My Lord in heaven. Who is Sarah's father?" Jake asked.

"I don't have a clue. That big mouth bitch is trying to see how much trouble she can cause."

"Emily, please watch your language."

"Someone has to do something about Kate. The woman is digging up skeletons faster than a Track Hoe," Renee said.

"Man, the cops are going to be really ticked off. That woman just told the world the cops and judges are being bought off. Carol better put some distance between herself and Littleville," Johnny said.

"She will carry her little ass down to West Palm and run straight to Don, as sure as I'm sitting here. I'd bet money she is on her way to the airport right now."

"My Lord, who is going to be next," Emily asked.

Well, they didn't have to wait long for the answer. The show was back on the air and Howard and Florence had brought Vicki back from the passing out spell.

"We're back with Sally Gentry from Decatur, Alabama," Tom said.

"Sally, what's on your mind?"

"Kate, I want to hear about the naked preacher's wife with the xxx videos."

"Oh my God, please don't Kate," Jake said.

"I'm going to kill you, Kate!" Renee screamed.

"I've had enough of your big mouth running trash!" Emily shouted.

"Sally, I have to cut the girl some slack. She was a wild ass in high school, but she settled down when she married old Jake. The story goes something like this, Sally. Emily needed to take a leak and fell in her own piss. She got in the van and rode home naked. No big deal, except a cop almost nailed both of them. The xxx video was a lapse in judgment. When the store got popped, she freaked out. She ran to Renee and paid her a grand to take the fall."

"You no good bitch!" Renee shouted.

"I'm as good as gone," Jake said.

"I'm going to step on her like a bug," Emily said.

"Thank God we didn't get on the witness stand and commit perjury. Your damn sister is going to take a bite out of everyone's ass," Johnny said.

Emily had enough and went in the next room. Before Jake knew it, she called the network. She probably would have gotten turned away except for Wesley's instructions. The next thing the world and Emily knew, she was on the air live with Kate.

"Sally, stay with us. We have Kate's sister, Emily, on the phone right here in Littleville. You get to hear her side of the story," Tom said.

"Oh no," Jake said.

"Let her take a bite of Kate's ass," Renee said.

"I think she is making a terrible mistake. She better not have any skeletons in her closet," Johnny said.

"Emily, go ahead and run your big mouth. I'm warning you before you start lying, you better think twice."

"Kate Manley, you ought to be ashamed of yourself talking about me. You can't believe Renee when she runs her big mouth. She rented the video and made up a big lie. What was I supposed to do, stay covered in urine?"

"Big Mouth, you are a lying piece of shit. You and Sally rented the damn video and tried to cover it up. Renee showed me the damn check you sent for a grand. Speaking of covering it up Emily, I think I'll tell the audience about you getting caught naked with your prison boyfriend in front of the whole high school."

"Don't you dare tell that story! I was overwhelmed and lost my head."

"Okay Emily, maybe the people would enjoy the story about you getting caught naked at the drive-in a lot more."

"I'm going to come over there and shut your big mouth."

"Bring it on anytime you feel up to it. Make damn sure old Jake has plenty of medical insurance. I'll be off the air at ten o'clock and waiting on your loud mouth. Meantime, I'll tell the audience about you getting caught naked in the bedroom by Daddy. You gave a whole new meaning to the expression, 'Couldn't keep her pants on.' You couldn't keep a damn thing on. You were as bad as Howard when it came to getting your big ass caught. You must have stayed overwhelmed with sexual desire. No wonder Daddy had to shoot the damn boy off the motorcycle. You were banging more than a porno star in the movies."

"How dare you accuse me of being a whore? Why don't you tell your damn audience about the men you slept with? Quit trying to be the innocent victim of a dysfunctional family!"

"I have no problem with that chick. Unlike you, I told my man about my past. What else do you want to talk about, Emily? You want to tell the audience how you single handily emptied a restaurant with your loud mouth?"

Emily slammed down the phone and saw the look of horror on Jake and Renee's faces. Johnny couldn't even speak, much less look at her.

"I think Emily had enough, Kate," Tom said.

"Are all of you starting to get the picture of my family? Now you understand why I keep to myself."

"I gave her a piece of my mind," Emily said.

"You made a fool out of yourself," Renee said.

"Emily, I'm turning in my resignation tomorrow. We are leaving the state. I should have known something was wrong when you got in the van naked that night."

"I didn't hear you complaining, Jake. You ran off the road four different times going home."

"I was worried sick about being stopped."

"You couldn't take your eyes off of me."

Florence and Vicki had both passed out on the couch. Jimmy couldn't move as the show continued. Amanda and her parents were glaring at poor Scooter. Sarah was like the rest of the world. She couldn't move an inch away from the television. Rufus looked at the two women out cold. Howard looked like he had seen a ghost.

"Howard, things are never going to be the same again."

"My dogs are the only friends I'll have, Rufus."

"I'll still be your friend."

Tom jumped in and introduced the next caller. "Well, that was an interesting call to say the least. Welcome to Brenda Patterson, who joins us from beautiful Maui, Hawaii."

"Kate, I swear on my first born child I will never miss your show. I'm calling my cable company tonight when the show is over and buying the Wes-Star package."

"Brenda, you are a girl after mine and Wesley's heart. What else do you have to talk about?"

"I want to know about you, your husband and kids."

"Brenda, I have a damn good man. He has provided for me from day one of our marriage. He was driving a truck five nights a week, until Wesley came into our lives. He's a country boy and I couldn't ask for a better husband. My kids are a different story. My son is a damn pill head and stays in jail half the time. He has a smart ass mouth and he doesn't come around me. My daughter tries to eat for four people and is big as a cow. She has worked for thirteen different companies in the last four years. All she wants to do is bitch and complain. I'm a plain ass redneck girl. I don't cotton to bullshit and gossip. I had myself four lovers before I met Chuck. I've been guilty of drinking too much. I don't go to church and I keep my ass at home. I ain't anything special to look at, and I like real people. My favorite thing, next to sex, is chewing tobacco."

"We love you, Kate. Keep telling it like it is baby."

"Brenda, that's the one thing you can count on."

Wesley stood outside the studio with a phone in his ear. The Wes-Star switchboards were being flooded with phone calls from people. The cable networks had sold over three million packages of Wes-Star to subscribers in the first four days. In New York, network executives were in full blown panic. The audience for the shows in Kate's time slot was dropping like a brick falling from the sky.

Don and Faith sat watching the show at home. Don looked at his text message and almost fell out of his chair. He looked over at Faith who had a worried look on her face.

"Faith, you are not going to believe this. Kate just blew every show on television away."

"Jake will be fired and Emily is ruined. Vicki will probably never recover from the shock."

"Have another glass of wine and relax. Jake can have any damn church in the country. You are not hearing what I'm saying to you. Kate is headed for the number one show in all of television. Wesley and I are going to make billions."

"You're going to do what?"

"I said we are going to make billions."

"How much stock in Wes-Star do we own?"

"We own forty percent of the company. When Wesley sold the radio stations, all the other investors took a powder. They thought he was going to bust his ass trying to start a new network. I put our profit of forty million back in Wes-Star. Wesley just sent me a text message saying he expects to sell thirty million subscriber packages at ten bucks a month. We will gross around three hundred million a month. Two hundred and seventy million is pure profit. Thank God that boy ran into her damn house."

"Don't you feel bad profiting off my families misery?"

"The woman is telling the truth. They don't know it now, but they will all be kissing her ass before it is over."

The show was back on with a caller from Orange County, California. "Linda Charles, you are live with Kate in Littleville."

"Kate, what was the whole story on the son-in-law who stole the police car and walked away a free man."

"Linda, sit your ass down. This is the best story you are ever going to hear. The amazing thing about the whole damn story is it is true. The odds of it happening have to be a trillion to one. The boy's ass was looking at three to five in the state pen. He was drunk, doing 120, and smoking dope. He literally drove off and went home in the state police car. The family tried to hire the boy a lawyer and they all turned us down. Along comes the third richest man in the country, who it turned out was the damn boy's grandfather. He hires Don Hudson and pays the freight. Hudson comes in and makes a fool of the state trooper who arrested the boy. The damn cop was foaming at the mouth on the witness stand. I honestly thought the bastard was going to have a heart attack. Then he proceeds to undress every woman on the damn jury. The Judge, District Attorney, and Governor didn't know whether to shit or go blind. The Mayor and a fat ass councilman got in Hudson's face and went down for three hundred years. The boy walked away without a scratch on him. His stupid ass wife divorced him before she saw the light. The woman is suffering from deep depression every day of her life."

"So Hudson came in and turned the good old boy network on its head?"

"Hell no, girl; he buried their asses ten feet under the ground without a grave marker. Linda, I have never had much until Wesley gave me a job. I never bet on anything in my life. If you had seen those twelve women on the jury the second day, you would understand what I'm about to say. I would have bet my life against a hundred dollar bill the boy was going to walk free."

"What the hell happened on the second day?"

"Honey, every woman on the jury showed up eighty percent naked and praying for a night of action with Don. I'm here to tell you; the government had as much chance of winning as I do of flying. It got so bad; the state just flat out dropped the charges in front of God and everybody. It was the most amazing thing I will ever see in my life. The boy moved to New York and works for the old man."

"What is Mr. Hudson like in person?"

"Well, how would I describe him? He is one of the nicest and kindest people you will ever meet. He is definitely the smartest man you will ever meet. He is so damn handsome they need to outlaw him. Sexy, doesn't even come close to doing him justice."

"My word, no wonder the women went crazy over him."

"The damn man has never lost a case. There is another part to the story, Linda. He will never lose a case as long as a woman is on the jury."

"Thanks Linda, our next call comes from Marty Aaron in Cleveland, Ohio. Girl, you are on live with Kate," Tom said.

"I'd like to hear about all the men and their shirt chasing. I saw the clip where you said it was like a sport."

"None of them can keep their dick in their pants, Marty. I only have one brother, but he carries the load for five or six men. He's been married several times and keeps half a dozen girl friends.

He loves two women at a time. The old brother in laws chased women hard forever. Howard got religion and gave it up when he hit seventy. He holds the record for being shot at a dozen times by different men. I guess he had something against single women. He always got caught with married women. Old Rufus still runs it hard if someone will open the door. The preacher keeps his dick in his pants. The nephews run like thoroughbreds at the race track."

"Damn, what about the women?"

"The young ones roar like a lion. They get messed up on drugs and dance naked in the cage at the clubs. They have been barred from almost every club in the state. The old ones gave it up years ago. Renee was servicing two men at the same time. They pulled up to an intersection in town and shot it out one day. Her new boyfriend had to chase an old naked one out of her house this week. She's the only one of us kids still on the make. Her other daughter is a real looker and men go bananas when they meet her. She must be bad in the sack because they always leave after they sample the merchandise. Her real name is Anne, but we call her slugger. She is always busting some man upside the head. She calls Don and he bails her ass out of trouble."

Well, the show broke to sell the Wes-Star subscriptions and Shirley had heard enough. Violet Blue and Mona had heard enough as well. Scooter had dodged the bullet and sat quiet as a church mouse. Renee started to throw her glass at the television screen, but Johnny grabbed the glass. They say bad news spreads like wildfire and the news was definitely spreading. The phones were ringing off the wall all over Littleville and around the world. Wesley had a phone in each ear as the ratings soared and the subscribers went crazy. Jake and Emily's kids called to say how embarrassed they were about Emily's past. Some fool who went to Littleville High School called the local radio station to say he saw the whole performance behind the basketball arena. Hell, Pedro even called from New York to tell Howard how sorry he was to hear about the situation.

The show came back on for the final segment of the night. Tom introduced the caller from New Orleans. Her name was Edna Falk and she came right out with her question.

"Kate, your sister Renee must drive the men insane. I can't believe they shot it out in the middle of town over her."

"Edna, it's the damn truth. It was like the Wild West right here in dip shit Littleville. They carried one man to the jail and the other man to the funeral home. Some shit head sent me a bunch of pictures of her having sex at her house. I told her to get some heavy drapes and put an end to that crap. The girl ain't much to look at, so she must be a tiger in bed."

"Kate, tell us some funny stories about the family."

"They are a dime a dozen, Edna. The old ones went to New York and wound up at a nude show. They freaked out when the place got busted. Howard and Rufus caused a big commotion at the country club. They thought someone was shooting at them and ran for their lives. People out there thought they were going to die and called for the cops. It turned out no one was shooting at them or anyone else. Birds shit on both of them all the time. Honey, they are telling me we have to call it a night."

"I can't wait for Monday night."

The first week of Live with Kate from Littleville had come to a close. Renee poured her a double shot of whiskey. For the next two hours, the family was burning the phones up with each other. You can just imagine the conversations were quite lively.

The next morning, Sarah sat down at Cracker Barrel and waited for the mystery man. Rory was an old seventy eight and he barely made his way to her table. Sarah was shocked when he sat down.

"Sarah, I'm Rory, and it is a joy to finally meet you."

"Rory, I don't want to be rude. Will you please tell me what this is about?"

"Sarah, I used to live in this town years ago. My business failed and I was pretty much told to leave by the men who ran the place. I left and years later found my calling on Wall Street. I am now a very wealthy man. I'm not here to embarrass anyone or cause a problem."

"Kate said a man was claiming to be my father. Are you that man and do you have proof?"

"The answer to both your questions is yes. I want you to have real money and no one needs to know, including your mother."

"Were you married when the affair with my mother was going on?"

"Yes, and I divorced my wife. Vicki refused to leave Howard and I never remarried. You are my only child and I want you to have everything. May I ask you a question?"

"You may ask anything you wish."

"Are you happy in your marriage, Sarah?"

"I'm miserable in my marriage. My life is work and no fun."

"I want you to get a divorce before I give you the money. I bought a house in Twelve Trees for you. I want to have some fun before I pass away. I'd like to repay the bastards that humiliated me and ran me out of town. Do you still talk to Kate?"

"I talk to her almost every day."

"Well, we are going to turn Littleville upside down and have a ball. I know this is awkward for you, and I want nothing but a friendship. I'll give you my numbers and you call me when you are ready for your house. I have a mansion in Chicago and you are welcome to come see me if you so desire."

"I'd like that a lot, Rory. May I ask you a question?"

"You may ask anything you wish."

"How much money should your daughter expect to inherit?"

"You will inherit north of sixty million in cash and another forty million in assets. I have a cashier's check for a hundred thousand dollars to help you with the transition."

"I'd like to quit my job and come spent time with you in Chicago. My attorney can get my divorce completed fairly quickly."

"That would be wonderful, Sarah. Would you like to see the D.N.A. results?"

"There is no doubt in my mind you are my father. I always knew I didn't belong and something was wrong. Why did you wait so long to tell me?"

"I've asked myself the same question ten thousand times."

They left the restaurant together and she walked him to a waiting limo. They said their goodbyes and Sarah headed for home. Shirley called a friend and left Jimmy's ass. It took a good twenty minutes before Violet Blue moved in. Renee took Johnny to bed and tried to put the nightmare out of her mind. Carol hit the ground in West Palm and made a bee line to Don and Faith. Howard and

Vicki went to the church and prayed for things to get better. Florence busted R.E. for a new car the very next day.

Jake and Emily drove back to Lilleyville to face the music. The deacons had called for a meeting Sunday morning to determine the fate of poor Jake and Emily. Most of the men felt it was all Emily's fault, but the embarrassment might be too great for Jake to overcome. I mean if you think about it, would you want one forth of America knowing your preacher's wife got caught naked three times. The meeting was scheduled for ten o'clock and Jake's sermon at eleven. The deacons started to arrive, but there were no parking spaces. They all wound up having to park three hundred yards from the church. They made their way to the church and noticed three out of every four cars had out of state tags. The little church only held four hundred people and it was packed. At least a thousand people stood outside.

"I can't believe my eyes and ears. What on earth is happening at our little church today?" Deacon Brown asked.

"Brother Jake and Emily must have called on their friends from all over the country," Deacon Miller said.

"I believe it is the television show that has brought all these people to our little town," Deacon Autry said.

"How are we going to accommodate all these people? We need a church five times this size," Deacon Butler said.

"Oh my goodness, the television people are here. It's that Wes-Star network and they are filming everything. Our church is going to be on national television this week," Deacon Brown said.

They looked up and Jake and Emily were making their way through the crowd. The Wes-Star newsman had cornered them for an interview. Jake was a wreck, but Emily was relishing the moment. She didn't hesitate when the man asked for an interview. He introduced himself as Bobby James. The crowd gathered around to hear what was being said.

"Emily, thank you and Jake for the opportunity to speak with you. I know you were rushed Friday night. We wanted to give you an opportunity to explain everything in your own words."

"Well, I thank you for the opportunity to set the record straight. Kate only got half the story from Renee. My friend Sally and I were running a sting operation to weed out pornography in our community. We did, in fact, rent the video and took it home. We planned on tapping it for evidence to turn over to the authorities. Of course, we didn't know our fine Sheriff was one step ahead of us. The reason I wrote Renee the check is simple to explain. She had been bitching and complaining for years about Jake and I not paying rent to stay overnight with her. She is very cheap and has no conception of how you treat your family. Jake insisted I write her a check for one thousand of our hard earned dollars. When I told her about renting the video, she just freaked out and started running her big mouth. The woman needs help badly. She just cannot keep her mouth shut and makes up the worst stories on people. I'm sure Kate wanted to know why she had a check for a thousand dollars from me. The truth is she, was ashamed and made up a big story about me getting her to take the rap. Any fool knows you have to show your drivers license to open an account. The woman never left Littleville the day we rented the movie.

"Well, that certainly explains the xxx movie rental. Do you care to comment on Kate saying you were caught naked three times?"

"Kate is telling the truth, but she left out the reasons and implied I was having sex. I have a terrible problem with my bowels and I hate to discuss it. However, my husband's job is on the line as well as my reputation. My daddy caught me running for the bathroom, but it was too late. I had made a mess of myself and was getting all my clothes off. The same thing happened at the drive-in and the school. It happened to me in the van with my husband. You just cannot imagine how embarrassed you are when it happens. You have to remove your clothes and get cleaned up."

"Jake, do you have a comment."

"I think Emily has covered everything. I don't have anything to add."

"Thank you both so much for your time."

"Thank you, for letting me set the record straight, Bobby," Emily said.

The deacons made the decision to stand by Jake and Emily on the condition she never call Kate again. Jake was amazed at the crowd of people and preached his ass off. The collection plates set a new record by a mile. Jake and the Deacons started plans for a bigger church.

Wesley had an idea and he called Don in Florida. He saw a movie deal and massive souvenir sales. He was now completely sure Kate was going to be a mega star. It was time to cut the rest of the family in on a little piece of the action. Don sat in his study preparing for a trial. The phone rang and he saw it was Wesley.

"Wesley, you are a genius."

"Don, I have an idea to run by you. I see a low budget feature movie that grosses four to six hundred million in the United States. It will do the same overseas and the DVD sales will top everything. I see souvenir sales making tons of money."

"You know you can count me in."

"I want you to make a trip to Littleville and lock everyone up. Pay them fifty grand for the rights to use their names and pictures. Let them open their own little business selling the crap and taking people on tours of their homes. I don't want any problems with lawsuits. Create a new company and name it Arnold-Hudson. I'll keep sixty percent and you can have forty percent."

"How quickly do you want this done?"

"I want it done as fast as you can make it happen. Don, we can sell the network for thirty billion in a year. Kate is blowing away the competition. This is going to get out of hand very quickly. I don't want some network coming in and making a move on the family."

"Alright, I'll get to work on it immediately. I'll stay in touch and let you know how I'm coming along."

"There is one thing you have to commit to, Don. Kate tells me you are still driving women insane. I want your ass on with Kate the full two hours. Check your court dates and give me a week's notice when you are available. I'm going to come watch you in a courtroom one time. "

"You better make it fast, Wesley. With twelve billion, my ass is finished practicing law. Do you think I'm ready for prime time?"

"You son-of-a-bitch, you were born in prime time."

"You got a deal, Wesley. I'll be there two weeks from tonight."

He walked in the living room and sat down with Faith and Carol. "We need to fly up to Littleville the day after tomorrow. Faith, call the family and let them know we are coming. I'll call each of them and explain why we are coming."

"Okay baby, I'll call everyone."

"Carol, I'm going to get you fifty grand for the use of your name. I'll draw up the contracts tomorrow."

"God almighty damn, Don, for fifty grand you can have anything you want."

Faith looked at Carol and shook her head. "He just wants the use of your name, Carol."

CHAPTER NINETEEN

Well, it didn't take long for Don to get up to Littleville. Trust me when I tell you some court cases got moved around real quick. He was making a small fortune practicing law, but Wesley was making them a large fortune. Sarah was moving full speed ahead with her divorce and Carol joined her. It was barely a week later when Anne jumped her ass out of bed one morning and joined the other girls at the courthouse. The family was all excited about Don and Faith coming to see them. Florence and R.E. waited for Vicki and Howard at their house. Don was due to arrive in an hour and they all smelled money. He had told them about an opportunity to make some easy money.

Florence had the floor and she was excited. "R.E., what is a personal service contract?"

"The way Don explained it, you lend your name to a company and they pay you. He said the key is if Kate will go along with it. Her show is taking the world by storm, according to Don. He said he was confident Kate would give her blessing."

"How much are these personal service contracts worth?"

"He said we would never have to worry about money again."

"I bet we have to kiss Kate's ass to get a shot at the money. I could kick my ass for not running my mouth to the damn newspaper. I know more shit than Kate. I blew my chance."

"Damn woman, bite your tongue. If Kate finds out you are running your mouth, she will cut us out of the action."

"Well, you're right for once in your life. I'll zip it up and take the money."

"Howard and Vicki are here, Florence. Let me get the door and show them in. Howard said Vicki is still in shock about Sarah. The girl quit her job and left town without a word. She filed for a quick divorce and Ben is handling it. Her damn husband must have freaked out about the news. I never liked that boy worth a damn."

"She's better off without the piece of trash."

R.E. showed Vicki and Howard in and brought them a coke. Florence poured her a shot of Jack Daniels and sat down with them.

"Howard, I think Don is going to bring the roast duck and sit it on the table. I knew from the beginning that Faith had hit the jackpot. That girl did real good marrying that boy."

"I don't mind lending my name to a company. I didn't think anyone would have anything to do with me after Kate threw my dirty laundry in the front yard. The boy probably feels sorry for us and is reaching out to help. The good Lord is going to answer my prayers."

"He says we are looking at good money," Florence said.

"Sarah called from Chicago today. She told me not to worry about anything. I can't believe the girl is so happy about getting a divorce and losing her job."

Florence looked at Vicki and smiled. "She found her a sugar daddy in Chicago."

"Don is here, Howard," R.E. said.

"I'm on my way to greet him. I just love that boy."

Don got out with Faith and they walked up to the front porch. All four of them were waiting with open arms. They came in and Don got right down to business. They were all ears as he started to explain the offer.

"Kate has created an opportunity for all of you to make some money. The company wants to sign you to a personal service contract. You give them the right to use your names for stories, pictures, and movies. They pay you for the right to use everything on an exclusive basis. If it works, you can set up your own company to sell the stuff. You can charge money for people to come see your house. I have the contracts with me and a check to each of you."

"How much bread are they willing to lay on me?' Florence asked.

"Fifty thousand a year to each of you is guaranteed. You get a royalty of three percent of any merchandise sold. If the sales take off, you could make hundreds of thousands if not millions. You all better pray Kate stays hot."

"What do we have to do, Don?" R.E. asked.

"You have to sign the contract giving them a five year exclusive and have your pictures taken. A photographer will come out and take the pictures. They will take one individually and different ones of all of you together. I'd set up my own gift shop if I were you. The tourists will flock to Littleville to see the town. You are the main attraction next to Kate."

"I can't believe we are finally catching a break," Howard said.

"I'm ready to sign and get the money," Vicki said.

"Damn Don, I ought to kiss your ass," Florence said.

"Ain't that the damn truth," R.E. said.

They all signed and got their fifty thousand dollars. Don and Faith headed over to Renee's to meet her and Emily. Anne was there and Carol had flown up and joined them. Jake had already given his okay on his fifty thousand. Don gave the girls a hug and they all took a seat. He went through the same spill he had given the old crew.

"I will not stand for any nude pictures. I'm at a disadvantage. Jake and I don't live here."

"No one will be asking you to take nude pictures."

"Do we get to wear what we want?" Renee asked.

"As far as I know, you can wear what you want."

"I'm putting on something hot and sexy. I am going to find me a sugar daddy," Carol said.

"I'm getting decked out with a pair of boxing gloves around my neck. I'm milking this for every dime I can get," Anne said.

"I want my grand back, Renee. You take forty nine and I'll take fifty one. You need to split your sales with me."

"Are you completely crazy, Emily? I'll bill you fifty dollars a night for every night you and Jake stayed in my house. One hundred and six times comes to fifty three hundred. Hell will freeze over before I give you any of my sales."

"Alright, forget it then, Renee. Just cut us both a check for fifty and we'll call it square."

Don smiled and pulled the checkbook out of his briefcase. He wrote all of them a check and put the checkbook back in his briefcase. "I'm happy for all of you."

"We love you, Don. You are the best thing that has ever happened to this family," Renee said.

Emily looked at Don and then Renee. "Thank you so much, Don."

"You are very welcome."

"Renee, I hope you have enough sense to not blow your money in the casino."

"Kiss off, Emily, and mind your own business."

R.E. and Florence headed across town to the bank with a vengeance. Florence stood at the bank window with R.E. making the deposit. Katherine Lawrence, took the check and deposit slip.

"Mrs. Florence, you must have hit the jackpot."

"Honey, I am a star now and so is Rufus. Vicki and Howard rode my coattails and got some action too. You are looking at a woman who has a personal services contract with big money. I'll make more money than you can imagine with my mouth. Kate has a head start, but I'll catch her ass."

"Wow, are you going to be like your sister and get on television?"

"Honey, I don't have to do a damn thing, but have my picture taken. I got a deal working right now with Jack Daniels to promote their liquor."

"Mr. Cage, here is your deposit slip, sir." She looked at the copy of the deposit slip. "Arnold-Hudson. I never even heard of the company. It just shows you how stupid I am."

"Don't feel bad about it, Katherine. Those Hollywood types don't want anybody knowing their business. There are things I know about, but I have to keep it to myself."

"We are so excited about having big stars banking with us. Mr. Johnson said we are not to charge you for any of our services."

"Johnson is a smart man. We are going to be big stars. For a fee, I'll let you use my name," Florence said.

They walked out of the bank feeling mighty good about the sudden turn of events. Florence got in the car clutching her deposit slip. She looked at it and spoke to R.E. as he got in. "I bet the damn boy owns a piece of the company and cut us in on the action."

"You are probably right, Florence. Beverly told me Bobby Jack's grandfather paid him ten million. He has a good heart. Sure as hell, he is giving us a break. Why didn't you tell me you were working a deal with Jack Daniels?"

"Rufus, don't even try to break in on my territory. You and Howard need to find a condom company and cut your own deal."

"How the hell did you hook up with Jack Daniels?"

"I'm smarter than everyone else. I got me an agent to work my deals."

"You are full of shit woman. You called the damn company and put the sell on them. The next thing I know, you will be drinking that crap on television."

"Don't you say a word to me about anything? Myrtle Lee is running her mouth all over town about you screwing her. I can't even go to my beauty shop anymore."

It didn't take a full day for Don to have everyone signed on the bottom line. Faith and Don took everyone to dinner. Jimmy and Scooter went to the bar after dinner and celebrated their good fortune.

"Damn, I never thought I'd be happy about Kate dropping the dime on our ass, Scooter. I wish she had spoken up sooner."

"I know damn well I'm next in line with Sarah to get a divorce. She is happy as a pig in shit these days. I'm pretty sure she has found her a sugar daddy. She's moving to Twelve Trees as soon as the divorce is final."

"We need to find us a rich woman ourselves. Daddy said that was the biggest mistake he ever made. We all keep winding up with broke women. He must have told me a hundred times not to make the same mistake."

"Amanda is rich, but she won't share a penny. It's not as simple as you are making it out to be. I'm not telling her ass a damn thing about my money. If I ever hit the jackpot, my ass is out the door and gone."

"Your tanning bed place will take off when all the promotions start. You may want to bring back the hooker."

"How is Violet working out so far?"

"I really like the girl, but she ain't as good as Mona. Man, I just can't trust that woman after she flipped out and threw the damn skillet. I may break down and give her a call."

"Jimmy, you better stay away from that crazy bitch. She may pop a cap in your ass the next time she catches you."

"You are right, Scooter. I just wish she wasn't so hot in bed. I need to be on my way."

Another week passed by and Kate was still smoking the competition. Sarah got her divorce and moved in her new home. Rory came down and they sat talking about his plan to get even. It was really quite clever and unique.

"Sarah, I have a recorder buried on the sixth tee box. You can trigger it by pushing this button."

"What does the recording say, and who are we going to use it on?"

"We are going to use it on J.R. Fair and Charles Seaman. They ran my ass out of town and we are going to return the favor. The bastards play every Wednesday afternoon at twelve o'clock. I want you to tip off Kate and have the Wes-Star cameras waiting on their butts."

"What are you going to do to them?"

"I'm going to deliver them to the world buck ass naked."

"How on earth are you going to do that?"

"The recorder will take care of everything. You don't need to know what is on it."

"Hell, I'm game to give it a shot. You will damn sure ruin their ass driving around naked on national television. I'll call Kate right now and give her a heads up. She won't believe it when I tell her."

Don called Wesley and gave him the good news. The family all had their pictures taken and got to keep a copy. Kate was on the air and feeling more and more comfortable. Wesley had already hired the screen writer to start the script. He was close to cutting the deal for the shirt sales. Man, what we all wouldn't give to trade places with Wesley and Don. I'll tell you one thing I know for sure. Those bankers better not let Rory get their asses naked on T.V.

J.R. and Charles were bad ass bankers. They had built a small empire beating customers out of their land over thirty years. The table was set as they teed off for their round of golf at Twelve Trees. Rory had made sure no one was behind them for twenty minutes. The starter stood with his one hundred dollar bill on the first tee. I can assure you of one thing. No one was going off before twelve twenty. The men were cruising along drinking some beer and having a good round. It was a little after one o'clock when they got out and walked up to the sixth tee box. Rory and Sarah sat looking out the window. The Wes-Star cameras sat on number seven waiting for the scoop they had been promised. J.R. and Charles had pulled out their drivers and were getting ready to hit their next shot.

"Push the button, Sarah," Rory said.

Sarah hit the button and both men froze. The voice was harsh and the message was clear. "Don't move a muscle. I'll blow your asses away. If you turn around, both of you are dead men. You stole my farm and I'm stealing from you. Take your clothes off and leave your billfolds in the pocket. You have one minute to strip naked and drive away. If you stop, or look back before you hit the clubhouse, I'll kill both of you."

Sarah and Rory watched as both men striped naked and took off in the golf cart. "Good Lord, they are buck naked."

"The best is yet to come, Sarah."

The Wes-Star crew watched as the two men came flying down the hill. "Son-of-a-bitch, here they come," Wally said.

"I got them and we're filming," Bruce said.

"How the hell does Wesley come up with this stuff?"

"I don't know, but you better drive the hell out of this golf cart."

J.R. and Charles were flying by in their birthday suits. The Wes-Star crew went hauling ass in behind them. Suddenly, out of nowhere, a police helicopter came down and started chasing them. Charles looked up and they started to stop, but gun shots went off and they hit the petal and ran for their lives. Rory had positioned four men out on the course and wouldn't you know it, they were unleashing the cherry bombs right on cue. Both the men sure thought guns were being fired. They were not about to stop and find out. They came up on the number eight fairway and four women were playing. The women looked over and screamed as they came roaring by completely naked. Susan was about to take a break when the phone rang in the pro shop.

"Twelve Trees Golf Shop. This is Susan."

"Susan, J.R. and Charles have lost their minds. They are riding around the golf course naked. There is a film crew following them and they are driving like a bat out of hell," Rosie Hill said.

"Let me put the pro on the line." "Tom, please come quick and listen to this. We have naked men riding around the course and they have a crew filming them."

Tom got up from his desk and stared at Susan. "What the hell are you saying? Give me the phone." He took the phone and was clearly agitated. "This is Tom. What are you seeing?"

"Two naked men riding around in the golf cart. They must be proud as punch, Tom. The sleazy bastards have a film crew following them. They think their crap doesn't stink. Can you believe the nerve riding around naked in front of Christian women?"

"Where are they at now?"

"They are almost to number nine. A police helicopter is trying to head them off. If this is J.R. and Charles' idea of a joke, they are both crazy. Vida is passed out on the ground."

"I'll call 9-1-1 right now and get someone out there to help Vida."

Well, word had spread and everyone stood outside the clubhouse waiting for the naked men to arrive. The newspaper folks were trying their best to get there in time to capture the men on film. J.R. and Charles had no intention of stopping for anything or anyone. When they came up to number nine the cart path was blocked. They ran right across the number eight green and almost ran over Mitchell and T.J.

"You prick. I'll kick your ass!" Mitchell yelled.

"Those bastards have lost their minds," T.J. said.

"Get in the cart. I'm going to chase those assholes down and beat the living hell out of them."

"We are almost back to the clubhouse," J.R. said.

"Keep going as fast as you can," Charles said.

Mitchell was a bad ass and used to drive race cars. He had his own supped up cart and he put the petal to the metal. The Wes-Star boys were right on his bumper. J.R. was almost to the clubhouse when Mitchell rammed the rear end and the cart flipped. By now, there were at least a hundred people watching. The restaurant had emptied and the cooks and waiters joined everyone to see the sight. Rory and Sarah drove up and sat taking in the whole scene. Mitchell was beating the living hell out of J.R. and Charles as the police helicopter landed. The Wes-Star crew was filming away as Mitchell put the Mike Tyson workout on their ass.

"Jesus Christ, Wesley is not going to believe this scene," Wally said.

"That dude is putting the hurt on those two queers," Bruce said.

Man it was quite a scene as the cops arrested J.R. and Charles. There wasn't a whole lot left to arrest when Mitchell finished. They were desperately trying to explain what had happened to them. The cops went to the sixth tee and of course they found nothing. Rory's people had taken the clothes and gotten rid of them. They went to jail and were kicked out of Twelve Trees. They caught a bad break when the Judge threw the book at them. It turned out they had screwed his family years ago.

Of course, Wes-Star showed their naked asses off to the world. Kate had Mitchell on live that night. Tom was all hyped up after the film chip ran for five full minutes.

"Let us extend a warm welcome to the man who cornered the two naked men today at Twelve Trees here in Littleville. Mitchell, we are damn glad to have you on," Tom said.

"Thanks, I'm glad to be on. My wife never misses the show."

"Mitchell, what the hell did you think when you saw the two fools?"

"I first thought it was a show about gay men being filmed at Twelve Trees. When the bastards tried to run over me and T.J., it pissed me off. T.J. had me down two hundred and I was about to get my money back."

"That was some kind of ass whipping you put on those boys. I'm damn glad you did and hopefully we can get those assholes run out of town. Twelve Trees is always having some crap coming down."

"You can say that again, Kate. I've almost been shot on the course. It is a rough ass part of town."

"Take care of yourself, Honey. We need to take another call now."

"Warren Taylor from Reno, Nevada is on the line. Warren say hello to Kate," Tom said.

"Kate, I used to think golf was a gentleman's game until recently. I heard the stories from the ladies on your show. Yesterday, I got to witness a golf story play out right before my damn eyes."

"Warren, we are waiting to hear the story."

"Kate, my wife and I live on a golf course, but I'm like you. I never played the game and I don't pretend to understand it. Our next door neighbor's house keeps getting hit by golf balls. The poor woman sued the people who own the club to put up a screen, but she lost. This afternoon, I heard a lot of commotion and went to check it out. Three men were laying head first on the ground. My neighbor was standing over them with a shotgun."

"Holy shit, what the hell happened, Warren?"

"It turns out they hit her house and went in her yard looking for the ball. The damn fools decided to relieve themselves in her yard. They all got in a cussing match. She pulled a shotgun and put them on the ground. It was a hell of a scene when the cops got here. My wife and I thought it was all over for those men. The cops almost never got her to put the gun down."

"I'll be damn, can you even believe it. I have to tell you if they came in my yard pissing all over the place, I'd kick the living shit out of their sorry asses. My husband, Chuck, has been thinking he wants to take up golf. I told him from the little I know; it would be a bad idea. I never heard of anybody getting shot at a football or baseball game. I used to play basketball and no one got shot. Hell, this damn golf is a rough ass game full of pissed off people."

"I certainly don't want any part of it."

"Honey, we need to take another call."

"Sadie London joins us from Charlotte, North Carolina," Tom said.

"Sadie, welcome to the show. What's on your mind tonight?"

"My aunt lives in Littleville. She is screwing one of your brother in laws. She is ready to come clean and get it off her chest."

"Hell, tell her to give me a call and take a load off."

"I'll give you her name, but she wants you to call her when we are finished. I hope I'm not stepping out of bounds, Kate."

"Sadie, it's time for a commercial break. Stay on the line and you can give me her name and number."

The microphones were dead and Kate looked at Tom "I can't believe we are going to get this on the air," Tom said.

"It's why Wesley hired me, Tom."

Well, now here we go again with drama. Florence sat glaring at R.E. Vicki was uptight herself. Jake was not the least bit worried, but Emily felt a little knot in her belly. Faith was fit to be tied at the thought of what was coming next. Hell, even Don sat up and took notice. The show came back on and the shit hit the fan.

"Welcome back folks. I have Myrtle Lee on the horn and she is full of piss and vinegar. Myrtle, your niece says you need to get some things off your chest. Start talking and go hard until you are through."

"Kate, I hate to do this, but I'm sick of people accusing me of trying to wreck a marriage. Rufus Cage and I have been lovers for fourteen years. He moved in on me when my late husband died. Florence and I were best friends. I caught her ass cheating with my husband. It is wrong for her to cheat and me not be able too. I'm a single woman and Rufus tells me she hadn't put out in twenty years."

"Damn girl, I think you are going to tell it all."

"All Rufus gives me is two hundred a week. I think it's wrong for Florence to be constantly running her mouth about me."

"Honey, let me see if I can get Florence to pick up and we'll have a three way. Florence was going crazy and throwing everything in the room at R.E. The phone rang and she grabbed it.

"Kate, this is Florence. I've been listening to every word Myrtle said. I was about to kill this no good bastard, but he ran for his worthless life."

"I can't hold that against you, Florence."

"Myrtle, has that sorry bastard really been giving you eight hundred a month?"

"Yes, and you have been saying bad things about me at the beauty saloon. I never ran my mouth about you when you were screwing Elwood. He swears you will never give him any. He comes over here begging for some."

"The son-of-a–bitch's dick is three inches long. I told the bastard, I can't get any satisfaction. It's not my fault he shriveled up to nothing. I'm sorry if I offended you and you can have the piece of shit."

"Oh Lord! I don't want him. He is the worst lover on the planet. I have to fake having an orgasm. You are so right, the man has nothing down below."

"I could have told you fourteen years ago."

R.E. had hid behind the door and taken it all in. He took off out the back door like a man running for his life. Florence heard the car roaring out of the driveway.

"Okay girls, we got everything on the table. It's not going to be a good evening for Rufus," Kate said.

Now that would qualify for the understatement of the century. Have a little pity on the man for goodness sakes. Try for a second to imagine sixty million people being told by two women you had a three inch dick. If that wasn't bad enough, they both say you are the worst lover on the planet. I have to say it would break many a man. I mean, who doesn't love Kate, but for heaven sakes the man didn't rob the damn bank. Man, where is the dude even going to spend the night? How the hell did Florence get a pass?"

"I don't think Rufus has a three inch peter," Howard said.

"I wouldn't know, Howard. Both the women are claiming its true," Vicki said.

"Rufus is in a tight spot, Vicki. I'm going to call him and tell him he can stay with us."

"Howard, if Florence finds him she is going to start shooting. The man is on his own tonight."

"I been shot at and it ain't no fun."

"Howard, if all the stories are true, you had more rounds fired at you than a soldier in war."

Kate was back on the air and R.E. was on the run. He was one shook up dude as the night progressed. Tom was trying his professional best to hold it together as the next caller came on.

"Pamela Byrd from Memphis, Tennessee you are on the air with Kate Manley."

"Kate thanks for taking my call."

"Pamela, what's happening in Memphis tonight?"

"I'm one shook up bitch, Kate. I had something happen last night that I'm never going to get over."

"It sounds like you almost stared death in the face."

"I thought me and my sister both were going to buy the farm. My sister and her husband spent the night at my house last night. I had just met the man for the first time and didn't know much about him. We went to bed about eleven thirty and I had just fallen asleep. I heard my sister starting to yell at the top of her voice. It was terrifying as she kept yelling, "Bob, stop it. Don't do this to me, Bob." I heard a blood curdling yell from Bob that lasted forever. It was pitched dark and I couldn't find the phone. I was pretty damn sure my sister was a dead woman, and I was probably next."

"Holy shit, girl, what happened next?"

"Bob quit screaming and it got very quiet. I eased out of bed and started down the hall. My sister came out of the bedroom and I was quite relived to say the least. I asked her what the hell happened. The bitch told me the man was having a nightmare. I told her, in no uncertain terms, she had scared the living shit out of me. I asked her stupid ass if she ever thought of just turning on the lights and telling Bob to wake his ass up. I told her she made it sound like the man was going to kill her."

"Honey, I think I'd tell both their asses to get a motel room. Chuck starts that nightmare crap about twice a year. I throw a bucket of cold water on his ass. That stops the howling on the spot. Then, I have to go get the damn dogs settled down. It usually takes an ass whipping to calm them down. It ain't so bad now that we moved, but it used to be a damn nightmare. We had about thirty dogs on our street. They all wanted to put their two cents worth in. Every light in the damn neighborhood would come on."

"I'm telling you Kate, I'm never going to get over it. I thought my ass was fried for sure."

"Pamela, get you a can of mace and a thirty eight. Put it out of your mind. There will be better days."

The show ended another episode of Live with Kate in Littleville. R.E. was trying his best to stay alive in Littleville. The little dude called Beverly for help, but she was no fool.

"Daddy, Mother just called me. You better lay low for a few days. She is threatening you with death on the spot if she finds you. I know damn well she is coming over here looking for you. Please don't get within a mile of my house."

He called Myrtle and got the iceberg treatment. When he reached Howard, he found no relief. His son told him in no uncertain terms to keep his ass away. He went in the I-Hop and sat down by himself. Damn, if it wasn't two minutes and everyone was pointing at him. Two men walked over and sat directly across from him. Dan Bennett and John Bernard had just finished their shift at the Ford plant.

"That's the man with the three inch dick. They flashed his picture up on the screen. We saw him on our break," John said.

"I think I'd tuck my tail and hide out. Both those women said he was bad in bed," Dan said.

"The poor man looks like he doesn't have a friend in the world. He just looks pitiful sitting there all beat up."

"Life can sure deal you a dirty blow sometimes. You know it might not be all bad. My wife is always calling me a big dick asshole."

The waitress, Ginger Welker, came over to R.E. She stood with a cigarette hanging from her mouth. "What can I get you, Little Fellow?"

"Those women are both damn liars. I don't have a three inch dick."

"Honey, I don't give a shit about your dick. Are you going to order?"

"You must be the only person in America who doesn't watch Kate's show."

"I can't watch T.V. on the job. I tape it and watch her when I get home. I ain't got time to shoot the shit, mister. Order something or I'll have to ask you to carry your ass."

"Give me a waffle and a cup of black coffee."

"Now we're getting somewhere."

R.E. looked at his cell phone ringing and it was Sarah. He picked up and answered in a whisper. "Sarah, I guess you saw the show tonight."

"Do you need a place to hang your hat tonight?"

"Honey, I ain't going to lie. I'm in bad need of a place to lie down and rest. This has been a bad day for me."

"I live in Twelve Trees on the sixth fairway. Drive up Twelve Trees Lane to the top of the hill. It's the two story gray house on the right. You can't miss it. I have someone who is looking forward to seeing you when you get here."

"I'm having a waffle at the I-Hop. I'll be right over."

"Take your time. We will be up late."

The man finished his waffle and felt better knowing he had a place to stay. He paid the bill and started out for Twelve Trees. Dan and John watched as he reached the door.

"Hold your head up high and don't be embarrassed. It could happen to anyone old timer," Dan shouted.

R.E. looked over and shook his head. He was in a real bad mood as he started his car. He was only about a mile away from the entrance to Twelve Trees when a damn car went sliding off the road. He pulled to a stop and called 9-1-1. Five minutes later, the ambulance got there and loaded the man in for the ride to the hospital. The press showed up and damn if they didn't recognize him. You think they wanted to talk about the man calling 9-1-1 to save someone? Hell no! They wanted to talk about Kate's show. The damn reporter was on him like a rabbit on a carrot. Carol Reed was no fool and knew she had a big scoop on her hands. She walked right up and stuck the mike in his face.

"Mr. Cage, this has to be a rather rough night for you. How are you taking the allegations made against you tonight on national television?"

"Young lady, I never thought I would have to defend my manhood. For your information, I have sleep with well over fifty women. The two women on Kate's show don't like me a damn bit."

"Mr. Cage, are you looking at a divorce?"

"Listen, I'm looking for a damn bed and I found one. Florence can do any damn thing she wants. Myrtle Lee can kiss my ass goodbye. I'm leaving before I say something I might regret."

"Mr. Cage, before you go, would you like to disprove the assumption the size of your private is quite small."

"Lady, I ain't going to take my pecker out in front of you. I think I best be on my way."

R.E. got in his car and took off to find Sarah's house. It was past midnight and he hadn't seen ten o'clock in thirty years. He thought he found Sarah's house and went to the door. He rang the doorbell expecting to see Sarah. Rory opened the door and spoke to him.

"Rufus, I can't believe I'm seeing you."

"Rory, I'm a hell of a lot more surprised to see you. I didn't even know you had moved back to Littleville. You can't even believe how bad my day has been, old friend. I'd love to stand here and visit with you. I'm looking for Sarah's house and I came up on yours. I'll come over tomorrow and we can catch up on everything."

"Rufus, you are at the right house. Come on in, we have been expecting you."

"I don't understand, Rory. Have you and Sarah been friends for a long time?"

Sarah walked up to the door. "R.E., welcome. Please come in and make yourself at home."

Here we go again. The man is being subjected to more drama. The man's mind was racing faster than a bunch of NASCAR drivers gunning for the finish line.

"Thank you, Sarah. Are you and Rory old friends?"

"Sit down and I'll tell you all about it."

R.E. noticed Rory was moving very slowly. "Rory, can I give you a hand?"

"Rufus, I thank you, but I'm fine."

They all sat and Sarah brought them all a stiff drink. "R.E., can you keep a secret?" Sarah asked.

"It probably depends on what the secret is, Sarah. Since you saved my ass tonight, I owe you to keep the secret."

"Rory is my biological father. He has given me a new life of joy and security I have never known. I don't want my father or my mother to be hurt."

R.E. looked like he had seen a ghost. "You can bet your little ass I'll keep my mouth shut. Jesus Christ, who the hell knows about this; I hope to God you haven't told Scooter or Vicki."

"Rory told Vicki, but no one else knows. Kate has given me her word it will never be spoken about again."

"Damn, this has been some kind of day. Rory, I need to carry my ass to bed before I pass out. Don't either one of you worry about me. If I can just make it to tomorrow, I'll be happy."

Well, there is always another day and Rufus had put a real bad one behind him. The next morning, Rory gave him the scoop on how to get Florence off his ass for good.

R.E. stood and shook his head. "I'll be damned, Rory. I have voted for that son-of-a-bitch for years. That big mouth bitch can't hold my women over my head again."

"Rufus, there were more men and women running around in Littleville than the boys running track."

Myrtle Lee, with all her farting, was just a bad memory. Florence took the man back in after giving him a little hell. Wesley cut the deal on the merchandise and the tee shirts went to press. Faith was probably the least pleased about the turn of events. Don just went right on smiling at the girls and loved Faith more every day. Jimmy just couldn't help himself and gave Mona another shot. Scooter was praying for Kate to be the world's biggest star. He was a slick little rascal and had already figured out he was the only one with a license to sell the merchandise. Howard shook off the shock and went right on being Howard. Vicki could never get Sarah to confirm anything and went on herself. R.E. damn sure never opened his mouth. Everybody was getting ready to make an old fashioned killing. Wesley had cut the deal with Kate and she and Chuck got another million dollars a year. The Martin's were a happy bunch.

CHAPTER TWENTY

The merchandise had arrived and Scooter was set to go hard. All the other family members couldn't get a permit to sell from their homes. He had taken out a full page ad in the paper and it was paying off big time. The lines outside the tanning bed were growing by the second. Scooter had three girls collecting the money and bringing out more shirts. Florence was about to have a fit watching the money roll in for Scooter. The shopping center owner and all the tenants were thrilled with all the cars and people.

"One out of five shirts being sold is mine," Florence moaned.

"I'm trying to get a rezoning started, but it will take months. We have to break down and rent a building. I'll see if Howard and Vicki will go in with us," R.E. said.

"Scooter is making all the money while we stand here with a finger up our ass."

"That boy has out foxed us, Florence. We need to get off our ass before he sells everything. Jimmy told me he ain't going to fool with trying to sell the stuff. I think Scooter cut him in for a little piece of his action."

"The only thing Jimmy cares about is women. He would have passed Daddy long ago if he hadn't had himself clipped."

Doris Campbell, and her husband Sam, walked over and poured salt in the wounds. "Florence, we just bought twenty five shirts to send to our friends. Why haven't you opened your store? We would have bought from you," she said.

"Thanks for saying that, Doris. The truth is we got caught with our pants down. We got no one but ourselves to blame."

"You better get moving before it is too late, Florence. Scooter is raking in the money faster than a hay bailer," Sam said.

Over the next twenty minutes, the scene repeated itself no less than eighteen times. R.E. and Florence were both having a cow. Scooter walked over to visit. "Aunt Florence, you are making sixty cents on every one of your shirts we sell."

"How much are you making?"

"I'm making eleven dollars and forty cents on every sale. I already sold two thousand shirts today. Lord, I can't believe I've already made over twenty two thousand today. I'm sending Kate ten dozen roses."

"Who's buying all these shirts?"

"I'm getting a lot of tourists and locals. The thing is they buy ten at a time. They are being sent to friends all over the damn country. I just called the company and ordered twenty thousand more shirts.

"Damn son, I didn't know you had that kind of money," R.E. said.

"Don told me when he was here to buy whatever I wanted. They are real good about extending credit. Don must have a lot of clout with the company."

"The man must be guarantying the payment."

"Son, I'm afraid we are going to have to give you some competition," Florence said.

"I don't blame you one bit. If this keeps up, I'll make over a million dollar profit in one month."

"Son, I'm happy for you. It looks like everyone is getting rich but us."

Well, R.E. and Florence hauled ass to the real estate office looking for a building. R.E. called Howard and he and Vicki agreed to join them. They spent the rest of the day looking at buildings. That evening, they tried to figure out how much money they were going to need to open the doors. R.E. went down to city hall the next morning to check on the permits with Florence. The new Mayor had fired all of Huey's people and hired new people in every department. His instructions were very clear to everyone. There were to be no short cuts or special favors to anyone for any reason. But, you and I know there was one exception, and his name was Ben Rollins. They walked up to the window to pay for their permits.

"I'm R.E. Cage, and this is my wife, Florence."

"I know who you are, Mr. Cage. I never miss Kate's show. What can I do for you?" Candy asked.

"We found a building and we need a license to operate. We need to get open fast, before Scooter gets all the money."

"I never heard of Scooter's. He better have a license to operate."

"He has a license, and that's the damn problem, lady," Florence said.

"What kind of business are you opening?"

"We are going to sell tee shirts of the Martin family. Me and Rufus are on the tee shirts."

"You will need a C/O before you can open."

"Lady, I've been out of the army for over fifty years. I wouldn't have a clue where my C/O is or even if the man is still alive."

"Mr. Cage, you need a certificate of occupancy. All of our inspectors must approve the building. The state fire marshal will have to approve the plans. We will need a set of plans and they must be approved as well by the city staff. I'm afraid if you started today, it will take four months."

"I'm losing twenty two thousand a day," Florence said.

"I'm very sorry, but you must get everything in order before we can issue you the C/O."

"Scooter has us by the balls," R.E. said.

"There ain't going to be a son-of-a-bitch left that doesn't have a shirt in four months. Candy, we just got it stuck up our ass. I got all this fame and no fortune to go with it. The damn boy is going to make millions. I ain't making a plug nickel," Florence said.

"Well, I'm very sorry about your misfortune. When you have completed everything that is required, come back and see me."

Now, I don't know about everyone else, but I was born and raised in a small town. One thing you learn early on is people love to gossip. They talk about the good, the bad, and the ugly. They talk about family and friends. In short, they talk about everyone. The good is discussed about ten percent of the time. The bad makes it into discussion about twenty percent of the time and the ugly clocks in at a good seventy percent. The Martin family had always fallen in the ugly category. You can just imagine the local's feelings now that Kate was a world wide star. Rumor had it that Kate was making millions. The rest of the lucky devils were getting big money hanging on to her coattails. It didn't take long for people to start the age old tradition of begging for some of that money. Florence was grocery shopping with R.E. when the minister of a local church, James Akin, cornered them.

"Brother Cage, how are you and your lovely wife?"

"Do I know you?" R.E. asked.

"I'm Reverend James Akin, with the Church of Journey. We are out on Highway 309 ministering to the flock. I've been hearing and reading about you and Florence's new found success. The young lady at your bank told us Sunday morning that Florence told her she was going to be a big star and pass right by Kate."

"Preacher, don't believe everything you hear."

"I would like to extend an invitation to both of you to attend our service next Sunday. We have a fund raising drive and I hope we can count on you for a large donation from your new found wealth. I'm sure you both want to give back to the community that has been your home since birth."

"Listen, we ain't got any money, James. Vicki's boy, Scooter, is raking it in over at the tanning place. Kate is getting all the bread from the show. Rufus and I don't get a plug nickel. You are barking up the wrong tree."

"The girl at the bank said you told her you were getting big money. She even said you were going to be doing commercials for Jack Daniels."

"My wife has a big mouth and loves to show off, Preacher. The only deal she has with Jack Daniels is drinking the crap. You need to move on down the isle and try to find someone else. What little money we got has to go towards opening a store."

"The young man with the tanning bed has the money?"

"He's raking it in faster than a jet plane can fly, Preacher," Florence said.

They took off with their cart down the isle. "Florence, you need to shut your mouth. Every damn preacher in town is going to be knocking down my door begging for money."

"Rufus Cage, do I have to remind you half that door is mine. I was just trying to get the bank to comp some free stuff. I didn't know the girl was going to run her mouth to the damn preacher."

The chamber lady, Billie Braintree, who ran the place, was plotting to take advantage of Kate's success. The chamber bought billboards promoting the city with a picture of Kate. Billie and Renee were not on speaking terms. It seems Renee had caught Billie with her former husband and bad blood still existed. Billie loved to gossip and word got back to Renee. Billie was only speaking the truth when she said Kate was the star. She could have left out the other stuff about the rest of the family being a bunch of free loaders. To make matters worse, she implied Renee was a very loose woman. I guess it was bound to happen. Renee and Billie came face to face in Roy Jones' drugstore on Thursday night. The store was packed when they rounded the corner and started in on one another.

"Billie, I ought to whip your big ass right here in front of God and everyone else. How dare you call me a slut and a free loading jerk."

"I wouldn't stoop so low as to give you the time of day. Move out of my way."

"There is only one slut in this isle and it damn sure ain't me. I seem to remember it was you in bed with my husband."

"Carson was in my bed, bitch. The man told me he hadn't had an orgasm in two years. He said you were the worst piece of ass on the planet. You need to go out to Kate's mansion and see how many times you can kiss her ass. All of you worthless Martin trash need to kiss her ass."

"I don't have to kiss anybody's ass, chick. Unlike you, I don't have to screw half the chamber members to have a job. You could write a book on who has the biggest dick in town."

"You are nothing but a lucky jerk. If you're drug crazed kid hadn't run into Kate's house, you would still be begging for money.

Everyone in town knows you raised three idiots. You were born in the gutter and you never came out. You are nothing but white trash!" Billie screamed.

Well, Mr. Jones and three customers had to pull them apart. Renee managed to get in two good licks upside Billie's head. The word, of course, traveled from one end of town to the other in minutes. But, the really big rumor was circulating that a movie was going to made right smack in Littleville. The Governor had spoken with Wesley and a deal was in the works. The locals were all quite excited about getting a part in the movie. The family was being besieged for help in securing a part. Jimmy and Scooter assured every good looking woman in town they would secure them a role. Florence was bragging to everyone she was the answer to their prayers. Lord, people were even begging Jake for a role. R.E. and Howard couldn't even fish in piece.

Over at the mansion, Wesley and Kate were having a coke and discussing everything. Chuck was still in a state of shock over their good fortune. He came in and sat across from Wesley.

"Kate, I'm taking your advice. Friday night, I got Don Hudson to be on with you the whole two hours. I'll start the promotion tonight."

"The boys' better hope there is two T.V. sets in the house. You can bet your ass every woman in the damn country will be watching. There will be some ass whippings if the boys don't give up the T.V. sets."

"Y'all can shoot the bull about the movie and the family. The shirt sales are taking off like a bat out of hell. I think you and Chuck can expect a big royalty check. The subscribers just keep signing up."

"Wesley, you have turned mine and Chuck's life into a dream. You mark my words. Don will sell more subscribers in one night than we did in a week. You won't get a damn one until we go off the air. You better have a ship load of people ready to answer the phones when we sign off."

"I have to see this show play out. You have never steered me wrong, Kate."

"Wesley, are you in the stock market?"

"I invest from time to time. Why do you ask?"

"I don't know shit about the market, but I'll tell you this much. You find out the name of the company that sells the best vibrator. You take Kate's word and load the boat."

"The man must drive women crazy."

"I've seen it with my own two eyes, Wesley. You better have your censors ready, because they are damn sure going to proposition the man. When word gets out, there will be a boat load of women at my front gate."

"Damn, did you see Don in action, Chuck?"

"Kate is not bull shitting you, Wesley. You just have to see it with your own eyes to believe it. My dad told me women used to act this way when they saw Elvis."

"I better beef up our security at the front gate."

"You can take that to the bank. Those four men you have out there will be trampled to death. I'll bet you anything every woman under forty in this part of the state will be waiting to see him."

"Wesley, don't think for a second Chuck is blowing smoke. The damn cars will be parked a mile down the road."

The confrontations were starting to become a regular occurrence around town. I think a lot of it was petty jealousy, but some was the real deal. Vicki and Florence were on their way to see Sarah and her new home. They stopped at the Home Depot to pick up some things. They were standing on isle thirteen when they ran into two of Howard's old flames, Betty Calhoun and Lillian Camp. Both of the women's husbands had a restraining order against Howard for years.

"Well, if it isn't the lucky ass Martin women. I bet neither one of you runs your big mouths about Kate anymore," Betty said.

"Watch your big mouth, you low life hussy," Vicki said.

"I ran into Sarah the other day shopping her ass off. Imagine my surprise when I saw Rory with her," Lillian said.

"Lillian, don't start any shit. I'll kick your ass," Florence said.

"I think Sarah found the lucky sperm and is cashing in. How else can you explain going from a working stiff to living in a million dollar home fully paid for," Betty said.

"How dare you imply Howard is not her father? Rory and I were nothing but good friends. You bitches were the sluts in this town."

"Are you still having an affair with Jack Daniels, Florence," Lillian asked.

"I keep my pants on, you low life bitch."

Things went from bad to worse. I mean, half the people in the store had quit shopping and were taking it all in. The manager had to ask all of them to leave. They were both fit to be tied as they drove out to Twelve Trees. Florence always had a heavy foot and the red lights went off two miles down the road.

"Where in the name of God did that cop come from?" Florence said.

"Pull over, Florence."

The police car pulled in behind them and the officers got out. They were greatly relieved to see it was Herb with his partner,

James Jackson. He walked up to the car and asked to see a driver's license.

"Herb, what is the problem?" Florence asked.

"You were driving twenty miles over the speed limit in a construction zone. I'm sorry, but I have to write a ticket with a four hundred dollar fine."

"This is your family, Herb. Why don't you walk back to your car and we will be on our way."

"Write her another ticket for trying to coerce an officer," James said.

"Joan is going to pinch your head off."

"I think it would be wise for you not to say another word. We are close to taking you in to the station."

"Buster, you don't know who you are screwing with."

"Florence, please don't say another word," Vicki said.

"You better leave me the hell alone. I'll bring my brother in law in here and rain fire down on both of your stupid asses!"

"You just threatened a police officer, Fat Ass," James said.

"You dumb shits are never going to learn. Be my guest and take me in, if you have the balls. You wimp ass dickheads will be heading off with Huey when Don gets through with you."

Well, that did it for the cops. She wouldn't shut up and the next thing Vicki knew, Florence was in handcuffs and heading off to the jail. She got behind the wheel and headed for Sarah's house to call Rufus. Sarah answered the door and showed her in. Rory was sitting in the living room looking out over the golf course.

"Sarah, I have to use your phone and call Rufus. Florence ran her mouth and got arrested."

"My God; what on earth did she do, Mother?"

"She got a damn speeding ticket and wouldn't shut up. She tried to get Herb and another officer to not write the ticket. She crossed the line and they arrested her."

"Here is the cordless phone, Mother. You better call Rufus right now."

R.E. saw Sarah was calling and almost didn't pick up. He and Howard were fishing and had found a hot spot. Imagine his surprise when Vicki was on the line telling him Florence was in jail.

"What the hell did the fool do now?"

"She got a speeding ticket and threatened Herb and the other cop."

"I'm in the boat with Howard. I'll pull out and head back in."

"You better get down there as fast as you can. Thank God she wasn't drinking the Jack Daniels."

She hung up and looked at Sarah. "Surely my day cannot get any worse."

"Mother, Rory is here. It is time for us to have a little talk."

"Good God, Sarah, I don't think my heart can take another shock. Where is Rory for God sakes?"

"He is in the living room. Let's go in and talk."

Vicki eased around the corner and looked in to see Rory sitting in an over sized chair. He looked around and smiled at her. "Please have a seat Vicki and just relax."

"Florence got arrested and I need to go to the jail."

"Mother, please sit down for a moment. No one is going to bite you."

"Vicki, we just wanted you to know that no one is going to embarrass you or Howard," Rory said.

"I've got news for both of you. Lillian Camp already confronted me this morning about the two of you. How the hell do you explain a million dollar home fully furnished. She saw the two of you out shopping. It doesn't take a rocket scientist to figure out what is going on."

"Mother, tell all of them to go straight to hell. I am happy and secure for the first time in my life."

"I have to go now before Florence winds up in the pen."

"Mother, Rory is giving me a hundred million."

"Rory is giving you a hundred million what?"

"He is giving me a hundred million dollars."

Well, it took a good five minutes to bring Vicki back from passing out. She had to go lie down on the couch and regroup. The poor woman went seventy years without passing out one time. It seemed like she was passing out once a week now.

Rufus and Howard were off the lake and on the way to the jail. Florence was raising more hell than a rock band in concert. By the time R.E. and Howard got to the jail, she had insulted every cop in the station. Chief Thomas and Herb met R.E. with the list of charges filed against her. The fines were now up to twenty five hundred dollars. Florence was right about one thing. Nobody wanted another taste of Don Hudson and they let the poor man pay the fines. Florence was released and still raising hell on her way out of the police station. They got in the car with Howard in the back seat.

"I hope you're satisfied, Florence. You made an ass out of yourself and cost me twenty five hundred dollars."

"I know it has to be killing your soul, you tight wad son-of-a-bitch. I'm going to crawl all over Joan's jealous ass when I see the bitch. That little piece of shit she raised told me to shut the hell up. I wish Don had put him on the stand and cut his nuts out."

"Jesus, cut the damn boy some slack. He was just doing his job, Florence."

"Did you give them a good piece of your mind?" Howard asked.

"I told the jackasses I was calling Kate and telling everything I know on the bastards. I'm going to put all their asses in jail with Huey."

The word was out and Don and Faith boarded the jet for the flight up to Littleville. Carol had hit the jackpot with one of Don's assistants and they flew up for the show. The twelve women on the Cullen jury were all plotting to get to Don. The husbands had finally figured out the story and were watching them like a hawk. Wesley took Kate's advice and positioned a mobile crew at the front gate to film Don's arrival. The jet landed and Don got in the limo for the ride over to Kate's house. Faith got in the car with Renee and Emily. They drove over to Renee's home to watch the show. Anne picked up Carol and her new boyfriend and headed over to her house. Needless to say, the cops had been warned and showed up in force. I mean the State Police, Sheriff Deputies, and Littleville Cops were everywhere. All twelve of the husbands stood outside the gates with eight hundred screaming women. The limo arrived at the gates and out jumped Don. He started hugging the women and signing autographs. Wesley stood looking at the monitors with Kate. Damn if two of the female cops didn't run up and hug him.

"Jesus Christ, what in the name of God is he doing?"

"He's playing the women, Wesley. The man is smarter than hell. He knows every woman in the country is watching. He told me after the trial he never stops working. He said, "Kate, if you create the illusion, it becomes real. I want every woman to love me. You never know when a trial will be held in their area."

"I hope they don't tear his clothes off before he gets on the set."

"It could damn sure happen, my friend. He ain't any fool, Wesley. You can bet your last dime he has another suit in the limo. My sister is one of the ten best looking women in America. You will never see her with Don in front of a camera. He wants every woman to think he is available."

"The man is a better promoter than me. Look at those women going crazy out there."

"Wesley, I don't know how much money you are making. It is none of my damn business. I'm telling you one last time. The boy is going to blow your mind. Women are stone cold crazy about him."

After thirty minutes of hugging and signing autographs, Don got back in the limo. The driver drove up to the house. Kate walked outside with Wesley to greet him as he stepped out of the limo. Man, out of nowhere, here came Denise and the eleven other jurors from the dark. They were hugging Don like a puppy licking his momma. Wesley stood glaring at his security people. They all stood with a shit eating grin on their faces. Don invited them all in after clearing it with Kate. Wesley walked over to Don and acted like he was introducing himself.

"You crazy bastard, Faith is going to kill you."

"Wesley, I wouldn't cheat on Faith for a billion dollars. I'm just doing my job and she knows it."

"Where are we going to put these damn women?"

"I'd appreciate it if you would put them on the show for a few seconds. I'm sure with your genius mind you will figure out how to capitalize on it."

"Damn, do you ever stop hustling?"

Wesley had a live shot of Don with the girls and they were seated in the living room to watch the show. The husbands all went home thinking everything was okay. Tom was introduced to Don and sat down with Kate on the set. It was show time and Tom did his thing.

"Welcome to an evening with Kate and her special guest, Don Hudson. Don just happens to be America's top criminal defense attorney. We are going to open the phone lines now with our first caller. "Rita Collins, from Longview, Texas you are live with Kate in Littleville."

"Kate, I've been looking forward to your show tonight."

"Rita, of that I have no doubt. What's on your mind tonight?"

"I'd like to ask Don if he has considered doing a movie."

"Don, have you considered going into the movie business?" Kate asked.

"I just practice law, Rita. I believe Mr. Arnold is going to shoot a movie called Littleville. I might get lucky and score a cameo role."

"I followed every minute of the Cullen trial. You were just breathtaking and I would have voted to acquit."

"Thank you so much, Rita. The jurors were nice enough to come out for the show tonight. I think Kate has a clip of them with us a little earlier tonight."

Kate talked while the girls were shown with Don. "I'd have to say those women are now big fans of yours, Don."

Well, I don't have to tell you twelve cars were pulling out of garages a minute later. The dudes had been had and they all knew it. Faith sat watching and having her wine.

"Every damn woman in America thinks they can have him, Faith," Renee said.

"I sure as hell hope they all keep thinking they can have him. God I love that man."

"My Lord, the courts are going to have to create a dress code for Don's trials. Those women showed up tonight like they did the second day of Bobby Jack's trial," Emily said.

"They always do, Emily."

Wesley was on the phone to his people in New York. The switchboards were flooded with callers and Dave George was in panic mode. "Wesley, we are going to have some pissed off women. I have five hundred women holding on the lines trying to get through to Kate."

"We will do the best we can, Dave. Cut out the commercials tonight until the end of the show."

"Molly Hanson from Canton, Ohio, you are live with Kate," Tom said.

"Kate, my husband passed away a year ago. We have a thousand acre farm we own. Some S.O.B. planted marijuana on three acres and the cops busted me. I'm on the verge of losing everything to the damn government. I didn't even know what the plant looked like and never got one penny. The bastard they busted even said I didn't know anything. I'm out on bail and scared to death."

"Well, that sucks for sure. Maybe Don can give you some advice."

"Molly, had you ever met the man they caught growing the plants?"

"Don, I wouldn't know him if he walked up to my door."

"You need to find a good criminal and civil attorney. The government has no right to seize your property. Some damn United States Attorney is trying to make a name for himself. Molly, you have grounds for a multi-million dollar lawsuit. You need to clear your name and then go after them."

"The attorneys I spoke too are scared of the government. I'm stuck with a court appointed attorney who has never tried a case."

"You call my office Monday morning and we will put the hurt on the government's ass."

"Mr. Hudson, I'm dead broke."

"You will not be for long, Molly. Call your attorney and tell him you just hired me."

"Molly, you can rest easy my friend. I've seen Don in action and the government will be begging for him to get off their ass. Trust me on this one sugar; you will not have a mortgage when he is finished."

"Don, I'm about to break down and cry. You have taken the weight of the world off my shoulders. I thank you from the bottom of my heart."

Don looked directly into the camera and cut the billion dollar smile. "Don't you worry another second, Molly."

The boys were back at the front gate demanding to be let in. The cops listened to their sad tale and told them to hit the road. When they refused off to jail they went kicking and screaming. Denise and the girls were having a fine time watching Kate and Don.

Susan Morgan was watching the show. Her husband was the United States Attorney for the Canton district. She picked up the phone and called her husband who was working late in Cleveland. Henry Morgan was a hard charging man on the way up the ladder. His secretary passed Susan through immediately.

"Susan, what's on your mind?"

"Don Hudson is on my mind."

"That man is one bad ass attorney. I've got a ninety nine percent conviction rate, baby. We don't want that prick coming in and messing it up."

"Do you have a case working against a woman named Molly Hanson from Canton?"

"We damn sure do sweetheart. Why do you ask, Susan?"

"The woman just hired Hudson on national television. Let me see if I can quote exactly what he said. I believe to put it in the simplest terms he said, 'we will put the hurt on the government's ass.' He also let the world know you, my dear, were trying to make a name for yourself."

"What the hell do you mean she hired him on national television?"

"What part of 'hiring him on national television' don't you understand?"

"Jesus Christ, what show are you watching?"

"I'm watching Kate Manley's show on Wes-Star."

"Mother of God, we better take another look at her case."

"You better drop the damn case like a hot potato, Henry. Her court appointed attorney is history and you are staring Don Hudson dead in the face. The jurors in the Cullen case, if you can call them that, showed up to see Hudson tonight. If the show was on network television, they would have been banned. Henry, can I share something with you?"

"By all means, tell me what's on your mind."

"Your conviction rate is getting ready to take a drop along with your reputation. I understand why you took the job as a stepping stone. If you don't want to be pushed off the cliff into the rocks down below, I strongly suggest you drop the case against Molly Hanson. This son-of-a-bitch is the best looking man on the planet and smoother than silk. You don't want any part of him in a courtroom.

Baby, I'd have to vote against you if I was on the jury. I have to run, the show is back on and I don't want to miss a second."

Well, Kate was right as rain once again. Every woman in the world wanted to talk to the man. The censors were on red alert and blocked three different women offering the man a night in their bed. Wesley let the show run for an extra hour and the ratings looked like the Super Bowl. The damn subscribers went completely crazy after the show. Don hugged all the girls and headed over to Renee's house to pick up Faith. The cops got the women in their cars and called it a night. Wesley was so damn excited, he couldn't sit down. Kate made them a drink and Chuck and Tom joined them.

"I've never seen anything like that in my life. You would think they were teens at a rock concert."

"I told you, Wesley. You just have to see it to believe it. Did you find the vibrator company?"

"I damn sure did, Kate. I bought two hundred thousand shares. They don't report for four weeks. I'll just sit tight and wait for the results."

"It's money in the bank, Wesley. If Don could get a buck for every woman wanting to bed him, he would be rich."

"Kate, you can trust me on this one. The rascal already has more money than you could ever imagine."

"How the hell did those women get up to the house?" Chuck asked.

"Chuck, you have been out of the game far too long. The only way they would have been turned away is if the guards were gay."

"I think we can start shooting the movie next month. The script is finished and the cast is being chosen."

"This damn town will go completely crazy. If you want to see people make fools of themselves, go watch the filming. Do me a favor and cast a three hundred pound woman as Florence. I want to hear the old bitch scream bloody murder."

Huey had watched the show from his cell in the federal pen. He was carrying on to the other inmates about how Littleville was his town. One of the men, Dave Johnson, had just been transferred from another jail. Would you believe his cell mate was none other than C Jacob himself? The dude was in no mood to hear some convict running his mouth about being a big shot.

"You loud mouth asshole. If it's your town, what the hell are you doing behind bars?" Dave shouted.

"That no good bastard, Don Hudson, dropped the dime on me. I had everything under control until he showed up and nailed me."

"Your old buddy told me the same sad story. Both of you are full of shit as a Christmas turkey."

"I ran the town my way for fourteen years."

"You better enjoy the memories, because your ass is grass from now on. Don Hudson wouldn't piss on you if you were on fire."

Don picked up Faith and they boarded the plane back to West Palm. Emily drove back home the next day and everyone started in with bragging rights. The family wondered out loud who would be playing their characters. The visions were dancing in their minds as to who would be selected. Florence and Vicki were holding court at the beauty salon and it was packed with women. Florence had a few drinks before she arrived and was feeling mighty fine about herself. She rattled off the names of a half dozen young and beautiful actresses who should play her character.

"Honey, those girls could be your granddaughters and they are a third your size. You must be getting yourself confused with Faith and Anne," Mabel Craig said.

"Mabel, you better bite your tongue before I get up out of this chair. For your information, the movie is about our entire lives. Need I remind you, Vicki and I were the biggest catches in Littleville."

"How did you wind up with Rufus Cage? My husband said they would have to find a midget to play Rufus," Marie Law said.

"You are a bunch of jealous old bitches. I don't think I'll let either one of you in the movie. Rufus was a very handsome man in his youth. He shrunk when he got older."

"You don't have a damn thing to say about who is going to be in the movie. The Jack Daniels must be getting to your brain cells," Marie said.

"Who is going to play you and Howard, Vicki?" Janet Holden asked.

"I don't know who they will choose."

"Are they going to have scenes with Howard being shot at, Vicki?"

"Janet, why don't you go straight to hell."

It just went on and on for an hour and a half. Florence had lost her damn buzz and Vicki was not happy as they left. They were on the way home when Florence looked over at her sister.

"Have you ever seen bitches that jealous in your whole life? I was wondering to myself about something."

"What were you wondering?" Vicki asked.

"If they use the scenes with Emily, I bet the movie will have to be x-rated."

"Florence, the Martin family has been xxx rated forever. Daddy made sure of that before he died."

CHAPTER TWENTY-ONE

The film crews arrived and the little town was buzzing. Auditions were being held at the local basketball arena and almost everyone showed up. Wesley had booked the hotel for thirty days and the owner was ecstatic. Scooter had his new mobile van outside, selling the living hell out of the shirts. Amanda and her parents were stunned when Scooter walked in and paid off the note. She was becoming a little uneasy with the sudden turn of events. Her parents had her sign a pre-nuptial agreement before she and Scooter were married. The good news was he couldn't touch her money. The bad news was she couldn't touch his money. It seemed like a damn good idea at the time, but this Kate Manley show had changed everything. When she offered to change everything, Scooter blew her off like the wind. When he blew her off in bed, she knew there was big trouble. The boy had found a sudden streak of independence and it was obvious to her and her rich parents. Truth be known, Scooter was well on his way to putting their bad ass memory in the past.

The Governor, being the publicity hound he was, showed up with everyone else. He was a little taken aback when no one gave him the time of day. They had bigger and better things on their minds. Besides, the prick had just pushed through and signed into law a bill banning smoking in public places. The family had been informed who the cast was going to be. They were extremely unhappy. No one knew any of the actors, but they sure as hell saw their pictures. The women had congregated at Renee's house and the talking began over breakfast.

"My Lord, the woman who is playing me weighs over three hundred pounds. She is ugly as hell. The bitches in this town are going to have a field day making fun of me. She looks like she belongs with C. Jacob. Christ, she must wear a size fifteen shoe. Her hair is so bad I'm sure she has never been to a beauty saloon," Florence said.

"Florence, I feel so badly for you. The woman is just awful looking and there is no getting around it. Sammy Joe saw her at Target and she was spitting tobacco in the parking lot. He said the lady is all bent over and she pulled her false teeth out right in front of him. She caught him looking at her and asked him what the hell he was looking at. She started over to him and spit at the boy. Sammy said he took off and ran across the parking lot to his car," Renee said.

"The man they choose to play Howard looks like Elmer Fudd. Do I really look as old as the actress playing me?"

"You don't look nearly that old. We need to find out how they went about getting these actors. We should have given them a picture of ourselves so they had something to go by. They choose the biggest and ugliest people they could find," Emily said.

"I've never looked as bad as the woman playing me. The woman looks fifteen years older than me. She has her mouth closed in the picture trying to smile. Christ, I'm afraid to even read the script. Kate called to tell me the shooting scene is in the movie. She thinks your naked days are in the movie, Emily," Renee said.

"I should never have agreed to give them the right to use my stories. The woman playing me looks like a linebacker on the football team. Moose met the woman at the airport. He said she has a set of lungs like a bullfrog. He said she was down right intimidating and one rough looking woman. He told me I was going to freak out when I met her."

"Rufus is going to be very upset with them for using a midget. He is a good five inches taller than the man. The damn three inch dick is in the movie and I'll never hear the end of it."

"That was a terrible thing to say about any man. It would have been bad enough just saying it was small. R.E. will never get over it. You should know how easy it is to crush a man's ego. I still can't believe you said that about the poor man," Renee said.

"I lost my temper and it just came out."

"The man they chose to play Jake is six foot six. I think he is from a foreign country. His accent is clearly not that of an American. I would never be married to a foreigner."

"The man is from Vancouver, Emily," Anne said.

"They chose two nice looking men to play Jimmy and Scooter. The girls playing Anne and Carol are pretty," Renee said.

"The movie is a comedy for goodness sakes. Why are all of you so uptight about the actors?" Anne asked.

"I can't believe they chose a good looking woman to play Kate. I think she is fooling around with the producer. The woman does have a slight resemblance to Kate. Her eyes and mouth are the same. At least they are the same size for God sakes," Florence said.

"Why are they making a big secret of who is playing Don and Faith? I'm calling Faith and see if she knows," Emily said.

"I'm going to just die if it's two big Hollywood stars. We already look like hell," Renee said.

"You know damn well they will be drop dead beautiful. I'm ready to go see these actors," Vicki said.

The girls all loaded up and headed down to the auditions. They wanted to meet the director and put their two cents worth in. Wesley sat with Tim Hamel conducting interviews. Needless to say, the first twelve locals hired were Denise and the other eleven women on the jury. It is pretty safe to assume Wesley interviewed each one personally. Jackie Simpson and Judge Harrison had no interest whatsoever. I mean, it's like Kate once said; a good old fashion ass whipping will give a man religion. They had no interest in reliving the nightmare called Don Hudson. Florence had no sooner got out of the car when an old enemy walked right up to her and pounced.

"I just met the actress who is playing you. She looks just like you, Florence," Amy said.

"The woman does not look a thing like me. Did you come down here to get in my face?"

"I came to laugh my ass off at you fools. Go over and meet your husband, if you can find him."

"R.E. is fishing with Howard today."

"How did you ever get out of high school? I'm talking about the actor playing Rufus."

"You old cold hearted bitch, get out of my face. You are jealous as hell and showing your ass."

"You know, I think I'll do just that, Florence. God forbid if you sat on me. I'd be a dead woman."

"You have always been a trash talking bitch. Your husband begged me for some until the day he died."

"I thought you gave him some and that's why he died."

Florence was hot as the girls started walking. They saw Jimmy and Scooter surrounded by young women. Scooter had the shirts and was gladly helping the girls put them on. Jimmy was right there with him smiling every second.

"The damn boys are in their element. Jimmy can't get the smile off his face. Sarah told me he ran Violet off and has a different woman or two over at his house every night," Vicki said.

"Their both going to start a harem," Renee said.

"Scooter is really getting flagrant running women. He must be ready to check out from Amanda," Anne said.

"Here comes a big limo with the film crews following. I wonder if it is the mystery stars," Vicki said.

"I can't wait to see who it is, girls. I bet your right, Vicki," Renee said.

The limo stopped and Wesley walked over and got in. A minute later, out stepped Kate dressed to the nines with makeup on. The crowd went wild and the cast came rushing over to shake hands.

"Son-of-a-bitch, can you even believe it? She doesn't even look like Kate. My God, they have given her a whole new look," Anne said.

"What is the man saying to the cameras? Get over there Anne and see what is happening," Vicki said.

Two minutes later, Anne was back with the news. "Kate is staring as Kate in the movie. I guess being a television star was not enough. Now she is going to be a movie star."

"I'm going to kick my ass until the day I die for not running my mouth."

"Florence, you have run your mouth since the day you came into the world. You just ran it to the wrong people. You should have run your big ass down to the newspaper and television station," Renee said.

The women made their way over to the actors. They were eyeballing them to beat hell. The lady who was cast as Florence introduced herself. "Florence, is half this script the truth?"

"I haven't read it, but nothing would surprise me."

"I'm thrilled to death to get the role. I hope when you see the movie, you will be happy. I'd really like to spend some time with you before we start shooting. This is my very first role in a movie."

"Well, it's going to be a hard role to play. You got lucky when you got to play me. I'm certain you will be the star of the show."

"My part will not be big enough. Kate is the star of the show, as you would expect. Anyway, I'll do my best and it was nice to meet you."

Some egos are hard to deflate and Florence moved right on to meeting the rest of the cast. Renee was just beside herself when she saw the woman playing her. The actress looked worse in person than she did in the pictures.

"Momma, this is not going to be flattering to you. The lady's two front teeth are missing. She talks real country, but she is real nice. She doesn't wear makeup and has a big scar on her face. You need to get control of yourself and be prepared for a shock," Anne said.

"You know, I thought something might be wrong. Johnny hasn't come over for three nights in a row. He called me and said he met the woman who was playing me. I wondered why he just blew me off when I asked what she looked like. He told me last night on the phone he would be traveling a lot this month."

"The lady wants to meet you and get to know you. Her name is Sharon Henry."

"How could this happen to me?"

Anne led them over to the actress and everyone was introduced. "Renee, you have led quite a life."

"I'm sure the script doesn't really tell the whole story. How did you lose your teeth, if I may ask?"

"I had bad teeth since I was a kid. I usually wear caps, but they told me not to wear them for the movie."

"Were you in a car accident? I'm so sorry about the scar on your face."

"My former husband freaked out on acid one night. I fell through the window trying to get the hell out. I have to run and study my lines. It was nice of you to come by and say hello. This is the break I've been praying for all my life. I'll do my best to make you proud."

They watched her walk away and Renee was fit to be tied. "Now I know why Faith has been so mad about the movie. She keeps saying all they care about is the money. She said Kate came out smelling like roses and she was happy about that."

"The rest of us are going to come out smelling like the goose shit Howard and Rufus keep landing in," Vicki said.

"I'm afraid we have been had girls. We got fifty thousand for letting the world see the Martin family," Florence said.

"Daddy would be proud of all of us for telling the story. I wonder why they cast a ghost as Daddy," Vicki asked.

"I don't know, but again Faith is mad as hell about it. She said as long as Wesley is making big money he will never stop. I think she knows something, but can't tell us. I can always tell when she is holding back on me. I sense there is a little friction between her and Don," Renee said.

"Daddy's sister, Aunt Thelma, told me a man came by and talked for hours about Daddy. She said he couldn't hear enough stories about Daddy and our Aunts and Uncles. The fellow took her to lunch three different times. He even said he had identified all the children from the other women. Thelma said all the kids would love to get together and meet. The man told her he had someone willing to pay for everything. She said we should get together sometime. Why would someone go to all that trouble?" Florence asked.

"Someone wants to know everything about Daddy. The man is dead, so nobody can sue him. Kate is the trustee of his affairs. He didn't have a damn thing when he died. It must be one of those kids and they are rich as hell," Vicki said.

"I smell a rat and he's getting ready to steal the cheese. It would be funny if you think about it. We become the laughing stock of the world, but the little royalty from the sales makes us rich," Renee said.

"Something is going to jump up and bite us on the ass when we least expect it. Faith knows something and it's not good," Florence said.

"Vicki, the old woman playing you is walking over here. My God, she looks like she came out of a nursing home. The lady has to be ninety years old," Emily said.

"This is a nightmare," Vicki said.

The actress walked up and introduced herself. "Good morning, I'm Brenda Johnson. You have to be Vicki."

"It's nice to meet you, Brenda. How are you today?"

"Vicki, my damn arthritis is about to kill my old ass. They told me this morning I could use my cane and I'm really grateful."

"Have you been in a lot of movies?" Emily asked.

"No. I get one about every ten years. I need to get back over there before they fire me."

They watched her walk away and Florence looked at Vicki. "Something peculiar is going on here and I don't like it a damn bit. What do you think, Vicki?"

"We have all been had in the worst possible way, Florence. I think we need to go over and see Kate if we can get to her. How in the hell did Wesley convince her to change her look?"

"Money talks and bullshit walks. Kate is enjoying her new life as a rich and famous person," Renee said.

"I can't believe how good she looks," Anne said.

Kate was surrounded by people, signing autographs when they walked up. Everyone ignored them as they stood waiting to visit with her. After ten minutes, she was shown into a trailer. The girls started to follow her in, but two security guards stopped them. Kate looked out and told her security guard to let them come in. They were a little taken aback as they entered the trailer.

"Did y'all have a chance to meet the actors playing your characters?" Kate asked.

"I couldn't miss mine unless I was blind. How did they go about picking the actors?" Florence asked.

"I don't know, Florence. I can't believe Wesley and Don talked me into being in the movie. What do you think about my new look? Wesley flew some famous hair stylist down from Los Angeles with a makeup artist."

"You look wonderful, girl. I didn't even recognize you when you got out of the car," Renee said.

"Chuck almost fell out when he saw me. It is amazing how money makes you change your mind. Wesley is creating my own clothes and cosmetic line. We are up to twenty six million subscribers and Wesley is giving me a third of the new company."

"What does that mean in dollars and cents?" Florence asked.

"I don't know about the cents, but he guaranteed me ten million a year. He and Don are getting to be asshole buddies. For some reason, Don can't seem to do enough to help me and Wesley."

"Damn, you are living a dream," Renee said.

"Emily, someone wants to meet you," Kate said.

"Is it the actress who is playing me?"

"She is a crazy chick, Emily. Judy, come in here and meet Emily."

The woman came through the door and looked exactly like her picture. She looked at the women and let out a howl. "I can't eat a whole chicken!" she screamed at the top of her lungs." I got to stay thin. I like to be naked!" she bellowed.

"Oh no. Please tell me the script is not calling for that."

"You damn right the script is calling for that and a hell of a lot more. I am going to grab that skinny ass boy playing Jake and throw him on the floor. I'm going to tie him up and watch a porno movie."

"Judy, that didn't happen."

"This is the movies, Emily. Its fiction, baby. So, just sit back and enjoy it."

"Go on and get your crazy ass out of here," Kate said.

"Kate, please tell me she is not serious."

"Emily, relax. She is pulling your leg. She is all fired up about doing the nude scenes. The crazy bitch offered to give Wesley a blow job for the part. He told her he didn't like big women."

"Kate, we are all so happy for you," Vicki said.

"Thanks for saying that, Vicki. Florence, do you want to do a Jack Daniels commercial? I can get you a gig for seventy thousand if you want it. Wesley don't want me doing any commercials."

"Sign my ass up and I'll pop the top. I damn sure appreciate it too. Scooter caught our dumb asses flat footed on the shirts. The boy is selling more shirts than Wal-Mart. I need the bread in the worst way."

"Girls, I have to get my ass home. Wesley has his girlfriend flying in for dinner tonight at the house. Don and Faith are stopping in on their way home from New York. I'll see all of y'all later when we start shooting the movie."

The women started back to the car watching Kate get in the limo. Renee and Emily were a little taken aback at Faith not calling to say she would be in town. Old Florence had about figured out that Don might own a little more than a small piece of the action. Vicki was just not pleased at the age of the actress playing her part. Renee had one splitting headache thinking about the woman playing her.

It was Wednesday morning and the cast was busy filming the movie. Renee's worst fears had come to pass. Two big stars were playing Don and Faith and I'm not even going to tell you who they were. R.E. and Howard were taking it hard over their characters. The poor men couldn't go anywhere without being made fun of by their so called buddies. R.E. was all bowed up and bent out of shape at the barber shop.

"Rufus, you need to make some money like Florence. She has the Jack Daniels deal and we all got together and figured out how you and Howard can cash in," Ralph Jones said.

"Ralph, I ain't in the mood for any of your shit today. I just need a haircut and so does Howard."

"Suit yourself, but we got a winner for both of you. You ought to cash in on your fame boys."

"Alright, but no more jokes about us," Howard said.

"I got a friend who owns a plant that manufactures things for people. You could hook up and make a killing selling you and Howard's stuff. The man is wired in with all the big chains."

"We signed away our souls on any merchandise to the company," R.E. said.

"That's too bad my friends. You could have made millions according to my friend."

"That's just mine and Howard's luck. We sell out for fifty grand and leave millions on the table. What was the fellow wanting to sell for us?"

The boys were all waiting for Ralph to deliver the punch line. "He wanted Howard running from a man with guns drawn. With you, he wanted a three inch dildo."

The men cracked up, but R.E. was madder than hell. He stormed out and swore he would never return. Howard felt the same way and followed him to the car.

"Now, I know how the Americans felt when the Japanese starting making fun of them," Howard said.

"I'll never forgive Florence for running her mouth about me. I have to find a way to prove I don't have a three inch pecker."

"Why don't you have a bunch of women stand up for you? That way it will be ten against two."

"Ain't any damn woman going to stand up and tell the world the size of my pecker? Florence just called to tell me she got seventy thousand from Jack Daniels. I have to watch the big rhino drinking on television now."

Sometimes you just find yourself in a bad situation with no way out. Oh well, at least they still both had their fifty thousand. You can bet your ass R.E. got his twenty-five hundred back from Florence. They drove home and R.E. stopped at the mailbox and got his mail. They went inside and sat down over a cold beer. He noticed there were two envelopes from Arnold-Hudson. One was made to him and the other to Florence. He opened his and saw a check for six hundred dollars. He thought Florence's check would be the same. About that time Florence showed up and came in with her chest puffed out. Florence saw her envelope and picked it up.

"I got my first royalty check for six hundred dollars," R.E. said.

"I'm sure mine will be much more. Sarah told Vicki the people are buying my shirts. I told the actor today she would be the star in the movie."

"I'm sure you are full of shit."

Florence opened the envelope and let out a howl that would have made Emily proud. "I told your jealous ass I was the star. My check is for twenty thousand. You better hope I don't decide to leave your ass. Men are going to be chasing me like hell when the word get's out I'm rich. I'm thinking I better call Don and have him put together one of those pre-nuptials for me."

"You're fifty three years late, old fool. I ought to sue your big fat ass for telling the world I have a three inch dick. You are making a killing because you ran your mouth on Kate's show about me."

"Well, you are an ungrateful little bastard. Did you forget I kept you out of jail when you made a fool out of yourself?"

"You never talked to the damn Judge. Come on Howard, I've had enough and we are out of here."

"Go on and take your little midget ass out of my house."

Man, they both hit the door without looking back. I guess fifty three years of marriage doesn't mean that much. R.E. called Sarah and she invited him back to spend the night. He dropped Howard off and took off for Twelve Trees. The man was mad as a hornet and plotting to get even. Sarah told him there was only one way to clear his name. He had to go on Kate's show and set the record straight. He shook off his fear and placed a call to Kate, who agreed to have him on. Hell, she even invited Howard to be with him the same night.

Three nights later, R.E. and Howard were on the set. The old boys looked like two deer caught in the headlights when the cameras started to roll. You can bet your last dime Florence and Vicki were glued to the television set. Matter of fact, half the country was glued to their set. Tom did his thing once again and Kate got right to work.

"Good evenings to everyone. I have two of my brother in laws on tonight. One of them is about to become an ex brother in law after fifty three years. Boys, welcome to the show."

"Thanks for having us over, Kate. I'd like to clear the record and get my manhood back. Howard has a few things to say himself."

"Hell! Let your hair down and fire away. We have two hours for you both to get it off your chest."

"I measured myself and I'm five foot five. Howard measured me, too. I'm not a midget like the fellow playing me in Littleville."

"Folks, the men are shooting straight with us. I'm looking at him and he is no midget. What else do you want to clear up, Rufus?"

"I know this is delicate, but I have to clear my name. My wife Florence and Myrtle Lee both told the world I had a three inch you know what. I went to three doctors and they measured me for length. I brought the results and had them notarized. I ain't really into anything, but you telling the audience the three inch is a lie."

He handed Kate the results and she laughed. "Folks, the man is telling us the truth. Both my sister and Myrtle were pulling our leg. Let's take some calls for the boys now."

"Marie Law from Kansas City, Kansas is on the line," Tom said.

"Howard, did you really get shot at a dozen times?"

"Yes, I'm afraid I did Mrs. Law. You see, I was a sinner before I found the Lord. I'm in the flock now and the good Lord has given me a pass. One of my boys is the pastor of our church. He used to be a sinner too."

"What was it like having men shoot at you?"

"It was scary as hell. It was almost as bad as when the Japanese attacked the Americans."

"Howard, you weren't in World War Two."

"I was damn sure on the boat in New York when they attacked. There I was in the middle of the water and can't swim a lick. They were coming from every direction, Kate. R.E. and I had to run for cover and felt real bad. R.E. told Pedro we were just too damn old to help."

"R.E., what the hell is Howard talking about?"

"We went out on the boat to see the Statue of Liberty. Pedro couldn't drive across the water. The Japanese started making fun of the Americans and all hell broke loose. Florence tried to get me to dive off the boat, but I couldn't leave Howard to die at the hands of their fighters."

"Were Florence and Vicki on the boat?"

"They were shopping at the store across the street from where the saints live. They gave it up when they found out the britches cost two grand. They drove up with Pedro to get us and saw the war going on. My mouth was dry, but I didn't dare buy a bottle of water.

Can you even believe they sell water for twelve bucks a bottle in New York City?" Howard asked.

"Is Pedro one of your sons?"

"Scooter is my son. Pedro is Don and Faith's driver. He took us around and tried his best to keep us out of trouble. I forget what you call the places, but you can't go there. I think you can go uptown and the middle is okay. The lower part is supposed to be okay, but we almost got killed there. I think Pedro said you can't go east or west without running into big time trouble."

Marie signed off and the next call came in from Tucson, Arizona. Mack Byrd was anxious to get started and plowed right in after Tom introduced him. "Kate, could the boys talk about the time the family thought Don was a killer?"

"Which one of you wants to take the lead?"

"It was all just a big misunderstanding, Mack. My wife has bad ears. I have to say I'm in the same boat. We thought Faith said the boy was going around killing people and beating drug raps. Vicki called Florence and I told R.E. the boy was killing people faster than a speeding bullet. One thing led to another and we convinced ourselves our own lives were in danger."

"Mack, let me just give it to you straight. We proceeded to scare the shit out of ourselves. When it was all said and done, we were the laughing stock of the damn county. I have to call it like I see it, Mack. If someone told me the story, I'd laugh my ass off. By the time we finished making a fool of ourselves, the whole town was in an uproar. We had a killer on the loose wiping out four men at a time in the local motel. Scooter's gun went off in the house and everyone hit the floor. Howard and I were running for our lives out at the local country club and Howard was covered in goose shit."

"How did you feel once you realized the man was the top defense attorney in the country?"

"I felt like a damn idiot. I've never been so embarrassed in my entire life."

"I thought I'd done fooled around and lost my mind," Howard said.

Things were moving along and R.E. felt like he was finally putting all the bad stuff to rest. The calls kept coming and the boys were making quite an impression. Kate saw her producer flash a card saying Florence was on the line. She couldn't pass up the opportunity and passed her through.

"Rufus, your wife is on the horn," Kate said.

"What the hell do you want, woman?"

"Why don't you tell everyone how much room you had to spare big dick?"

"Why don't you tell everyone the last time you ever saw it?"

"Hey, that's enough about that subject," Kate said.

"Kate, have the fool tell you how he almost got his stupid ass indicted betting on football games."

"Do you want to tell us about your near fatal mistake?"

"My buddy offered to fly us to court. On the way down, he blacked out and we almost died three different times. I was so shook up I almost misspoke on the witness stand. It wasn't nearly as bad as Florence is making it out to be."

"You old bullshit artist, you were scarred to death. I had to walk in the courtroom myself and save your lying ass. If the Judge hadn't been taken with me, they would have sent your ass right off to prison. The old devil has been chasing women his whole life."

"Saint Teresa, why don't you tell everyone about the Congressman?"

It went on and on, until Kate called a truce. It turned out the timing for Florence's call was not so good. The call no sooner ended when the two hookers from New York called in. Wesley had been tipped a day earlier the gals would be calling. It turns out they were both big fans of Kate. They watched the show every night it was on when they were not working.

"We have Maria and Joyce on the phone from New York City. It seems they are both coming to speak up for R.E. Girls, welcome to the show," Tom said.

"Hey sugar, I told you to tell those old bags to kiss off. Were those hot dogs any good?" Joyce asked.

"I couldn't even touch them they were so cold. Frank was off chasing women, but I told James you sent us over."

"Kate, this son of a gun is hung like a horse and frisky as a rabbit. You put him with a couple of good looking young women and he is almost too much to take. I'd jump a plane in a second if R.E. said the word," Maria said.

"Lord in heaven, you are on a roll girl."

"Why don't you call Jimmy and Scooter and send us a couple of plane tickets. We'll show those bitches how to have a good time," Joyce said.

"Those boys have their hands full now, Joyce. Howard and I would love to see both of you again."

"Honey, we will be down there in a split second. I'll give the man our number when we sign off," Maria said.

"Thanks for calling girls and I damn sure will not forget what you did for me. You can bet you're pretty asses I'm done with looking for hot dogs. Y'all come down to Littleville anytime. Howard and I will show you around."

"Bye Sweetie. We both miss you," Joyce said.

The girls rang off and Florence was a wild woman. Frankly, the family couldn't believe the old boys were running hard in the big apple themselves. Scooter and Jimmy were proud as punch and slapping high fives. The boys had two girls each and they didn't seem to mind at all. R.E. made quite an impression before it was all said and done. Howard made an even bigger impression with the folks at home.

Let me tell you that Wesley is one smart son-of-a-gun. Don wasn't bull-shitting when he told Faith the man was the smartest executive he ever met. The entire movie was shot in less than a month for a million dollars. The Kate Manley show was now the most watched show on television and you had to pay for it. Wesley had cut a deal with all the no name actors for another movie. The Return to Littleville was already written and the star was none other than Wild Buck himself. You probably guessed by now that Scooter became a millionaire several times over. He left Amanda and moved on down the road. He and Jimmy signed a pact to never get married and see who could score the most. The boys even put it in writing and had it notarized. I'm pretty sure Jimmy is going to win the bet, but you never know. Sarah freaked everyone out when she bought Twelve Trees and took up golf. Rory was happy as hell watching the girl enjoy herself.

Kate and Chuck took up the game, but Chuck's back wouldn't hold up and he had to give it up. Anne and Carol both moved to West Palm and got married. They both claimed their wild ass days were over, but only time will tell. I'm like Forrest Gump, I'll believe it when I see it and that's all I have to say about that. Joan got jealous and broke up with Elmer. It turned out the old boy couldn't hear a lick, but was quite the ladies man.

Denise didn't get Don, but she sure as hell got the actor playing his part. I guess she must have popped a couple of pills because the actor took her back to Hollywood with him. Chief Thomas decided he would make a good Sheriff and threw his hat in the ring. It turned out to be an embarrassment like few men have experienced. Sheriff Holley got fifty one hundred votes and the Chief got fourteen. He would have got fifteen, but he accidentally pulled the wrong lever and voted for Holley. R.E. and Howard did much better on their royalty checks after the appearance on the show. Sarah invited them back to play a round at Twelve Trees, but they thanked her for the invite and passed. Howard stayed straight and R.E. gave it up himself. The boys bought a brand new fishing boat with a top on it. They never got hit again by another goose and had a large time.

Jake and Emily wound up with the biggest church in the state. Jake stayed cheap and Emily stayed loud. Renee never saw

Johnny again, but hooked up with a much younger man. They spent a lot of time gambling in Metropolis of all places. The Governor lost his bid to be reelected and it wasn't even close. Florence went on to become the spokesperson for the liquor brand. The old girl was quite a hit and sales soared. She and R.E. stayed together, but still gave each other hell. She even got a call from the Congressman congratulating her on her new found fame and success. Florence was real pleased until the man asked for a campaign contribution. Needless to say, if the boy is waiting for her check, he is a fool. R.E. swore he never slept with Joyce and Marie, but Florence knew better. Vicki refused to take Florence's advice and stayed with Howard. Rory got ticked off at the newspaper and bought the damn thing. He fired nearly everyone and brought in new folks to run it. The family got a bunch of big royalty checks and learned to live with fame. It wasn't what they had envisioned, but what the hell. It turned out just like Don told them and none of them had to worry about money again. Kate made out like a bandit driving off in a Brinks truck. The woman was a household name around the world. Wesley was right as usual and a major network tried to cut a deal with Kate. Let me just say from what I was told there are not enough four letter words to describe what she told them.

Rumors flew that Wesley and his mystery partner were buying a movie studio. It turned out they couldn't get the price they wanted and started one. The legal community was stunned to hear Don had quit practicing law. Would you practice law if you were worth twelve billion dollars? Faith's living room looked like a funeral home with flowers coming from prosecutors all over the country. The local Florist made so much money he sent an arrangement himself. All the love letters and pictures got tossed and Faith finally had her picture taken with Don. Women around the world were hugely disappointed when Kate showed the two of them together. Just when you thought you had heard it all, Wesley went and sold Wes-Star for thirty billion dollars to a big entertainment company. The company was public and out came the disclosure that Don owned forty percent. Florence put the pencil to paper and out jumped twelve billion dollars. R.E. couldn't wait to tell everyone he knew Don was one of the hundred wealthiest men in America. Wesley, being the gentleman he was, gave Kate a new contract at five million a year before he signed the deal. Huey and C. Jacob settled in to spend the rest of their worthless lives in prison. Ben kept right on making a fortune practicing law and running the show. Don made Pedro a loan and the man started his own limo service. It turned out real good and the man wound up with twenty limousines.

Henry Morgan, the U.S. Attorney, took another look at the Molly Hanson file after Susan called. The next morning, he called his staff together and informed them he had decided to drop the charges. Don got one of his buddies to file suit against the government. Molly ended up without a mortgage and Henry wound up without a job. Bobby Jack Cullen became a household name in the business community. It seems the boy had quite a knack for spotting a commodity trade. When he made three billion on a bet the stock market would fall, it became news around the world. On a sad note, Mr. Warrington passed away, making Bobby the third richest man in the country overnight. I told you he was the luckiest man alive. Beverly never got over showing the boy the door and I can't say I blame her. On a positive note, Bobby upped the child support big time and it was just wonderful every month when the check arrived. The movie distribution deals were cut and guess what? Littleville should be coming to a theater near you very soon. Oh, I guess I forgot to tell you where Littleville is located in all the confusion. Well, now that I think about it, shame on me for being so full of myself. That is downright foolish on my part as y'all already know exactly where it is.

ABOUT THE AUTHOR

Ain't any way I'm going to tell you my real name, folks. I'm all about living and people could take this the wrong way. Hell, they might think I'm talking about them. We'll just call me, Jim Bob Sally and leave it at that.

Made in the USA